"*Faceless* teased and taunted me until I stayed up all night reading, only to be stunned by the astounding ending. This is a blockbuster thriller screaming to be told in the movie theater, and I'd be the first person in line for a ticket. A Perfect 10 you're sure to enjoy."

—*Romance Reviews Today*

"The intricate nature of this story increases the tension as numerous unknowns gradually come to light. With every new revelation, Debra Webb weaves the yet-unsolved issues more deeply into the lives of her hero and heroine to create a gripping thriller." —SingleTitles.com

". . . [E]ven an experienced mystery solver will never see this ending coming." —TheMysteryReader.com

"The collision of a straight-arrow hero and a fascinating anti-heroine gives a unique twist to an already complex and gritty novel—one that shows how truth and justice can be twisted, often with frightening results. In this town, murder, lies, and power are inseparably bound. Webb's tale reeks of corruption and deadly manipulation—an impressive brew." —*Romantic Times BOOKreviews*

TRACELESS
A *Cosmopolitan* "Red Hot Read" of the Month

"Skillfully managing a big cast, Webb keeps the suspense teasingly taut, dropping clues and red herrings one after another on her way to a chilling conclusion."

—*Publishers Weekly*

I0669212

"A steamy, provocative novel with deep, deadly secrets guaranteed to be worthy of your time."   —Fresh Fiction

"*Traceless* is a riveting entanglement of intrigue, secrets, and passions that had me racing to its breathless end. I loved this book!"   —Karen Rose, author of *Die for Me*

"*Traceless* is a well-crafted and engrossing thriller. Debra Webb has crafted a fine, twisting thriller to be savored and enjoyed."   —Heather Graham,
          New York Times bestselling author of *The Dead Room*

"The talented Webb has built a wide fan base that should be thrilled with her vengeful and chilling new tale."
          —*Romantic Times BOOKreviews*

"Betrayal, secrets, lies and passion lead to murder in a small town . . . *Traceless* is a breathtaking romantic suspense that grabs the reader from the beginning and doesn't let up. Riveting."   —*New York Times* bestselling author
          Allison Brennan

NAMELESS

"A complex plot and an eerily compelling villain make this fast-paced chiller outstanding reading. Take a deep breath and enjoy!"   —*Romantic Times BOOKreviews* (4.5 stars)

Also by Debra Webb

Faceless

Nameless

Traceless

Available from St. Martin's Paperbacks

FIND ME

DEBRA WEBB

St. Martin's Paperbacks

This is a work of fiction. All of the characters, organizations and events portrayed in this novel are either products of the author's imagination or are used fictitiously.

FIND ME

Copyright © 2009 by Debra Webb.
Excerpt from *Everywhere She Turns* copyright © 2009 by Debra Webb.

Cover photo of woman © Herman Estevez. Cover photo of scene © Masterfile.

All rights reserved.

For information address St. Martin's Press, 175 Fifth Avenue, New York, NY 10010.

ISBN: 0-312-53295-4
EAN: 978-0-312-53295-6

Printed in the United States of America

St. Martin's Paperbacks edition / January 2009

St. Martin's Paperbacks are published by St. Martin's Press, 175 Fifth Avenue, New York, NY 10010.

10 9 8 7 6 5 4 3 2 1

I have dedicated more than one book to my family. But this story simply must be dedicated to those wonderful souls. First, to my incredible husband, who drove that giant U-Haul truck 1400 miles, ensuring that we were surrounded by the things we loved while living in Maine. He chopped firewood, kept the fire blazing and shoveled snow every single day. Thank you, honey, I love you so much. You went above and beyond the call of duty. Secondly, I have to thank my daughter, Melissa, for agreeing to leave all her friends behind and move to the middle of nowhere with dear old Mom. I, of course, also appreciate the cooperation of my three dogs. They too made this long journey and survived the winter in Maine. Lastly, I must express my sincerest appreciation to my older daughter, Erica, and her beloved, Ashley, for holding down the fort until we returned to Alabama. I love all of you and appreciate all that you do.

ACKNOWLEDGMENTS

The coast of Maine is hauntingly beautiful. My family and I had the pleasure of spending five months in the dead of winter near Camden while I pounded the keys to bring this story to life. We lived in a century-old farmhouse surrounded by glorious mountains and the icy waters of lakes as well as the magnificent ocean. While we were there we learned many things about the folks who populate the proud state of Maine. Hardworking, enduring . . . but most of all caring about others as well as about this planet. The atmosphere was steeped in tradition and history. Exploring homes dating back to the early 1700s was utterly fascinating. More than once I found myself looking over my shoulder and double checking what I thought I saw from the corner of my eye. The cemeteries are amazing and if one is going to believe in ghosts, this is the place to believe. The very air vibrates with the centuries of living and dying. And the snow! Having grown up in the South, I could never have fathomed just how much there would be. All I can say is thank God for a husband handy with a snow shovel and good old four-wheel drive. But the simpler, slow-paced way of life in Maine made me feel right at home. A roaring fire kept the cold at bay while the old wood floors of the house creaked and groaned the same way those in my grandmother's house did.

The village of Youngstown in *Find Me* is somewhat of a collage of the lovely villages we frequented: Camden, Rockport, and Rockland. I borrowed many of the street names and the Chapel of the Innocents, as well as the enthralling cemeteries. Every day brought new inspiration and the fire to get the story on the page. The characters are purely fictional products of my twisted mind.

Thanks to Reny's, Scott's Place, Cappy's Chowder House and Hannaford's for providing us with all the essentials of daily life. A very special thanks to Rite Aid Pharmacy for taking care of us so far from home. My daughter had the misfortune of becoming very ill during our time in Maine, and we didn't have a clue which doctors were taking patients or where to go. Since we patronize Rite Aid here at home, I called the pharmacist at the Camden store. I explained the situation, and the pharmacist had my daughter an appointment with a local physician within the hour. That is old-fashioned neighborliness at its finest.

As always, thanks to those who protect our communities: city and county police officers, as well as the state police and the Federal Bureau of Investigation. Though we fiction writers at times like to cast a bit of a bad light on the occasional character representing law enforcement within the pages of our stories, it is no reflection on those outstanding folks in real life who serve. We would be lost without you.

Thanks to all those Mainers who graciously answered my questions and welcomed me into their homes. Big, big thanks to our closest neighbor, Peter Green, and his lovely daughter, Rachel, who befriended my daughter Melissa.

I hope all who read this story will appreciate the stunning beauty of Maine's southern coast. I worked hard to capture that genuinely natural splendor. Keep in mind that in doing my research, I literally made every step through the snow right along with Sarah Newton. But it was my pleasure.

Lastly, thanks to the many readers who continue to make my dream of storytelling come true.

FIND ME

CHAPTER 1

Footsteps echoed in the darkness. Faint at first, then louder.

Her breath stalled in her chest. Was he coming back? Yes! Oh, God, he was coming back. A scream rushed to the back of her throat. The tape on her mouth imprisoned the sound.

She struggled to loosen her bindings. The ropes or bands cut into her skin. Her wrists burned. She couldn't get loose! Couldn't reach up to tear away the blindfold.

The devil was here . . .

Oh, God!

Wait. Wait. Wait.

Be still. Her body trembled. *Be still!* If she didn't move maybe he would think she was already dead.

Don't move. Don't move. Don't move.

A sob ripped at her chest. *Please, please don't hurt me.*

She could hear him coming closer.

Closer.

She'd gone to church every Sunday of her life. Why hadn't she listened better? Maybe then she would know what to do . . . how to save herself.

A kick to her side made her gag. She tried to cough. The restraining tape stung her lips. Instinct curled her forward into a protective ball, her face pressed against her knees.

Don't move. God, don't move. Don't even breathe.

Be still. Be still. Be still. Quiet. Quiet. Quiet.

He crouched next to her, the rasp of fabric grating her eardrums.

Her heart thumped harder . . . harder.

His repugnant lips rested against her hair. "I told you I'd come back." The harsh whisper exploded in her brain.

He's going to kill me.

She whimpered.

Shhh. Be quiet. Stay still.

"Don't worry." That exotic, lusty voice resonated thick and rough and sickening. "You won't die today. Maybe tomorrow."

Her body seized and she trembled no matter how hard she tried to stop it. Don't move. Don't move! Her muscles refused to listen. They convulsed and quaked with a will of their own.

His fingers twisted in her hair. Snapped her head back. Those mocking lips grazed her cheek. She cried out, the desperate squeak muffled by the chafing tape.

Rich laughter echoed around her. "Don't cry. It won't be long now."

A sob surged up her throat, died in her mouth. Then another erupted. She tried to choke back the sounds. Couldn't. Oh, God, she couldn't keep quiet.

What did it matter? She was going to die. No one was coming to save her. Just like no one came to save Valerie.

What had she done wrong? She'd walked home alone after cheerleading practice dozens of times. She should have listened to her mother . . . *never walk home alone after dark.*

She was stupid. Stupid! Tears streamed down her cheeks . . . dampened the place where those full, disgusting lips touched her skin.

"You'll hardly feel a thing," he promised softly, sweetly, almost femininely. "When it comes to pain, there's a certain point where your mind begins to block just how excruciating it really is."

The hiccupping of her sobs made the repulsive mouth still pressed against her cheek curve with triumph.

"First, I'll sew your eyes shut." Taunting fingers dragged across her blindfold. She shuddered. "It'll be so much better that way. You can't covet what you can't see."

Somebody please help me! The silent plea resonated through her soul . . . but no one would hear.

"The end result makes perfect sense."

What made perfect sense? She didn't understand. Why was this happening to her? Why couldn't she remember how she'd got here? One minute she was walking . . . the next she woke up here. Cold, damp . . . and the smell. She shuddered. Like stagnant water.

The devil pressed closer, the heat from his vile body drawing hers even as she wanted to scramble away. To run. But she was so cold. So very cold.

"Everyone will be so much happier," the seemingly disembodied voice promised, its texture becoming velvety . . . soothing almost. "You've been such a selfish girl . . . such a rotten snob. The devil knows everything you do . . . and you've been so, so bad. Now it's time to pay."

Terror relit in her veins, igniting her need to escape. She shook with the force of it, jerked at her bindings. *Let me go! God, please, please help me!*

Her screams rammed against her throat . . . the sound silenced by the tape over her mouth.

"I'll do things to you . . ."—his disgusting tongue flicked in her ear; she tried to draw away—"that will make you understand just how toxic you've been."

Urine gushed free. Warmth soaked and spread around her bottom. The final humiliation. She had no control . . . she was completely helpless.

Defeat drained the last of her fight and the fear let go of her heart. The certainty that no one was coming . . . that she was going to die . . . won the battle. One by one her muscles went lax. Her mind drifted from this awful place.

"Lastly," he said gently, dragging her fleeing attention back to this dark, damp, evil place, "I'll mark you as a sign to ensure that no one ever forgets how beauty can conceal such poison." He hummed a satisfied sound. "Then, I'll leave and you'll die, cold and alone."

The ruthless grip released her hair. Her head fell forward.

The devil walked away, the scrape of steps on the stones growing distant, then fading entirely.

Her body twitched and she collapsed onto her side against the cold, hard rocks. Vomit surged into her mouth and nose, strangling her with its bitter burn.

No one was coming to save her.

Not even God.

She was going to die.

Tremors quaked her powerless body.

She didn't want to die.

No. No. She didn't want to die.

Find me. Please, God, just let them . . . *find me*.

CHAPTER 2

Find me!

Sarah Newton's eyes flew open!

The air raged in and out of her lungs. For one endless second she felt paralyzed.

A dream. Just a dream.

She sucked in a ragged breath and sat up. Shoved the hair out of her eyes.

"Shit." She forced her respiration to slow. Long, deep breaths. Hold it. Let it go. Breathe in slowly, count to ten, let it go slowly . . . slowly . . . slowly.

Find the calm. *You're awake now.* No more dreams. Just relax. Pull it together.

Little by little her body responded to the technique she'd used half a lifetime. She stretched her neck, then rolled her shoulders. The digital numbers on the alarm clock taunted her. She slapped the off button despite having another thirty or so minutes of sleep coming to her. That wasn't happening. She might as well get up and get ready.

Kicking the covers back, she rolled out of bed. She needed coffee. Lots and lots of coffee.

She stumbled to the kitchen in the dark. Guided by the glow of the streetlight invading her narrow-but-prized kitchen window, she went through the necessary motions to get her favorite Colombia blend brewing. On the counter next to the microwave, the answering machine's blinking red light warned that she had a message. Probably a lot more than one. A closer inspection confirmed her speculation.

Four messages.

Answering the phone at home was something she rarely did. Once locked away in her personal space, she preferred not to be disturbed. The rest of the world could just go away.

If only that was possible . . .

Knowing who had likely left the most recent message, she reached over and pressed the play button. Get it over with. If she failed to hear whatever instructions he'd left before she headed north, he'd bitch at her.

Hearing was vastly different from listening and she only listened when she really wanted to. One would think he would have learned that lesson by now.

"Sarah," her aunt's voice sang out, "you should be ashamed of yourself, dear. You never call anymore. I—"

Skip. Next was her shrink. Definitely skip. Then the airhead of a guy she'd made the monumental mistake of dating a couple of weeks ago. Permanently erase.

And finally the newest message.

"Newton, what the hell is wrong with your cell phone?" a booming male voice demanded.

She rolled her eyes. Yep. Her editor. Sometimes he treated her like a child. He should have had kids of his own decades ago. She was damned tired of him using her as a surrogate.

"Remember, this is February. You're going to Maine. There are certain essentials you will absolutely need. Pack your gloves and winter boots and wear your fucking parka, for Christ's sake. I don't want you coming back here sick. Call me when you get to Youngstown."

"Right." He would hear from her when he heard from her. Probably when he called her cell phone. And when she decided to answer, which was rarely at the same time.

Sarah hit erase then turned back to the only essential she absolutely needed right now.

Hot, steaming coffee.

The mere smell was like sex, only without the awkward postmortem chitchat.

Was it good for you?

Sure. You?

Cradling the warm cup, she sipped the stiff brew and moaned as satisfaction and the caffeine infused her blood, wiring her for the day. Youngstown. The Weather Channel had reported snow on the coast of southern Maine last night. Perfect. She hated snow. That was the one thing she deplored about living in New York, the winters. Still, she'd take a New York winter any day over a Maine winter.

"But we go," she muttered, "whenever and wherever the work takes us."

That was another thing she was beginning to hate. The work. She refilled her cup and hoped like hell a second shot of caffeine would get her on the way to feeling remotely human. Three or four more cups between now and flight time and she might just attain that elusive goal.

She trudged back to her bedroom. Pack, get dressed, then take the train to LaGuardia. A short flight to Portland, then a ninety-minute rental-car drive to Youngstown. Whoopee.

No doubt a welcoming committee would be waiting for her.

Something else she intensely disliked. Sarah downed the last of the coffee. *The people.* Wherever her work took her she could always count on being the passing freak show.

The locals would stare at her. Whisper behind their hands. Make up weird shit to say about her in their insignificant little newspapers. Bring up crap from the past and call her unreliable. Then, when she was finished, they would really go for the jugular.

A charlatan who just got lucky when she stumbled upon what no one else had found. A burned-out pessimist who got off on damaging the lives of others with her harsh, tell-all reports of truth in relation to so-called real life in small-town America.

The truth she worked so hard to uncover was never what

anyone wanted to see or hear, no matter that the mystery was ultimately solved in the process.

Sarah's view on the subject of truth was simple. It was fact. No amount of steadfast determination, relentless hope, or desperate prayer changed it.

It is what it is.

Once she revealed the facts, her job was done. She left and then for months or even years the good citizens would blame her for their every misfortune.

She stared at her beat-up old suitcase and shook her head. "Man, I love this job."

CHAPTER 3

From the broad expanse of windows in his parlor-turned-lobby Barton Harvey gazed out across the sleepy harbor below. Morning mist still shrouded the vessels docked there. Floating aimlessly in the chilly water like abandoned pirate ships, the schooners waited patiently for their protective covers to be removed. The scraping and painting and other maintenance work that had gone on the better part of the winter was finished now. The fishing boats were already venturing daily into the icy waters.

The peaceful village that had been his home from the day he was born clung to the side of the gently ascending cliff, rooftops jutted stubbornly through the lingering fog. Chimneys puffed the smoke of survival.

As stubborn as the houses their ancestors had built centuries ago, his friends and neighbors were ready to plunge into the work they loved—dredging the sea for its generous bounty and playing host to tourists from far and wide.

In a couple of months or so his inn would be filled to capacity. For most folks life would move smoothly into the tourist season as it did every year.

His jaw hardened. But not for Barton. Not this year.

A young girl was dead. Another was missing.

And *she* was coming.

Barton turned away from the picturesque view. He had

duties to see to. No matter how he worried. The facts would not change.

Murder was murder . . . new or old. Didn't matter.

Someone would have to pay.

She had a reputation for finding the truth, however crude and dispassionate her tactics.

Barton glanced at the blazing fire he'd meticulously prepared to chase away the morning chill. Guests loved arriving in the lobby of his inn to a glorious fire roaring in the massive stone fireplace. One guest or an innful, he never liked to disappoint.

He crossed the quiet room and stepped behind the two-century-old registration desk. His grandfather's grandfather had imported the intricately carved mahogany greeting-counter from Spain. The matching hutch that hung on the wall behind the counter and housed messages for guests and room keys had been designed and handcrafted by the same artisan. Every square foot of this inn echoed centuries of history from near and far. It represented all that Barton was. In good times and bad, he never neglected his responsibility to his heritage.

After slipping his reading glasses into place, he opened the leather-bound reservation book. He despised computers. Refused to use them to this day. He liked making reservations the old-fashioned way, the way his father had and his father before him.

Scrawled in the block for today's date was one name.

Sarah Newton.

He closed his eyes and fought to calm the emotions warring deep in his chest.

No matter how good she was, he had to make certain she didn't find the one secret he had kept carefully hidden for so very long.

No one could ever know.

No one.

Squaring his shoulders with determination, he dismissed the worry. Failure was out of the question. He would not allow her to destroy all that he had worked for his entire life.

All his forefathers had carefully preserved for those who
came after.

He would stop *her*.

Whatever it took.

CHAPTER 4

"Amen." Reverend Christopher Mahaney lifted his head and gazed at the beautiful crucifix adorning the wall beyond the modest altar.

He had prayed for most of the night. A sweet child was still missing. Christopher's eyes pinched shut in agony. Another lay dead beneath a snow-covered blanket of earth.

The devil had ascended upon the community of Youngstown with devastating impact, igniting a ripple, the full effects of which were building, broadening, threatening . . .

"Forgive me, Father," Christopher murmured, the anguish seizing his faulty heart yet again.

He'd begged for forgiveness over and over during the days since the first girl had gone missing. Though his heavenly Father forgave His children freely, Christopher was not so sure he would ever truly be forgiven for this despicable mistake. A sin for which he had no acceptable excuse.

Except that he was guilty of just one thing—*giving her what she wanted.*

She had cried on his shoulder and told him of her desperation . . . of her darkest desires. She had needed him. He had surrendered to the temptation. Then, afterwards, she had changed her story. Insisted he had misunderstood her needs.

Anger trickled into his veins. He served his congregation

selflessly . . . was always there for each and every one of them. Did no one see his own needs? He was, after all, only human.

Christopher resisted the frustration and anger. The error was his . . . no matter the excuse. The path of repentance was the only road to forgiveness.

Perhaps forgiveness was not the issue . . . but punishment.

He squeezed his hands together in supplication.

"Give me the strength, Father . . . to stand firm during the coming trials."

When the chosen time came there was no escaping God's wrath. As a faithful servant, he would not be so bold as to wish to escape. He was not entitled to mercy. The wherewithal to endure would be gift enough. He must humbly accept whatever punishment his dear Lord decreed.

But not this . . .

His chest heaved with a burdened breath.

She would arrive today.

Mere hours from now.

He had read accounts of her exploits in other towns, with other cases. She left many desolated lives in her wake. Not even the innocent stood in her way. As God had sent forth his faithful servant Ezekiel amid the children of Israel to reveal their sins and to give warning . . . *she* too came forth as a revealer and to give warning.

The truth would be exposed, naked in the light, for all to see and be outraged.

There was no escaping . . . no hiding . . . not when one's fate had been ordained.

Christopher genuinely feared that the Divine decision regarding his having succumbed to the sins of the flesh had already been made.

He was as certain as a lowly human could be.

She was his punishment.

How would he endure?

CHAPTER 5

Youngstown Municipal Offices, 1:55 P.M.

She was here.

Kale Conner stepped outside Youngstown's Municipal Offices as the Budget rental car pulled into the lot. Mayor Patterson owed him one for this. No one on the village council had wanted this job, but not a single member was willing to allow Sarah Newton to roam the town unsupervised.

Her reputation preceded her.

By several hundred miles and endless newspaper headlines.

"Ms. Newton?" Kale ordered a smile to go along with the cordial tone he managed. There was work he could be getting done. Running a decent-sized fleet of lobster boats kept him plenty busy. But, as Patterson had so graciously reminded him, he also had an obligation to the citizens and to the village. There would be times that obligation would need to take priority over all else. Like now. Since Kale was the first in all the generations of Youngstown Conners to hold a political office, he doubted his father would be particularly proud if he screwed it up this early in his new career.

New . . . right. His *career* was the same as it had always been—pleasing everyone but himself.

Get over it. There were worse things. Doing the right thing was something to be proud of.

"That's me." Newton thrust out her right hand.

Kale gave her hand a quick, polite shake. Her grip was

firm, self-assured. He'd expected nothing less. "Kale Conner. I'm certain you're anxious to get settled at the inn."

Zipping her coat against the chill, she glanced around. "Actually, I'd like to go to the scene first." Her gaze reconnected with his. "If you'll give me directions, I'll be fine on my own. I wouldn't want to inconvenience anyone."

The offer was tempting but he had his orders. "You're our guest, Ms. Newton. We—"

"Sarah," she cut in.

Kale hesitated.

"That's what people call me," she explained, obviously mistaking his pause to modify his strategy for confusion at her suggestion. "At least in the beginning."

He nodded. "Sarah," he repeated. "We appreciate what you've come here to do and we want to facilitate your efforts any way we can. I'm completely at your disposal." Good for him. He'd gotten out the whole backup spill without a glitch. He couldn't see any reason why she wouldn't grasp the logic in that explanation.

Except maybe for the skeptical look in her eyes. Clearly he'd needed a Plan C. She was nowhere near convinced of his sincerity or the sensibleness of his offer. Great.

"That's very nice of you, but I'm used to working alone."

He just bet she was. She had that whole martyr-with-a-cause attitude about her, from the defiant tilt of her chin to the wide set of her feet. At all of five three or four, maybe ninety lean pounds, and full of spit and fire, she was ready for battle. Blond hair hugged her neck and would probably hug her face if it weren't so haphazardly tucked beneath a black ski cap. Shaggy gold wisps curled this way and that. But it was the eyes that put him on guard. Bluer than any body of water he'd navigated, and he'd navigated plenty. Intense, high-octane blue. And totally suspicious of his motives.

"But leaving you to fend for yourself wouldn't be very neighborly of me." *When all else fails, go for the basics.* "I insist on making your visit here as pleasant as possible."

That analyzing gaze she skillfully wielded claimed another few seconds to complete its scrutiny of him, then she presented half a smile. "You mean you don't trust me so you want to babysit me."

Well, hell. "Ms. Newton—Sarah—" he amended, "we've had a murder. The first in twenty years." The irritation he'd kept tightly compartmentalized seeped past his guard. She didn't want him hanging around and, in truth, he had better things to do. But that was just too bad for both of them. "We've got an eighteen-year-old girl missing. We want her found and this case solved. The whole village is living in fear of who might be next and, so far, the police don't have a shred of evidence, much less a suspect. If you can figure this thing out, I'm all for it. So's the rest of the town."

As if she'd read his mind when he visually sized her up, she tugged off the ski cap, finger-combed her hair, then pulled the cap back into place before settling her full attention on him once more. She sighed as if she had to trawl long and deep for patience before responding. "Let's be completely frank here, Mr. Conner, I—"

"Kale," he interrupted.

Her eyes tapered with more blatant suspicion. "Kale," she acquiesced. "I know who you are and why you're here."

He resisted the impulse to brace his arms over his chest. Keep it relaxed. No telltale body language. He should have anticipated that she would look into who's who in Youngstown before showing up. As much as she clearly wanted to give that impression, people like her didn't dive into a situation blind. To the contrary, they calculated every move.

"You're a fifth-generation fisherman with a good-sized operation," she said. "Like so many other small Maine fishing companies, you turned the greater part of your attention to lobsters when the fish stocks became largely depleted. Last year you got yourself elected to the Youngstown Village Council. I imagine your family's very proud. But I also know that you're the youngest and newest member of Youngstown's esteemed council, so you get the menial jobs no one else wants to deal with. Like the potentially unpleasant task of handling me."

He opened his mouth to regain control of the situation but

she held up a hand to stop him. "In the past ten years, I've been down this road more times than I care to recall. I'm well aware of what people, like you and your fellow council members, think of me."

She sent a pointed look across the street at Cappy's Chowder House where most of the patrons had their noses plastered to the windows. "I know what the citizens in your town think of me when they haven't even met me. And that's okay." Another of those half-smiles slanted one corner of her mouth. "I didn't come here to make friends. I didn't even come here to make nice. I'm here to clarify the facts in an unsolved case swaddled in naïve myths. Nothing more." She made one of those facial expressions that said *whatever*. "It's quite simple. You don't get in my way and I won't get in yours. Capiche?"

Don't say anything you'll regret.

Though he'd passed impatient and was barreling toward ticked off, he took a breath. Kept it contained, as challenging as that proved. He inclined his head and countered her lengthy discourse with a somewhat shorter one of his own. "I know a little something about you, too, Sarah Newton. But I won't trouble you with the details. Whether you believe me or not, we're on the same side. If you can figure out what our chief of police, a fourth-generation lawman, and all his deputies can't, then by all means, let's get to it."

She searched his eyes one long, pulse-pounding moment. "All right. We'll play this your way. Since," she qualified, "we're on the same side."

The muscle in his jaw throbbed from the hard set of his teeth. Stay cool. *Don't let her get to you.* He gestured to his Jeep. "Why don't we take my vehicle?" He patently scrutinized her mid-size sedan. "I think you'll find that four-wheel drive comes in handy around here." Although the temperature was fairly mild, they still had upward of two feet of snow on the ground. Last night's misforecast storm had dropped six inches instead of two. The snowplows had been out in earnest this morning, ensuring the roads were cleared.

"Good point." She gifted him with one of those looks

that said he'd earned a measly point, then she did an about-face and hustled back to her rental car.

She grabbed the keys from the ignition and a black shoulder bag before locking the doors. The bag was nearly as big as she was. With her back still turned, she draped it over her head, allowing the strap to fall onto one shoulder while the bulky bag settled against the opposite hip. A good stiff breeze and she'd surely topple over.

No question the lady was from New York. Black coat, bag, and cap. His gaze traveled down the slim-fitting black jeans. Judging by her shapely legs, he would wager she had one hell of a great ass.

"I know."

His head snapped up. Busted. He was supposed to be representing the Village of Youngstown. The last thing he wanted was for her to think he was some kind of pervert scoping out her assets.

"I was supposed to bring snow boots but I forgot."

He glanced down at the black Converse sneakers. She turned her palms up in a what-can-I-say gesture as she backed toward his Jeep. "I'll pick up a pair while I'm here."

"That wouldn't be a bad idea." He'd dodged the bullet on that one. She didn't strike him as the type who wanted to be looked at. At least, not that way.

He rounded the hood and climbed into his Jeep. As determined as she was to stick to her own agenda and methods, she seemed reasonable enough. She had agreed to ride with him. That was a step in the right direction. "You might want to get gloves, too."

She made an agreeable sound as she settled into the passenger seat. "Definitely. Forgot those, too."

"We've set a record for snowfall this winter." He started the engine, turned up the heat, and snapped his seat belt into place. Backing out of the slot, he added, "Hopefully the weather will cooperate for the next few days."

No comment.

"Lucky for us, last night's snowstorm hit well after the

collection of evidence at the scene had ended. It can make things a little tricky when the weather gets in the way."

Not even a grunt of acknowledgment.

He was done making attempts at conversation for now. He didn't doubt for a minute that she would let him know whatever was on her mind. For the time being, she appeared absorbed in taking in the details of the environment. Might as well give her the scenic tour. Through the middle of Youngstown's thriving, however small, business district and past the harbor. Across the wooden bridge that connected Route 1 to Main Street. Tourists always stopped near the bridge for pictures.

"The candles in the windows," she said, breaking her silence. "Are those for the missing girl?"

Kale considered the houses along the street, tried to see them as she would. Most of the homes along Main were historic, with the accompanying plaques boasting the names of the original owner and dates as far back as the late seventeen hundreds. Trees, even older, guarded the picket-fenced yards.

"Some," he said in answer to her question. "Others are always there in the winter." He made brief eye contact. "A number of the folks who were born and raised here choose to head for a warmer climate in the winter. It's tradition to leave candles in the windows until their return. Electric ones, of course," he added.

"To keep evil away while they're gone."

And so it began.

"I prefer to consider the candles welcoming beacons for their return."

"The wind chimes dangling from porches? The sprigs of heather and rosemary hanging over front doors?" She twisted to stare at the house on the corner they'd passed. When she resettled in her seat, she tacked on, "And the glass bottles hanging from trees."

He braked for the four-way stop at the intersection of Main and High. "The family with the ornamental bottles moved here from Louisiana after Katrina. Don't folks down there consider that art?" He shot her a look that dared her to prove otherwise.

"The bottles are for warding off evil spirits, Conner. As are the rosemary and the heather. And the wind chimes."

Hadn't they decided to call each other by their first names? "Don't you have wind chimes in New York?" Lots of homes were adorned with those accents. It didn't mean the occupants believed in witches and demons or any damned thing else.

"Face it, Conner, this is New England. The place is steeped in ghost stories with vengeful spirits."

"I guess you don't have those in New York, either." He wasn't going to argue with her. Damn straight, New England was steeped in many things, first and foremost history and tradition. He wasn't ashamed of it. He just didn't want her ridiculing the town and the people he loved in her heartless magazine. She hadn't been here twenty minutes and she was already looking for ways to twist that history and tradition into something sinister and simpleminded.

Case in point, she didn't say a word about all the yellow ribbons. Folks had started putting those up the very next day after Valerie Gerard's disappearance. No, that was too normal to mention.

He rolled through the intersection, continuing east on Main. Newton's attention lit on Bay View Cemetery.

"You see the crow on the headstone?" She turned to face him. "People associate crows with death. But there's perfectly logical reasons they hang out in cemeteries."

"Is that a fact?"

"Pull over."

He'd asked for that one. "Sure." He eased to the side of the street. Stellar job so far of setting the tone for her visit. She was right. He'd definitely gotten a raw deal on this assignment.

But then, that was the story of his life.

"Tell me if I'm off course here," she allowed. "People believe there's something evil about the person buried in that grave because of the crow."

Oh, she was going to love this one. "Mattie Calder," he confessed. "According to village history"—he met his passenger's expectant gaze—"she was a witch."

"I rest my case."

"But," he continued with a listen-carefully tone, "she was a good witch. Her remedies cured the sick and enlivened the sex lives of many of our forefathers."

"Fascinating stuff, Conner."

He was on a roll now. *Why not give her what she wants?* "You're right, you know. People are a little afraid of cemeteries so they compensate. Take the six-foot iron fence, for example." He nodded to the subject of his topic. "That wasn't erected for the visual aesthetics. Its original purpose was far more important than keeping out the neighborhood kids and dogs." He turned fully toward her, leaned in slightly as if to ensure she didn't miss a nuance of what he had to say. "It was erected to keep the dead inside. Iron was the strongest metal at the time. The accepted notion was that it could withstand the fires of hell itself."

She stared into his eyes for one, two, three seconds. This close he could see the silver flecks gathered around her irises. The silver seemed to flare and darken into the deepest, purest blue he'd ever seen. That he found her eyes so damned distracting was annoying as hell.

"You're quite the tour guide."

Her lips tightened as she said the words. That was when he noticed how ordinary yet strangely unusual that feature of her face was. Plain, not particularly richly colored or plump . . . but there was something challenging about the shape.

"Or maybe you're a comedian."

Withdrawing the inch or two he'd encroached, he set both hands back on the wheel. "I'm making a point, Ms. Newton. Just because folks honor a tradition, whatever its roots, doesn't mean they're any different from you."

"Actions speak louder than words, Mr. Councilman." She faced forward. "They always have. Always will."

Kicking himself for antagonizing her, he mentally groped

for a way to redeem himself as he pulled away from the curb. "You were going to tell me the real reason crows hang out in cemeteries."

"It's the trees."

"Trees?" There were trees all over town. Thankfully he had the self-control not to mention that obvious detail.

"They're attracted to the larger, old-growth specimens. Unlike in residential areas, the trees in the cemeteries are rarely removed for progress. They just bury the dead around them."

He nodded. "Interesting." But then, there were a lot of old trees in Youngstown, period. Something else he wouldn't point out.

"They're social creatures. Where there's one, there's usually more."

Social. Yeah. "This"—he made a right turn—"is Calderwood Lane. The witch's namesake." A fitting tribute considering how the narrow road snaked along the countryside.

"You, of course, know she wasn't actually a witch."

He flashed his charge a smile. "George Washington may or may not have chopped down a cherry tree, but that's the way the legend goes."

"I liked you better as a tour guide."

Guess his comedian days were over.

"Sorry. I couldn't help myself."

She fixed her attention back on the passing landscape.

He did the same. Although he had lived here his whole life, for better or worse, he never once took for granted the rugged beauty of the land. Grazing pastures elbowed out the trees in places, sprawling on both sides of the road, the left disappearing into the ocean, the right merging with the treed mountainside.

"Appleton Farm?"

He nodded. "Grandparents of Alicia Appleton."

That bleak reality settled deep in his gut. That was the real story here. The one that needed everyone's attention . . . if this woman, whatever her motives for coming here, could help that was all that mattered.

Alicia had gone missing four days ago. Less than two days after Valerie Gerard's body was discovered. Emotion swelled in his throat. It seemed impossible one of them was dead and the other was missing. So young. So damned young. Alicia was the same age as his little sister.

"You know her?"

Kale kept his focus on the winding road; mostly it was easier to maintain a hold on his emotions that way. "Everybody knows everybody around here." No matter that the number of year-round folks got smaller each year. "I can't name a handful of Youngstown residents I didn't grow up with."

"With no unknowns or variables, that kind of limits the suspect pool, don't you think?"

He looked at her then, the instant dislike he worked to ward off filtering in. She was either angling for information on the people he knew and cared about, or, worse, making an outright accusation. "There's no one here who would . . ." He tamped down the emotion that threatened to overwhelm him and his ability to keep his voice firm. "We don't grow killers in Youngstown, Ms. Newton."

"And yet," she countered. "You have one woman heinously murdered and another missing with few or no newcomers to the area. According to my research, you had basically the same scenario twenty years ago."

He braked hard for the next turn but didn't take it, cut to the side of the road instead. "Let's get something straight right now." He let her see and hear exactly where he stood on the matter. "We have strangers passing through, just like any other coastal town on Route 1. Three seasons a year we get hundreds if not thousands of tourists from all walks of life and all kinds of places. The man who did this may have been here before, may even somehow know one or both of the victims. But he isn't one of us."

"What evidence do you have to suggest the perpetrator is a he? My impression is that it could go either way."

Was she purposely trying to piss him off? "That the killer is male is the predominant view in the investigation," he clarified. "Male or female, bottom line, the people in this community are God-fearing, compassionate, and trusting. Maybe that makes us easy targets, but that's the way we are."

She shifted her attention to the deserted road that lay before them. "I'll let you know in a few days just how compassionate your friends and neighbors are."

Give it up. Don't argue. She was from New York. Trying to convince her that the world outside the Big Apple was different was a waste of time. Just drive.

The right onto Chapel Trail led them deep into the woods. The canopy of trees blocked the noonday sun and the dirt road narrowed the farther they traveled. Evergreens far outnumbered the hardwoods, ensuring the thick mass of trees were mostly green even in the dead of winter. The lesser-numbered hardwoods were tall and broad with age and bare of leaves. A few weeks from now they would bud, heralding the official arrival of spring as marked on the calendar. But New England springs returned a bit more sluggishly than most. Still, when the worst of winter passed life changed dramatically in Maine. It was like a resurrection. Of both activity and spirit.

"Any houses back here?"

"Only one on this road. It's at the other end." Kale gestured straight ahead. "Through the woods in that direction"—he hitched his thumb left—"is BeauChamp Road. It runs parallel to this one but doesn't connect. There are seven or eight houses along that private road." He shot her a knowing glance. "The big houses next to the water."

"Rich folks," she offered.

"Very rich."

As he caught sight of the crime-scene tape ahead, his foot touched the brake. The tape fluttered in the cold wind, waving its too familiar colors like a caution light between the trees. That tightening sensation he suffered each morning on awakening and remembering the ugliness that had descended upon his hometown took hold of his chest now.

Who would have done such a thing? Couldn't be any of

the people he had grown up with. Not possible. He didn't care what anyone thought or said. Unlike some of the older folks he'd heard talking, he didn't really believe in curses or legends. This wasn't the work of the devil. The person responsible for this was out there somewhere. All they had to do was find the bastard.

Whatever he believed to be the truth, he wasn't about to disrespect those who believed otherwise—as his passenger made her living doing. However the facts lined up, folks had a right to their own spiritual viewpoint, religious or otherwise.

The path that led up to the chapel was too narrow and steep for a vehicle. He parked in the designated area along the side of the road and was about to explain the reason when Newton hopped out and headed up the path.

Stay calm and focused, he reminded himself as he emerged from the Jeep. Do the job. Keep the peace. The less controversy the less likely the media was to latch onto Newton's presence here. He knew all too well what a circus this tragedy would turn into if that happened.

Problem was, he didn't see how keeping this quiet was possible considering the lady's reputation. She appeared to piss off just about everybody she met wherever she went. There was an arrogance about her. He hadn't decided yet if it was real or just a defense mechanism. Didn't really matter. The end result was the same.

He followed the route she'd taken. As brisk as the air was today he could still smell the death permeating the area. He understood that it was his imagination, but his gut seized just the same.

"Stay between the lines of tape," he called after Newton.

"I've done this before, Mr. Conner," she tossed back over her shoulder without slowing her progress. That big black shoulder bag bounced against her hip.

With her moving upward and well ahead of him, he had a decent view of her lean hips. Nicely rounded. A runner's butt. He'd suspected as much. A woman didn't get legs like that any other way.

Way to go, Kale. Get distracted with the lady's ass. Step right on your dick.

He berated himself and stalked after her. The area had been thoroughly searched for evidence by the state forensic team. Though that part of the investigation was officially completed and a guard was no longer posted to preserve the scene, the tape had remained out of respect for the victim's family. The villagers wanted it that way. They wanted visible evidence of the investigation continuing until the killer was found.

The tape discouraged entrance into the chapel, but the small open-air structure was easily viewed from any side without crossing that line. Bare of leaves and blooms, the vines crept around its perimeter, except for the end where they'd been trimmed back for viewing the ocean.

"Give me some history, Conner."

Surely she'd researched the scene of the crime. Maybe she wanted the local folklore. That was something she'd have to dig up on her own. He'd given her all of that he intended to give.

"In 1885 Gracie Kingsley persuaded her husband to build this chapel in memory of their daughter who died at age sixteen of what's believed to have been complications from pneumonia. Mrs. Kingsley proclaimed this the Chapel of the Innocents."

" 'To all the innocent ones who pass through this world,' " Newton recited.

Oh, yeah. She'd done her research. That line was emblazoned upon the plaque at the end of the chapel that overlooked the ocean but she couldn't possibly read it from where they stood.

"The chapel is used for weddings and family reunions," he went on. The last Conner family reunion had been held here. "Basically all kinds of gatherings. Most tourists end up out here sometime during their stay."

"To get a glimpse of the bride they claim wanders the cliffs on summer nights?"

So she'd learned about that one, too.

When he didn't comment, she added, "They say her veil floats around her whether or not there's a breeze."

"That's what they say," he admitted grudgingly. As if that bride had abruptly appeared and slapped his face, the chilly air stung his cheeks. He shivered. Cold as hell out here. The image of Valerie Gerard lying on that cold stone floor kept appearing in his head, reminding him of the horror that had taken place here. His internal thermometer plunged several more degrees.

"She walks the cliffs looking for the groom who never showed." Newton peered toward the ocean and the cliffs of which she spoke.

Was that wistfulness he heard in her voice? He considered the woman. Nah. Not this tough-as-nails chick.

He guessed that setting the record straight would be the right thing to do. "According to village history, when her groom didn't show, she climbed down the hillside, walked through the woods and straight into the ocean. Her body washed up the next day." He'd heard that story his whole life but he'd never seen the lady in the white wedding dress. And he'd been up here plenty of times, usually with a girl. That was another thing this chapel was known for, a make-out spot.

"Fact or fiction? I doubt anyone really knows," Newton muttered, her attention seemingly still lingering on the cliffs.

"Stories like that have a way of surviving through the generations," Kale suggested, hoping to stay in that neutral zone. Some folks believed the stories, others didn't. "It's hard to say what's fact and what's fiction." The one certainty was that most of the tales were embellished over time.

Newton suddenly faced him. "Twenty years ago the bodies of two young women were found here. You have any facts on that case?"

"Some." The chief had briefed the council on any possible similarities between Valerie's murder and the ones twenty years ago. "Other than location there are no real similarities. But we're not ruling—"

Newton lifted the tape and ducked under it.

"Hey, you can't do that." What the hell was she thinking?

She turned back to him and gave her head a little shake. "Don't get your boxers in a wad, Conner. This scene's no longer officially sealed."

"But—"

"We're alone." She sounded distracted now, as if she was totally focused on the place and could care less what he said or did. "No one will ever know unless you tell." She walked slowly around the perimeter of the stone floor, seemed to study every crack and crevice.

"Damn it." Short of physically hauling her ass back over to this side of the tape, what was he supposed to do?

She glanced at him. "Relax, Conner. I know what I'm doing. I'm not breaking any laws."

He hadn't meant to say that out loud. He surveyed what he could see of the road, listened for traffic. Shit. If Chief Willard found out he'd allowed her to cross that line. Shit. He would be in a buttload of trouble. Whether the techs were finished here or not, it was the fucking principle of the thing. Oh, yeah, how had he forgotten? This lady had no principles.

"You have pictures of how the body was positioned?" Newton pointed to the center of the stone floor where the darkened bloodstains remained.

Kale tamped down the urge to drag her back to this side of the yellow tape. "The chief has a complete file on the case." How did she think they did business up here? "We could go—"

"Have you seen them?" She looked at him when she asked the question. Really looked. As if she was watching for a certain reaction.

He nodded.

"What did you see?"

"You didn't read those details in the newspaper?" Just about every damned thing about the murder scene was outlined in print as well as on every news channel from here to

L.A. Except for the one detail they had excluded from all reports. Nausea roiled in his stomach as the grotesque letters scrawled on the victim's body shimmered in front of his retinas.

"I want to know what *you* saw that morning."

His guard went up. How did she know he'd been at the scene that morning? His presence hadn't been reported in the media. She was fishing again. Had to be. He could lie. But, as she studied him like an amoeba under a microscope, he understood with complete certainty that she would recognize the lie. It was more than the way she looked at him. It was her too-laid-back-and-yet-completely confident posture. The cool, I-see-everything look in those eerie blue eyes.

"I didn't say I saw anything *that* morning. I said I saw the crime-scene photos."

"But you did . . . see something that morning. You were here."

"Why the hell would you say that?" She was pushing his buttons and it was working.

"You have that look, Conner. The one that says I was here and I saw things I never want to see again."

He started to take a stab at a subject change by reminding her to call him Kale, but the way his gut churned he wasn't sure he wanted to open his mouth.

"So"—she turned her attention back to the chapel with its cold stone floor and century-old wooden canopy—"when you stood here in the freezing cold with the tang of coagulating blood rushing into your lungs, tell me what you saw."

When he didn't answer right away, she went on. "You told me we were on the same side. Now's your chance to prove your claim."

He thought about that for a few seconds.

Then he caved. Cooperate as much as possible, that was what the mayor had said. "There was a lot of blood." He closed his eyes and forced his mind to relive that morning. He and the chief had been having coffee at Cappy's. The same way they had a thousand times. Fate, bad luck, whatever, the call had come in and Kale had ended up riding out here with Willard.

"She was lying here, right?"

Kale opened his eyes and stared at Newton. She lowered into a crouch, studied the place where Valerie Gerard's mutilated body had been positioned.

"Yes."

The lone word echoed around him, haunted him. He shouldn't talk about this . . . not with her . . .

"Was it unusually cold that morning, Conner?"

He nodded, then remembered that she wasn't looking at him. "Damned cold. The stone path was icy." The chief had fallen twice in their haste to scramble up the slope.

"The medical examiner said she'd only been dead a few hours," Newton prompted.

"Between three and four, but the temperature made it difficult to nail down a more exact time frame." Kale stared out at the ocean, couldn't bear to look at the bloodstains any longer. "No one should die that way."

"The medical examiner's preliminary assessment," Newton said as she pushed to her feet, "indicated that the victim was alive while her lips were sewn closed."

Kale didn't want to hear this. He'd seen it in his dreams every night for almost a week.

"But that wasn't the worst of it," Newton continued as she moved around the place where Valerie Gerard had gasped for her final agonizing breath. "She lived through more than a hundred lacerations and gouges. Some seemingly pinpointed to nerve centers to optimize pain."

"That's right." His heart pumped harder with each passing second. He wanted to puke each time the images from that morning floated before his eyes.

"And yet, no real evidence was left behind. Just a few footprints. Too indistinct or contaminated to make a decent impression."

That was partly his fault. He'd been so shocked, he'd rushed to help. The chief had tried to hold him back. The next thing Kale remembered there were people everywhere and things got out of control. He'd never seen grown men cry like that, then he'd realized he was crying, too.

He felt sick.

Enough. "We done here?" She obviously knew the facts the same as he did.

Newton crossed to where he stood, lifted the tape and slipped beneath it.

He hoped that was a yes.

"That's the thing that bothers me, Conner." She folded her arms over her chest and stared directly at him. "How is it that some twisted piece of shit brought that girl up here, sewed her lips shut, then played psycho surgeon without leaving a single piece of evidence."

Anger ignited amid all those other emotions churning in his gut. What the hell was she saying? "That's what we're trying to figure out." He reached deep for calm, couldn't find it. "That's the thing that has folks believing this somehow relates to a curse." Or the devil himself. He hated to bring that up, but, after all, that was the reason Sarah Newton had come. The rag she worked for, *Truth Magazine,* had made its place in the print world by allegedly exposing the truth wherever the unexplained was sold.

This sure as hell was unexplained so far.

Newton stared at him without saying a word for about ten more trauma-filled seconds, amping his tension to an explosive level. "This was no paranormal event, Conner. This was plain old carefully planned and painstakingly executed murder. By someone who knew the victim well enough to hate her enough to do all that you saw that morning."

She made it sound so neat and easy when no less than twelve cops, local and state, had been working this case and not one had reached such a concise deduction. "That's just another theory, Ms. Newton. What makes yours so special?"

She laughed softly but there was no amusement in the sound. "There's nothing special about it. But I will do one thing as damned fast as I can."

He shouldn't have let her bait him. "And just what is that?"

"While everyone else is still running around in circles trying to do the PC thing"—she inclined her head and stared at him another long moment—"I'll prove my theory."

He shook his head, couldn't help himself. "I sure as hell hope you can. But I have to tell you that's a pretty damned ballsy statement."

She wasn't put off in the least. "It's actually quite simple. You see, I don't have any friends or family here. I don't even know anyone except you. I'm not ethically bound by the same rules and restrictions as your fourth-generation chief of police. So I'll step on toes, I'll piss people off, I'll do whatever it takes to find one thing."

She held his gaze a second, then another. "The truth."

CHAPTER 6

2312 Beauchamp Road

She was here.

Jerald Pope adjusted his telescope lens to narrow in on the faces. Kale Conner looked a little green around the gills. The woman, on the other hand, looked focused and determined. She was here and she'd dug in her heels. If her skill could be accurately measured by her media reputation, she would find what others had missed.

Many of the villagers were upset by the idea that her magazine had chosen to get involved, but Jerald didn't have a problem with this turn of events. Her tactics were a bit unorthodox and her empathy somewhat lacking, according to the articles and blogs he'd read, but neither had affected her success rate.

Only her popularity . . . or lack thereof.

Sensing that he was no longer alone, Jerald straightened and stepped away from the telescope.

"What has you so captivated, darling?"

He turned to acknowledge his wife Lynda's presence. "Come see. Our young Mr. Conner has been saddled with the duty of escorting the controversial Ms. Newton about town."

Lynda crossed the expansive great room and took a look for herself. "She only arrived this afternoon." Lynda adjusted the setting of the far-reaching zoom lens. "It certainly didn't take her long to plunge right into the investigation." She peered through the delicate but powerful instrument. "What do you suppose they're doing up there?"

Jerald gazed beyond the floor-to-ceiling window to the chapel perched high on a hilltop in the distance overlooking his home. "She's getting a feel for the scene."

His wife moved away from the telescope and allowed her interest to follow his. "Do you think she's really as good as they say?"

A local woman was dead. Another was missing. If the police couldn't find the murderer, then more power to anyone who thought he or she could. "Time will tell."

Lynda turned to him, her respect and admiration for him still as strong as it had been in the beginning. "It always does."

His wife was still as beautiful as she had been when they'd married twenty-eight years ago. Coal-black hair and eyes the color of rich jade. Her skin remained flawless even as she neared her mid-fifties. Her figure . . . well, he was a very lucky man indeed. She worked hard to stay in shape. Her eating habits would be envied by the finest nutrition experts. Her willpower was nothing short of militant.

And yet they had drifted further and further apart.

"Is this why you haven't been sleeping well?"

He considered his lovely wife at length. Was there a particular reason for her concern? "I sleep as well as any man with a life-changing decision before him."

That much was certainly true.

Designing and producing elegant schooners and yachts was more than what he did. It was who he was. Few true artisans remained in the business. Painstaking craftsmanship had been replaced by assembly lines and the need to expand. He built each vessel by hand only after weeks, sometimes months, of carefully planning each design detail. That his work was considered the best of the best domestically and internationally had garnered him a fortune many times over. But no amount of money could replace the immense satisfaction he gained through his work. The creation of each design was as intimate to him as the birthing process to any mother.

Though he might not know that particular process firsthand, he had shared with his wife every intimate nuance of his daughter's development during pregnancy and then her birth.

The most integral part of him was being threatened by his own body's weakness. Recently he had been forced to face a hard fact, he was neither immortal nor immune to infirmity. The numbness in his hands was the first sign of trouble. There were steps he could take but those steps carried significant risk. How could he gamble with even the slightest change in his ability to touch the wood? To judge its potential in raw form and then to slowly coax forth its utter luxury and beauty?

He could not.

The occasional weak tremors and more frequent bouts of numbness were two things he would simply have to live with . . . until he had no other choice.

"We should do something special tonight," Lynda suggested as she wrapped her arms around his waist and pressed her firm, high breasts to his chest. She'd always been able to read his moods. "We haven't gone out in a long time," she urged. "We could drive over to Camden and have dinner at Sydney's. You love that quaint little place so much."

"Sounds pleasant. I'll text Jerri Lynn and invite her to join us. Perhaps she hasn't already made plans." An evening away from the house would do him good.

His wife tensed. The change, though subtle, was undeniable. "I'm sure she'll be busy with her friends. It is Friday, after all. We should just hop in the car and drive. Remember? We used to do that all the time. We haven't done anything impulsive in years."

"I'll extend the invitation," he countered, keeping any hint of impatience from his tone. "If she has plans she can decline."

Lynda stepped away from him, the distance claimed emotional and physical. "You'll let me know then." Her disappointment was palpable.

When she would have turned to go he asked, though he

knew well the answer, "Why does it annoy you so whenever I insist on including our daughter?"

The incensed expression appeared almost genuine. "Don't be ridiculous, Jerald."

She folded her arms over her low-cut silk blouse. The blouse and the slacks fit her toned body as if the designer had fashioned them precisely for her. Jerald wouldn't even attempt to hazard a guess at the exclusive labels inside that delicate gold fabric. From the shoes to the hairstyle, her entire appearance demonstrated a taste for the extravagant. No one in Youngstown dressed as well as Lynda. Probably no one in New England did. Yet, as self-centered as that one flaw made her seem, she gave of her time and money generously. There wasn't a high-profile charity organization in the region that she failed to avidly support. When it came to giving, Lynda rivaled, if not surpassed, Stephen King's generosity.

If only she had once given their daughter that kind of attention.

Lynda sighed in that long-suffering way that warned she was weary of the subject. "There are simply times when I would like an evening alone with my husband. We don't do that often enough anymore."

Anymore, meaning since they'd had a child. Almost nineteen years. Lynda had not been satisfied since Jerri Lynn developed her own personality and became more than an extension of her mother.

He should have learned long ago that this was not a battle either of them would or could win. They had gone head-to-head on the subject of their one child far too many times in the past to believe otherwise. He could allow the tension to escalate into a full-fledged battle of wills or he could defuse the tension here and now.

Considering he had more than enough on his mind at the moment, the latter was by far more appealing. "I suppose you're right."

She latched on to that small concession with renewed fervor. "I just want things to be more like they used to be.

That's all." She curled her arms around one of his. "I miss the way we once were, Jerald."

BC . . . before child.

Why couldn't she be like other mothers and put her child above all else? Not that Lynda had been a bad mother . . . she was just a selfish, at times indifferent, one who refused to share what she felt was rightfully hers.

Perhaps twenty years ago when he had insisted they have a child, he had made a mistake . . . but he'd had his reasons. He pushed that thought away.

"She won't be with us much longer," he placated, knowing exactly what she wanted to hear. "After college, we'll hardly see her." His chest ached at the thought. His life would be empty without his little girl around.

Admittedly, he had his flaws but he would do anything to protect his daughter. She was his heart . . . the heart he had never possessed, hard as he had endeavored, before her birth. The potential, however remote, that she may have inherited a life-altering weakness from him caused a kind of anguish he had not known existed.

Lynda lifted her chin in abject disapproval. "She would be away at school now if you hadn't insisted she attend a university so close to home. You hold the apron strings far too tightly, Jerald."

He took his wife's hand in his and fixed a firm gaze on hers. "My decision was based on what was right for our daughter. She still needs us. She'll be gone soon enough and you'll have me all to yourself." He kissed her hand, then her cheek. The subtle scent of her perfume stirred his loins. He resented her lack of emotional attachment to their daughter but he did love her so very much.

A seductive smile slid across her lips. "I miss that." She drew away from his touch. "But you can't distract me from the real problem here."

"What does that mean, Lynda?" He was no longer able to conceal his own weariness of the subject.

"She's strange, Jerald. I'm very concerned." Lynda turned

to stare out the window. "She's not normal. I've told you this before but you refuse to listen."

"We have discussed the issue many times and I am not in agreement with your conclusions," he offered, drawing on a well of patience that should long ago have ceased to produce.

"She has no friends except that odd Tamara girl. Of course, that's not so surprising considering where we live."

That was something else Lynda would change if he would only agree. She hated the cold . . . hated this place. This place was his home . . . too much of him was here. He could not leave.

He moved up behind her, put his arms around her waist and pulled her against his body. Her well-maintained rear snuggled him. "I'm certain our daughter will grow out of her awkwardness," he assured before leaving a soft kiss on her shoulder. "After all, she has you for a mother. How could she not blossom into perfection?"

Lynda folded her arms over his. "I hope you're right. Otherwise . . ." She sighed. "I don't know what to expect from her next."

As if the worries she voiced had drawn him there, he gazed across the snow-laden branches, rested his thoughts on the chapel and the visitor there. Sarah Newton had come to find the truth, but would the truth serve the true purpose?

Every small town had its secrets. Secrets that could destroy carefully constructed lives. Youngstown was no different. But would uncovering those secrets stop the evil that had already chosen two victims in as many weeks?

One could only hope.

Jerald would do whatever necessary to protect the women he loved. He would not allow the evil to take them from him.

Ever.

CHAPTER 7

Sarah assessed Youngstown's law-enforcement setup. A receptionist who apparently served as the chief's secretary manned the lobby. From what Sarah could see down the corridor behind the reception desk there were four or five offices. At the end of the corridor the door was open and the larger room there could be a conference room.

Judging by the telephone on the desk, there were six incoming lines. Sarah had expected a small operation. Any forensic work would be passed on to the state police and the new lab that had garnered much praise for its cutting-edge technology. A county medical examiner handled the routine autopsies.

Utilizing the same parking area as the Public Safety Office was another building that housed the Fire and Rescue Services. Not a bad setup, just not state-of-the-art.

Conner had been chatting with the receptionist a good twenty minutes. The chief was out of the office and the deputy he had assigned to serve as Sarah's liaison was on her way back to the office. Sarah and Conner's arrival had caught her on the tail end of a call regarding a possible break-in on West Street. She would be back any minute, according to the receptionist.

While Sarah waited, she watched Conner in action. He was one of those easygoing guys who got along with everyone. Charmed the ladies if the receptionist's captivated reaction was any indication. Tall, lean build with broad shoulders, longish black hair framing a classic square jaw that, despite a close shave each morning, would likely sport a five-o'clock shadow by noon. He dressed like the typical Down East kind of guy. Rugged jeans, plaid flannel shirt, and Sorel boots. His only concession to popular fashion was the North Face jacket.

A walking, talking Mainer cliché. And yet, there was something about him that made her curious. Maybe it was that whole I'm-just-a-regular-guy façade he wore like a badge of honor. Every second they had spent at that chapel had visibly shredded his emotions. Refreshing, she decided, a good-looking, successful guy who didn't try to pretend he was immune to emotion. So far he didn't appear the least bit interested in playing the role of hero. That had to be the draw. He intrigued her because he wasn't what one expected at first look.

Possibly.

But Sarah knew her weaknesses and she was brutally honest with herself about them. She and good-looking men did not mix. Experience had taught her not to go there. Pick the chubby, unattractive, balding guy every time. Be smart. Don't go down that other road.

Off-loading Kale Conner as soon as possible would be essential to staying on track with this case.

The bell over the door jingled, drawing Sarah's attention to the lobby entrance.

"Sorry to keep you folks waiting," Deputy Karen Brighton announced as she scrubbed her boots on the welcome mat. Nose and cheeks red from the cold, she tugged off her gloves and stuffed them into her coat pockets.

"Hey, Karen." Conner smiled one of those broad, pearl-white smiles that could have easily been an advertisement for the next season of *American Idol.*

The gleam that instantly brightened the deputy's eyes told Sarah that he effortlessly elicited that response from all the ladies in town. And probably anywhere else he passed through.

If Sarah had needed any more evidence, there it was.

He had to go.

"Sarah Newton," Conner said, "this is Deputy Karen Brighton."

"Good to meet you, Sarah," Karen enthused as she pumped Sarah's outstretched hand.

"Same here." Sarah reminded her lips to tilt into a requisite smile. People were put off when you didn't smile at the expected times.

"Come on back to my office." The deputy glanced from Sarah and Conner to the receptionist. "If the chief calls, let him know Ms. Newton is here."

"Will do." The telephone buzzed, dragging the curious receptionist, who since Brighton's arrival had been transparently sizing up Sarah, back to the business of receiving.

Didn't bother Sarah. She was used to being analyzed.

Down the hall, Karen cleared a couple of chairs in her office. "Have a seat." She shed her coat and hat then settled into the chair behind her desk. "Where would you like to start, Sarah?"

That was certainly original. A cooperative cop?

Yeah, right.

More like a cordial cop who had been given a strict script.

"I'd like to be brought up to speed on whatever your investigation has uncovered. Particularly the parts not released to the press."

Surprise flared in the deputy's eyes.

Well, she'd asked.

If Sarah got even a fraction of that she'd be overjoyed. But, she knew from experience, what she would get was what they wanted her to know. No matter how cooperative the deputy appeared, she wouldn't be any different than all the rest.

"Good deal." Karen leaned over her desk and shuffled through the files there. "Here we go." She opened a folder and spread it on the desktop between her and Sarah. "We got copies of the reports made by the chief and the other folks involved in the investigation. Interviews with family members and friends, Valerie Gerard's as well as Alicia Appleton's." She shuffled through a couple more pages. "Forensic reports from the scene and possible related cases from the surrounding area. Though, so far, none seem even remotely similar." She leaned back in her chair and gestured to the pile. "That's what we've got."

Sarah shuffled through the reports, skimmed the neatly typed accounts of what each investigating officer had seen and/or discovered that day and since. Just as Sarah had suspected. Whitewashed just for her. "Where are the crime-scene photos?" She watched the deputy's eyes and expression for signs of the lie she was very likely about to pass off as the God's honest truth.

The deputy made one of those faces that said she didn't understand why the question had been posed. "I haven't been authorized to show those to you just yet." She gestured to the file again. "This is, as I'm sure you know, a good deal more than we're required to share in the middle of an ongoing investigation."

Not an outright lie, but nothing Sarah hadn't expected. "That's a shame. I was really hoping to get a feel for the scene as it was when the victim was discovered."

"If the chief gets here before you leave," Karen offered, "we can ask him for authorization. I got no problem with it. The sooner we get this ugly mess solved, the happier I'll be. But I will warn you, that level of cooperation isn't likely to happen."

Deputy Karen Brighton gave every appearance of being sincere about wanting to share more were she not restricted by the rules. Sarah didn't buy it for a second. "Why don't you walk me through what's been going on in the community for the past week or so, since the first girl went missing."

Confusion lined Deputy Brighton's forehead but her eyes gave her away. She'd just locked down like the Pentagon during an unexpected alert. "I'm not sure what you mean. I think you'll find everything you need in the reports there."

The proverbial Mexican standoff.

Conner repositioned in his chair twice in the ensuing silence.

This was going to take a while. "Let's see . . ." Sarah plopped her bag on the floor by her chair, then unzipped her coat and shrugged it off, letting it drop onto the back of her chair. "Talk in the village is that this case is related to the one twenty years ago. One reporter interviewed five Youngstown citizens and got the same story. The new property development coming to town awakened a curse the village founder predicted would befall anyone who desecrated sacred ground. Sacred, apparently, primarily translating into whatever he held dear."

Karen glanced at Conner. Sarah waited patiently for her to decide how she intended to evade giving an answer.

"It's true," she said finally. "Thomas Young, Youngstown's founder, warned the settlers some two hundred fifty years ago that a horrible fate would befall the village if its history was disregarded or otherwise disrespected." She shrugged noncommittally. "Some believe the development going in on the Young estate has spurred that curse. They point to the out-of-season storm we experienced a few weeks ago as the first warning."

"Like twenty years ago," Sarah suggested. "The unearthing of a cemetery set off a chain of events that culminated in murder."

"That was a mistake," Conner chimed in. "The cemetery wasn't recorded. No one knew it was there. The high school expansion was well under way before the problem was discovered. What happened after that was no curse, Ms. Newton. It was just a run of nasty weather and bad luck that ended in tragedy."

"But the murders," Sarah countered, "were somewhat similar to Valerie Gerard's." Earlier Conner had argued that they weren't, but that wasn't exactly accurate.

Again that look was exchanged between the deputy and the newest village councilman. "The similarities aren't consistent with a repeating M.O.," Karen allowed, "even though on initial examination they might appear to be."

"How so?" Sarah wasn't giving up until she knew all that the police knew. If Deputy Brighton wanted to test her staying power she could have at it.

The deputy pressed her lips together for a moment, ensuring she appeared to give ample thought to the question before responding when her real intent was to keep the unauthorized answer from popping out. "All the victims"—she looked straight at Sarah—"then and now, were mutilated. But not in the same ways. This kind of murder is never pretty, but the hack-and-slash act of killing doesn't mean that every hack-and-slash case is related."

Now she was patronizing. "No evidence then or now. It's my understanding the killer didn't leave a message last time."

Another of those she-couldn't-possibly-know-this shared glances. "According to what we've been told by the chief," Brighton said carefully, "who was involved in the investigation twenty years ago, there was no message left by the killer back then. The files on that case were lost in a fire in the old Public Safety building."

Sarah might have considered that rather convenient except that the timing didn't really lend itself to a conspiracy. "But this time was different," Sarah prompted. She resisted the urge to lean forward in her intense examination of the other woman. Karen Brighton wasn't a very good liar; it would be easy to spot. "This time the killer left a message."

Conner stood. "We should get you settled at the inn."

Relief flooded the deputy's face. "I'll let the chief know you have more questions. I'm sure he'll make time for you."

Sarah felt sure he would do exactly that. "Thank you, Deputy Brighton." She poked her arms back into her coat and pulled it on. "I'll look forward to meeting with Chief Willard." Giving the appearance that she intended to let it go at that, Sarah grabbed her bag and pushed to her feet.

"You're welcome, Ms. Newton. We want to cooperate all we can."

Ms. Newton, not Sarah. Lines had been drawn. Before following Conner out the door of the office, Sarah hesitated.

She turned back to the deputy who immediately got that trapped-in-the-headlights look on her face. "Just one more thing."

Conner did an about-face and towered in the open doorway.

When the deputy didn't raise a protest Sarah said, "Your investigation doesn't appear to be focused on any specific suspects. People have been interviewed, but—"

"Sarah."

That he called her by her first name startled her, he'd already drawn his line as well. That he shifted that boundary now warned that he wanted her full attention. Sarah ignored him. "There seems to be this overriding assumption that the killer isn't anyone from your community."

All the uncertainty and apprehension vanished. Deputy Brighton leveled a stare on Sarah that could only be called categorically cold and unyielding. "That's because the perpetrator responsible for this *is not* one of us. There isn't an officer of the law in this department who doesn't know every single citizen in this village and most of those in the nearby communities. When this case is solved, and it will be, you'll see that we were right to stand by that conclusion."

"So you're sticking with the curse theory."

Brighton's expression turned to stone as she pushed back from her desk and stood. "I believe you'll need to address the rest of your questions to the chief."

"I'll do that." Sarah draped the strap of her bag over her shoulder. She started to turn away but she hesitated one last time. "You know," she said to the deputy, "considering the first girl went missing a week ago and you basically have nothing, it looks very much like we won't ever know the truth. I guess history's going to repeat itself."

Deputy Brighton didn't say good-bye or come again or even kiss my ass. Conner couldn't get Sarah out of the building fast enough.

He didn't say a word to her until they were in his Jeep.

He was pissed.

So much for the easygoing guy.

"Was that necessary?" He twisted the key in the ignition and jerked into reverse. After a jarring three-point turn he rolled onto the street. "You couldn't have been more diplomatic?"

"There's a time for diplomacy, Conner. And this isn't it." Sarah snapped her seat belt into place.

He moved his head side to side as if he couldn't decide what to say next and maybe if he were lucky that maneuver could shake something loose.

No point in dragging out his misery. "I don't like being lied to." Why not put her cards on the table and get it over with? He would hate her soon enough, just like everyone else in this too-happy little town would before she was finished.

"There's something called protocol, Newton," he roared. "Karen can't tell you something she isn't authorized to tell. Bullying her, or anyone else for that matter, isn't going to get you what you want."

"In my experience," Sarah countered, her tone calm and even enough to piss him off all the more, "it does exactly that. When you put someone on the defensive they speak before they think. That's how you learn secrets."

He fumed. Silently, but he couldn't have proclaimed his fury any more loudly.

Any second she actually expected to see steam rolling from his ears. "If you plan to follow me around, Conner, you should know that I don't play nice. It's not my style."

"Maybe it should be."

"Been there, tried that. It doesn't get the job done."

He whipped into the parking lot of the municipal offices and shoved the gearshift into park. When he'd drawn in a deep breath and let it go real slow he looked at her. "I'll follow you to the inn and see that you get settled." His voice was lower now but still taut with frustration.

Not necessary, but whatever. "Suit yourself." She released the seat belt and reached for the door.

"It doesn't have to be like this," he argued, waylaying her. "Just because a tactic has worked in the past doesn't make it the best strategy in every situation."

Wow. A guy with a conscience. She considered this anomaly of the male species. Particularly odd reaction from a handsome specimen. Could he really be such a nice guy? One who genuinely cared about his community, wanted to do the right thing? A guy who actually didn't want to part with anyone, even the enemy, on bad terms? Could he be as good inside as he was to look at on the outside? No way. All she had to do was hang around him long enough and she would find the flaw. There was always a flaw.

Since he waited, his gaze glued to hers, for an answer, she gave him one. "Of course it has to be this way." He had the darkest eyes. Completely brown. The kind where the color was so dense and rich that it didn't even reflect light. "This is what I do, Conner. I find the truth. The sooner the powers that be in this town admit there's no curse or passerby who murdered that girl, the sooner they'll start looking for the person who did. The person who is *one of you*."

He stared at her another quarter of a minute more. She should have gotten out. Should have left it at that, but somehow she couldn't walk away without ensuring he fully understood her position.

"You won't save Alicia Appleton this way," she warned. The words would only add insult to injury, but it was true. That was the saddest part. "You and all these God-fearing, compassionate people"—she gestured toward the heart of the village—"can't pray that girl to safety. If someone doesn't figure out why a person she knew, a citizen of Youngstown or a nearby community, wants her dead, she's going to die."

He looked away then. Just sat there and waited for Sarah to get out.

Whatever.

She opened the door, got out and strode to her car.

He was wrong.

They were all wrong.

CHAPTER 8

The Overlook

The innkeeper thrust the key at Sarah.

Not a key card. The old-fashioned kind. She accepted it. "Thank you." Room 13. Ha-ha.

The innkeeper, Barton Harvey, glanced expectantly at the man who'd followed Sarah from the municipal offices. "I'll show her to her room," Conner offered.

"Thank you, Kale," Harvey said, making no attempt to conceal his relief that he would be in Sarah's presence no longer than absolutely necessary.

Funny. Sarah was the one paying for the room and he hadn't thanked her.

More of that compassion Conner spoke of so ardently.

Sarah followed him up the stairs to the second floor. When Connor hadn't driven away after seeing her to the inn, she'd been surprised. Evidently he'd decided to ensure she didn't go off nosing around town without him. Once she'd gotten out of her rental car, she'd expected him to speed away then. Instead, he'd insisted on carrying her suitcase but the show of chivalry hadn't been necessary. She'd wagged that damned thing all over the country by herself plenty of times.

She gave the inn's high ceilings and intricate architectural details a cursory survey. Nice place. As long as there was hot water and a comfortable bed, she would be happy.

At the door marked 13, he moved aside for her to unlock it. She hadn't used a hotel room key like this since Charlotte,

North Carolina. Once the door was open, he took two steps
inside and set her bag on the floor. He was ready to split. As
it was, he'd lasted longer than she'd estimated.

"Call me . . ."—he looked anywhere but at her—"in the
morning."

"I don't have your number."

"I'll give you my cell number."

Monotone, uninspired. Yep, still ticked off. She dug out
her phone and entered the number he recited.

"If you need anything, you can . . . let me know."

He turned to the open door.

She should say something. It wasn't like she'd wanted his
company today. She hadn't asked for it. But she couldn't
deny that he'd made things marginally more interesting.
Even if the way in which he'd made them interesting wasn't
in her best interest.

Say the words. "Thank you."

He hesitated but didn't turn around.

What now? She glanced around the room, didn't find the
answer. Fuck it. "Good night."

"Good night."

He walked out, closed the door behind him.

For one long moment she stood there staring at the closed
door. "That was weird."

Why?

She had no reason to feel guilty about disappointing this
guy. She'd done pretty well today. She'd only pissed off two
people. Not counting the innkeeper. In all fairness, the mere
fact that she'd shown up appeared to have pissed him off.

Whatever.

Sarah picked up her bag and tossed it on the bed. Then did
the same with her shoulder bag. She set her hands on her hips
and turned all the way around to view her room. She hadn't
been surprised that she'd been given room 13. What did surprise her, however, was that it turned out to be quite nice.
Generally, when she met with the kind of hostility she'd
sensed in the innkeeper she wound up with the worst room in
the place. Bad plumbing, drafty windows, no air-conditioning,

she'd had it all. If this was the worst, then it was no wonder the inn was the most popular one in the county.

Four-poster bed with a lace canopy. Lots of big fluffy pillows and lush bedding. Antique furnishings. Cable television. High-speed Internet service. Her own private bath and a nice big bowl of fruit.

She sat on the mattress and bounced.

"Not too bad."

'Course, a good mattress didn't guarantee she would sleep.

She pushed up and wandered over to the massive window. Kale Conner strode down the front steps and across the parking area to his Jeep. Long, confident strides. She felt a prick of disappointment that he didn't spare a glance back at the inn as he got into the vehicle.

There it was. The most fundamental reason she should avoid him at all costs.

Attraction.

He really did have nice eyes. She didn't usually pay attention to eyes other than for assessing intent and emotion. As good-looking as Kale Conner was his best assets were definitely his eyes. Looking at him from a purely physical perspective, she had to confess that he fell into the hot category. He had a good voice, too. Low and deep, and he was obviously intelligent.

As his Jeep moved down the twisted road leading back to town she wondered if he really believed that sales pitch he'd given her about the citizens of Youngstown. Was he really that naïve?

Then again, his life didn't revolve around murder.

Whatever he thought, the fact was that a murderer could crop up anywhere. Their reason for becoming a killer could be environmental, could be genetic.

Yet this whole village appeared to be convinced that their troubles were not related to a local. At least not one from this century. Give them a curse or a stranger, but not one of their own.

When Conner's taillights disappeared, she shifted her attention to the village and harbor. It was dark now but the collage of lights around the waterfront twinkled in the clear night. The sailboats drifted like ghosts with their white covers shimmering in the moonlight. Squares of light glowed from the homes that clung to the hillside flanking the inlet. She could only assume that the lack of sun in the winter prompted the owners to forgo curtains or blinds on their windows. She couldn't imagine, even on the fourth floor, leaving her windows naked for anyone's viewing pleasure.

Though it had melted on the pavement and had been scraped from the parking lots and driveways, snowbanks loitered beneath trees and against the corners of buildings and rooftops. The winding street up to the inn's hilltop station had reiterated Conner's point about four-wheel drive. The first icy or snowy morning she would regret not having gone with a fully equipped SUV.

Kale Conner. She unzipped and shed her coat. Her research indicated he was thirty, the eldest of three children. After his father became disabled ten years ago, the full responsibility of the family's fishing business had fallen upon his shoulders. He'd left his university studies behind and returned home. She wondered if he regretted that choice.

His younger brother was twenty-three and in his final year at the University of Massachusetts. His sister was eighteen and a senior at Youngstown High School. The matriarch of the family attended to the disabled father and took care of things at home, leaving the business to her eldest son.

The four other village council members were much older than Conner, married with grown children and, of course, pillars of the community. Sarah hadn't been able to find any dirt on the four. Typical small-town politicians with their fingers in every pie.

Chief of Police Benjamin Willard, sixty, was, from all reports, born with steel blue in his veins. A wife and two grown children. Mayor Fritz Patterson was the former principal of Youngstown High School and a widower. No dirt on the chief or the mayor, either.

Squeaky clean.

The whole village population appeared to be just what Conner said, good, God-fearing, compassionate folks.

But that was impossible.

Good, God-fearing, compassionate folks didn't mutilate and murder young women.

Nope.

Someone here had a secret. A dirty, disgusting secret, and she was going to find it.

Sarah dragged off the ski cap. She threaded her fingers through her hair and braced her elbows on the window. Randall Enfinger, the bicoastal developer who'd purchased the Young estate, was clean. As clean as a guy that rich and with that many connections could be. He'd bought the extensive property for the purpose of building a resort. He didn't care that the village's founding father, Thomas Young, had been born there. The greedy heirs didn't appear to care, either, since they had sold to the highest bidder with no thought as to what happened after the sale.

As soon as the deconstruction had started, so had the village's trouble. At first there were protests from the residents. Local media aired the controversy. Then Mother Nature stepped in. Hurricane-force winds had struck in the middle of the night. No lives had been lost but the property damage had been significant. Sarah had seen the trees along Calderwood Lane and Chapel Trail that had been snapped by the out-of-season storm. As an encore, full-on winter arrived early in the form of heavy snows in December and January. All construction work had stopped for a couple of weeks.

When even the forces of nature didn't stop Enfinger completely, Valerie Gerard went missing. A few days later her body had been found and a faction of the village residents had jumped on the curse bandwagon. Enfinger's temporary office at the development site had burned.

"Just like twenty years ago" the headlines had read. The accidental unearthing of a historic, and previously undiscovered, family cemetery had set off the chain of events back then. A hurricane had struck, doing substantial damage and killing four Youngstown residents. Almost immediately af-

terward, two women, one eighteen and one nineteen, had
been murdered in a very similar manner as Valerie Gerard;
their bodies discovered at the chapel. As if that wasn't punishment enough, according to those who clung to the curse
theory, the winter that followed was the worst in Youngstown
history.

Until now.

Though Conner and Brighton hadn't mentioned it, the tale
went that the devil himself had been commissioned with
punishing the villagers for any infractions of this nature.

"Bullshit." Sarah pushed away from the window and
scoped out the minibar. Wine. Bottled water. She frowned.
No liquor?

Frustrated and tired, she opened a personal serving bottle of white wine that had been grown, bottled, and aged
right here in a Youngstown vineyard.

"Probably poisoned."

She took a long, deep swallow anyway.

Not bad. She drifted back to the bed, plunked the bottle
on the antique side table, and opened her suitcase. She
shoved her stuff into a couple of drawers and tucked the bag
under the bed. Cosmetic bag in hand, she shuffled to the
bathroom and tossed it onto the counter. "Cosmetic bag" was
a misnomer in her case. She didn't wear unnecessary cos-
metics. Deodorant, Chapstick, toothbrush and paste, and
hairbrush were all she packed.

Finishing her wine, she kicked off her shoes and climbed
onto the bed. It was early still but she was tired. She needed to
think, to review the research she'd done before she crashed
for the night.

Tomorrow she would get started with the interviews.
That was when she would really make friends. She would
be watching for that compassion Conner spoke of.

The buzz of her cell phone vibrating reminded her that
she hadn't called her editor. Tae Green would be pissed. She
rolled off the bed and dug for her phone in her coat pocket.

"Newton," she answered without checking the number
first as she usually did.

"Sarah, you missed your appointment today."

Big mistake.

"Sorry about that, Doc. I had an unexpected assignment. I completely forgot the appointment." Shit. Dr. Ballantine. Her shrink. She would never get off the phone without answering endless, probing questions.

"You know our deal, Sarah. You can miss one appointment but if you miss two, we have the session by phone. Is now good for you?"

Sarah fell back onto the bed. Damn it. Damn her editor. This was his fault. She'd had that little meltdown a couple of years ago and he'd blackmailed her into therapy. One session per week or no field assignments. Even worse, he kept Ballantine abreast of Sarah's assignments—just to ensure she wasn't working too hard or going against the doc's orders.

Damn it.

"Sure." She made a face. "Now's fine."

"Excellent."

The sound of a page turning told Sarah the doc was preparing to take notes. At least she wasn't recording it. Sarah hated recorded sessions. What if someone broke into the doc's office and stole the tapes or the notes? The dirt-bag killer here in Youngstown wasn't the only one with secrets.

Sarah would just as soon hers stayed where they belonged. In the past.

"How have you been sleeping?"

"Great." Lie one.

"Good. Any dreams or nightmares that wake you or unsettle you?"

"Nope." Lie two. She usually made it all the way to four before Dr. Ballantine called her on her lack of cooperation.

"Any night sweats or headaches?"

"Nada." Three. Sarah reached up and righted the painting of the harbor hanging over her bed.

"Have you been taking your medication?"

"Absolutely." Four.

"When did you last eat?"

Hey, this was going pretty damned good. Maybe she should do this over the phone more often. "About two hours ago. This hot guy took me to a cozy restaurant right on the water. It was nice." Five. Six.

Damn, she was on a roll.

"I'm impressed, Sarah."

She was, too. "I try, Doc."

"Now." Paper rustled as Dr. Ballantine flipped to a new page in her notepad. "Let's start from the beginning once more. This time I'd like the truth."

Sarah rolled her eyes. Fooling Ballantine had been wishful thinking. "Shitty. Yes. Yes. No. And I can't remember."

"I see."

Honesty was never the best policy when it came to shrinks.

At least not for Sarah.

"So, you're not sleeping. You're experiencing those same nightmares. You're having night sweats and headaches. Not taking your medicine. And you haven't eaten today."

"I had coffee and wine. Does that count?"

"Sarah."

She sat up and opened the drawer on the bedside table. A room service menu mocked her. "You know I hate to eat at these places. They could poison me."

"Paranoid already? You haven't even been there twenty-four hours. Doesn't it usually take forty-eight?"

There was nothing worse than a shrink who knew everything about you. "Okay. I'll eat. Then I'll take my medicine and go to sleep. I won't dream or sweat or any of that other shit. Okay?"

"I wish I could trust you to do exactly that." Dead air pulsed between them. "Sarah, if you stay on this track you're headed for trouble. Following my advice is the only way to avoid it. You know this."

Sarah pulled out the menu and scanned the items available after seven. What else would one eat in Maine? Chowder.

"I'm ordering something right now. You can listen." Sarah

ignored whatever the doc said and placed her cell on the table while she made the call on the room phone. She ordered
the chowder and hot tea. A young, female voice promised to
deliver the order within fifteen minutes. Sarah recradled the
receiver and picked up her cell. "You happy now?"

"Sarah."

Here it came. The talk.

"Have you forgotten what happened last time?"

Sarah scrubbed her free hand over her face. "Of course
not." How could she? She'd spent seven days in a padded
room with voices that weren't hers screaming in her head.
Then another seven days under close observation.

"This is the way it starts," Ballantine scolded gently.
"You stop eating and taking your medicine. You stop sleeping and then you become vulnerable to the break."

The break. That was the official diagnosis. A break in
reality. The inability to control one's thoughts or actions and
to discern the real from the imagined.

Not exactly a trip to the islands.

"I'll check in with you tomorrow," Sarah promised. "I'll
be fed and fully medicated. I swear."

"I've seen the news reports regarding the case you're
working on, Sarah. You let yourself be vulnerable and you
could end up a victim. You know this. It's one of the hazards
of your work. Not to mention the fact that you're not going
to win any popularity contests while you're there. Stress can
be an overpowering enemy."

"Yeah. Yeah. I got it, Doc. I'll do better."

"Tomorrow," Ballantine reminded. "Five o'clock. You call
me and give me an update."

Sarah gave her assurance and ended the call. She pitched
her cell aside and lay there for a long, disturbing moment
considering all that Ballantine had said.

The medicine made Sarah groggy, slowed her reactions.
She just forgot to eat. It wasn't on purpose. And the dreams
et al, she had about as much control over those as she did the
rest of her life. Shit happened.

She'd always dealt with it just fine except that once.

Maybe the case had been too close to home. The murdered kids had been between eight and ten years of age. Sarah had empathized too closely with their vulnerability. Gotten in too deep . . . nearly gotten herself killed.

She touched her right side. Shuddered.

Put it away. Don't even look.

In her experience the best medicine for her was work.

As long as she remembered not to trust anyone but herself.

With that in mind, she sat up and reached for her shoulder bag. She never left home without it. Inside she carried a folder on whatever case she was working, a flashlight, compact pair of binoculars, an ultrathin digital camera, pepper spray, matches, and toilet paper. Oh, and a bottle of water. The bag was her life preserver.

She pulled the folder from the bag and thumbed through her handwritten notes and the newspaper clippings and police reports she'd gathered. As if she'd gone blind and couldn't see any of those things, her thoughts wandered back to Conner. If she opted to keep him around, how long would it take her to win him over to her side? A couple of days? Maybe. Right now he was just doing the job he'd been ordered to do. But he wanted the truth just as badly as she did. Maybe more. He wouldn't find it until he backed off that high horse of his and admitted that the killer could be anyone.

That could be expecting too much. Maybe winning him over wasn't possible.

She'd learned in the past couple of hours that he wasn't quite as easygoing as he appeared.

Not twenty minutes ago she had reminded herself what trouble she could get into hanging around with a guy like him. Suddenly she was leaning in that direction.

Kale Conner was a means to an end. He could help her get into places she might not get into otherwise. He could be useful. Keeping him around another day or so couldn't hurt.

The last piece of research material she had in her file was a photograph that had cost her editor a pretty penny. A copy

of a crime-scene photo taken of Valerie Gerard's body on
the cold stone floor at the chapel.

Why hadn't Conner told her the truth about the body?

Maybe he'd been instructed not to. After all, that detail
hadn't been disclosed to the public. Nine days and counting
and there hadn't been a leak yet. But that wouldn't last. Eventually someone would get smart enough to bribe the same
tech she had and then the proverbial shit would hit the fan.

That one detail was more telling than any other related to
the condition of the body. It also told something significant
about the killer.

A single word had been written along the victim's torso
in her own blood.

That one word shifted this homicide to a whole different
level.

A very personal level.

Sarah stared at the photo of the young woman who had
died such a slow, painful death.

"Who hated you enough to call you that?" Sarah murmured. "Then killed you for it?"

One word, four seemingly innocuous letters that when
aligned together carried profound meaning.

L I A R.

CHAPTER 9

Kale spread the invoices across the kitchen table. Christine, his secretary, had done an outstanding job organizing the paperwork he needed to sign. He penned his legal signature on one document after the other, then leaned back in the chair and considered that was about all he needed to do for now.

Truth was, the business could basically run itself without him. The tension that admission generated flexed in his clenched jaw.

What did that say about his life?

Maybe not a whole hell of a lot. He'd called his father and reviewed this month's ledger. All was satisfactory considering it was the end of February and still damned cold. Business would kick into high gear as spring neared.

His crew didn't need him holding their hands or overseeing their work. Kale's absence around the office during Sarah Newton's stay in Youngstown would scarcely be missed though he would never admit as much.

He should be glad. He should be damned thrilled that he had reliable employees and loyal customers.

But those things didn't fill the emptiness expanding inside him with ever-increasing steadiness lately.

Pushing back his chair, he stood and paced his kitchen. His golden retriever, Angie, swished her tail across the floor, her big eyes following her master's movements. He could take her for a walk or load the dishwasher. Taking care of a load of laundry or two wouldn't hurt. He never had to worry about cooking. His mom always made enough for him when she prepared the family meals. If he failed to stop by and pick up dinner, his sister delivered it each evening before dark. He would come home and find a home-cooked meal waiting for him.

Kale stopped, hands on hips, and surveyed the home he'd bought seven years ago. Seriously spacious for a bachelor. Ocean view across the street. Two-car garage, small, easily maintained yard. He had every reason to be proud of his accomplishments.

Why wasn't he?

He threaded his fingers through his hair and heaved out a disgusted breath.

It was her.

She'd stormed into town and shaken up his carefully constructed, strictly maintained routine.

Kale shuffled into the living room and plopped down on the sofa. He stared at the leather bench-style ottoman that served as his coffee table. If he lifted the lid, photos and school yearbooks were stored inside. His mom had been so proud when he became a homeowner. She'd made sure that what she considered important lifetime memorabilia was safely and conveniently stored in his new home.

But Kale never looked at any of it. It no longer mattered that he'd been the valedictorian of his class or that he'd gotten a full scholarship to the University of Maine. Responsibilities and obligations had derailed all that.

As much as he at one time had wanted to . . . there was no going back to the past. He couldn't go back to being a student now. He was thirty damned years old. He should be married and raising a family.

That was another thing he'd forgone the past few years. Relationships. At first he hadn't had time. Then . . . he didn't know . . . maybe he'd lost interest, other than the occasional date that usually included meaningless sex.

What had happened to him?

And why was he only just now paying attention?

Her. It had to be her.

When the mayor had asked him to take on this "public relations" role, Kale had taken the responsibility seriously, as he did all obligations. He'd done his research. Sarah Newton was a free spirit who never let anything hold her back or slow her down.

As interesting as her background was, it was the woman, in the flesh, who made him feel inadequate about his own life. She'd charged in and gone straight for what she was after. No second-guessing, no hesitation. No apologies.

When had he lost his enthusiasm for what came next?

He dropped his head on the back of the sofa. Maybe about the same time he'd realized that the only thing that came next in his life was a repeat of the same old thing.

He closed his eyes and cursed himself for being so selfish. His father was paralyzed. Kale's family was solely dependent upon him. He had no right to resent his obligations.

Valerie Gerard was dead. Alicia Appleton was missing.

He damned sure had no right to feel this way when others were suffering real tragedy.

Kale opened his eyes and pushed away the self-pity. He had no one to blame but himself for his lack of a real personal life. He could have a wife, a steady girlfriend at the very least. The rut he lived in, on a social level, was of his own choosing.

He could have changed that situation long ago.

But he'd been waiting . . .

Funny thing was, he couldn't label what it was he'd been waiting for.

The telephone rang. He didn't have to check the caller ID to know it would be his father.

There was no reason for anyone else to call him.

Just another indication that there was absolutely nothing he should be waiting for.

This was it.

Angie sauntered into the living room, her nails clicking on the hardwood.

"You wanna go for a walk, girl?"

Her tail wagged.

"Let's do it." Kale stood and headed for the door, Angie on his heels.

Fifteen minutes of fresh air and then he would call his father back and talk about whatever he wanted to discuss.

Like he did every night.

CHAPTER 10

Youngstown Public Safety Office, 9:00 P.M.

"You still at it, Chief?"

Ben Willard glanced up from the mound of reports on his desk. He didn't bother manufacturing a smile for his old friend. They knew each other well enough and had been friends long enough that social protocols weren't necessary. "Looks like I will be for a while yet." He leaned back and his chair squeaked. "Have a seat, Fritz." He motioned for the mayor to come on in.

Fritz Patterson settled into the only clutter-free spot in the office, an extra chair that one of Ben's deputies had rolled in for working with him on these damned reports. Between the evidence and interview reports, the faxes and photographs, not to mention old case files, that danged chair was the only space save for scattered sections of the floor that wasn't used as a holding place.

"Anything new from other agencies?" Fritz asked.

Ben had expected that question. He'd answered that same one ten or twelve times today. He shook his head. "We're still comparing MOs with homicides all over the country. So far we've got nothing." The process had been a waste of time. His gut clenched. As prepared as he'd thought he was . . . he hadn't been anywhere near ready for *this*.

This was far worse than he'd expected.

Fritz nodded thoughtfully. "Nothing new on the search for Alicia Appleton?"

Ben shook his head. "We've interviewed all her friends a second, some a third, time. Her family. The FBI has her name and face plastered all over the Internet and on billboards. And nothing. It's like she just vanished into the mist. The grandparents offered a reward today so we can hope that'll help." Even as he made the statement his mind whirled with all that could go wrong . . . yet, nothing about any of this was right. His gut twisted. God help him. There was no way to make it right.

"Can't hurt," Fritz agreed. "So far we seem to have been successful in keeping that . . . detail from the homicide scene out of the media." Fritz tugged at his tie. The man had worn one every day of his adult life. Didn't seem to matter to him that no one else bothered.

"So far." Ben was terrified that the single detail they had saved from the beginning of the investigation might get leaked. That was the one piece of evidence with the potential to end this nightmare. The only part that made it personal enough to connect to a suspected killer.

Images from the murder scene zoomed into horrifyingly vivid focus before his mind's eye.

God help me.

"Conner's going to bring the Newton woman over to meet with you in the morning, I hear," Fritz commented.

The chief pushed aside the agonizing thoughts and images. He had heard about *her* visit with Deputy Brighton. The way his deputy had gone on, it was clear Ms. Newton was already up to her usual theatrics. Sarah Newton was a loose cannon. He didn't need that right now. This case didn't need that right now. What he needed, what the folks of Youngstown needed, was for everything to fall into place so this nightmare would end.

He redirected his attention to the conversation. "She giving him any grief?"

Fritz shrugged. "Not so much. Conner says she has her own methods and he's doing all he can to cooperate with her wishes. If he gets in over his head he'll let me know. I think she gave your deputy more trouble than she's giving him."

Ben shifted in his chair, earning another squeak of protest. If he was lucky, Conner would keep that woman under control. That was all Ben could hope for at this point. Unless he got lucky and the news he had to pass along now helped her to see that she wasn't needed here.

Get on with it. This part had to be done. Beating around the bush wasn't going to change this vital step. Ben wasn't looking forward to what he had to do. Had put it off a good two hours already. But it had to be done.

Only two people besides the killer knew this part. Ben and Carl Saxon, the medical examiner. Ben had ordered him to keep this quiet until they had more information. A couple of hours ago Carl had called with what he'd learned. Another pivotal step in reaching the end of this nightmare. It was time for Ben to share that information with Youngstown's mayor.

Ben pushed to his feet, stepped to the door and closed it. What he was about to say to his old friend was something he didn't dare let out, not even among his own deputies. Not until he'd run it by the FBI . . . not until the time was right.

"I'm relatively certain we're alone, Ben," Fritz offered, obviously puzzled at the covert behavior. "The only light on in the whole building is yours. I let myself in." He patted the ring of keys on his belt. "We can speak freely."

Fritz would understand when he'd heard what Ben had to say.

Dropping into his chair once more, Ben studied his lifelong friend before saying what would change everything for him as well as the citizens of Youngstown.

"You're making me more than a little nervous."

Ben dragged in a heavy breath. "This is not like twenty years ago, Fritz. For more reasons than we already knew."

The mayor's eyes narrowed. "What do you mean?"

Those two young women had been murdered in a manner every bit as heinous as Valerie Gerard. Ben had made the initial discovery at the chapel that cold, January morning two decades ago. But he'd never told anyone. Not a single soul. Not even Fritz. If he had, how on earth would he have explained going out to the chapel at that hour of the morning?

If he'd known then . . .

Guilt congealed in his gut. But then, there were some things he couldn't make himself regret.

He'd told William Boggus, the chief at the time, that he'd gotten an anonymous tip on his ham radio at home. Back then there hadn't been any way to trace that kind of thing. At least none a small village like Youngstown knew about.

Not unlike the morning he and Conner had trekked up to that chapel, what Ben found had shaken him to the core. For months afterward he couldn't close his eyes without seeing that horrific scene. Those poor girls . . .

"Ben."

Fritz's urgent tone snapped him back to the present. "Sorry. I was thinking about . . . last time."

"What's going on, Ben?" Worry furrowed his friend's brow. "You said yourself that sometimes a killer changes his MO."

"We can only stretch that theory so far. This is . . . more personal. When Carl Saxon performed the autopsy on Valerie Gerard he found something . . ."

Fritz sat up a little straighter. "Why am I only hearing about this now? The autopsy was concluded yesterday."

Ben nodded as a new layer of guilt descended. "Just hear me out, Fritz." He should have told Fritz earlier, should have gotten this part over with. "There was a foreign object lodged in her throat."

"Good Lord, man. What sort of object?"

"At first Carl wasn't sure." Ben heaved a weary sigh. "I asked him not to divulge this information to anyone until he could determine exactly what we had."

Fritz gestured for him to get to the point.

"The object was round, like a large coin. There appeared to have been a cloth necklace attached to it. The medal was inscribed but the acid in the esophagus had made it difficult to make out. I wanted the state forensics lab to try and salvage the inscription if possible. The tech from the lab made the call a couple of hours ago." Ben felt sick at the thought of what had been crammed in that poor girl's throat before her mouth was sewn shut like a rag doll's. No telling how long after that before she surrendered to death. Long minutes of merciless suffering.

How could . . . Jesus, he didn't want to think about how anyone could do that. To go that far . . .

Ben cleared his throat. "It's a ten-year-old medal from a spelling bee. The year was engraved on the damned thing."

Fritz sat forward, his face arranged in bewilderment. "Did you say a medal?"

"Yeah." Ben scrubbed a hand over his face and met his friend's expectant gaze. "There's more."

Fritz Patterson had been Youngstown's mayor for five years. He'd done great things. Most considered him the best and the most popular mayor in the village's history. Before seeking political office he had served as the principal at Youngstown High School. He loved this community. Loved the kids. This next part was going to be especially hard for him to accept. Ben regretted being the one who had to tell him . . . but it was essential.

"The medal was presented by a fourth-grade teacher . . . from Youngstown Elementary."

Realization of exactly what that meant sent a kaleido-scope of emotions across the other man's face.

Fritz shook his head. "That can't be right."

"I've considered this six ways to Sunday, Fritz, and it comes out the same every time."

The mayor's gaze locked with the chief's.

"The killer is one of our own."

CHAPTER 11

Sarah's eyes opened.

Her heart raced. The blood roared in her ears like a train.

She couldn't move.

Fear ignited, flaring along her helpless limbs.

Run! Hide! She'll find you.

She always finds me.

Sarah stalled, stared down at her hands. Blood dripped from her fingers. Her gaze followed a big, fat droplet as it fell from her finger to splatter on the tile floor. She blinked. Three feet . . . her two and . . . another. She stared at the larger foot—the one that wasn't really hers. Red-painted toenails matched the blood draped like a crimson ankle bracelet around the top of it where it had been severed from a leg.

Her body started to shake. Urine slid down her thighs.

Don't look! Move!

Sarah lunged upward in bed, hugged her knees to her chest.

"Just a dream. Just a dream."

Breathe. Slow. Deep.

Just a dream.

She looked at the clock. Blinked. Then took a moment to get her bearings.

Maine.

The missing girl.

The *dead* girl.

Sarah was okay.

Safe.

And pissed off.

She threw back the covers and climbed out of bed.

She glared at her cell phone. "Yeah, I know. I should have taken the fucking medicine." And eaten the chowder. The bowl of now cold soup sat on the bedside table, untouched.

Her body shivered. She was soaked with sweat. Muttering profanities, mainly at herself, she peeled off her T-shirt and shed her sweatpants. She hated this shit. Nineteen years and she still fought the demons of her past every damned night in her sleep.

Three different shrinks or was it four; five . . . no, six separate drug trials. Nothing stopped the dreams unless it knocked her out cold. Then she couldn't function the next day.

A vicious cycle that sucked ass!

In the bathroom, she flipped on the light and reached for a towel. Midnight was a hell of a time to take a shower but she felt dirty. As much from her dreams as from the sweat.

Sarah stared at her reflection in the clouded-with-age mirror. She looked old. Dark circles under her eyes from lack of sleep. Lines at the corners of those weary eyes. Maybe from all those years she'd spent trying to smoke herself to death. Twenty-nine. She looked forty. And felt fifty. Thanks to her amazing childhood.

And the lack of sleep.

She twisted the knob and set the water temperature. Shoving her panties down her thighs, she wondered if Kale Conner would mind getting an early start. Say at one in the morning?

Not very likely.

She stepped into the claw-foot tub; the hot water felt good against her skin. She yanked the curtain around the tub and dropped her head back to enjoy the heat. Despite her intention to relax, images from Valerie Gerard's crime scene flicked one after the other through her head. This was no random killing or sacrifice related to some curse. Valerie Gerard had been a target. The killer was someone who thought she was a liar. The stitched lips made it personal. The distinct message made it undeniable. A message specifically for Valerie.

At only nineteen, who had the girl pissed off that royally?

A freshman in college. Honor student. Award-winning high school student who had graduated valedictorian. President of the class. Et cetera, et cetera. No history of drug use or promiscuity.

Then there was Alicia Appleton. High school senior. Cheerleader. Miss Popular at school. Rich kid. Got a Range Rover for her sixteenth birthday. Had an iPhone and all the other cool gadgets teenagers loved. Won beauty pageants far and wide.

The kind of girl you loved to hate.

The two victims had nothing in common. Not friends. Not hobbies or goals. Not tax bracket. Nothing.

Same perp involved? Sarah's gut said yes.

Could be a copycat in Alicia's case. Since Alicia hadn't gone missing until after Valerie's body was found, it was possible someone had used the murder as an opportunity to get rid of someone he or she despised.

But, like Conner said, Youngstown was a small place where everyone knew everyone else. The likelihood that two killers could be lurking about was a stretch.

Not to mention that only two days separated the events.

Realistically, that element could shift Sarah's theory either way.

Too early to tell.

Sarah shoved the dripping shower curtain aside and stepped out of the tub. When she'd dried her skin and hair sufficiently, she went in search of clothes. Going back to bed would be a waste of time. Any possibility of sleep was long gone. She did much of her best theorizing and deducing in the middle of the night. For years now she had had one simple but firm motto, she could sleep when she was dead.

Jeans, heavy-duty wool socks, T-shirt, and hooded sweat-shirt. Good to go. She shivered in spite of the thick clothing. Where was the thermostat in this joint?

She moved around the room, but didn't find one. What-ever. She pulled her ski cap on, figuring that would help since her hair was still a little damp.

The innkeeper evidently didn't have a crappy room to give her so he'd decided to freeze her out.

On the bed, she spread the notes and photos out around her. She hadn't been able to get anything on the autopsies from twenty years ago. The files weren't available she'd been told before coming, and according to Deputy Brighton they weren't only not available, they had been destroyed. Those details she would at some point have to get from Chief Willard.

Valerie had been a pretty girl. Blond hair, blue eyes. A little plump but not fat by any means. Astigmatism forced her to wear prescription eyeglasses. Smart, obviously. No history of trouble of any sort. Sarah wondered if the girl had stuck with the glasses rather than going with contacts as a way of hiding from the social world she didn't quite fit into.

Sarah considered the photo of the victim naked on that cold stone floor. Exposed, humiliated. Mouth sewn shut so she couldn't lie anymore.

Why would a good girl with seemingly nothing to hide lie?

Digging through the other documents, Sarah picked up the photo of Alicia Appleton. It was easy to get photos of just about anyone these days. Most had a MySpace or a Fa-cebook page. Type the name in a search box and voilà. All sorts of images and personal information. Far too many of these kids didn't set their profiles to private, allowing any-one who wanted to look to do so.

Sarah set the borrowed Facebook image of Alicia aside and studied the ones she had of Valerie. Sarah would bet her ass that Valerie's killer had known her personally. Maybe even gone to school with her at U-Mass.

It was possible that some psycho had focused his obsession

on the girl. Picked her out of the crowd for no other reason than some aspect of her appearance.

But Sarah's honed instincts were screaming otherwise.

"Who hated you so much, Valerie?"

Sarah stared at the photo from the ME's office.

Wait.

If the victim bled out at the scene . . .

How was she restrained?

No drugs were mentioned in the preliminary toxicology screen, indicating she hadn't just lain there of her own free will.

Sarah hadn't been able to get a copy of the autopsy. When she'd asked the first time the stock answer had been that the report wasn't ready for release. Which meant the ME hadn't completed the report. Then, upon her second request, the contact who'd provided the crime-scene photo at significant personal gain had chickened out on her and refused her calls. The results of the tox screen had been given in a press conference late yesterday.

Sarah stared at the victim's wrists, then her hands. Those markings on her wrists could have been tape or rope burns. But how had the killer kept the victim's arms out of the way while doing his or her evil work? There was nothing to tie her arms to on either side of her torso or above her head. Unless ropes had been stretched from the center of the chapel floor to the support beams at the sides of the structure. Sounded like a lot of extra effort to Sarah and why would the restraints have been removed before the crime-scene photos were taken?

Not standard protocol.

What were the other markings on her hands? The tops of Valerie's hands appeared skinned or scraped. The tissue certainly looked torn. More patches of torn skin left a path up her forearms. All the way to the bends of her elbows.

Sarah studied the markings, then she knew.

"Son of a bitch."

She scrambled off the bed and pulled on her Converses. Her theory couldn't be confirmed without a copy of the autopsy and that wasn't happening in the middle of the night. But there could be something at the scene.

All she had to do was remember how to get there.

Sarah braked to a hard stop.

"Dammit."

She'd passed it again.

After dragging the gearshift into reverse once more, she hit the accelerator. The car lunged backward. She slammed on the brake. Jerked forward.

Puffing out a frustrated breath, she let off the brake and eased down on the accelerator with a little less force. The tires spun, then grabbed onto the icy dirt and propelled the car slowly backward. When she'd reached the halfway point along Chapel Trail, which she now recognized after passing it twice, she moved cautiously to the side of the road and slowed to a stop. Shutting off the engine, she peered through the darkness. With nothing but the aid of the moonlight she could barely see the cluster of broken trees she'd noted on her first visit. Yep. The chapel was close by.

She grabbed her shoulder bag and climbed out of the car. Once she'd fished out the flashlight, she slung the bag over her shoulder and headed into the woods.

The wind had died down, but it was still as cold as hell. She shrugged her coat up around her neck. Man, she'd give a hundred bucks for even a cheap scarf and pair of gloves right now. Back home, vendors dotted the streets of Manhattan. Forgot your umbrella? Not a problem. Check any street corner and you could buy a piece of crap for five bucks that would get you through the day.

If she'd had any sense she would have waited until daylight. But she'd never been accused of possessing any patience much less any common sense.

She hated waiting.

Maybe it was some kind of phobia related to all those nights she'd waited for her mother to come and find her.

Until that last time . . .

"Yeah, yeah. I'm totally screwed up." *Just like my daddy and mommy.* DNA was a bitch.

Once she spotted the yellow tape hanging from a tree branch she was good to go. If the wind had been blowing as it had earlier she would have spotted the tape fluttering midair from the road. As it was, the long strips flanking either side of the path up to the chapel lay impotently on the ground.

She accidentally veered off the path and stepped into ankle-deep snow, swore a couple of times and found her way back to the path Conner had used. If she stepped in the indentions others before her had made, the snow didn't rise above her Converses. The wind had blown the strands of tape wide apart, making it more difficult to stay on the path in the darkness. She didn't have the patience to take it slow and let the narrow beam of her flashlight do its work.

Luckily for her wherever there was a break in the tree canopy the snow reflected the moonlight, making her trek somewhat less difficult than it could have been. She slipped once or twice but quickly regained her balance.

She held on to the railing and climbed the steps up to the chapel. With the drop in temperature since nightfall the damp stones were slick with a coating of fragile but slippery ice. By the time she reached the top step she wished again that she had brought her gloves. Her hands were freezing.

"And the boots," she muttered. Her toes were numb.

Ducking under the tape, she used her flashlight to scan the chapel's floor until she found the spot where the victim had lain. Instead of wasting time scouring the entire area around the bloodstain, she lay down next to it. The cold instantly permeated her clothing.

The victim had been about Sarah's height. Since the tissue damage was on the top of her hands, Sarah stretched her arms up over her head. Satisfied her position was close enough, she rolled onto her right side, keeping her arm stretched above her head. She set the flashlight, beam down, on the area next to her hand.

When she'd scooted up onto her knees, she reclaimed the flashlight and began scanning the area around where she'd stationed it. Slowly, inch by inch. Then she found what she was looking for.

She leaned closer to inspect the spot where there appeared to be tissue left behind. The darker part was dried blood; the lighter, skin. More spots of varying sizes spanned about a twelve-inch path.

Oh, yeah. She was on to something here.

Sarah sat back on her haunches and stared at the residue left by the victim's hand and forearm. Some fifteen to eighteen inches to the right was a matching sequence of spots.

The victim's hands and forearms had been glued to the stone. That was why she hadn't tried to escape . . . or to fight her attacker.

Or to rip the stitches from her lips so she could scream.

Valerie Gerard couldn't move without ripping off her own skin.

Sarah positioned herself on the cold floor once more, placing her hands parallel to the spots where the victim's hands had been. Then she rolled up into a straight-legged sitting position and leaned down to set the flashlight between her feet. She crawled back onto her knees and searched until she found the corresponding spots where the victim's heels were likely glued to the stone as well.

"There we go." Sarah grimaced. There were traces of tissue and dried blood higher up, where the meaty parts of the calves had been glued down, too.

Sarah shook her head. What a sick son of a bitch. And why the hell hadn't the crime scene photo reflected that "glued down" positioning of the body? Had the body been touched or moved prior to photographing?

Sitting back on her heels, she roved the flashlight over the stone floor. Whatever the crime-scene techs had missed was likely history after the snowstorm that blew through last night. Not that she'd expected to find anything other than what she had. But it never hurt to look. Sometimes a fresh set of eyes detected something others missed.

Mostly, she lingered after finding what she'd come for, to absorb the vibes of the place.

Though she definitely didn't believe in the paranormal, she did believe in atmosphere. There was a perfectly logical explanation, in her opinion, for all things that went bump in the night. She didn't believe in spirits or the devil, maybe not even in God. She waffled most of the time on that last part. Her aunt had taken her to church every Sunday from the time she was about ten all the way until she left for college at eighteen. So it wasn't like she hadn't been exposed to the Good Book or its teachings.

She just wasn't convinced anything beyond the human sphere of things existed.

It was too easy to blame bad things on the devil or on God. When the fact was, most bad things were carried out by humans. Every single event that people called miracles or plagues, dating back to Noah and before, could be explained by science. Not that she was a scientist by any means. She'd dropped out of college and her bid for a forensic science degree after three semesters to go to work for *Truth Magazine*. But she'd spent a lot of time studying the sciences. Men of science had a theory for everything just as men of the Bible had their legends and myths and parables.

It all boiled down to personal choice.

Whether one believed in heaven or hell or demons or angels, there was one truth here and now that could not be denied. A human being had killed Valerie Gerard and there hadn't been any angels around to save her.

Just like there hadn't been any to save Sarah when she was a little girl.

A shudder quaked through her. From the cold, she reasoned. The cold had leached deep into her bones.

She dug around in her bag until she located her digital camera. The picture quality wouldn't be that good, but she wanted documentation of her findings.

With the flashlight's beam aimed on the place where a limb had been positioned, she snapped a couple frames of each location.

Surprisingly, the images turned out better than she'd ex-

pected. She tucked the camera back into her bag and got to
her feet.

Had the victim been walked up the path? Was the perp
wielding a gun?

Wouldn't the techs have found tracks? Where had the
killer left his vehicle? According to Conner any footprints
left by the perp had been ruined. Had the same thing happened with tire imprints? Another question to ask the chief.

Or maybe the perp had come from an alternate direction.
There was another road, a private one Conner had said, that
ran parallel with Chapel Trail. Where the rich folks lived.

Sarah ducked under the tape on the other side of the chapel. The slope was steeper here. Lots of snow and ice. The
trees were thicker. This didn't seem like a good route for
marching or dragging a hostage.

Unless the perp had been going for as much camouflage
as possible. Sarah made her way down the slippery slope,
dodging saplings and monster evergreens.

She walked for maybe ten minutes and didn't stumble
over any paths or broken branches that might indicate anyone had traveled that route recently. After an about-face, she
moved back toward the chapel in a zigzag pattern. Still no
indication of a used path. But it was dark, she could be missing something.

The recognized entry path leading up to the chapel was
on the opposite side. That left the side adorned with the crucifix and the other side that looked out to the sea. The crucifix side was a sharp drop. The chances of making it up that
incline with or without a hostage in tow were slim to none.

She stared out at the sea, moved to that end of the chapel.
This route wasn't much better. Pretty steep slope. A few
hundred yards beyond where she stood, past the expanse of
woods, was the narrow gravel road Conner had told her
about, beyond that a house that sat on the rocky shore. No,
not a house. A mansion.

Someone was up late. Lights glowed from the massive
windows. Maybe they couldn't sleep, either.

Reaching into her bag, she fumbled for the binoculars. She could only be labeled a Peeping Tom if she was caught, right?

She rested the binoculars against her eyes and focused the lens to the longest zoom setting. A soaring window came into view. The room was . . .

A man stared at her.

Sarah jumped. Jerked the binoculars away from her face.

A man stood at the window gazing toward the chapel . . . or maybe toward her.

She sucked in a deep breath. "Okay. He can't see you."

It was dark as hell where she stood. She was wearing a black coat and dark jeans.

No way could he see her.

Another deep breath and she set the binoculars back into place. There he was. Perfectly still, gazing out the window like a statue.

He wore dark clothes. Navy maybe. He was older. Fifty-ish. Dark hair.

She stepped closer to the edge of the rock floor and studied the man. Was he lost in thought? Had he seen her flashlight and was curious as to who would be up here this time of night?

Strange. He seemed to be looking right at her.

Couldn't be. It was dark and he wasn't using binoculars.

No sooner than the thought had formed, he moved to his right.

A telescope.

A big, powerful telescope.

She stepped to the side, close to where the vines had encroached, despite ambitious pruning. The thick, rebellious vines snaked about in no particular pattern, weaving in and around the wooden pillars supporting the chapel's roof.

He had to know someone was up here. He'd seen her flashlight. She was sure of it. Now he was looking for the owner of that light. He would likely call the police. Damn it.

If she knew his name and number she would call him and

tell him not to worry. She was a little weird but she was no threat to him or his prestigious property.

The hair on the back of Sarah's neck lifted.

She tensed.

The rasp of leather on icy rock whispered in her ears a split second before she recognized the danger.

Turn around.

Something slammed into her back.

She was propelled forward.

Cold, thin air met her.

She was over the edge.

The oxygen evacuated her lungs.

Falling.

She clutched at the vines.

The sudden jerk told her she'd managed to grab on.

Don't move.

Be calm.

Think.

The vine was holding.

Her heart bumped hard against her sternum.

She wasn't falling anymore. She had a death grip on a couple of vines and she wasn't letting go for anything.

You're okay.

Take a breath. Stay calm. The bag she always carried pulled at her neck like a millstone.

Stay still? Or climb up?

It was dark as pitch below her but she was pretty sure there were trees and rocks. Nothing she wanted to land on.

Up was her best bet.

Reach up, she ordered her right hand.

Her body refused to obey.

Do it!

Her right hand released the vine. Adrenaline shot through her veins.

Her hand shook as she reached up. A foot or so higher, she latched on to the vine once more. Then the other hand. Reach up. Higher! Grab on.

Pull!

One methodical, achingly slow foot at a time, she pulled herself upward. Until she was within reach of the stone ledge.

Then the memory of the impact that had sent her over the edge paralyzed her.

What if someone was up there . . . waiting to push her again?

Her body trembled violently. Her fingers started to burn.

She had to do something.

Couldn't keep hanging there.

She tried to look down . . . couldn't see shit.

Up was her only option.

She reached up, hoped like hell no one stepped on her fingers. She clutched the ledge. Pulled. Her arms trembled. All she had to do now was turn loose of the vine and reach up with the other hand. No hesitation. Do it fast.

Using her right hand since it was strongest, she released the vine, grabbed the ledge. After a moment to steady herself, she reached and clawed and pulled with both hands until she hauled herself up, her arms quivering violently.

Sarah collapsed on the cold-as-ice stone floor and caught her breath.

She was okay.

Safe.

Not dead.

A new surge of adrenaline fired her blood.

Someone pushed me.

She rolled to her side. Shot to her feet.

Listen!

She peered through the darkness. Held her breath. Listened beyond the persistent pounding in her chest.

Silence.

Darkness.

Time to get the hell out of here.

Her legs wobbled, weak and seemingly boneless. After straightening her bag so that it no longer dragged at her neck, she crossed the stone floor, careful not to make a sound.

She pulled out her cell phone and checked her service. Shit. No service.

Perfect.

As quickly as she dared, she moved down the slope. It wasn't that far to her car. Whoever had pushed her evidently had taken off.

Probably just someone who wanted to scare her.

Yeah. Enough to kill her.

She stilled. She could have been killed. Dr. Ballantine's warning about ending up a victim rang in Sarah's ears.

Okay, but she hadn't been. She was safe.

Keep walking.

Just get to the car.

Get out of here.

Not far now.

Something rustled to her right.

She darted left. What the hell?

She stilled. Listened.

More rustling. The soft crunch of snow.

Someone was close . . . coming in her direction.

Sarah couldn't see shit. She couldn't turn on her flashlight. All the hell she could do was move as quickly as possible with her arms extended in front of her so she didn't collide with a tree.

Faster.

She bumped a gnarled trunk. Pain streaked through her shoulder, across her chest. Shit.

The pepper spray was in her bag . . . wait . . . no . . . keep going . . . don't take time to look for it.

Move. Don't stop. Don't dare stop!

Don't even slow down.

The sound behind her was louder now.

Closer.

Whoever was after her wasn't taking his time.

How the hell could he see?

He had to know the area.

Heart pounding, she burst into a run.

Barely missed a head-on collision with another tree.

Don't think. Feel. Run!

He was practically on top of her now.

She braced for impact.

Hands grabbed at her coat.

She slammed her elbow backward as hard as she could.

The contact jarred all the way up to her shoulder.

A grunt told her she'd connected with something vulnerable.

The hands stopped clutching at her.

She rushed forward.

Stumbled.

Fell flat on her face in the underbrush and snow.

She scrambled to get up.

Strong fingers manacled her ankle.

She screamed.

The sound echoed through the woods.

She kicked at her attacker.

Twisting her body, she kicked harder.

She couldn't see his face.

He wore a black ski mask. His eyes glittered.

She kicked hard at his head. Rammed a hand into her bag. Her fingers couldn't locate the metal canister.

She kicked again.

He let go.

She scrambled to her feet.

Ran.

Fuck the trees.

She butted a tree trunk full-on. The air whooshed out of her lungs.

She shook herself, dragged in a breath.

Keep going.

Her head spinning, she moved around the tree.

Ran as fast as her legs would go.

She burst free of the woods.

The road.

Where was her car?

She turned around.

Couldn't see it.

Fuck it!

Run!

She didn't know which way she was running. Toward Calderwood Lane or away from it. Was she even on Chapel Trail?

Didn't matter.

Run!

Her feet flew out from under her.

Her ass hit the ground.

She scrambled up.

Keep running.

Faster.

Don't look back.

Listen.

Hold your breath.

Listen!

The only sound was her own steps echoing behind her.

Or was he still coming?

A burst of adrenaline sent fuel to her muscles. She lurched forward, tried to run faster still.

Her feet hit pavement.

She glanced around. Saw the green street sign.

Couldn't read it. Had to be Calderwood Lane.

She lunged left.

Not daring to slow down, she dug her cell from her pocket.

Bars glowed.

Relief burst inside her.

Full service.

All she had to do was put through the call and hide until help arrived. She ducked for cover under a thick evergreen. Pulling up her contact list, she hit *C* for Conner.

The slap of soles on the pavement in the distance sent fear throttling through her.

He was coming.

Don't even breathe.

CHAPTER 12

Kale drove like a bat out of hell along Calderwood Lane. What in God's name was she doing out here at this time of night? It was twenty degrees! As soon as he found her he would damn sure ask.

This only confirmed his conclusion. People from New York were crazy.

A dark figure appeared in front of his headlights.

He slammed on his brakes.

The Jeep skidded to a stop.

She stood in the center of the road.

Didn't move.

Shit.

He shoved into park and flung his door open.

"What the hell were you thinking?"

She still didn't move.

He stepped between her and the front of the Jeep. His gut roiled at the idea that a few more feet and he would have run her down.

"Thank you for coming." Her voice sounded small and way more humble than usual.

What the hell had happened to her? Before he could shout that and the other questions bombarding his brain, she walked, her movements unnatural, around to the passenger side of the Jeep and climbed in.

Kale threw up his hands, then dropped them to his sides. This was not what he'd signed on for. He was supposed to be a tour guide, not a freaking search-and-rescue service.

Or a peace mediator. Or . . . whatever the hell else she needed.

He marched to the driver's side door and plopped behind the wheel. "Where's your car?"

"Near the chapel somewhere."

He glanced at her. She sat like a stone, her gaze fixed on the road. Her voice sounded flat.

"Put on your seat belt."

Her hands shook as she followed his order.

He shifted into drive and rolled forward. When he'd located her car and determined it wouldn't block traffic, not that there was much out here, he pointed his Jeep toward home. There hadn't appeared to be any damage to the vehicle so she hadn't run off the road. What he could see of the tires hadn't given the impression she'd had a flat. Maybe the battery had died on her.

She started to shake. The adrenaline he'd heard in her voice when she called was wearing off. Not to mention she was likely freezing. He turned up the heat and drove a little faster.

He didn't ask any more questions. She didn't ask where he was taking her. Shock, he supposed. But from what?

She didn't utter another word until they arrived at his house. "I apologize for the trouble."

"Not a problem." He braced for Angie's attack as he unlocked and opened his front door.

As he'd anticipated, the dog reared up to greet him. "Hey, girl." He scratched her head and ushered her down. He glanced at his guest. "She's harmless, but a little aggressive with her curiosity."

Sarah Newton blinked, still looking damned dazed.

"Down, Angie," he ordered as he opened the door wider for Newton to enter his domain. He swiped the wall switch and the lamps on either side of the couch illuminated.

Angie wagged her tail and smelled their guest's sneakers. Newton stared at her as if she was an alien life-form.

Kale closed the door and cast around for what to say next. He didn't bring strangers home too often. How about never?

In fact, he couldn't remember the last time he'd had a female in the house who wasn't his dog, his mother, or his sister. He tried to visualize his place as she would see it. Not exactly rustic, but definitely on the ordinary side.

Like everything else in his life.

"I should have brought my gloves."

Startled from his ludicrous musings by her odd statement, he looked her over again just to be sure he wasn't missing something that required immediate medical attention. "You've lost me." He dragged off his coat. "What about—"

She reached toward him, turned her hands palms up. The red marks on her palms looked like burns. "I should have brought my gloves," she repeated.

"How did you do that?" He reached out, inspected the marks more closely. Her hands were like ice. Angie, hearing the tension in his voice, barked. "Settle down, girl."

"The vines." Newton exhaled a shaky breath. "That's how I broke my fall."

He shook his head, totally confused. "You're going to have to start at the beginning." She opened her mouth but he stopped her. "First, we should get you warmed up." What was wrong with him? She'd stood out in the cold inadequately dressed for God knows how long. "Take off your coat."

She looked as puzzled as he felt but she did as he said.

He pointed to the couch. "Sit. I'll be right back."

He strode to his bedroom, Angie on his heels, and gathered a wool blanket and down comforter and a couple of pillows. By the time he reached the living room once more her teeth were chattering. He swaddled her in the blanket and ushered her down onto the couch. He tucked the pillows behind her and tugged off her sneakers. Her socks were wet so he pulled them off, too.

"Down, girl," he scolded as his curious companion attempted to sniff his guest's half-frozen feet. "I'll get you some dry socks." When he'd covered her with the down comforter, he snapped his fingers for Angie to come and hustled back to his bedroom for socks.

Angie trotted alongside him as he returned to the living room. "Put these on." He tossed the socks to Newton. "I'll make some tea."

Backing slowly toward the kitchen, he was almost afraid to take his eyes off her. She was too quiet. Her movements mechanical. Definitely out of character. *What the hell had happened to her out there?*

"Come, girl." He patted his leg and Angie joined him at the stove. He checked the kettle and turned on the burner beneath it. His mom had sent over chicken and sausage gumbo that he hadn't bothered eating tonight. Newton looked as if she could use a few good meals.

As soon as he had her warmed up, he would have some answers. If Mayor Patterson learned that she had been running around in the middle of the night—without Kale—he would not be happy. He didn't even want to consider what the chief would say.

Maybe his life was ordinary—boring even—but considering his guest's demeanor there was something to be said for boring.

Sarah Newton had been here less than twenty-four hours and already she was causing havoc.

He slid the soup into the microwave and searched for a tray. He had one. He knew he did. By the time the microwave dinged he'd found the tray and checked on his guest twice. The need to know what had gone down tonight made him hurry. If there was trouble out on Calderwood Lane he wanted to know about it before the chief or the mayor heard the news.

Angie sat at attention, her nose raised high as the scent of gumbo filled the air. "In a minute, girl," he promised.

Soup, tea, sugar. He needed a napkin and spoon. He grabbed both, added them to the tray, and headed back to the living room.

"This should warm you up," he announced as he settled on the ottoman-style coffee table in front of the couch. He set the tray beside him and offered the mug to his guest. Angie stayed back. She knew better than to crowd her master or his guests when food was served. "Sorry there's no lemon or cream." He didn't use them so he didn't keep them.

Newton accepted the tea, holding it in both hands. "Thanks. This is fine."

More patient than he'd known he could be, he let her drink and eat her fill. When the emptied dishes were back on the tray, he pushed it aside and braced his forearms on his knees. "Okay, Ms. Newton, let's hear it."

She'd stopped shivering and looked a little less rattled. "My car died. The battery, I think."

He arched an eyebrow. He might not be an expert but he knew a flat-out lie when he heard one. "Is that how you burned your hands? Trying to start your car? I thought you said you broke your fall."

She shrugged, some of that characteristic indifference glimmering back through. "Maybe I was confused."

Like hell. "What were you doing at the chapel?" He'd taken her there first thing today. He'd given her a minitour of the village. He'd sat by and let her bully Karen Brighton. He wasn't standing for anything less than the truth.

As if the full, uncut version of Sarah Newton had suddenly kicked back in, she gave him one of those quick half-smiles. "I was bored. I thought I'd hang out at the scene to see if the killer showed up for an encore."

Fury whipped through Kale. "The truth, Ms. Newton."

She rolled her eyes. "You sound like my shrink."

Oh, that was good news. The lady had a shrink? Why was he surprised? He didn't repeat his demand. He let the pissed-off glower on his face speak for itself.

An impatient sigh hissed past her lips. "Fine. I had an epiphany."

"What kind of epiphany?" Was she really going to make it this hard?

"The victim had to be restrained at the scene. So I went out there to see if my hunch about the manner of restraint was right."

His brow furrowed with utter confusion. "What are you talking about? What hunch?"

"Her arms and legs were glued to the rock floor at the chapel." She stared straight into his eyes. "Super Glue. Krazy Glue. Something like that."

Dread formed a rock in his gut. Anything he said from this point had to be carefully worded. This lady had a way of dredging information from thin air, it seemed. He'd been briefed on the autopsy results, he knew all too well how Valerie had been restrained. "How can you be sure she was restrained . . . in that manner?"

"I found blood and tissue residue." A frown tugged at her lips. "You haven't seen the final autopsy report? Surely that detail was mentioned."

How could she have known that? "You couldn't have waited until daylight? I would have gone with you."

"I couldn't sleep."

Jesus Christ. She was going to be a pain in the ass. "So you followed your hunch. Good for you. What really happened to your car?"

She averted her gaze again. "I got turned around in the woods. Couldn't find my way back to it."

That sure didn't sound like the cocky woman he knew her to be. "You could have gotten completely lost and frozen to death. This isn't New York, Ms. Newton, there isn't a taxi waiting at the corner of every block."

"Believe me, there isn't a taxi waiting at the corner of every block in New York," she snapped. "Only in the movies."

"I'm going to ask you once more. If you keep yanking my chain, I'm going to have to excuse myself from being your escort."

That prompted a laugh. He couldn't decide if the sound reflected amusement or hope.

"You're my escort?"

"You know what I mean."

"I was checking out the house across the woods from the chapel and someone pushed me. I went over the edge. If I hadn't grabbed on to those vines . . . I'd still be lying out there. Frozen probably. Seriously injured for sure."

"Someone pushed you?" She had to be mistaken. Though no one in town wanted her here, there wasn't a soul he could think of who would do her harm.

"I was pushed, Conner." Fury glinted in her eyes. "Then someone chased me through the woods and down the road. He disappeared after that."

"Someone chased you and then just . . . disappeared?" He made no attempt to hide his skepticism.

"I hid in the trees. He gave up maybe." She shrugged. "I don't know."

Kale didn't know a whole lot about Saran Newton. Whether she was easily spooked or not. If she had a vivid imagination. Now wasn't the time to ask. She was on the defensive from whatever had happened.

He stood. "I'll get you something for your hands."

If her story was true . . . but it couldn't be.

Could it?

Folks were pretty upset about her presence. Someone could be watching her. Hoped to scare her off, maybe.

"I knew you wouldn't believe me, that's why I wasn't going to tell you." She looked directly at him. "Those compassionate folks you know would never push a girl over a ledge."

Irritation tightened his lips. "I'll be back."

Rather than argue with her, he stormed to the bathroom. He knew these people. Maybe some of them were capable of spooking her . . . but pushing her over a ledge. Not possible. There had to be another explanation.

He located the antibiotic cream and headed back to the living room. Angie stood at attention next to Newton, tail wagging.

Newton had pulled her sneakers back on and was reaching for her coat. "I apologize if I inconvenienced you." She produced a faint smile. "I appreciate your help. Now, if you don't mind taking me to my car, I'll get back to the inn. I'm sure you're ready to call it a night."

Oh, no. He wasn't letting her out of his sight again tonight. "Sit."

Angie obeyed instantly. Newton, however, stared at him

as indignantly as if he'd slapped her with a glove in blatant challenge.

"You're staying here tonight."

She scoffed. "I don't think so, but nice try."

Nice try?

Then he got it. "Don't flatter yourself, Newton. You're not my type."

She angled her head, stared at him with mounting defiance. "Why would I stay here?"

He searched her eyes, saw the faintest flicker of uncertainty. "Because it's late. We're both tired and you've had the hell scared out of you."

The fight visibly draining out of her, she lowered back onto the couch. "I guess it wouldn't kill me to stay."

He didn't bother asking what that meant. He thrust the tube of cream at her. "This will help your hands."

She opened the tube and spread a thin layer on both palms. "Thank you." She passed the tube back to him as she toed off her sneakers.

"Anything else I should know about tonight?" He was beat. He resettled on the ottoman as she stretched out on the couch and pulled the comforter around her. But he would stay up as long as he was getting information from her. Angie, the traitor, hopped on the couch and curled up at their guest's feet. She'd apparently lost interest in a midnight snack.

Newton gave her head a little shake.

"Did you get a look at the person who allegedly pushed then chased you?"

Those curiously blue eyes met his in challenge. "He wore a black ski mask."

"How tall was he? And you're sure it was a he?"

She thought about that a moment. "Your height or taller. Yes, definitely a he."

Kale was still skeptical. "Heavy? Thin?"

"Medium."

"When he was chasing you, did he fall behind like he was out of shape or did he keep up?" Physical fitness could be indicative of age.

This was nuts. Who would do this sort of thing?

She shook her head. "I don't think he was really trying to catch me. I think he might have been trying to scare me off but got a little carried away."

"What makes you think that?"

Uneasiness had started to nudge Kale. If she was telling the truth . . . if any of the villagers had decided to take matters into their own hands and go to this extreme . . .

Not good.

He would have to talk to Patterson and Willard about this.

Yet, not a single name came to mind of anyone who would be capable of such a thing.

"Because he was right behind me in the woods," Newton explained. "Didn't seem to have a problem catching up or keeping up with me. He was close enough that when I fell, he grabbed me by the ankle. But I got away and then he never caught up with me again. As if he'd accomplished what he'd set out to do."

"We'll talk to the chief about this in the morning." He rubbed his neck. No one was going to be happy to hear it.

"Who's the guy with the big house through the woods? The one you can see from the chapel?"

"Jerald Pope?" The Pope home was the only one visible from the chapel.

"Who is he?"

"Master boat builder. His work is internationally known. He and his wife and their daughter, Jerri Lynn, live there."

"I assume he was interviewed and had nothing to add that might prove useful to the investigation."

"Correct." Why would she ask about Pope? Sure, his house was close to the scene but that didn't mean he was involved or had seen anything. That was Kale's defensive side talking. Her question was perfectly logical.

She fell silent for long enough to make him start to feel anxious.

"He was watching me." Her voice cracked when she said the words.

"You think Pope pushed you?" That was seriously outrageous but if that was her perception, Kale needed to know right now.

"No. He never left his house."

"Explain," he ordered.

"I noticed him watching me from his window." She shrugged. "I guess he saw my flashlight and wondered what I was doing. Or maybe he was worried there was trouble at the chapel again." As if she'd just had a thought she asked, "No one called in about someone snooping around at the chapel?"

Kale shook his head. "I doubt it. If anyone had called it in, the chief would have called me first." It seemed both the chief and the mayor were expecting him, and him alone, to keep her out of trouble.

Newton looked unsettled by that answer.

"I'll take you to meet Mr. Pope tomorrow if you'd like," Kale offered, in hopes of making her feel more comfortable. "You can ask him if he saw you."

"I have a list of people I want to interview," she informed him as she snuggled deeper into her covers. She was exhausted and it was catching up with her.

Great. He couldn't wait. "We'll start first thing in the morning after I check in on my office." He stood. "You let me know if you need anything."

"You locked the door, right?"

"Believe it or not," he said, surmising that her question was a jab at life in Maine, "we don't lock our doors because there are no robberies in Youngstown."

"Only murders," she reminded.

Right.

Only murders.

CHAPTER 13

Saturday, February 28, 7:30 A.M.

Sarah's nose wiggled.

She inhaled more deeply.

Bacon.

Another deep draw of the sweet smell.

She opened her eyes and looked around.

Shelves lined with books, some haphazardly placed. A comfortable, however slightly wear-worn chair. White walls. She sat up, pushed the thick layer of covers away.

Conner's place.

Memories of rushing through the woods broadsided her. Her body ached from more than one full frontal confrontation with solid wood trunks. Her pulse reacted to an adrenaline dump.

Someone had pushed her over that ledge . . .

Her palms burned. She opened her hands and stared at the angry red marks there.

That certainly hadn't been a dream.

. . . running through the woods in the dark.

She shuddered. This had to be a new record. She'd scarcely settled into town and already someone wanted her dead or, at least, out of the way.

The aroma of fresh brewed coffee abruptly distracted her senses.

She turned toward the kitchen, then scanned the room for

the time. An antiquated clock sat on the mantel, its arms reaching toward the numbers stenciled on its face.

Seven thirty-five.

She'd slept at least five hours. And no dreams.

Another record.

Sarah pushed up from the couch, grimaced as pain radiated up her torso and across her shoulders. Swinging from vines and intimate contact with trees clearly weren't in her best interests.

Righting her clothes, she shuffled sock-footed to the kitchen door. Sprawled at her master's feet, Angie swished her tail across the wood floor but she didn't bother raising her head. The dog had slept on the sofa with Sarah as if she'd needed a guard. Considering last night's jaunt through the woods, maybe she did.

Sarah's host moved his spatula round and round in a pan of scrambled eggs. Crisp slices of bacon lined a nearby plate. The coffeepot had filled. As she took in the scene, two slices of browned bread popped up in the toaster.

But it was the man that held her attention. He wore jeans as he had yesterday. The same wooly kind of socks he'd lent her covered his otherwise bare feet. Her gaze traced a path back up those long legs. His shirttail hung loose and his hair curled around his neck.

He looked damned good.

But . . . *this* was not good.

She knew better and, yet, here she was. She should have gone back to the inn last night.

Just another dumb decision she would live to regret.

Might as well get the initial awkward moment over with. She couldn't loiter in the doorway all morning. She had places to go and people to see.

"Isn't this quite the domestic scene," she announced, moving away from the door and toward the coffeepot. The smell had her taste buds crackling with anticipation.

He glanced over his shoulder. "What's the matter, New York guys don't cook?"

She ignored the question. While she poured a cup of coffee, he scraped eggs onto the plate next to the bacon. He placed the toast alongside the eggs and dropped two more slices of bread into the toaster.

As good as his efforts smelled, she never ate breakfast. Maybe she would savor her coffee before breaking the news to him.

His long-fingered hands gathered two plates, two forks, and napkins. She watched with interest as he set the table. His shirt remained unbuttoned, the long-johns-style undershirt beneath molded to his chest. He had a nice profile. Strong jaw. Symmetrical nose. Nice eyes. She'd noticed them before. She'd noticed a lot of things about him before. Those dark eyes, for instance, likely hid a man with far more depth than he preferred to reveal.

Her instincts went on point. Where was the wedding ring? What was a guy like him, at age thirty, doing single in a small town like this?

What else was there to do?

Except—Sarah glanced at the animal on the floor—walk his dog?

"Let's try restarting the conversation," Conner suggested as his gaze met hers. "Good morning."

She managed a halfhearted smile. "Morning."

"One of my employees picked up your car and dropped it off at the inn." He jerked his head toward the counter. "Keys are over there. You left them in the car."

"Thanks." A chill slid along her spine at the memory of falling face first in the snow . . . then those strong, gloved fingers curling around her ankle. She shivered. At least she'd gotten in a couple of good kicks.

"Sit." He gestured to the table, drawing her mind from last night's strange events. "I'll serve."

Sarah couldn't help herself. She laughed. "You spend too much time with your dog, Conner."

He placed a plate in front of the chair he'd indicated, then a fork and napkin. "What's that supposed to mean?"

She pulled out the chair and sat. "You give a lot of one-word commands."

"I also have a younger brother and sister. It worked well for them." He shot her a smile and prepared his own place setting.

Sarah's cheeks warmed. It wasn't like he was the first guy to smile at her in recent history, but there was something extraordinarily charming about his smile. Who knew? Maybe she wasn't herself this morning. Maybe real sleep dulled her usual edge. Certainly made her as horny as hell.

But that couldn't happen.

No getting personally involved in cases.

Never. Ever.

No matter how tempting.

Personal could be hazardous . . . in more ways than one.

"Dig in," he announced as he settled the laden serving plate in the middle of the table. "See." He snagged himself a cup of coffee and dropped into a chair. "That was more than one word."

Yeah, all right. Two. "I hate to break this to you, Conner, but I don't do breakfast."

He spooned a heaping of eggs onto her plate, then flanked it with toast and bacon. "There's a first time for everything, Ms. Newton."

She speared a bite of egg and lifted it to her mouth. Yes, life was filled with firsts. First steps, first kiss, first . . . kills. Remembered terror slithered along her skin. She pushed the memories away.

Sarah would be curious to see how Kale Conner responded to the first currently plowing its way into his life faster than the dozens of snowplows she'd seen cruising the streets since her arrival. Learning that you were friends with or perhaps even related to a murderer definitely carried an impact.

She knew all too well.

Banishing the images that wanted to accompany the thought, she shifted her attention to the man and her curiosity about him. "So, what's the deal, Conner? No wife? What about a girlfriend?"

He stopped mid-chew, surprise flaring in those dark eyes. Cutting to the chase saved time and energy. He would learn that she valued her time above all else.

He swallowed. "Single and thirty seems odd to you?" He scrunched his brow as if trying to recall some fact. "Wasn't there a show about single women in New York, all of whom were over thirty?"

Yeah. Yeah. "But this isn't New York?"

"Ah." He took a slug of coffee. "So you think there's nothing else to do around here but get married?"

The thought had definitely crossed her mind. "Well?" No need to be shy.

"Well." He set his palms flat on the table. "I run a fishing company. And I'm on the village council. I stay pretty busy."

"Let me guess, the older council members talked you into that. New blood and all that jazz."

Another flare of surprise. "That about sums it up."

She'd thought so. "What about college?" She picked up a piece of bacon and took a bite.

"What about it?"

Ah, she'd hit a nerve. His entire demeanor changed. "You didn't finish." He'd been an honor student, too. Marine engineering or something like that. Halfway through the program when he quit.

He stared at his plate, rearranged the food with his fork. "My father had an accident and my family needed me."

Now there was something she hadn't learned in her research. "What sort of accident?"

"One of his fishing boats crashed into the dock. He tried to help." Conner shrugged. "Got in the way and his spine was fractured in about half a dozen places."

"Paralyzed?"

He nodded. "Now the only navigating he does is in his wheelchair from the TV to the table."

She grimaced. "That's tough."

Conner nodded again. "Like I said. My family needed me." He dug into his food, kept his attention on the plate.

And there was the first flaw. Sarah leaned back in her chair and watched the man devour his breakfast. Handsome, nice, always ready to do his part. But. He'd had to sideline his life and live his father's. She could guess all that went along with the assignment. He'd likely played a large role in rearing his younger siblings. Ran the family business. Did whatever Daddy told him to do.

And absolutely nothing for himself.

Five years. She'd give him five years tops before the resentment and bitterness took its toll.

That was the thing about life. Whatever your reason for avoiding living it—no matter your noble motive for taking a detour—life always got the last laugh.

And the final say.

2313 *Beauchamp Road,* 9:00 A.M.

"The Popes are nice people," Conner warned as he and Sarah approached the massive double doors belonging to the Pope mansion.

Enormous house, ocean-front property. Nice and seriously wealthy people. She paused at the door, peered toward the chapel on the hilltop in the woods. "And they live really close to the crime scene."

Conner sighed and pressed the doorbell. "Just don't do or say anything I'll regret."

Sarah flashed him a smile. "I can't make any promises."

He looked miserable. She didn't need to be able to read his mind to know he would rather be doing anything but this. Like seeing to that fishing company. He'd opted to call in rather than drop by. Business appeared to be running smoothly without him . . . another thorn in his side this morning, she imagined. If work had needed him, would he have used that as an excuse to beg off *escorting* her?

The door opened and the man Sarah had seen in the

window last night looked from Conner to her and back, a broad, welcoming smile on his lips.

"Kale, what brings our newest council member out for a visit so early on a Saturday morning?"

"Morning, Jerald." Conner gestured to Sarah. "This is Sarah Newton. I'm sure you've heard she's here to help with the investigation."

"Of course." Jerald Pope thrust out his hand. "It's a pleasure to meet you, Sarah. Won't you come in?"

Sarah accepted the offered hand, gave it a solid shake. "I'd love to."

Environment spoke volumes about a person. Hopes, dreams, goals, concerns . . . they were all there.

The Pope home certainly had plenty to say. The entry hall was every bit as grand as one would expect for a house of this magnitude. Marble floors gleamed. Wood moldings, intricately designed and glossy white, accented the bold, rich walls. Splendid art lined the walls, making Sarah think of a museum or a gallery rather than a home.

Position and power were immensely important to one or all of the Popes.

Jerald Pope led the way to a luxurious sitting room on the right. "Please make yourselves at home." He gestured to the sofa. "Coffee? Tea?"

Conner shook his head, Sarah declined the offer of refreshments as they accepted the invitation to sit, an entire sofa cushion between them.

"Are you making progress in your investigation?" Pope asked as he settled into a silk-encased wing chair.

Nice. Someone else who liked to cut to the chase. "I'm still getting a feel for the community."

Pope relaxed more deeply into his chair. "How may I assist your endeavor?"

Sarah liked this guy already. Straight to the point. "Last night I noticed you have a perfect view of the chapel. That's a very nice telescope you have, by the way."

Pope smiled knowingly. "Indeed. That was you up at the chapel last night, was it?"

"It was." Tension rippled through Sarah as she considered that someone had stolen up behind her and given her what could have been a fatal shove. "Did you notice anyone else there last night?"

Pope moved his head side to side. "Only you. And I probably wouldn't have noticed your presence there if not for your flashlight. I considered reporting the activity, but then you were gone and I let it go."

She'd concluded as much. "Do you view the comings and goings at the chapel often?"

"Not until recently." He gestured to the soaring windows across the room. "When my wife and I commissioned this home we wanted to take in as much of the views as possible, the ocean as well as the mountains. The windows accommodate us quite well. The telescope is for watching the stars with my daughter."

"I'm sure the police have asked you this question already," Sarah ventured, "but I wondered if you saw anything or anyone the night Valerie Gerard was murdered?"

Regret etched across Pope's face. "Unfortunately not. I wish I had been watching that night. Perhaps I could have helped. Since that tragedy struck . . ."—he closed his eyes, drew in a heavy breath—"I try to keep an eye on the chapel." He blinked twice. "That's why I saw you last night."

"But then"—Sarah searched his face, his eyes, gauged the sincerity there—"you can't watch every minute."

He held her gaze, something like defeat in his. "So true."

Conner cleared his throat, whether to let her know it was time to go or from the emotional impact of the moment Sarah couldn't say.

"I'm sure the chief appreciates your efforts," Conner offered.

"It's the least I can do."

Sarah had other names on her list. She'd gotten all she was going to get here . . . for now. She stood, giving Conner a cue to do the same. "Thank you for your time, Mr. Pope."

He rose. "Please." Pope smiled. "Call me Jerald."

"Jerald. If I think of other questions . . ."

"Stop by any time," he offered. "I'm completely at your disposal."

"I appreciate that." Sarah surveyed the room before moving toward the hall. "Your home is magnificent."

"We enjoy it." He paused at the front entry. "You'll have to visit again when my wife and daughter are home. Perhaps you'll join us for dinner one evening."

"Absolutely." Sarah hesitated when he opened the door. "Your daughter," she said to Pope, "was she close to either of the victims?" Unnecessary question actually. As Conner had pointed out repeatedly, everyone here knew everyone else.

"Not really." Pope seemed to weigh his words before continuing. "She attended school here in Youngstown with Valerie, but they were never close friends." He shook his head. "Such a tragedy."

Definitely a tragedy.

In the Jeep, Conner braked at the end of the cobblestone driveway. "Where to now?"

His enthusiasm was underwhelming. "The next name on the list. Marta Hanover."

Without comment, he pointed the Jeep in the direction of town.

Sarah found it quite abnormal that he didn't ask why she wanted to speak with the Hanover woman. Maybe he didn't want to open himself up to questioning. He'd been noticeably quiet since she'd questioned him about his personal life.

"In case you didn't know," he said abruptly, as if to defy any negative conclusions she might have reached, "Jerald Pope paid for Valerie's funeral. Paid off the mortgage on her family's home, too, so her father wouldn't have to rush back to work. The Popes are good people," Conner added without even a glance in her direction, "just like the rest of the folks around here."

"Interesting." Rich, powerful, and generous. A complex man. Sarah would keep that in mind as she assessed the people on her list. Each name was there as a result of having met one or more of the Big Three criteria.

Access to the victims was the primary reason Pope had made Sarah's list. He lived closer than anyone else to the crime scene. He had a daughter near the same age as both Valerie Gerard and Alicia Appleton.

Motive, means, opportunity. The Big Three.

No one committed a murder for anything less than one or all.

CHAPTER 14

"Ms. Hanover?"

Marta Hanover was busy restocking the produce in her general store when Sarah and Conner approached. She had decided that his presence might actually gain her more co-operation than if she'd showed up on her own. The tactic had worked reasonably well with Jerald Pope.

Folks in small towns didn't take too well to strangers.

She had learned that the hard way, too.

"Kale, morning. How's Mr. C?"

"He's hanging in there. Thank you for asking."

Marta Hanover wiped her hands on her apron, arrowed a brief glance at Sarah. "You let your mama know that I'm bringing some special goodies by this evening."

"Yes, ma'am. I'll do that." Conner gestured to Sarah. "This is Sarah Newton. She's here to look into Valerie's murder and Alicia's disappearance."

Judging by the pained expression on his face, Sarah estimated that he wasn't anticipating a favorable reaction from the seemingly pleasant lady.

As Ms. Hanover's scrutiny swung to Sarah, she jumped in with both feet. "I sincerely appreciate your time, Ms. Hanover." Sarah thrust her hand in the woman's direction. "I'm here to help." Marta accepted the offered hand and gave it a rather limp shake. "I have ten years' experience working cases very much like this."

The older lady's eyes tapered with suspicion. "You're the one from that magazine."

"Yes." Sarah nodded. "*Truth Magazine* is an investigative journal. We work particularly hard to find answers in tragic cases like this one."

Marta's hands settled on her hips. Not a good sign. "The problem here is simple," she said frankly. "That Enfinger fellow has barged in with his big plans and walked all over our history. Mark my word, things won't be right until he's gone for good."

"That may certainly be the case," Sarah placated. "I was hoping you might be able to help me confirm some of the facts."

The pleasant-looking, loose-tongued lady had been quoted in several newspapers. That was why her name was at the top of Sarah's interview list. The woman loved to talk.

Marta glanced around the store. A gentleman, probably her husband, was at the counter running the register. A couple of stock boys were filling the shelves. Five, maybe six customers milled about. No one appeared to be paying attention to the quiet conversation going on in produce.

"Let's go in the back," Marta said with another quick assessment of the man behind the counter.

"Of course." Sarah followed the lady through the double doors marked Employees Only; Conner was right behind her.

Marta went over to a large commercial sink and washed her hands. She pulled off a couple of paper towels and leaned against the counter. "Valerie Gerard was a good girl," she began. "I'm sure Kale told you that."

Sarah nodded to keep her talking. She had reviewed the history on the girl, as well as her MySpace and Facebook pages. She appeared to have been a great girl. Not the typical rebellious teenager.

"Her family's just devastated. She was their only child and they'd poured everything they had into that girl. They had high hopes for her future. There was talk of Harvard."

As any good parent would. Not that Sarah would know.

"She worked here during Christmas vacation," Marta offered. "She was a hard worker and always kind to our customers. We didn't have one complaint. She was never late and never missed a single day."

"She sounds like the ideal teenager," Sarah commented. She had this part already. What she wanted to learn was the flip side. Everybody had one. "Did she have a boyfriend?"

Marta moved her head side to side. "She was too focused on her studies to be fooling with boys. She didn't even date as far as I know."

"That's right," Conner cut in. "She went to her senior prom single." He said to Sarah, "Her friends have confirmed there was no boyfriend, then or now."

"What about her friends?" Sarah looked from Conner to Ms. Hanover. "Did she have a lot of friends?"

"Not that many." Marta pursed her lips a moment. "All you had to do was look at the *Youngstown Sun* to know that Valerie Gerard didn't bother much with a social life. She was always involved in activities that would further her education or that supported the community."

"How would you compare Valerie to Alicia, the girl who's missing?"

Marta tossed the wadded-up paper towel into the closest trash receptacle. "No comparison."

"Can you be more specific?"

"Alicia has herself lots and lots of boyfriends. Parties. Big social life." Marta threw up her hands. "Not that I'm talking bad about the girl. She's a pretty good kid. Just a little wild. But no one"—her gaze locked with Sarah's—"deserves this."

"You're so right. I certainly hope I can help find her." *Before* it's too late.

"Alicia's always in the paper, too," Marta went on. "She's won all kinds of beauty pageants and her grandparents have her in every kind of dance and theater activity around here. They take her to New York shopping about once a month. They've spoiled that child. Maybe a little too much."

"Do you know the name of Alicia's most recent boy-friend?"

"Brady Harvey," Conner cut in. "His family owns the inn where you're staying."

Sarah hadn't met the innkeeper's family. She'd have to make it a point to do that. Brady definitely went on her list.

"Thank you, Ms. Hanover." Sarah reached into the front pocket of her shoulder bag for a business card. "I hope you'll call me if you think of anything you believe might be useful."

Marta took the card, considered it, then set her attention on Sarah. "It's the curse."

Sarah started to let it go, but something in the woman's eyes made her rethink that strategy. There was something more there than idle speculation. "Why do you say that?"

"I saw the roses."

Conner and Sarah exchanged a look. "What roses?" he asked.

"The red ones. A big bouquet. Sandra Gerard got them the day before they found her girl's body."

Sarah noticed the new tension in Conner's posture. This was something he didn't know. "Who were they from?" Sarah inquired before he could.

"The card was unsigned. Just said, *Deepest regrets*." Marta shrugged. "When I took that fruit basket to Sandra I asked her about them. I didn't say nothing, of course. I didn't want to upset her."

"Did you speak to Chief Willard about this?" Conner was visibly agitated now.

Sarah was mildly intrigued.

Marta frowned as she shook her head. "I didn't really think about it. I figured the chief would remember same as I did. You're too young," she said to Conner. "But the day before those two missing girls were found twenty years ago, each family received a big old bouquet of red roses. They never did know who sent them. Could've been anybody, I guess."

"No one thought the flowers were relevant?" Sarah asked.

"I guess I can see why they wouldn't," Marta explained. "When there's an illness or death or something like that, most folks take something to the family. It's the community's way of helping. I just thought it was an odd coincidence."

Sarah scarcely took the time to thank the lady before walking quickly to the parking lot. "Take me to the Gerards' home." He wouldn't like her request. If she hadn't let him talk her into riding along in his vehicle, she could just go. She wanted to see those flowers. To touch them. Her instincts were humming.

"That's probably not a good idea." He paused on the sidewalk. "The family's been through enough. They've—"

Frustration lashed through her. "Their daughter is dead. What the hell do they expect? To just close the book and forget the last chapter? There should be more questions!" She was pissed now. "The questions shouldn't stop until we have all the answers."

For five seconds he stared at her.

She was the first to blink. Damn. That almost never happened.

"Fine. We'll go over there." He stepped off the curb. "But it's a waste of time. Like I was trying to tell you, Valerie's parents have gone to Florida for a couple of months to stay with friends." He looked at Sarah across the top of the car. "You're right, the investigation has to continue, they just couldn't be a part of it anymore."

"If they're not home, what does it matter if I snoop around? They'll never know." These people had to get past the whole "let's not inconvenience anyone" or "hurt anybody's feelings." A girl was dead! What did it take to wake them up?

"You wouldn't understand." He shook his head. "There's this thing called respect—"

"That doesn't make sense." How was trying to find their daughter's killer being disrespectful?

"Just get in the Jeep, Newton."

Sarah kept her mouth shut during the drive along Main. He turned onto Central Street and she mentally braced. Going to the victim's home was one of the worst parts. Seeing things the way they used to be and knowing it would never be that way again. Looking into the eyes of those left behind . . . but there was nobody home here.

That felt wrong. Maybe she just couldn't understand the reaction. Bury your child and then take off?

But then, she was definitely no expert on the interactions between parents and their children.

Conner parked at the curb in front of 1118 Central. It wouldn't have mattered whether or not Sarah knew the address already. The evidence of loss was all over the place. Hundreds of bouquets. Cards and stuffed animals. Candles. The front of the house and the porch were lined with gifts.

"I don't know about you," Conner said, "but I would find it difficult to come home to this."

They emerged from the Jeep simultaneously. Sarah couldn't take her eyes off the house. The rest of the neighborhood didn't matter. The feeling of emptiness, despite the visible outpouring of gifts, was overpowering.

Maybe he had a point.

Sarah climbed the steps. She didn't knock or ring the bell, she tried the door. Locked.

"That would be trespassing," Conner warned.

She didn't care. The need to go inside—to see—was overwhelming. She had to do it.

Her feet had taken her down the steps and around the corner of the house by the time he'd caught up with her.

"Ms. Newton—Sarah—don't push it. I'm not about to let you break the law," he cautioned.

At the side of the house, farthest from the street, she crunched through the snow and pressed her face to the nearest window.

Kitchen. Vase after vase of flowers lined the counters.

Her heart skipped a beat, then started to pound frantically.

On the center of the island was the only vase of red roses. A full dozen, at least. Clear glass vase, water almost exhausted. Several of the velvety heads drooped with the passage of time, but others still stood tall and open. Petals had fallen on the white counter, their deep crimson color like drops of blood.

She faced Conner. "You have to call Chief Willard. There could be prints on the card . . . on the vase." The possibilities raced around in her head. "This may be the only break the investigation gets."

Conner held up his hands. "Just wait a minute. We don't know that this means anything."

But it did. She knew it. Urgency swam through her veins. "Never mind." She considered what she was about to suggest. Definitely the best strategy. "We can talk to the chief later." She leveled a take-no-prisoners look on Conner. "We need to go to the Appletons'. Now. If they've gotten the roses already . . ." She swallowed back the threat of defeat. "It may be too late."

But they had to try.

The changing expressions on Conner's face told her he wanted to say no. But the possibility that she was right wouldn't allow him to.

"All right. But you watch what you say."

"I understand. Let's just go."

The ten-minute drive to Calderwood Lane had her literally suspended on the edge of her seat. Her hand was on the handle, ready to open the door and bail out of the Jeep the instant he stopped.

Two endless miles past the big sign proclaiming Appleton Farms land for as far as the eye could see, he slowed for the turn.

"That's the grandparents' home." He pointed to the rambling farmhouse on the left of the driveway. "Farther back"—he nodded toward the gravel road that served as a secondary drive beyond the paved one—"is where Alicia and her family live."

As soon as he braked, she was out of the car. She didn't slow but he caught up with her.

"Remember what I said," he cautioned as they climbed the steps to the front stoop.

Yeah. Yeah. Sarah pressed the doorbell and the door opened almost immediately.

"Yes?" An older version of the missing girl stared at Sarah a moment before shifting to Conner. "Kale," she said, acknowledging him personally.

"We're sorry to bother you, Ms. Appleton," he said with obvious shame. "This is Sarah Newton and she'd like to ask you a few questions about Alicia."

The hesitation that followed prevented Sarah from taking a deep breath. She needed to talk to this lady. She needed to see if red roses had been delivered.

"Ms. Appleton," Sarah blurted, unable to bear the silence any longer, "there are questions in your daughter's case that I believe haven't been raised yet. I'd like to speak to you about those."

Sarah was surprised that Conner didn't kick her or argue her suggestion. His silence and tolerance was all she could ask for.

"All right." Though clearly disappointed that good news hadn't arrived, Ms. Appleton stepped back and opened the door wider. "My husband isn't home right now," she explained as Sarah and Conner entered her home. "He took the boys in to town for lunch."

Alicia had two younger brothers who still needed parents. Sarah sympathized with how difficult this must be for them as well. "Thank you," she said with all the sincerity she could pack into the two impotent words.

The house looked lived in. Big overstuffed furniture, a little worn. Magazines and papers lying about. A home where people gathered and enjoyed each other's company. But it felt empty. Stark and empty. And too quiet.

Like the Gerard home.

"Would you like something to drink?"

Rachel Appleton's voice was empty of emotion. Her pale, drawn features spoke the same. How did one face the day knowing their child, however old, was missing, possibly dead?

"No, ma'am." Conner shifted uncomfortably. "We'll only

take a few moments of your time." The look he shot Sarah said it had better turn out that way.

"Well." Rachel stood in the middle of the room as if she wasn't sure what to do next. "All right."

"Ms. Appleton, have you received any gifts?" Sarah shrugged offhandedly. "Flowers?"

Rachel's head bobbed enthusiastically as if she were glad to have a question she could answer. "Oh, lots."

Sarah moistened her lips. "May we see them?"

Confusion lined the older woman's brow but then she gestured to the hall behind her. "They're in Lici's bedroom." She managed a shaky smile. "That's what we call her."

Sarah nodded. Rachel Appleton's next hesitation had Sarah ready to explode with tension.

The lady finally turned and led the way to her missing daughter's room. She opened the door. The light was already on inside. As with the exterior of the Gerard home, Alicia's room was filled with flowers and cards and stuffed toys. Sarah scanned the vases . . . her heart thumped harder and harder as she moved from one to the next. Dozens of mixed bouquets of pastel colors, some richer, bolder colors like purple and orange. Lots of whites and creams. Rows of pink, lavender, and yellow tulips.

If the roses had already been delivered . . .

Her gaze lit on a vase. The long-stemmed roses stood tall and proud amid the less revered varieties. The water level in the vase was barely an inch from the top. No fallen petals, no bowed heads.

These flowers were fresh . . . newly delivered.

"The red roses," Sarah said, barely resisting the impulse to run over and look at the card, "when did you receive those?"

"This morning." Rachel faked a smile. "They're very beautiful, but the sender forgot to sign the card."

"May I?" Sarah gestured to the flowers.

"Newton," Conner admonished.

Rachel blinked, the confusion was back. "It's all right." She swallowed with effort. "Alicia will love them. She loves flowers. We always got her pink ones on her birthday." Rachel's voice quivered as she said the last. "But the red is pretty, too."

Sarah heard Conner say, "They're very beautiful."

She dropped to her knees in front of the vase that sat on the floor amid the other arrangements. Her pulse thundered, had her blood rushing. The card wasn't in an envelope. Just tucked loosely amid the greenery and baby's breath.

Her fingers cold as ice as if the blood wasn't making it that far, Sarah used her fingernails to grasp the very corner and lift up the card just enough to see the written note.

Deepest regrets . . .

No signature.

She released the note, let it settle back amid the foliage, and pushed to her feet. "Ms. Appleton, do you recall which floral service delivered the roses?" Sarah's gaze connected with the lady's.

Rachel thought a moment, then shook her head. "They were on the stoop when my husband and boys were leaving. I'm not sure anyone rang the bell. I called Deputy Brighton like I was supposed to. She said it was okay to keep them."

This could be nothing. Sarah knew that for certain. Just because Marta Hanover recalled red roses from twenty years ago, and because a dozen had been delivered to Valerie Gerard's family more than a week ago . . . meant nothing.

But it didn't *feel* like nothing.

Conner sent her a firm look. "We should go."

"Did you see?" Rachel asked. She moved across the crowded-with-gifts room. "Alicia's senior portrait arrived yesterday." She admired the large portrait that sat on an elaborate stand. "She's beautiful, isn't she?"

Sarah studied the image in the portrait. The girl was stunning. She wore a delicate necklace that sported a small shimmering crown. "She's very beautiful. The necklace is lovely, too."

"That was a Christmas present," her mother explained, clearly excited to talk about something besides the fact that her daughter was missing. "She's won so many beauty pageants, her friends nicknamed her the queen." Rachel touched the flawless portrait, smiled.

"I can certainly see how it would be difficult to choose anyone else standing on a stage next to her. She is stunning." Sarah felt sick to her stomach.

Alicia's mother motioned around the room. "She has so many trophies and crowns." She sighed. "She was crowned Miss Youngstown High School at the homecoming game." She moved to an enormous curio cabinet and indicated a glittering crown sitting atop a velvet pillow. "She loved getting dressed up from the time she could walk."

Sarah surveyed the numerous crowns, would have shifted her attention back to the roses, but something out of place snagged her curiosity. A pink pillow, four shelves down, was empty. All the rest displayed a shimmering crown, but not that one.

"I don't know what happened to that one," Rachel offered, obviously noting Sarah's focus there. "I've searched this house twice over and I can't find it. I even accused her brothers of having misplaced it but they swear they didn't touch it."

Part of her needing to reach out, Sarah put a hand on the woman's arm. "I'm sure you'll find it." She wished she could say the same for her missing daughter. Sarah's every instinct blistered her senses with the impression that this would not end well.

"I sure hope so," Rachel lamented. "She won that crown in seventh grade." She drew her eyebrows together. "Or was it eighth? She'll remember and she won't be happy to learn it's misplaced."

Conner practically dragged Sarah out of the room after that. He kept apologizing for their having stayed so long. When they reached the front door, Rachel Appleton asked, "Are you going to put Alicia's picture in your magazine?"

Sarah paused. The other woman's expression was so hopeful that she couldn't say no. "Yes. With your approval, of course."

The woman beamed even as her lips trembled with fear. "Alicia would like that a lot. Just a minute." Rachel hurried off in the direction of the bedrooms.

"We have to go," Conner urged. "The chief needs to know about this. He's not going to be happy you touched that card."

Sarah didn't care what the chief thought, she couldn't stop obsessing on that missing crown. "We'll go in a minute."

This felt wrong. It was more than the missing girl . . . it was about the crown somehow. And the roses. She felt it deep in her gut.

"Here."

Sarah hauled her attention to Rachel as she burst back into the room. She held out a small photograph. Sarah accepted it. Alicia Appleton's Top Model smile radiated from the wallet-size photo as if it were ten times its size. This girl would walk into a room and own it with nothing more than that smile.

"That's her favorite." Rachel glowed with pride. "She would be mortified if you didn't use that one."

"This one's perfect." Sarah delivered her best attempt at a reassuring smile.

Rachel's face fell as if the weight of maintaining the hope was too much for her. "You don't have any more questions?"

The woman was lonely. Lonely and terrified. Terrified that no one would be able to find her daughter.

Before it was too late.

Emotion burned Sarah's eyes. "I may be back with more questions. If that's all right."

Rachel nodded. "Come any time. I'll be here." The distraught mother glanced around her living room. "When she comes home, I want her to find me right here waiting."

Waiting, Sarah knew, for things to be the way they used to be.

"Thank you, Ms. Appleton."

Rachel Appleton reached out this time . . . rested her

trembling fingers on Sarah's arm. "I know what other people say . . . but . . ." She moistened her lips, blinked back the shine in her eyes. "But I'm glad you're here."

There. Right there, Sarah realized, was the compassion that Connor spoke about so avidly. No matter that her daughter was missing, this woman still reached out to Sarah to make her feel welcome.

The look that passed between them as they stood, touching, was something else Sarah recognized all too well. Sheer desperation . . . absolute terror.

Sarah was unconditionally certain of one thing in all this . . . if she wasn't found soon Alicia Appleton would die.

Very soon.

And Rachel Appleton would never, not in a million lifetimes, recover.

CHAPTER 15

Kale closed his cell phone. Things at Conner and Sons were still rolling along smoothly without him. He didn't like spending this much time away from work . . . but it was the only way he could keep up with his new project. This time of year, Saturdays, sometimes Sundays, were required to prep for the coming season.

Sarah Newton paced the chief's office, annoyed that they were being made to wait yet again by a member of law enforcement.

That was the other thing about people from New York. They thought everything had to happen now. Life here didn't move at that pace. Patience was more than a virtue; it was a way of life. Like waiting for the snow to finally melt away for the last time each spring. Slowly hauling up a lobster trap, each turn of the hydraulic lift increasing the anticipation of a rich catch. Watching the sun slowly sink into the deep blue sea at the end of the day.

She wouldn't understand any of that.

Learning to appreciate those things was the only way he'd kept his sanity after his father's accident.

Long-buried emotions attempted to surface. He pushed them away and immediately adjusted his attitude. Coming back here and following through on his responsibilities had been the right thing to do. No regrets.

People like Sarah Newton wouldn't understand that level of commitment. They lived for the moment.

He followed her movements back and forth in the room. Maybe he wasn't giving her enough credit. Her life was . . . different from his. That was all. She had no family obligations. She apparently poured everything into her work. Ultimately, she was free to make her own choices. She could live her life the way she chose.

Maybe that was the appeal. He envied her freedom.

But he didn't regret his choices. He *couldn't* regret doing the right thing.

As he watched her, he wondered about the demons that drove her. Last night he'd gotten a glimpse of a vulnerable side. But only a glimpse. She was strong. Determined and deeply committed to accomplishing her goal here. What would it be like if that fierce determination was focused on a connection with another human being? Images of frantic sex acts transposed themselves in front of his eyes.

Kale blinked. What the hell was he doing?

Luckily for him, Chief Willard strolled into his office smelling of winter, cold air, and chimney smoke. "Sorry for the wait." He propped a smile into place and closed the door behind him. "I'm pleased to finally have the opportunity to meet you, Ms. Newton." He looked from her to Kale and back. "What can I do for you today?"

She glanced at Kale to see if he was going to start. He motioned for her to go ahead. This was her theory; he wasn't about to take her glory—or her derision when the chief dismissed her hypothesis with fact. Kale had had a chance to think about the scenario and he felt certain the chief, as the one before him, had investigated any anonymous gifts. Maybe they didn't do things around here the way they were done in New York, but things got done just the same.

Maybe if Kale stopped thinking about what a great ass Sarah Newton had, his conclusions would come to him a little faster and save the trouble of bugging the chief.

"Rachel Appleton received a dozen red roses from an anonymous sender this morning," Newton informed the chief. When that didn't get the hoped-for reaction, she added, "The message on the card was *Deepest regrets*."

The chief seemed to consider the news as he leaned against the closed door, the file he carried clutched in both hands. "Did you check to see if all the cards with all the flowers and the mountain of other gifts were signed? Seems to me that would be the only way your suggestion might be relevant in some way or another. Wouldn't you say?"

Frustration sketched itself across Newton's face, demonstrated itself in her posture. "There's a vase exactly like it sitting on the counter at the Gerard home. *Wouldn't you say* there's a strong likelihood the card will read the same way?"

The chief flicked a glance in Kale's direction.

"We looked through the kitchen window," he explained, resisting the urge to shift his weight from foot to foot as he'd done back in Sunday school when asked to stand and respond to a question to which he didn't know the answer. As he had then, he tried not to look as guilty as he felt. His job was to keep Sarah Newton out of trouble, not to let her run unchecked through the village.

"All that means"—the chief pushed away from the door and moved around behind his desk—"is that someone wanted both families to be aware of their concern."

"So you're not going to check it out."

This wasn't a question. It was a challenge. No, an outright accusation. Kale looked from her to the chief, braced for an explosion.

"The fact of the matter is we've already checked it out." He reclined in his chair, gestured for the two of them to have a seat.

Kale waited to see if Newton would accept. She didn't. So he stood.

"And?" she prompted.

"The deliveries were made by two different floral services. So you know"—he laid the folder he'd been holding on his desk—"there were seven anonymous gifts sent to the Gerard family. So far there've been four to the Appletons. Deputy Brighton is monitoring any contact with the families."

That blew her theory full of holes. "None of these anonymous gifts," Kale ventured, "have any connection to the murders twenty years ago?" He knew the answer before he asked the question. He'd been in on the briefing in the beginning. Aspects of possible connections had already been considered. But he wanted her to hear that.

Willard shook his head. "There are some similarities, that's true. But, so far, there's no reason to believe the two are connected."

"You don't think it's strange . . ."—Newton leaned forward and braced her hands on the front of his desk—"that the victims twenty years ago received the same flowers from an anonymous sender and now that exact scenario is playing out again?"

"Right now," the chief allowed with infinite patience, "the answer is no. If we could prove the cards from twenty years ago carried the same message and were signed with the same handwriting as the ones today, maybe. But we can't do that. The Burgesses moved away. No one knows where they ended up. And the Petersons have both passed on. There's no way to confirm or to rule out the possibility."

"What about the handwriting on these two? Were the messages written by the same person?"

"We believe they were. But so were two of the other anonymous gifts both families received. Some folks don't sign cards because they're not looking for a thank-you or any other sort of gratification. They just want to express their sympathy and concern."

Newton straightened, blew out a perturbed breath, and started that tension-building pacing once more.

"Chief." Kale hated to heap any more worries on the chief's plate, but he needed to know about last night. "Someone attacked Ms. Newton at the chapel last night."

Willard's face pinched. "At the chapel?" He shifted his attention to Newton. "Are you all right, Ms. Newton?"

She scarcely stopped her pacing to say, "I'm fine."

"Did you get a look at your attacker?" the chief wanted to know. "We'll need to file an official report so one of my deputies can look into this. I have to tell you, I'm genuinely surprised anyone would have done such a thing. I hope you'll accept my apology. Folks around here don't generally do such things."

She shook her head. "He was wearing a ski mask." She paused, then sent a pointed stare straight at the chief. "But he got a look at the bottom of my shoe." The pacing resumed. "Don't worry about a report. It doesn't matter."

The chief shook his head, worry sagging his shoulders. "Ms. Newton," he said wearily, "I'd like you to take a seat." She turned toward him. "And I'm going to go over a few details with you that until now haven't been released to anyone beyond those involved with the investigation. Then you'll see why we aren't putting any credence in any kind of connection to the murders from two decades ago."

Kale watched as Newton visibly conceded and took a seat. He settled into the one next to her. Tension crackled through him, making his pulse jump. Did the chief have something new on the case? Why hadn't he been informed?

"Twenty years ago," the chief began, "the bodies of two young ladies were discovered at the chapel." He rummaged around on his desk and selected another folder then passed it to Newton. "Each body was stabbed, slashed, or gouged sixty-six times. Precisely sixty-six times," he reiterated. "But the fatal wound was the one inflicted when the killer removed the victim's heart. The organs were never found."

Kale tried to take a breath, Failed. Why hadn't the chief told him that part? Did the others know? Newton said nothing to this revelation.

"Since those files were destroyed," the chief continued, I've written a detailed report of all that I recall." He paused for Newton to consider the in-depth report from those murders.

When she glanced up once more, he went on, "There were no other markings, no other evidence. Nothing. Other than the victims being female and the lack of evidence, these murders share no significant similarities to Valerie Gerard's."

Newton closed the folder and placed it back on the chief's desk. "This is the reason," she suggested, "you've been so certain the murders weren't related."

He nodded. "These"—he passed to Newton the folder he'd been carrying when he entered the office—"are the photos from the Gerard scene. There's more."

Kale tensed, startled. When had the chief made this decision? The last Kale had heard she wasn't to know that one detail. Now she would understand that Kale had not been completely honest when she asked him to describe the scene. Didn't bode well for their tenuous working relationship. Then again, apparently there was a lot he hadn't known.

She studied the photos briefly then shot a fleeting look at Kale before passing the file back to the chief.

Oh, yeah. He was going to hear about this.

"What's your theory on this undisclosed detail?" she asked. She didn't look surprised or moved in any way.

"I've spent the past two hours on a conference call with our Bureau liaison and the state forensics folks. The consensus is that Valerie Gerard likely knew her killer. This murder was personal. And that's the way we're investigating it."

A flicker of surprise showed on Newton's face. "No more curse theories?"

The chief adopted a long-suffering face. "Folks are going to believe what they believe, Ms. Newton. All we in law enforcement can hope for is to ferret out the facts."

"Is there anything else you're keeping from the press?" Her tone was nothing short of skeptical. Obviously she wasn't convinced she'd gotten the whole story even now.

The chief's hesitation had Kale turning to him. There was something new. Being kept in the dark, under the circumstances, put him at a serious disadvantage. Giving the chief credit, he was neck deep in alligators in this investigation. He didn't have time to hold Kale's hand by keeping him apprised of every update. Kale had to keep that in mind. In truth, he'd just as soon never have known that one part.

"There is one other thing." The somberness of the chief's tone set Kale further on edge. "Let me forewarn you, Ms.

Newton. If a single word of this gets out before I personally release it to the press, you will be sitting in jail for the duration of your stay here."

"You have my word," she said immediately.

Kale felt himself holding his breath.

"Valerie Gerard's cause of death was ultimately massive hemorrhaging and exposure. But the autopsy revealed another piece of evidence, not directly tied to cause of death." He unlocked the middle drawer of his desk, reached inside and pulled out an envelope. He passed it to Newton. "This item was found in the victim's throat."

What the hell? Kale got up and moved to stand next to the chief's desk so that he could look over Newton's shoulder as she withdrew a photo from the envelope.

The round metal object looked like a large coin. Parts of what might have been a narrow cloth band lay next to it in the photograph.

"It's a medal," Newton suggested. "Like in the Olympics."

Willard nodded. "The lab was able to raise the inscription. It's a medal Valerie received for winning a spelling bee in the fourth grade."

Kale couldn't believe what he was hearing. "You've confirmed that this medal"—he tapped the photo—"is in fact the one Valerie won back in fourth grade? Not some kind of duplicate?" This just wasn't possible. This meant . . .

"It's the one. The date and name of the school are inscribed. We checked with the Gerards and verified the location of where it was kept in the home. When we searched the home the medal was missing."

Kale put his hand over his mouth, then let it fall uselessly to his side. "That means it was someone here . . . someone we know."

"It would seem so," Willard agreed. "But we're not limiting our investigation by that factor. Yet."

"At this point," Newton spoke up, "you actually have no evidence to connect Valerie Gerard's murder with Alicia Appleton's disappearance. Or to the murders twenty years ago."

"None."

"She could have run away from home," Newton theorized. "Or been abducted for other purposes."

Willard nodded. "All we can do is react to the tips that come in and whatever we dig up, which, I don't have to tell you, is not looking good. We have absolutely nothing to go on in Alicia's case."

"If her disappearance is related to the murder, the sooner you nail a suspect the better chance you'll have of finding her alive. So," Newton pressed, "the real questions are, who would this medal have been relevant to?" Her attention lingered on the crime-scene photos. "Who would have known where it was kept and subsequently gained access to that location? And who among those might have had motive to dislike both girls?"

Willard chuckled, but Kale recognized its severe lack of enthusiasm and total absence of humor. "You keep it up, Ms. Newton, and I'll be recruiting you for my staff."

Newton pushed her lips into a forged smile. "I'm afraid you couldn't afford me, Chief."

"And I'm afraid," the chief suggested, "that you've wasted your time and your magazine's money on this one. I don't think you're going to find the kind of story you were looking for here now that the true nature of the crime has been revealed."

"That's the thing, Chief." Newton stood. "The true nature—the truth—*is* my story."

CHAPTER 16

The chief wanted her out of here.

Not surprising. The only real surprises were that he actually thought he now had the perfect grounds to send her packing.

And the fact that Kale Conner had lied to her.

By omission, but a lie nonetheless.

That shouldn't have surprised her . . . but somehow it had.

Maybe even she wasn't so jaded that she couldn't hold out hope.

Flaw number two . . . capable of withholding information.

When she'd snapped her seat belt into place and he'd backed out of the parking slot she made the statement his shuttered expression silently validated that he fully anticipated. "You lied to me."

"I didn't exactly lie. Some parts I didn't even know." He eased the Jeep into the flow of traffic, purposely didn't meet her eyes. "As a journalist you should understand how that works. I left out the part I wasn't authorized to share with you or anyone else."

"Same thing."

When he would have argued, she added, "Doesn't really matter. I already knew about the message the killer left."

He braked at the four-way stop, aiming a questioning look at her. "That detail wasn't released to the press."

She laughed softly, directed her attention forward just to

keep him guessing. "I have my ways, Conner. Secrets can only really be secret if no one knows them but you. That's the only person you can really trust."

Silence.

Next he would ask the question, no doubt pushing the limits of his well-ingrained sense of propriety. She'd give him another minute tops.

Through the intersection of High and Main.

Past Bay View Cemetery.

A right up the twisty, steep drive that ascended the cliff-side to the inn. Home sweet home. She expected to find snakes in her bed before this was over.

The Jeep rolled to a stop, he shifted into park, propped both hands on the steering wheel then stared out at the ocean. "Does this mean you're leaving?"

Forty-five seconds.

Not bad for a guy who no doubt wanted his life back. The commercial aspects of the whodunit mystery had been solved. There was no need for the debunking lady to hang around. Time for him to go back to being plain old fisherman Kale Conner. No more babysitting the crazy woman from New York.

Nothing was ever that simple.

Not for Sarah Newton.

Things had a way of dragging her deeper into the current.

She watched the seagulls float over the harbor, the occasional one or two skimming close to the cold water. No would be the simplest answer to his question, but that wasn't completely accurate and there wasn't any reason not to tell him the truth. She would leave when her instincts told her it was time to go.

Not when the chief or any damned body else suggested she do so.

"I could," she admitted, which she didn't usually do, particularly when in the presence of the other side. "Probably should, but I'm not ready to go yet." Maybe it was her visit with Rachel Appleton. Whatever it was, something about this place wasn't ready to let her go.

That was as close to the truth as she understood herself at the moment.

No comment.

Interesting. She'd expected a "why not," definitely a disappointed sigh.

"Lunch sounds good to me right now." He shifted that dark, dark gaze back to her. "You want to join me? Or did you have more names on that interview list? We can move on to the next name if you like."

Her lips itched to stretch into a smile. He'd done something few people were able to. He'd surprised her a second time. Rather than question her decision, he'd accepted it and moved on to the next point: keeping up with her every move.

As for her list, she had lots more names. For now, she needed to work alone. He'd answered her call for help last night. Taken her to his place and cared for her when he could have dropped her off here to fend for herself. She appreciated his hospitality, but he was still one of them.

And she was . . . the enemy. Pure and simple.

That didn't even cover the aspect that should actually have been at the top of her list. He was a distraction. Too good-looking. Too earnest. Too . . . fucking tempting.

"I have to check in with my editor," she lied. "He's called about ten times already." That much was true. "I'll catch up with you later."

His hesitation warned that he wasn't sure leaving her to her own devices was a good idea, but he had no socially acceptable or otherwise logical excuse for arguing.

He rearranged his face into an agreeable expression. "I guess I'll see you later then."

"Yeah." She climbed out of the Jeep.

"Don't go out in the middle of the night without me," he suggested when she reached for the door.

"Right." She gave the door a shove and trudged across

the parking area. He didn't leave right away. She didn't dismiss immediately as she should have the thought that lunch might have been nice. Resisting the urge to look back, she twisted the doorknob and pushed into the lobby. She didn't need Kale Conner to do her work.

She always worked alone.

No reason for that to change now.

"Afternoon, Ms. Newton."

A new face was behind the counter of the registration desk. Young. Male. The son.

And he was on her list. Excellent.

"You must be Brady." She gifted him with her best smile, the one some went so far as to call charming.

"Yes, ma'am." He returned the gesture with a pretty damned charming smile of his own. Totally opposite from his sour-natured father.

Sarah crossed the lobby and extended her hand. He gave it a shake. "I'm Sarah Newton." Tentative grip. Nervous, she decided.

"I know who you are." His pleasant expression slipped a measurable notch. "You're here about Valerie and . . . Alicia."

Alicia was his girlfriend.

"That's right." She searched those hazel eyes, noted the uncertainty and frustration. "I'm genuinely sorry about your friends."

He lowered his gaze, busied himself with something behind the counter. "Me, too."

"I'm glad to finally have the opportunity to meet you." Sarah hadn't seen the first sign of the wife or the kids. She'd begun to think the innkeeper's family was another of the village myths.

"I have school, you know." Almost reluctantly, he met her gaze once more. "After school I've been helping with the . . . search."

She'd suspected so. "Alicia is a beautiful girl."

That uncertain expression melted back into a warm boyish smile. Cute kid. With that blond hair, if he had a tan he would fit neatly into the surfer dude category. "She sure is. I'm lucky she took a second look at me."

Where had boys like this been when Sarah was eighteen? They'd all been jerks. "She's made quite a mark in the world of beauty pageants."

He nodded with unabashed enthusiasm. "But she's got a lot more going for her than just that kind of thing. She has big plans."

"Yeah." Sarah gave an acknowledging nod. "Her mother told me." Not exactly a lie.

"She's going to New York for the summer." He shrugged. "After graduation and all. She's trying out for one of those model shows. You know, the reality kind."

"I can absolutely see her winning." The girl had the look. If she had half the ambition, she would have a very good chance of breaking in on some level. Sarah dug in her bag for a card and passed it across the counter. "You and Alicia call me when you get to Manhattan. I'll show you around. Take you out to dinner. It'll be fun."

That got his full attention.

"Cool, thanks." He pulled out his wallet and tucked the card away. "She'll be real excited to hear that. We don't know anybody there and"—he glanced around as if ensuring no one overheard—"the thought's a little scary even for me."

He had no idea he'd just told off on himself. Sarah would wager that no one else knew he'd planned to escape the land of maple trees and moose with his girlfriend. She mentally marked his name off her potential-suspect list. The boy was in love. Love could certainly end in murder, but not this time. He was still holding out hope Alicia would return and their plans to escape would see fruition.

"It can be a little scary for anyone if you don't know your way around." Sarah laughed, recalling her first day in New York. "Trust me, the bark is bigger than the bite. Many of the rumors you hear are blown way out of proportion. New York is just a bunch of little villages clustered together, that's all."

He laughed, probably the first in several days. "Definitely good to hear."

"How long have you and Alicia been together?"

"Almost a year."

He blushed. Definitely something you didn't see often anymore. Sarah bit back a smile.

"Prom's coming up. That's our anniversary."

Senior prom. And Alicia wasn't going to make it. Sarah wished that wasn't the case but she had that feeling. Her gut never failed her.

Alicia Appleton wasn't coming home.

"I know this is difficult to talk about," Sarah said carefully, not wanting to sound like an interrogator, "but some people are saying that Alicia left for New York early." She watched his eyes very closely and hated herself for what she was about to do. "Without you."

Her pulse reacted to the instant change in his demeanor. The shy, naïve little boy vanished. Testosterone-fueled, out-raged man took his place.

"Whoever said that's a liar. Alicia would never do that to me." He looked around again, abruptly realizing he'd shouted, then he bent forward. "It's the curse," he said for Sarah's ears only. Another covert check of the lobby. "Some of the other guys make fun of me for believing it. But Alicia knew. She said somebody had been following her. She was worried that something was going to happen to her. She said it was the devil."

Her pulse thumping harder, Sarah leaned in closer. "That information could be very helpful to the investigation. Did you tell Chief Willard?"

He nodded, looked around again. "He thanked me, but didn't seem to take me all that seriously since I didn't have any other details. Alicia never saw the person. No notes or calls. Nothing like that. That's what makes it so creepy. She said she'd wake up at night and feel like somebody had been in the room with her. Or turn around and no one was there when she'd felt like someone was right behind her."

"Does Alicia have any enemies that you know of?"

He lifted his shoulders and let them fall with visible disgust. "That's what the cops are focusing on. But I can't think of nobody. Everybody likes her. I swear. She's the most popular girl in school."

"I guess when you're that gorgeous you get used to the jealousy." Even a girl with no enemies in the broadest sense of the term had to have experienced envy, particularly one as physically beautiful as Alicia. "After all, whenever there's a winner, there are always losers, too."

Another of those disheartened shrugs. "I don't think that really bothers anybody. Alicia is Alicia. If she walks across that stage she's gonna win. The other girls just accept it." His forehead lined as he hesitated, obviously reconsidering. "Except maybe . . ."

Sarah waited, the tension swelling in her chest. *Give me a name, Brady.* Some damned place to start!

"I don't think Polly likes Alicia too much. She sort of had a crush on me and that caused some trouble a while back. But it wasn't that big a deal."

Polly . . . where had Sarah heard or read that name? "What kind of trouble?"

"You know, the whole talking behind Alicia's back, saying she was a snob and crap like that. Polly's kinda got a reputation for running her mouth, so nobody pays much attention to what she says. Sometimes her mouth gets her in trouble, though. But she's okay."

Polly . . . *Polly.*

Damn. Polly Conner.

Kale's little sister.

Holy cow.

"Polly Conner is a senior this year, too, right?" Sarah asked, confirming her conclusion that the Conner girl was the Polly he meant.

He nodded. "She feels real bad about Alicia and the stuff she said in the past. I told her Alicia didn't take it seriously, but I'm not sure it helped Polly feel any better."

"Brady, I need you out back."

Sarah's attention swung to the corridor on the left of the

registration desk just as the owner of the very unhappy female voice appeared.

"Coming, Mom." Brady glanced at Sarah. "Gotta go."

"Fill the wood box and see that the cord Mr. Jacobs just delivered is stacked neatly in the barn," his mother ordered as he swaggered past her. "I'll take care of things in here."

That last part hadn't been intended for Brady. She'd stared straight at Sarah as she made the statement, disapproval and distaste radiating from every square inch of her petite frame. Sarah didn't let that stop her from pushing a greeting smile into place. If Brenda Harvey expected her to run for cover she could forget about it. Tougher broads than her had tried that tactic.

"Is there something you need, Ms. Newton?" Brenda took her son's place behind the counter. "I can help you if you're ready to check out."

News traveled fast. "Thanks, but I'll be staying a while longer." The tightening of lips told Sarah that Mrs. Brenda Harvey wasn't too happy to hear that.

"You stopped at the counter," she maintained, "you must've wanted something."

Touché. "Just checking to see if I had any messages." Good one. Sarah gave herself a pat on the back.

The silent stare dragged on. Gave Sarah time to analyze the lady. Well-fitting green dress that brought out the emerald flecks in her eyes. Brenda Harvey was slender, maybe five one, with blond, graying hair arranged in a neat braid that coiled around the back of her head. She wore small, wire-framed reading glasses that hovered on the end of her thin nose.

"You don't have any messages," she finally said with a distinct snap.

"Thanks." Sarah threw in another smile, just to be a good sport before turning away. She'd gotten two steps away from the desk when the innkeeper's wife spoke again.

"I don't want you talking to my children."

Sarah hesitated, considered ignoring the comment, but then she wouldn't learn anything that way.

She faced the indignant lady. "Rest assured, Mrs. Harvey, you have nothing to fear from me. All I'm looking for is the truth. Unless, of course, you're hiding relevant information that would help this investigation in some way."

Brenda's eyes flared wide and the indignation shifted the tiniest bit, to something more like uncertainty or maybe . . . fear. The transition roused Sarah's curiosity. She'd been fishing, casting lines wherever and whenever. It was her tried-and-true strategy. Seemed she'd gotten a nibble.

"The Gerards and Appletons are friends of ours," Brenda said firmly but without the fire and brimstone of before. "If we knew anything at all, don't you think we would have told the police?"

"I'm certain you would." And yet, there was something the lady worried about . . . something she wasn't about to tell a soul. Especially not Sarah.

"It's just that Brady"—Brenda glanced in the direction her son had gone—"is taking all of this very hard." She blinked several times but the shine of emotion in her eyes wouldn't be exiled. Nor would the palpable sense that she felt somehow cornered by Sarah's very presence. "It's difficult for us all . . ."

Don't say a word. As much as Sarah wanted to ask what she meant, she knew better than to break the spell. Let the woman talk. Don't even breathe.

"My husband and I are worried sick. We don't want our children exposed any more than they've already been. God only knows what might happen next. We don't—"

"Brenda, have you seen—"

The innkeeper strode into the room, drew up short when his gaze bumped into Sarah. He looked from her to his wife. Suspicion immediately narrowed his gaze.

"Is there something you need, Ms. Newton?"

Here she went again. "No, thanks."

He glared at his wife before cutting his attention back to Sarah.

That would be her cue to exit. Except that . . . she stared at his face, specifically his left cheek. A little puffy and the pale skin there was a deep reddish color as if he'd been punched or . . . *kicked*.

The tingle of adrenaline rushed over her nerve endings as the images from last night's encounter zoomed into high-def clarity in her mind's eye. Right height . . . right build . . .

"Barton slipped on the ice last night when he was carrying in firewood," his wife said. She sent a look of concern at her husband's face. "Poor dear, almost gave himself a black eye."

The innkeeper waved off her worries. "I should have been more careful." He stared straight at Sarah then. "You can never be too careful in the dark . . . especially this time of year." His meaning was crystal clear.

He'd been the one and, on some level, he wanted her to know it.

"I'm always careful, Mr. Harvey," Sarah returned, her own meaning unmistakable. "There's no telling what or who you'll run into."

Their gazes held a moment longer before Sarah turned her back and headed for her room.

If the innkeeper thought he could scare her off, he should give it his best shot. Sure, he'd shaken her up last night, but she wasn't running.

No way.

"I understand you're leaving us," he called after Sarah.

Was there an echo in this village?

Sarah paused near the newel post at the bottom of the staircase. She met the man's haughty expression. "Not yet, Mr. Harvey. When the time comes you'll be the first to know."

If looks could kill Sarah would have dropped dead right there on the polished hardwood. Instead, she mounted the stairs to the second floor.

The harsh murmur of voices told her that Mr. Harvey was letting Mrs. Harvey know that she was not to be fraternizing with the inn's one guest.

Nothing like being the most popular girl in town.

Happened every time.

The difference between her and Alicia Appleton was Sarah never got a crown.

After going through her research material and comparing what she'd learned before arriving in Youngstown to what she'd discovered firsthand, Sarah hit the streets. She need-ed to think without any distractions . . . particularly Kale Conner.

Without doubt she appreciated his rescuing her the night before, but that was the exception to the norm not the rule. Sarah wasn't in the habit of needing a rescue. She had been taking care of herself for a very long time.

As if the thought had triggered the wrong file retrieval, memories flooded her brain, swelled in her throat. Her fin-gers tightened on the steering wheel as she attempted to push them away. Blood-soaked earth. Bones . . . so many bones. Rotted dresses . . . disintegrating purses. Shoes with broken heels.

Her mind conjured the image of a little blond-haired girl—needy and vulnerable—hugging her pillow beneath the stairs . . . the sound of heavy footsteps on the wood floor . . .

That was a long time ago, she reminded herself. Sarah Newton would never be vulnerable again. And she damned sure didn't need anyone.

"No way in hell," she muttered.

Not even a guy who seriously stirred the desire for sex.

That was why she never let anyone close.

It was far too easy to become dependent.

She didn't like being dependent.

Dependency fostered weakness.

More clips from her childhood flashed in her head. Pray-ing that her mother would find her before the voices got her. Burrowing her way to the very back of the closet . . .

"Stupid."

The voices she later learned were those of her mother's victims.

The chill seeped deeper into Sarah's bones.

That was the thing about a really shitty childhood; you learned that prayer was a waste of time.

Sarah braked for a pedestrian crossing the street. She surveyed the village shops that lined the street. The people here were deep in denial. Certain that no one they knew would commit such a heinous deed and that earnest prayer would somehow turn this tragedy around. Didn't they understand that Alicia Appleton would die soon if she wasn't found?

According to the police reports she'd reviewed, every registered cave and abandoned or unused structure in the Youngstown area as well as the surrounding woods had been searched repeatedly. Neighboring villages had cooperated by conducting their own searches in similar areas.

With no results.

If it weren't for the roses, Sarah would take a hard look at the possibility that the kid had hitched a ride to New York. Less than eight hours' driving distance, it wouldn't be that difficult. Just risky when one took into account the freaks, kooks, and perverts on the road.

The bus lines, airlines, and trains that served the region had all received the bulletin with her photo as soon as she was reported missing. No one had seen her. If she'd left Youngstown, it hadn't been via public transportation.

Yet she was nowhere to be found. Alicia Appleton had simply vanished.

There were no suspects. No nothing. Not in Alicia's case or Valerie's.

Who hated Valerie Gerard enough to want her dead? Who hadn't forgotten that she'd won a spelling bee in fourth grade? Who considered her a liar? Chief Willard insisted friends and family had been interviewed repeatedly and that Valerie had no enemies. But that wasn't true.

The truth is what it is.

And someone killed Valerie with considerably more hacking than was necessary. Labeled her a liar in her own blood. After viewing all the crime scene photos, Sarah's confidence in the investigation had boosted a little. Photos of the victim before her arms and legs had been scraped loose from the stone had been taken. Maybe they'd done a better job than she'd first thought. The newly revealed detail about the missing organs from the victims in the twenty-year-old case confirmed her conclusions that they were unrelated to Valerie's murder.

Brady Harvey's sister, Melody, was nineteen. She would have known Valerie. But her mother hadn't mentioned Valerie's murder. Only Alicia's disappearance.

Strange.

Passing Bay View Cemetery, Sarah braked.

The big iron gates yawned open but that wasn't what attracted her attention.

That dumb crow on the headstone.

"Freezing your ass off, huh?"

She shook her head, told herself to drive on.

But she didn't.

She turned onto the narrow strip of pavement that cut through the middle of the cemetery. Snow encroached on either side of the asphalt, narrowing it even more. She shut off the engine and got out. Snow immediately poked up her pants legs and slithered into her Converses.

Massive oak trees stood like sentinels, their gnarled roots reaching out to the sleeping residents. A few newer headstones were interspersed here and there; near ancestors, she supposed. Woods bordered the back of the cemetery, while streets flanked the other three sides.

Sarah walked along the rows of headstones until she reached the last one. Beyond that final row, at the very back of the property, sitting next to two stone cross markers, was the witch's headstone. The crow perched there eyed Sarah before flapping its wings indignantly and taking off. It lit on a naked branch high above her head.

"So where's your friends?" Sarah scanned the nearby trees. Maybe he was a loner. Like her.

"Don't worry," she said aloud. "I won't be here long."

Sarah started forward again.

Then froze.

A girl stood on the other side of the headstone. Long black hair. Hooded sweatshirt and jeans, all black; goth style. She lifted her gaze to Sarah's.

For two stuttering heartbeats they looked at each other without moving or speaking.

Where had she come from? Sarah started to say hello but the girl spoke.

"You're Sarah Newton, aren't you?"

Didn't take a crystal ball to guess her identity. There weren't that many strangers around outside the two or three lingering reporters who appeared to prefer their lodging accommodations to trudging through the snow.

"Yes." Sarah took another step in the girl's direction. "And you are?"

Teenager, Sarah decided. Seventeen or eighteen. She watched as Sarah lessened the distance between them one step at a time, but she didn't answer the question.

Sarah stopped a few feet away, on the same side of the marker. Worn by time and the elements, the name on the headstone was barely visible.

Matilda Calder. Mattie.

Oddly, all three headstones on this final short row faced the back of the cemetery whereas all the rest faced the street. A way of indicating they were outcasts, maybe?

"Do you visit her often?" Sarah asked. No need to wait for her name to ask questions.

"I'm the only one who comes," the girl said.

If she was around eighteen, she'd be the same age as the missing girl.

"Some people don't like visiting their deceased loved ones. Too sad." Sarah hadn't been to her mother's grave since the pallbearers lowered her coffin into the ground. She'd never been to her father's. In her case, it didn't have a whole lot to do with sadness. That sickening emptiness she knew far too well sucked at her insides. She forced it away.

"You should visit."

Sarah's attention snapped back to the girl. "What's your name?" She still hadn't answered that question. And definitely shouldn't know *that* about Sarah. What was she? Psychic? The day someone proved ESP to her, Sarah would maybe consider the possibility. Then again, the kid could have meant *you* should visit as in people in general should visit their deceased loved ones.

"Matilda."

Okay, so this was officially weird. "Matilda?"

The girl nodded to the headstone. "She was my great-great-grandmother. I'm named after her."

Maybe not so weird.

Matilda pointed to the two cross markers. "Those were her friends."

"Is that your pet?" Sarah jerked her head toward the tree where the crow waited patiently, probably for them to leave.

Matilda stared at the crow, then shook her head.

Inept stab at making conversation.

"She was a witch, you know," the girl said matter-of-factly.

Sarah nodded. "I heard."

"But she helped people." Matilda's attention returned to the headstone. "She wouldn't have let this happen."

"You mean what happened to Valerie and Alicia?"

Matilda nodded once.

"I guess you go to school with Alicia?"

"Did." She glanced up at the crow again. "But I quit this year."

What kind of parents would let their daughter quit school? Particularly if she'd made it all the way to her senior year.

"You don't like school?" Another lame question.

She shrugged.

"Did you know Valerie?"

"She tutored me in math year before last."

The kid needed a coat. She had to be freezing. The sweatshirt couldn't be that warm even if she had layers on underneath.

"Would you like to sit in my car?"

Matilda shook her head. "I gotta get home."

Now or never. "Do you know of anyone who would have wanted to hurt Valerie or Alicia?"

"Lots of people are jealous." She searched Sarah's face with curious eyes that were the most bizarre shade of gold. Sarah hadn't noticed that before. "But none of the kids around here would hurt them. Not for real."

"What about the kids Valerie beat in that spelling bee way back in fourth grade?" Okay, that was a stretch.

Another indifferent shrug.

Who remembered what happened in third or fourth grade? If one of Valerie's classmates had held a grudge over a spelling bee that long, then he or she needed to get a fucking life.

That theory suddenly seemed about as farfetched as the curse theory. Unless mental illness was involved. In light of the mutilation that was a definite possibility.

"I sure hope the police find some answers soon." The statement wasn't really directed at the girl. Just thinking out loud. Keeping the silence from dragging on too long.

Thankfully Sarah hadn't said the rest of what she thought.

Before it's too late for Alicia.

The tree branches groaned and scratched as the wind picked up. Standing out here much longer was about as appealing as being mugged. But Sarah wanted to talk to the girl as long as possible. She mentally scrambled for a way to meet both goals.

"Can I give you a lift home?" Good idea.

Matilda shook her head. "It's not that far. I like walking."

"It'll be dark soon." Sarah surveyed the sky. Another clear night. Which meant it would be even colder.

"I'm not afraid of the dark."

One girl was dead, another missing. A young girl shouldn't be out walking alone. Especially at dark.

"Until the police catch the person responsible for what's happened, it's probably not a good idea to be walking alone in the dark."

"They won't catch him."

Anticipation prickled Sarah's chilled flesh. "They're trying very hard. I'm sure they will."

Those eerie gold eyes held Sarah's. "They can't catch him."

That feeling, the one that made your skin prickle and the hair on your neck stand on end, sent Sarah's instincts to the next level. "Why do you say that?"

"Because he's the devil. Cops can't catch the devil."

CHAPTER 17

A passing car drew Sarah's attention to the street. She turned back to Matilda. "What makes you think—"

The girl was gone.

Taken aback, Sarah scanned the cemetery. The only way she could have disappeared so quickly was to have headed into the woods behind her great-great-grandmother's grave.

Strange girl.

Cops can't catch the devil.

"Yeah, right, kid."

Sarah's cell vibrated.

Three guesses who'd show up on her caller ID, and the first two didn't count.

He'd called repeatedly today. Each time Sarah had ignored him. But twelve was the number. If she didn't answer this time her editor would send a search party. Her editor and shrink used the same strategy to keep her in line.

Sarah dragged out the phone and flipped it open. "Newton."

"You almost missed me," Tae Green warned. "I had my finger on my cell's speed dial for Frank."

Frank. Sarah curled her lip in disgust. Frank Sampson had been Tae's heavy for twenty years. Whenever Tae needed one of his reporters located, extricated, or reined in, Frank was the man he called.

"Your intimidation tactics don't work on me, Tae." Sarah wasn't afraid of Frank; she just didn't like him.

"Call me when you arrive means the second you cross

into the city limits, not the next day. Oh, wait, you didn't call me period. I called you."

Yeah, yeah, her editor was a comedian. Appeared to be lots of those around.

"Don't give up your day job, Tae. I'm here. I'm alive so far and I've only pissed off a couple of people." She almost lost her balance on a patch of ice. "Happy?"

"What's going on up there? The news channels are buzzing with word that the Youngstown chief of police is about to hold a press conference. What's up with that?"

Sarah halted a couple steps shy of reaching her car. "When?" Willard hadn't said anything about any news conference. If one was happening any minute, he had to have known when she was in his office. So much for cooperation. He and his buddy the mayor had been placating her. Giving her just enough slack to distract her from what they were really up to.

Unfortunately it had worked.

"Apparently the chief is one of the people you've pissed off—so far."

"He was pissed off before I got here." She opened the driver's side door and plopped into the seat. "I should go and find out where that press conference is going down." Damn Kale Conner for not calling her. He probably knew this morning when he was so happy to play the hero host. Why the hell had she trusted him, even a little bit?

"Answer one question before you go."

She knew the drill. Twenty-four hours on location, assess the situation, determine if there is a story. If there's no story, pack up and hit the road for the next assignment.

"There's a story here, Tae." She started the car and dragged her seat belt across her lap. "No matter what the chief says in his press conference, trust me, there's something else going on." She hesitated before shifting into reverse, her attention tugged back to Mattie Calder's headstone.

The black crow had resumed his vigil.

Wasn't necessarily the same bird. Probably not. There

could be something close by the Calder headstone that attracted the damned creatures. Maybe a shiny frame around a photograph on one of the headstones. Maybe some kind of prey that wasn't readily obvious. Didn't have to be the headstone or the person buried in that precise spot.

What the hell was she thinking? Of course it wasn't.

Spooks, goblins, and ghouls—including witches and devils—didn't commit murder. People did.

As Sarah watched, another crow landed on a tree branch not a dozen feet away. That creepy sensation she got when she was onto something big made her skin crawl.

Or maybe it was the need to find the press conference. And quite possibly the overwhelming urge to kick Conner's cute ass.

Still . . . her attention lingered on the headstone and its ominous visitor.

"I'm waiting, Newton."

"What?" She shook her head to clear it. "Oh . . . yeah. The whole curse thing was really hyped in the beginning. Other than a few who'd rather believe an unseen force is responsible for what's happened, at this point I think most folks understand they're dealing with a mere human here. But . . ."

How did she explain this part? Her job involved debunking myths, cutting through the lore and getting to the heart of the matter when no one else appeared so inclined. Hanging around a stereotypical murder investigation wasn't in her job description.

"But?" he prodded.

"It feels like . . ." She bit her lip as she waited for the right words. "There's something more than a cut-and-dried murder case going on here. I can feel it. It's maybe not about curses or legends or woo-woo stuff, but it goes deep and involves . . . more." Damn it. She couldn't pinpoint what she sensed. "Trust me, Tae. I have to stay." If for no other reason than to see how this turned out, she didn't add.

Sarah held her breath through the requisite dead air. He never agreed too readily. Made him seem soft. Not that he ever said as much but she knew his MO.

"Forty-eight hours, Newton. If you don't have something concrete by then, you should move on. There's a situation down in Louisiana with some missing bodies and a shitload of voodoo buzz. It's got your name written all over it."

"Forty-eight hours." She could deal with that. "Gotcha."

"But I want a call from you in twenty-four, understood?"

She turned her car around, guided it onto the street. "Understood. Thanks, Tae. You have my word, this story will be worth your patience."

He let her off the hook with that promise.

Tracking down the location of the press conference was even simpler. She followed the news vans. The media hounds were back in force.

"Willard, you asshole." She shook her head at her own lapse into the unsuspecting zone. No one understood human nature better than her and she'd been completely blindsided by this.

Just went to show she'd let herself get too comfortable with the handsome fisherman.

A crowd had already gathered around the steps of the public library. Must have been the mayor's idea. The library was the most prestigious, architecturally speaking, building in the village. Set against the backdrop of the harbor, the picturesque scene made for the perfect news clips. Clapboard-cloaked homes clung to the cliffside across the bay. Schooners drifted in the water. Seagulls floated in the air. Even the snow worked to set the scene.

Several reporters were already filming lead-in shots with their mobile crews.

Just great.

Sarah drove all the way down the block to a small parking area around the corner from Cappy's Chowder House. She dug around under the front seats until she found her ski cap. Pulling it low over her hair she wished for her sunglasses. Something else she'd forgotten to bring along.

Being a recognizable figure in cases like this had its downside. The prospect of some face reporter recognizing her and starting a line of questions Sarah couldn't answer ranked right up there with getting her wisdom teeth pulled out.

Frustrated at her ill-preparedness, she grabbed her bag and slammed the door. She climbed the hill to the sidewalk and scanned the shops. Rite Aid. The chain pharmacy would have sunglasses. Maybe even gloves. She'd frozen her ass, toes, and fingers off today.

Sarah crossed the street and entered the pharmacy. She glanced around, didn't spot any loitering reporters, and headed for the turnstile rack of sunglasses at the end of the snack aisle. Looking over her options, she checked for the best fit. Too big; too eighties; too . . . she made a face . . . bizarre. Then she found just the right ones. Slid them into place. Perfect. Black, wrapped around the face. Lots of camouflage. Exactly what she needed.

Now for gloves. She wandered the aisles, found some black woolly mittens with a waterproof outer shell, and headed for the check-out counter.

"Is that all today, ma'am?"

"Yes." Sarah scrounged for her wallet, then looked to the cashier for a total.

"You're that reporter woman from that magazine, aren't you?" The woman eyed her speculatively from behind big pink-framed eyeglasses. She could be someone's grandmother, silky gray hair, outfitted in a paisley print blouse. But the look she was giving Sarah right now was anything but grandmotherly.

Sarah did a quick sleazeball check around the store, then pasted on a smile for the cashier who looked not at all like a fan. "Yes."

"I hear you think one of us is responsible for that poor girl's murder."

Sarah wasn't about to go there. "The chief of police is preparing for a press conference right outside." She gestured to the street. "I'm sure he'll have the latest news on the case and any possible suspects."

The cashier's pale blue eyes narrowed behind the glasses.

"But you're not working with the police. You're running around talking to people on your own."

"I'm looking into the case, yes." Was it too much to ask to get a total here?

"Well"—the cashier leaned across the counter—"if you're smart you'll talk to the minister over at Living Word Church."

Anticipation of a new lead spiked. Another check to ensure no one was close by. "What makes you think I should talk to him?"

"Valerie Gerard attended that church her whole life." The cashier looked around as if she'd decided that what she had to say next shouldn't be overheard. "Then, last year she up and stopped going. When her folks tried to persuade her to go with 'em at Christmas, she flat-out refused."

Lots of teenagers ticked church services off their must-do lists as soon as they were old enough to make their own choices. "It's not unusual for teenagers to decide church isn't worth their time," Sarah reminded her. She'd made that decision by the time she was sixteen but her aunt hadn't let her off the hook until college.

The lady shook her head. "Valerie wasn't like that. She was a good girl. Refusing to go to church was not like her at all. Her mama worried about it for a while but then she figured it was probably the college influence." The cashier hit the total button. "I don't believe it, though. Uh-uh. There's more to it than that. Nineteen forty-eight."

Sarah handed her a twenty. "What's this minister's name?"

"Christopher Mahaney." She took Sarah's money. "It was probably his doing—that her folks believed she'd gone off to college and left God behind and all."

Something else the chief hadn't mentioned. A new name to add to Sarah's talk-to list. "Thanks." She dropped the change into her wallet. As an afterthought she pulled a card from her bag and offered it to the cashier. "You call me if you think of anything else that might be helpful."

The lady nodded. "I'll be glad to." She pointed a disgusted look toward the street. "There's something rotten in this town and I think it's that so-called man of God." She leaned toward Sarah again. "The old devil goes after ministers, too. Sometimes he's successful."

Sarah thanked her again and headed for the door. She ripped the tags from her purchases and slid the sunglasses into place, then tugged on the gloves and stepped onto the sidewalk.

More locals awaiting news had gathered at the library. Sarah slipped into the fringes and tried to make herself as inconspicuous as possible.

Snatches of conversation from the locals filtered through the rumble. Some folks believed Alicia Appleton's body had been discovered. Others insisted she had been found alive.

Ah, there was a mention of Sarah. *Troublemaker. Had Rachel Appleton in tears. Tried to force a confession out of Bart Harvey's boy.*

Oh, wow. Maybe she was the devil that kid had spoken of.

The cashier's mention of the devil nudged Sarah.

People around here needed to wake up. This killer was someone they likely knew. Assuredly not the devil. Not that she believed in the devil.

Silence fell over the crowd and a sudden forward surge announced the chief had made his appearance.

Sarah tiptoed to see above the shoulders of the men in front of her. Mayor Patterson stood next to the chief, his polished suit and deep navy tie making him look particularly distinguished in comparison to the chief's khakis and uniform-style coat.

"Ladies and gentlemen, members of the press . . ."

Sarah settled onto the soles of her Converses and waited for the important parts. The whole "I appreciate your support" and all that jazz she could do without.

Finally he got to the real news.

The silence that hung in the air hummed with tension.

Even Sarah stretched up onto her toes once more.

The chief didn't spell out the details of the evidence but he informed the crowd that there was reason to believe that the person responsible for Valerie Gerard's death was an intimate.

Sarah rolled her eyes. Come on, Chief, she silently urged. Tell them they'd better start paying more attention to what their neighbors are doing. Keep their young girls off the street after dark, et cetera.

"That's not very nice," a too familiar male voice whispered in her ear.

Sarah bolted forward.

Strong hands grabbed her shoulders in the nick of time to prevent her bumping into the guy in front of her. Sarah whipped around and came face-to-face with Kale Conner.

He put a finger to his lips and pointed to the chief.

Annoyed as hell, she turned her attention back to the library steps where the chief was assuring the crowd that no stone would be left unturned. How original. And, finally, he urged all citizens to be cooperative and aware. Hard questions would need to be asked—and answered.

Reporters started firing questions and Sarah was ready to go while they were distracted. She skirted the traitor standing behind her.

"Newton."

She glared at Conner. "Shhh!"

"Sorry." He started after her. "You're leaving?"

"Yes."

That he continued to follow her to the corner and down the side street to the parking area she'd used cranked up her irritation. Kale Conner was one of those guys who wanted everybody to like him. The kind who couldn't deal with the idea that someone held ill will toward him.

Tough.

She avoided the icy patches, opting for the crunchy snow instead. The cold, wet stuff poked into her shoes and up her pants legs all over again, but she didn't care.

She had a list of people to interview; Melody Harvey, for one. A man of the cloth named Mahaney, for another.

At her car, she faced her stalker. "What do you want, Conner?"

He seemed temporarily at a loss for words. Turning his hands palms up, he shrugged. "I thought you were going back to the inn. I went there looking for you but—"

Shoving her cell phone in his face, she waved it back and forth. "Ever heard of using one of these?" If he was going to attempt telling her he'd wanted to let her know about the press conference and couldn't find her he could forget about it.

"My cell died on me and I don't have one of those car chargers. I—"

"You lied to me. Again," she emphasized. "Have a nice evening."

She tried to open the car door; he braced his hand on it. "I was looking for you so I could tell you about the press conference."

"Right. Like you didn't know when we were at the chief's office."

Confusion furrowed the handsome features of his face into a questioning frown. "You think I knew about this?"

"You knew. The chief knew. And so did the mayor." When he would have argued, she held up a hand. "I know how these things work. You don't throw together a media delivery of this size without some prior planning."

He raised both hands surrender-style. "I swear on my mother's beef stew, which is what we're having for dinner tonight by the way, that I didn't know."

Funny. "No offense to your mother's beef stew, but I don't believe you."

"Ask the chief. Whether you believe it or not, he had no idea he would be announcing this news until about forty or forty-five minutes ago. Right *after* we left his office."

"Get real, Conner. I have things to do." She jerked at the door but didn't get it open before he, again, blocked her effort.

"The Bureau is sending a profiler to help with the case. He insisted the chief get the word out to set the stage for whatever he's got planned."

Sarah hesitated, her hand still on the door latch. Knowing the Bureau, she could see that happening.

She turned back to Conner. "The Bureau set this in motion and had the chief read their script, is that what you're saying?"

He nodded. "It's the God's truth."

Maybe she was a fool for believing him, but the scenario, with the FBI component thrown in, was believable.

"What's the profiler's name?" While she fully understood that there was basically zero probability it would be *him*—that rotten, low-life, bloodsucking, sorry-ass bastard—some part of her still feared it would be and braced. Quantico had profilers out the wazoo. The odds were astronomical. It wouldn't be *him*. Too big a coincidence—to be a coincidence.

"Let me think." Conner concentrated on the question a moment. "It was an odd name."

Her breath stalled in her chest. No way. No freaking way.

Recognition dawned on Conner's face. "Lex August. That was it."

Her blood drained to her feet. Three years, six months, and ten days since she'd seen or spoken to Lex August and still the sound of his name made her want to kick somebody. The Bureau knew she was here all right, and sending that bastard was an intentional, tactical move. Hell, he probably requested the assignment. Maybe she would kick somebody.

Conner was lucky she was no longer pissed off at him.

"You know him?"

"What makes you think I know him?"

Another of those "guy" shrugs. "I don't know. Maybe the way your face went white as a sheet when I said his name. Or the way your lips—"

"I get the picture." What the hell? There was absolutely no possibility that this was coincidence and no way she could avoid it, unless . . . "When will he arrive?" Her first thought was to go. Get the hell out of here before that part of her past had time to catch up with her.

Cops can't catch the devil. The girl from the cemetery flashed through Sarah's head but was quickly trumped by the memory of the agony in Rachel Appleton's eyes. If Sarah left . . . who would look at this case with complete objectivity? Who would step on toes, even those of the locals, and push to find the truth . . . the killer—before it was too late and Alicia Appleton was dead?

Her mother had received the roses today . . . time was running out.

"He arrives tomorrow," Conner said. "Flying into Portland tonight and driving up first thing in the morning."

Wonder Boy, that's what they called *him*. He could analyze a crime scene and whatever evidence there was and reduce the killer to twenty-five words or less in record time. And he was always right. Except for that once, but no one knew about that. He'd used Sarah's theory as his own to cover his mistake.

She should have sued but pillow talk wasn't always admissible in court. And she didn't want the world to know what a fool she'd been.

He fucked her then he fucked her over.

If Tae found out August was assigned to this case . . . he would definitely want her out of here.

Damn.

The gossip she'd heard from the cashier at the Rite Aid nudged its way into her troubled thoughts. "I have to go." First stop the inn, then the church. That should really boost her popularity.

"I wanted to—"

The crunch of ice and snow distracted Conner.

Sarah glanced over her shoulder.

Oh, hell.

Not good.

Two news vans roared into the lot, then screeched to abrupt stops around her car. A blond female reporter hopped out of one and hurried toward Sarah as fast as her high heels would carry her through the snow. Before she could reach

Sarah another, this one male, also blond but no heels, sprinted from the other van.

"Sarah, what's your assessment of the situation here in Youngstown?" This from the female.

Sarah held up her warm, gloved hands. "I have no comment."

"Come on, Sarah," the male reporter said as he elbowed his way in next to Conner. "You must have some conclusions. All we need is one sound bite."

"You've been here more than twenty-four hours," the female urged. "Our viewers would love to hear anything you've learned."

Cameramen, equipment directed on Sarah, crowded up behind their respective reporters.

The sound of more vehicles arriving had Sarah's attention swinging back to the entrance of the parking lot she'd thought was a secluded spot no one would notice. Another news crew in an SUV and one of Youngstown's official police cruisers. This just got better and better.

"Back off."

Sarah turned back to Conner who was ready to exchange knuckle imprints with one of the cameramen.

"Sarah!" The blond guy. "Do you think there's any merit in the curse that has folks in Youngstown shaking in their snow boots?"

Cute. "If you knew me," she said, cutting him a look that let him know how inept she considered his propaganda hype tactic, "you would know the answer to that question without having to ask."

"Did you lead the local police to the truth, Sarah? We all know your debunking reputation. You knew there was no hocus-pocus going on here before you came. Did you help the police understand what they were really dealing with?"

"The evidence led the Youngstown authorities to their conclusions," Sarah answered. "I'm only an observer."

"No ghosts in the mist, Sarah?" the newest reporter to join the fray shouted.

Whatever possessed her at that moment, Sarah couldn't name. "No ghosts," she said to the reporter. "Just the devil."

The realization of what she'd said sank in instantly. Her words fueled the frenzy.

Sarah held up her hands stop-sign fashion. "That's it. No more questions."

"Is it true," blond boy persisted, "that you bribed a morgue tech for copies of the crime-scene photos?"

Conner jerked her car door open. "Get in. I'll take care of this."

Was that fury throbbing in his rock-hard jaw?

Sarah didn't waste time mulling over the idea. She scooted behind the wheel, dug out her keys, and started the car.

With Deputy Karen Brighton's assistance, Conner cleared a path for Sarah to drive away.

Okay, so now he'd rescued her twice.

That earned him a second chance. Maybe he hadn't known about the press conference. It could have happened just as he said.

She slowed at the inn, got a glimpse of a news van in the parking lot, and opted not to turn up the drive. She decided to pay the minister a visit.

Five minutes later she was still driving around. Where was that church? She'd passed it at some point since her arrival. Taking a right onto Central Street, she followed it until it intersected with High. The church with its soaring steeple sat in the pie-shaped spot carved out of the community by the angled intersection of Central and High streets.

The house nestled next to the church, she assumed, was the minister's home.

Only one way to find out.

She parked in the church lot and took her time strolling toward the house next door. The parking area as well as the nearby sidewalks had been cleared of snow. Proud stained-glass windows flanked the church's double entry doors. The church looked about as old as everything else around here.

The house, too. Cedar-shake-shingle siding, and six-over-six windows.

Two wide steps up put her on the stoop. She pressed the doorbell and waited. A car sat beneath a carport at the side of the house. Hopefully someone was home.

The door opened and a teenage girl peeked out. "May I help you?"

Brown hair and eyes. A little plump. Dressed in the expected preacher's-daughter attire. Loose-fitting jeans and a bulky sweater. Other than the soft oval face and long hair it would be difficult to tell if she were a boy or a girl.

"Hello." Sarah produced that pleasant smile folks expected. "I'm Sarah Newton and I'm here to see Father Mahaney. Are you his daughter?"

"No, I'm his niece." The girl blinked, seemed to consider her options, then opened the door wide. "Come in. I'll let my aunt know there's a visitor."

At least Sarah was through the door.

"Wait here, please." The girl gestured to the sofa.

"Thank you."

As the girl walked away, Sarah took in the decorating. Simple. Wood floors, the occasional colorful rug, subtle blue flowers in the wallpaper. Gas fireplace blazed, making the room overly warm. Homey.

"How can I help you, Ms. Newton?"

Sarah turned to the woman who'd entered the room. Middle-aged. Same brown hair as the niece except sprinkled with gray. Different eyes. More green than brown. That she wore gloves indoors seemed odd.

"I'm here to see Father Mahaney." Sarah thrust out her hand. "It's a pleasure to meet you."

"Deborah Mahaney."

The woman barely touched Sarah's hand, but even for that fleeting moment Sarah felt the gnarled digits hidden by the gloves. Arthritis?

"I'm sorry," Deborah said without the slightest remorse, "but the *Reverend* is out visiting an ill member of our congregation. Is there something I can help you with?"

Father, reverend, whatever. Sarah could never keep up
with that stuff. "Actually, you might be able to." Sarah
paused, expecting the invitation to sit. Didn't come. "I was
hoping to learn a little more about Valerie Gerard."

The lockdown couldn't have been any plainer if the reverend's wife had closed her eyes and taped her mouth shut.

"What would you like to know?"

In her peripheral vision Sarah got a glimpse of the niece
peeking around the doorframe leading into the hall.

"It's my understanding," Sarah said, refocusing her interest on the wife, "that until about a year ago Valerie was a
longstanding member of your church. Can you tell me what
happened that prompted her to leave?"

"Every congregation suffers losses, Ms. Newton. Now
and then one loses faith and falls away, lured by the sins of
this old world, I'm afraid."

Sarah paid particular attention to her eyes now. "Is that
what happened to Valerie?"

A glance to the right, then a blink. "It's difficult to say.
The Reverend urged her to cling to her faith, but sometimes
the best counseling and most earnest prayers aren't in align-
ment with God's intentions. Our view is limited, and we
must rely on His. He always has His reasons, and ours is not
to question why."

As expected. One of *those*. "So nothing happened in
church," Sarah redirected. "Maybe with one of the other
members or with the Reverend?"

Deborah's eyes widened a fraction. "I'm not sure what
you mean."

Sarah gave a little shrug. "You know. A falling-out or a
misunderstanding of some sort. Things happen. People
react."

"I'm afraid there was nothing like that."

Emotionless. Her voice was dull, monotone. The self-
righteousness she'd exhibited when Sarah first arrived was
gone and replaced by . . . absolutely nothing.

"That's strange," Sarah said, deciding to interject
doubt. "Several people have mentioned that there was a

falling-out. Maybe it was just a rumor." She let the possibility dangle.

"I'll let the Reverend know you wish to speak to him
about this." Deborah moved toward the door. "I'm sure he
can answer your questions better than I can."

Definitely a falling-out, not a rumor. Sarah hesitated at
leaving, looked the wife in the eyes to garner the most impact. "It's very important that any and all aspects of Valerie's
life be analyzed to get to the bottom of why she was murdered. The smallest thing could turn out to be immensely
important."

"I'll have the Reverend call the inn to make an appointment with you."

"Thank you."

Again Sarah delayed making the exit the woman wanted
so desperately for her to make. "Someone who knew Valerie
did this," she reminded. "The Reverend probably knows the
folks who were most closely associated with her. Perhaps
even those her family didn't know about. Young girls have
secrets." Sarah smiled. "As a spiritual leader in the community, your husband keeps lots of secrets, I'm sure."

The flames of hell couldn't have thawed the icy stare
Sarah got for that remark.

"Have a nice evening, Ms. Newton."

The door closed promptly behind her.

Sarah walked back to her car, got in and turned the key.
As she backed out of the driveway, she glimpsed the
front-window curtain falling back into place. Confirming
she was leaving, was she?

Some would call Sarah's tactics unconscionable. But that
was the way this game was played. She planted the doubts
and suspicions and then the reactions began. Just like tip-
ping that first domino. All the rest were helpless to do anything but fall.

Sarah checked the street, started to back out, but a figure
standing at the church doors drew her attention there.

Brown hair, bulky sweater. The niece.

She waved timidly to Sarah.

Sarah glanced at the house before pulling deeper into the church parking lot. Once her car was hidden from view by the church, she climbed out. "Hi." Sarah presented a wide, friendly smile. "I didn't catch your name." She didn't rush toward the steps where the girl waited, didn't want to startle her.

"Tamara." The girl glanced toward the corner of the church as if she expected her aunt to appear, then she settled a wide-eyed gaze on Sarah's. "My aunt didn't tell you the truth."

"About what?" Sarah asked carefully. Don't lead. Even if anticipation was sending her pulse into overdrive. Let the girl tell her story.

"Valerie left the congregation because of something my uncle did."

Sarah kept her expression schooled. "What did he do?"

Tamara bit her lip, looked toward the corner of the building again. "The same thing he did to me."

Disgust welled in Sarah's chest. "Can you be more specific?" She knew what the girl meant, but she needed her to say the words.

"Tamara!"

The aunt.

The girl's eyes widened. "I have to go!"

Sarah reached for one of her cards. "Call me and—"

Tamara rushed away before Sarah could finish. She dropped her hand to her side and waited until she heard the front door of the house slam before going back to her car and sliding behind the wheel again. She exited the church lot, careful to ensure she stayed out of view of the house. No need to get the niece in trouble. If Sarah could get a chance to speak with her again, alone, she would get the rest of the story.

Not that she needed another word to figure it out.

The reverend was a pervert.

Fury charged through her. Had Alicia Appleton attended the same church? That would be easy enough to verify.

Why the hell hadn't someone checked into this?

Because no one in this God-fearing village would ever suspect their divine communications link of such a thing.

Sarah abruptly slowed as she passed Bay View Cemetery. Dusk had chased the sun away. Another ten, fifteen minutes and it would be completely dark.

She couldn't shake the idea of what that reverend might be guilty of. Sure, she could be jumping to conclusions but . . .

Sarah's foot stalled on the brake. She squinted to peer through the gloom. Couldn't be sure of what she was seeing so she pulled to the curb and got out of the car.

Like a curious kid she bellied up to the big old iron fence and stared through the pickets.

Her seeking gaze found its mark. The witch's headstone.

Sarah's heart bumped hard against her sternum.

Two crows sat on the aged headstone.

Two dozen roses: one for the Gerards, one for the Appletons.

Two crows . . .

One for Valerie Gerard . . . one for Alicia Appleton.

CHAPTER 18

Kale still wasn't sure how he'd managed to do it but he'd gotten Sarah Newton to agree to dinner with his folks.

He had to admit, the lady cleaned up damned good.

Black was still her color, but the dress was an interesting departure from the usual slacks and tee. When he'd noticed she'd stuck with the Converse sneakers, even wearing the dress, he'd almost laughed. She hadn't missed his stifled mirth. She'd informed him that along with her snow boots, gloves, and sunglasses, she'd failed to pack a pair of heels. The dress, she claimed, went everywhere with her . . . just in case.

Didn't matter. She looked good in the dress that contoured to her shape like shrink-wrapped plastic. The curves he'd recognized even beneath that bulky parka were every bit as tempting as he'd anticipated.

She might be as stubborn as any man he'd ever met but, from those shapely calves to the curve of her cheek, she was all woman.

When she threw her head back and laughed at something his mother said, he smiled. The silky, thick mass of loose blond curls usually previewed by the wisps peeking from her ski cap made a man want to run his fingers through them. His fingers twitched as if the thought had gone straight from his brain to those tips. Other thoughts, far less polite thoughts, were barging straight to his—

A hard knock on the shoulder snapped him from his obsessing.

"Help me set the table, Kale," his little sister demanded. She pushed her glasses up her nose. "You think just because you brought company that you don't have to work?"

Kale straightened away from the counter. "Okay, okay. Don't be a pain in the—"

Ellen, his mother, cut him a look that closed his mouth. Newton belted out another of those throaty laughs.

He liked her laughter. The tough New York girl vanished and this soft, sexy woman emerged.

What had sent that side of Sarah Newton into hiding? That sweet, earthy female was right there hidden beneath all that streetwise urban attitude.

A stack of plates poked him in the abdomen.

He grunted, grabbed the plates before Polly dropped them on his feet. "Thanks."

"Anytime."

Kale had to work at keeping his eyes off his guest as he rounded the table, leaving a plate in front of all but one of the chairs. Polly followed his path, leaving silverware and linen napkins. Their brother wouldn't be home for spring break for a couple more weeks.

"The chief has no idea where to start with this investigation, does he?"

Kale glanced at his father, whose wheelchair already had been parked at the head of the table. "He's doing the best he can," Kale reminded his father. "There's not a lot to go on."

Peter Conner made a disparaging sound. "He'll do about like he did the last time."

Kale divided a look between his father and Newton, who had turned her attention from the cook and the dinner rolls in the oven to listen in. "Let's hope not," he commented, hoping to defuse the conceivably volatile topic.

"What do you say, Sarah?" his father asked their guest.

That was exactly what Kale had hoped to avoid.

Peter Conner never had been friends with Ben Willard. Kale hadn't been able to get the story from his father on what went wrong between the two men, but something was there and it went back as far as Kale could recall.

Newton walked over to the table and pulled out a chair. "This could take some time, Mr. Conner," she said.

"Obviously I've got nothing better to do." Peter gestured to the wheelchair that was his prison. Although he was paralyzed from the waist down, the devastating injury hadn't altered his sharp intelligence in the slightest. The man didn't miss a thing and he never thought twice about having his say. Who was going to slug a guy in a wheelchair?

Newton nodded. "Valerie Gerard was murdered by someone she knew who had a vendetta against her. The act was personal. The grudge deep and fierce. This was no random act."

"I'll bet you've been telling Willard this since you got here."

She smiled, not that indifferent gesture she'd tossed around on first arriving. This one was full lipped and completely genuine. "You would be right."

Peter shook his head. "That hardheaded man never listens. He's got to do every damned thing his own way."

"Watch it," Ellen warned.

"It's the truth." Peter dismissed his wife's counsel with a wave of his hand. "The only reason he's still the chief is because that's what folks think they're expected to do. Elect or commission a Willard. They've been doing it for four generations."

"Dad," Kale pressed, "let's not make tonight about bashing the good guys."

His father harrumphed and promptly ignored his son. He was clearly enjoying the pretty lady's attention. "And Alicia Appleton?" he queried. "You have a theory about her as well?"

Polly suddenly adopted a model pose. "Don't hate me because I'm beautiful," she crooned. "I can't help myself. I was born that way."

"Polly!" The reprimanding tone of his mother's voice was nothing to compare with the admonishing stare that accompanied it. "You should be praying for that girl, not making cruel remarks."

"It's true," Polly sassed, "and you know it. Alicia thinks she's all that and nobody else in the world matters. She's a snob. Nobody at school will tell her because they're afraid of being shunned. But they all secretly say it behind her back. I don't know why Brady follows her around like a stupid puppy. Alicia thought I liked Brady and got all mad at me. It's Jerri Lynn Pope she should be worried about. If Alicia gets killed, Jerri Lynn will dance on her grave."

"That's enough, young lady," her father growled. "It's one thing to discuss the flaws in the investigation but quite another to speak unkindly about the victims."

Polly rolled her eyes and shuffled off to get the water glasses.

Peter turned his attention back to Newton. "As much as I hate to speak ill of the poor girl, Polly's got a valid point. Alicia Appleton's mother has spoiled her beyond all reason."

"Peter," Ellen scolded him and tossed her oven mitt aside. "You're as bad as Polly."

"According to Brady Harvey, Alicia has no enemies." Newton draped one arm over the back of her chair and crossed those shapely legs. "Under the circumstances, I find that a little odd."

"You mean"—Kale pulled out the chair next to her—"because she wins everything and all the kids orient their social lives around what she's doing or planning."

"That's exactly what I mean. Jealousy is a part of human nature. Enemies go with the territory when you're the most popular girl in school." She looked from Kale to his father. "There is no way Valerie Gerard was murdered and Alicia Appleton was taken hostage by a person who hated them both enough to carry out that kind of action without someone noticing something. People see, sense, and ultimately talk. All we need is for those who know to start speaking up."

"Unless it's the devil," Polly tossed in as she settled a glass at each plate. "Matilda Calder says it's the devil."

Kale groaned. His father's brow furrowed. But it was his mother who came unglued. "Don't tell me you've been talking to that girl again."

"Tell me about Matilda." Newton addressed her question to the room at large. "I ran into her at the cemetery today. What's her story?"

"She's nice but weird," Polly said despite her mother shaking her head in abject disapproval.

"That little girl," Ellen explained, "is a fifth-generation illegitimate child. Those Calder women have repeated the same mistake time and time again. No husband. No marriages period."

"At least they had the good sense to stop at one," Peter offered. "That alone is a miracle considering the number of gentlemen callers they've all entertained."

"Calderwood Lane," Kale pointed out, "was named after Mattie's father who was supposedly an illegitimate great-great-grandson of Thomas Young, the village founder."

"That's never been proven," Peter interjected.

"What does Matilda's mother do?" Newton wanted to know.

Kale and his father exchanged a knowing look. "The oldest profession," Kale said quietly.

"She's a prostitute," Polly piped up. "They say she uses drugs, too, but Matilda doesn't do any of that stuff. She's just that creepy kind of weird. Reads about witches and stuff all the time. She has a pentagram in her bedroom. It's kindda scary but really cool and—"

When the room fell tomb-quiet, Polly realized she'd stuck her foot deep into her mouth. Her face flushed.

Kale groaned.

"And how would you know this, young lady?" Peter demanded.

"I . . . I . . . ah," Polly stammered.

She looked to Kale for help. No way was he getting in the middle of this.

"Don't you ever go back to that house again," Ellen ordered. "Why, there was a nine-one-one call over there just yesterday."

Newton's radar visibly rose. "Someone sick?"

"No," Ellen said, dragging out the vowel. "Matilda's mother claimed someone had broken in and taken some of her personal belongings, but she refused to say what exactly they took."

"And you think that's . . . not quite right," Newton suggested.

Ellen shrugged. "We all know there's nothing in that shack anyone would bother with except what she couldn't report."

"Drugs?" Newton speculated.

"That's what folks say," Peter said with a somber nod. "It's a very bad situation."

"She lives on West Street," Kale explained. "That was the call that held up Karen yesterday."

"Polly," Newton said, "where does Alicia go to church?"

Polly slid into the chair across the table from their guest. "Methodist. Same as the Harveys. Why?"

"Just curious."

The topic of discussion shifted. Grateful, Kale went back to watching the lady from New York. As she smiled and nodded at his father's every comment about the weather and life in general, Kale got the distinct impression that something about Matilda's circumstances had struck a chord with her.

He didn't know a lot about her history, but he had a feeling that tough, city-gal exterior was just a shield she used to protect herself. Most likely he was overanalyzing. She lived her life, trusted her instincts, and went after what she wanted with no regard to rules, social or otherwise. Somehow he was attracted to that. Quite possibly because she would be gone in a few days or a couple of weeks. There was no risk . . . no expectations. Just the possibility of amazing sex.

What man still breathing wouldn't be attracted to that?

Ellen set the steaming pot of beef stew in the center of the table. The rolls came next. She took her place beside her husband and sighed. "Kale, say grace and let's feed this girl. She's wasting away right before our eyes."

Kale reached for his sister's hand, then for Newton's. She stared at him, then at his hand, and finally put hers in his. He smiled. She looked away. He wondered at that. Did the lady not like to be touched? Or did prayer unsettle her? More mystery to nag at his curiosity.

When all hands were joined, he offered the blessing, adding a plea for the safe return of Alicia Appleton and an extra outpouring of strength and courage for her family.

"Amen," his father announced. "Now, Sarah, you'll see what beef stew is supposed to taste like."

Polly launched into a series of adolescent tales about the kids in school, particularly Alicia Appleton and Jerri Lynn Pope. Ellen gently scolded her from time to time for being less than sensitive toward her peers. Kale's father shook his head and pointed out regularly that Polly was not to be sending text messages during dinner. Each time she would feign obedience and pretend to put her cell phone away. Kale wasn't fooled. Like most teenagers, the girl was glued to that phone. She could probably text with her toes.

Newton interacted with his family, but watched and listened more than she talked. Absorbing, assessing, analyzing. He wished he had an inkling of what was going on inside that head of hers.

Chances were he would never know.

The lady kept her secrets, and she would be gone soon.

Just yesterday he'd dreaded her arrival.

Now he couldn't exactly say he looked forward to her leaving.

At times, life could sure twist a guy's balls.

Hard as he tried, he couldn't keep his mind from wandering back to the investigation. How could anyone be so warped as to cut out a person's heart? The idea that the killer from twenty years ago had never been caught seemed even more horrific given that detail. Kale considered the idea that Valerie Gerard had been murdered so heinously by someone she knew and his chest tightened. As crazy as it sounded,

that made it all the worse. How could this have happened
here?

As much as he wanted to believe, and as often as he
prayed for it, his optimism that Alicia would be found safe
was losing oomph fast.

After wine and the homemade chocolate layer cake his
mother had insisted they all had to try, Kale helped Newton with her coat. She said her good-byes to his folks, got
a hug from Polly before the kid rushed off to the computer
and MySpace.

"I'll walk you out," he offered.

That she didn't protest surprised him. She usually made
no bones about her ability to take care of herself. Not tonight. She led the way across the porch and down the
steps.

At her car she turned to face him. "Thanks, Conner. Tonight was nice."

"My sister's a little kooky," he admitted.

"Your sister is sweet and hilarious." Newton smiled.
"She speaks her mind. I like her."

That smile, the one he hadn't seen until tonight, did
things to him he was sure Sarah Newton didn't intend. Man,
when her unusual lips tilted that way . . . amazing. They
kept his attention lingering far too long. When he met her
gaze she was watching him . . . the way she'd been watching
his family all night.

He swallowed, yearned to . . . No. No. Not a good move.

"It's really not that complicated, Conner."

An alarm echoed in his head. "What's . . . not . . . that
complicated?" Busted. Again.

"If you want to kiss me, just do it. Life's too short to
spend it wondering if you should have, could have, or if you
ever will have the chance again."

The lady read minds, did she? "I don't usually—"

"Gimme a break, Conner."

Before he could put together a witty comeback, she
grabbed him by the face, pulled his mouth to hers and kissed

him. His body reacted in ways his brain had no chance in hell of catching up to. He didn't even want to try.

She kissed him fast and furiously. It was over way too soon.

"See." She licked her lips. "That wasn't so hard."

Whatever he should have said, he didn't. He threaded his fingers into that silky hair he'd been dying to touch all damned night and he kissed her back. Slower, deeper. She tasted a little like sweet chocolate and tart wine. Mostly she tasted like soft, hot woman.

He leaned into her. She reclined against the car and her soft curves cradled his rigid frame.

This kiss was never going to be enough.

Her palms glided down his chest, one sliding around his hip to pull him closer. The other molding to his cock.

"Now that," she whispered between desperate kisses, "however, is extremely hard."

"This . . ."—he gulped the cold air—"is going to sound like a seriously bad line, but your place or mine?"

"You didn't get your coat," she reminded. Her knee inched between his thighs. Higher. Higher.

He groaned. "I'll . . . ah . . . come back for it."

"Hop in."

She reached behind her and opened the driver's side door. Sliding behind the steering wheel and across the console, she settled into the passenger seat.

He got in, started the engine. "Where to?"

Her eyes were closed, those lush curls crushed against the headrest. "I don't care. Just go."

He roared out of the driveway and headed toward his place. That was closer than the inn.

At the first intersection, he turned onto Main.

She was watching him again. Not analyzing this time, savoring . . . maybe devouring.

"Just park somewhere," she urged, her hand skimming his thigh.

He took the next left, pulling into Bay View Cemetery.

Shit. Why did he turn here?

"There's no parking here after dark," he explained, his voice thick with need. Dammit. "I should—"

"Stop talking."

She was coming across the console before he got shifted into park. He didn't argue. He shoved the gearshift forward, hit the switch, and turned off the headlights.

"Seat," she ordered.

He reached around her and down, pulled the lever to send the seat sliding as far back as possible. She pulled the recline lever, pressed him downward. Without another thought or even a breath his hands were under her dress, caressing those sleek thighs and that perfect, tight ass.

Her fingers trailed up his fly, then down. His found their way to hot, damp panties.

"Condom," she murmured.

Shit. "Wallet."

He wanted to reach for it, but he couldn't take his hands off her. One finger slipped into that incredible slick heat. She moaned her approval. He closed his eyes and imagined his cock following that scorching route.

She dug into his pocket, pulled out his wallet. When she had the condom in her hand he snagged it, ripped it open with his teeth. She pulled his dick free of his jeans. He groaned at the feel of her cool fingers on him.

"Hurry," she urged.

He slid the condom into place and she sank onto him with a satisfied sigh.

Her lashes fluttered downward. She whimpered this little sound that made him crazy. He wanted to kiss her again, but he couldn't stop looking at her. Couldn't stop squeezing those firm, smooth thighs.

She started to move. She arched her torso, never slowing down the rhythm. He had to touch her breasts. His palms molded there. Had to taste her. He pulled the scoop neck of her dress aside, and the lace of her bra, then dragged her forward until his mouth closed over a firm nipple.

She cried out.

He caressed her legs, rubbed her ass, stroking that intimate seam. She felt so good. So soft and hot. And . . .

She was coming.

He didn't interfere. Let her maintain control, let her keep moving up and down, up and down, until she captured that explosion of sensations.

Her breathing ragged, she leaned down and kissed him. Her hot, tight cunt was slicker than ever, pulsed with pleasure.

When she'd savored her own pleasure as long as he could bear to wait, he lifted her hips, then slowly lowered her. He groaned with the effort, couldn't manage anything but that one back-and-forth movement. Up. Down. Slow. Jesus, she was tight. Hot. Wet.

She made those sweet sounds again . . . her body tensed.

She came again.

His cock pulsated with every squeeze of her amazingly taut muscles.

Then he came.

She sagged against him until their breathing slowed and the cold started to invade the car.

He touched those silky curls, loved the feel of her hair, the lavender smell.

She raised her head, looked at him. He couldn't read her eyes in the dark, but he felt her tension. Not the kind they'd just shared, either.

"Don't get any ideas, Conner." She pulled free of him, taking his breath, then slid across the console and righted her clothes. "For me, that's it. No relationships, no attachments period. Just sex."

A little disoriented by her sudden about-face, he shoved his gloved dick back into his jeans and zipped up. What the hell did he say to that?

Totally at a loss for words, he fired up the engine and backed out of the cemetery.

By the time he'd reached his parents' house he'd managed to pull together a reasonable response. "I shouldn't have

let things get out of control. I don't do casual sex, Newton."
He parked her car next to his Jeep and turned to face her.
This time he could see her eyes in the dim glow of the dash
lights. "That won't happen again."

She shrugged. "Fine by me."

"Fine," he snapped back, but the word was lost to the sound
of her slamming the door.

He sat there a moment then got out. It was her car. She
walked around him, got behind the wheel and drove away.

He watched her taillights fade in the night.

Yep. People from New York were definitely nuts.

Or maybe he was the crazy one.

CHAPTER 19

The Overlook Inn, 10:50 P.M.

Barton watched from the window as Sarah Newton parked her car, then hurried inside. He stayed in the shadows on the far side of the lobby as she rushed up the stairs. He touched his cheek and fury tightened his lips.

There was no reason for her to stay in Youngstown now.

She should have left today.

But no. She wasn't finished ruining lives.

He shuffled across the lobby, around the reception desk, and into his office. He closed and locked the door. For a full minute he stood staring at his desk.

What did he do now?

If she wouldn't leave . . .

With a burdened breath he ambled behind his desk and dropped into the chair.

What the hell did he do?

His hands shook as he unlocked the desk and reached into the bottom drawer on the left. He withdrew the journal and held it in his hands without opening it.

He didn't have to open it.

He knew the words by heart.

. . . the first plunge of the knife split the porcelain flesh and blood bloomed forth like a river of crimson . . . the heart quivered . . .

Barton shuddered. Squeezed his eyes shut. Tried to stop

the words. But they would not go away . . . they were permanently etched in his brain.

   . . . the tip met bone and he was forced to grind and slide sideways until the blade sank deep into muscle and tissue . . . each plunge of the knife sent blood gushing, spilling onto the cold stones . . . yet he did not stop . . . not until he was done . . .

   . . . and they were both dead . . .

Dear God . . . what had he done?

CHAPTER 20

Jerald peered through the powerful lens of the telescope, surveying the chapel and the woods that surrounded it like a natural fortress.

Half an hour ago the police officer charged with overseeing a local youth group's prayer vigil at the chapel had climbed the stone steps and walked the length of the structure several times. Eventually he had sought the warmth of his cruiser. Jerald presumed the officer would remain for a time to ensure none returned with mischief in mind.

Jerald stepped away from the telescope. It was almost midnight and he was tired.

. . . you can't watch every minute.

Sarah Newton was right. He couldn't keep a constant vigil. Jerald sighed. That was someone else's responsibility now. But he could protect his own.

He moved quietly to the second floor. The door to his daughter's room was open, the television blaring at its sleeping audience. A smile touched his lips as he neared her bed. He loved her so very much. Until she'd come into his life he hadn't known it was possible to feel so thoroughly connected to another human being.

She slept so peacefully. Worry tugged at his heart. He wanted her to have a rich, full life. Unburdened by his weaknesses. As if on cue his hands trembled, felt numb.

Whatever it took, he reaffirmed, he would protect his daughter and his wife.

He slipped from her room, closing the door behind him. He would keep those he loved safe . . . no matter the cost.

Down the hall he paused at the double doors leading to the master suite. Still closed. His wife remained angry with him. They had argued again over what was best for their daughter.

He walked away, chose a guest room for the night. It wouldn't be the first time he and his wife had taken a night apart. After more than two decades of marriage it wasn't so unusual to need space. It was the subject of their disagreements that grieved him so deeply.

She would never understand.

This was a situation Jerald would have to handle alone.

No one would understand.

Except . . . perhaps Sarah Newton.

CHAPTER 21

Midnight

Hours passed before it was clear to proceed.

The cold finally had gotten to the inept cop hanging around and he'd gone home.

Five minutes more and tonight's work would be complete. Fear and remorse would paralyze them all. Efforts to find the killer would intensify.

The bitch whimpered.

"Shut up!"

Stupid, stupid, snobby bitch.

The needle pierced her right eyelid. The nylon thread slid easily through. *Pull tight.*

Last stitch.

Very nice.

Six stitches each. Neat. Not nearly as much blood as the lips. Or maybe the pills had helped.

Another disgusting moan.

Fury ignited. "I know how to shut you up."

One, two, three, four carefully prepared pieces. Everything had to be exact. Even in the near darkness, the jewels glittered.

"Now. To crown the queen."

Tug the mouth open. The bitch had better not bite.

"This is the last time you'll ever be beautiful."

One, two pieces tucked deep inside.

The dying bitch coughed. Gagged.

"Don't you puke on me!"

Three, four. Done.

Shove the mouth closed. Press the tape into place.

"Perfect. Now comes your punishment, you bad, bad girl."

After having lain long minutes on the stone floor, the knife was cold.

Raise it high. Thrust it deep. Over and over.

The wounds gushed, spouting crimson and making the excitement build and build and build with each precisely numbered and placed plunge into smooth, flawless flesh.

And then the message they would all see.

The blood was hot. Formed the letters as if it had been made for just this purpose.

Sit back and assess the work, no mistakes.

"Perfect."

Soon it would be done.

Gazing across the treetops a triumphant smile formed. "Now who's the devil?"

They would all see.

But their eyes would deceive them.

Exactly as planned.

CHAPTER 22

Christopher Mahaney's hands shook as he lifted a mug to his lips.

Father, forgive my sins. Give me peace, heavenly Father.

For days, Christopher had silently chanted that petition over and over. Still he felt no peace.

Rather, each day, the turmoil inside him continued to surge, increasing in intensity.

His hand wobbled. Coffee sloshed onto his skin. He plunked the cup onto the counter.

"Father, forgive me . . ." His urgent whisper faded into silence. He closed his eyes and begged for mercy.

How much longer could he bear this immense cross?

Hadn't he been punished enough?

The sin was not his alone. *They* had tempted him. Drawn him to the darkness . . . to the evil sins of the flesh.

"You're up early."

Christopher whirled around. Met his wife's accusing gaze. His heart lurched, ached. He tried not to hold her partially responsible. Had she been any kind of mate, perhaps his gaze would not have strayed . . . perhaps he would not have failed the test. Now she insisted that he protect her. Protect the niece he'd been forced to support. Fury twisted deep in his blemished soul.

He should go. Pray for forgiveness for his selfish thoughts. This was not the time to place blame or to resent his respon-

sibilities. This was the time for action . . . for seeking guid-
ance.

"I'm going to the chapel to pray." He'd only just made the
final decision. That Valerie's body had been placed there
was a sign. Christopher must pay attention to the signs.

"Do you think that's a good idea?" His wife rubbed her
hands together and grimaced.

The pain. He understood. She suffered so. Perhaps that
was her punishment for failing to do her wifely duty.

"It's necessary," he insisted, forcing his faulty heart to
dispel the selfish emotions.

Deborah shook her head. "The only necessary thing,
Christopher, is for you to find a way to stop *her*. She's going
to keep digging until she finds something." His wife's worried gaze settled on his. "You know she won't give up.
Something has to be done."

Her words were far too true, but he did not want to hear.
Movement in his peripheral vision distracted him. He
frowned, inclined his head to the right so that he could see
past his wife. His niece hovered just beyond the doorway.
"You should go back to bed, Tamara." She was always
lurking about like that. No matter that Christopher had attempted to cleanse her of her impurities . . . she would no
doubt turn out to be a whore just like her mother.

Deborah twisted toward the girl. "Stop eavesdropping,
child, and go back to bed."

Tamara slinked off to the stairs. She had no one else in
this world. Only him and Deborah. Christopher had taken a
solemn oath to guide her in the Lord's path. He could not
fail in the task. That would only add to his mounting short-
falls.

If . . . things took a turn for the worse, what would Tamara do? What would Deborah do?

"That girl is into something," Deborah charged. "I caught
her sneaking back into the house at quarter of one this
morning. That's twice in as many weeks."

Worry heaped heavy onto Christopher's already burdened shoulders. "Was she with her friends?" Dear God,

could his wife do nothing to help herself and her sister's child?

Deborah untethered her long braid of hair in preparation for arranging the meticulous bun she always wore, her once nimble fingers struggling with the effort. "She won't say. Apparently she thinks just because she's eighteen now she doesn't have to answer to me. I think she's running with the Pope girl. You know that child is wild. You're going to have to do something, Christopher." Deborah arched an eyebrow. "About both those worries."

What did she expect him to do?

He shook his head before dropping it in shame. "What else can I do?"

"I don't know," Deborah exclaimed, then paused and buried her emotions. "But you have to do something. I've done all I can to help you already. More than I should have," she charged. "The rest is up to you."

His wife turned sharply and padded out of the room.

She was right, of course.

Christopher closed his eyes and repeated the petition for forgiveness.

He was to blame.

So many had suffered already.

Surely God would not continue to punish those who were innocent.

What was he thinking?

The Old Testament was filled with far too many examples of exactly that for Christopher to dare doubt.

He pulled on his coat, picked up his keys, then reached into his pockets for his gloves but decided he did not deserve that comfort. His hands should be exposed to the harsh cold while he clasped them in prayer. His grievous errors warranted far worse.

Driving to the chapel, he viewed his village as if for the last time. His flock trusted him, depended upon him to ensure that God's blessing showered upon them and their homes. And he had failed. His failure would shed a bad light on his Heavenly Father. An unforgivable sin.

By the time Christopher reached the rustic chapel tears had dampened his face. If only those salty fluids were acid. Perhaps the scars from the burns would ensure he never fell short of his faith again. Even that was not punishment enough. His eyes should be plucked from his head.

To blame his wife and his niece was the coward's way out. Christopher was not a coward. Sin had confused him, twisted his mind. He was, after all, only human.

Emerging from his car, he made the cold, lonely journey toward the chapel.

He would pray long and hard, until his knees and hands stung from the cold and went numb.

He would kiss the icy stones where her blood had spilled.

To attain forgiveness, he would do anything his dear Lord required of him to stop this heinous chain of events.

He prayed that somehow his merciful Father would see fit to give him a second chance. Christopher would not fail again. He would be strong.

Pausing to catch his breath, he reached for the hand railing before ascending the steps.

He paid no heed to the snow and ice beneath his soles. If he fell, it would be nothing less than he deserved.

Pain would be a welcome punishment.

Punish me, Father, he implored, *and give me peace.*

The smell of death remained in the air.

The ache in his chest swelled, pressing against the weak organ there.

As his boot rested upon the final step, his eyes widened and his breath deserted him.

Pale flesh splattered with the deep crimson of blood. Letters scrawled in that same lethal hue. He drew back, lost his balance, and tumbled all the way to the ground.

The impact against the frozen ground forced a grunt from his hoarse throat.

"No, no, no, no!"

His wail echoed through the surrounding woods. Haunted his very soul.

Fresh, hot tears streamed from his sinful eyes. He scrambled onto his hands and knees, crawled to the steps. He dragged himself up each tread, his body trembling with denial, seizing with agony.

Squeezing his eyes shut, he reached the top once more and prayed fervently that his impious gaze had deceived him.

"Please, please," he whimpered. "Please . . . no."

Slowly, he opened his eyes.

Terror apprehended his throat. His scream strangled him. This was his doing. His punishment!

His sinful desires had brought this plague upon his neighbors.

Christopher covered his face with his hands and howled in misery.

It was him. It was him. It was him.

Yet his heart continued to beat . . .

. . . and hers did not.

CHAPTER 23

A persistent vibration rattled her eardrums.

Sarah pulled the covers over her face.

Another buzz of hard plastic against harder wood.

She jerked the covers down and picked up her cell phone.

Conner.

The last person on earth, besides maybe her shrink, she wanted to talk to again in this lifetime.

At least before eight.

She dropped the phone and sat up.

If she had a cigarette she would smoke it.

Even after two years of nicotine abstinence.

That damned vibrating hum started up again.

She glared at the screen.

Conner.

If she didn't answer he'd probably just show up at her room. Then she'd probably want to drag him into her bed and fuck him stupid.

He definitely didn't need to show up here.

She pushed the hair out of her face and opened the damned phone. "Newton."

"I'm waiting for you in the parking lot."

The mere sound of his voice prompted an instant recap of last night's lapse into temporary insanity.

"I'm not interested in breakfast, Conner. Call me in a couple of hours."

"Sarah."

She stilled. He rarely called her by her first name.

"We have to get down to the chief's office."

The silence that followed made her gut clench.

Then she knew. Oh, hell no.

"Alicia's body was found this morning," he said flatly, confirming the conjecture squeezing the air out of her nicotine-deprived lungs.

"I'll be right down."

Sarah closed the phone and slammed it back onto the table.

Fury detonated deep, deep in her belly.

"Motherfucker!" She grabbed the same jeans she'd had on yesterday. Tossed through the drawer for her hooded sweatshirt, dragged it over her head.

"Son of a bitch." She tugged on socks and her Converses.

When she'd grabbed her phone and her bag she hit the door.

"God damn it." She took the stairs two at a time.

She didn't slow to see if the innkeeper's daughter, Melody, might be at the registration desk. Later.

Barely out the door the wind hit her head-on, sending her body temperature plummeting.

Shit. Fuck. Hell. She'd forgotten her damned coat.

"Screw it."

She hopped in the passenger seat of Conner's Jeep. "Who found her?"

"Reverend Mahaney."

What the . . . ? His niece's accusations echoed in Sarah's ears. She started to demand the time of discovery when Conner asked, "Where's your coat?"

"Forget about it. Let's go."

He hesitated.

"Let's go, damn it!"

He held her gaze half a second then turned his attention to getting them the hell out of here and over to the chief's office.

But in that ephemeral instant he looked directly into her

eyes she saw the agony. As pissed off and upset as she was about this, he knew this girl, knew her family. He, like everyone else in Youngstown, was devastated. Sarah thought of Rachel Appleton . . . there were no words to describe how she must feel.

Sarah closed her eyes and banged her head against the headrest. This place wasn't that big. How long could this go on before the cops identified the killer?

Forever.

Just like last time.

She thought of Rachel Appleton again and Sarah's misery sharpened. She had to do something.

. . . *I'm glad you're here.* Rachel Appleton had said that to Sarah . . . when everyone else wanted her to go.

Sarah's jaw clenched. She would find the truth. For Alicia and her family. For Valerie and hers.

The parking lot at the Public Safety Office was packed with reporters and probably locals wanting to hear the facts. Conner parked up the street.

Sarah climbed out.

"Let's go this way," he suggested as he set a course leading between two buildings. "We'll cut over to the next street and go around back."

"Good idea."

She hustled to keep up with his long strides. They made it to the rear entrance of the Public Safety Office without being spotted—an outright miracle.

The deputy posted at the door to ensure only authorized personnel entered greeted Conner then sent a disapproving glare at Sarah.

"She's with me," Conner said bluntly.

The deputy didn't like it, that was clear, but he nodded and let them pass.

Though Sarah was thankful to have gotten inside without time-wasting complications, Conner's automatic assumption that he had to take care of her grated. Like showing up to pick her up this morning. And asking about her coat.

A phone call would have sufficed. She could have driven here. Could have talked or bullied her way past the guard.

She would set Conner straight. Later.

Cops were rushing from office to office in the small police station. All six phone lines appeared to be ringing. Sarah glimpsed Karen Brighton and a couple other deputies she'd seen before and a lot of them she hadn't. Reserve deputies, Sarah surmised. Not the first sign of a fed. She thought of running into Lex August and her gut clenched again.

Two city councilmen she recognized entered the conference room. She elbowed Conner and pointed in that direction. He headed that way.

Before they reached the door, the chief's booming voice competed with the bustle. So did Mayor Patterson's hushed cadence.

Conner let Sarah go in first. To say that the tension in the room upped about twenty notches would be an understatement. Six sets of eyes glared at her with the same disdain as the back entrance deputy's. Those scornful gazes belonged to the chief, the mayor, and all four of the other village councilmen. This morning she was no longer a tolerated nuisance. She was an unwelcome intruder.

"Ms. Newton, this is a closed briefing," Willard barked. "You'll have to get your information at the next press conference just like the rest of the general public."

"Chief," Conner spoke up, "we—"

The mayor held up a hand. "Conner, we'll talk later. Right now, Ms. Newton has to go."

Conner looked from the chief to the rest, eyeing each in turn, before doing an about-face and walking out.

In the corridor Sarah stopped him. "You should stay. I can walk to the inn. It's not that far."

He glanced back at the door.

"You need to be in there," she urged. She wanted to yell, *Don't be stupid!* Get the story. Fill me in later. But she said none of that.

"You didn't wear a coat."

More of that whole protective-guy syndrome. "I'll be fine." She backed away a couple of steps. "Go before you miss something."

He dug into his pocket and snagged his keys. "Take my Jeep."

She shook her head. No more allowing him to do that thing he was doing right now. She was a big girl. She didn't need some guy taking care of her. "Call me later."

"You want my coat?" he called after her.

Sarah didn't turn around.

This was way too intense.

She just kept going.

Outside she didn't acknowledge the deputy on guard duty. He'd likely already gotten word not to let her back into the building and was feeling an ego rush at the idea that he'd been right to question her arrival.

Taking the same route she and Conner had used, she avoided the crowd of reporters in front of the Public Safety Office. She took a moment to get her bearings. Back to Main Street and then left. Follow it directly to the inn. She should have brought her car.

Dumb. Dumb. Dumb.

Taking off without her coat was even dumber.

Determined not to be cornered by roving reporters or any damned body else, she strolled down to the harbor and stuck with the small back streets and parking lots. If she stayed on that path she would avoid the traffic on Main as well.

The docked schooners groaned, shifting with the gentle undulation of the water. Sea gulls chatted in their high-pitched language, floated down close to the water and then soared up and away. The wind bit her skin through the sweatshirt. She pulled up her hood but it didn't help much. Since her trip to the chapel the morning of her arrival her Converses hadn't really dried out. Her new gloves were in her coat pocket—back in her room.

It was cold, damned cold.

Her cell phone vibrated once to let her know she had a voice mail. She checked the screen. Her shrink. Three missed calls from her already. Sarah hadn't called her back as ordered. The doc wouldn't be happy.

Definitely not in the mood for that.

"I told you the cops couldn't catch the devil."

Sarah spun toward the voice.

Matilda Calder leaned against the rock wall of the public restrooms, a half-smoked cigarette tucked between two fingers.

"You did." Sarah walked toward her. "You heard about Alicia, I guess."

The girl took a deep drag from her cigarette. Sarah watched with more interest than she cared to admit, even to herself.

"She was dead even before she disappeared."

"Why do you say that?" Sarah waited while Matilda blew out a lungful of smoke.

"He picked her out way before she went missing. Just like he picked out Valerie." She glanced toward the dock and a couple walking hand-in-hand. "They just don't want to see it yet."

"*He* being the devil? That's what they don't want to see?"

Matilda nodded. "He's here." She took a final drag and tossed the cigarette. "He's always been here. They hold onto their old stories about maidens jumping from cliffs and ghost brides walking the shore, but they pretend *he* doesn't exist."

"You've seen him?" Sarah tried not to put the girl off with her skepticism, but she needed her to be more specific. Was she talking about a person? Or an entity?

Matilda held Sarah's gaze for a long moment as if contemplating how she wanted to answer that question, then she said, "I can't point him out to you, if that's what you're asking. But I feel him." Her eyes tapered as she studied Sarah's. "Can't you?"

Sarah's defenses locked into place. "You must have your suspicions?" *Keep the focus on her.*

She stared at the cigarette still smoldering on the ground. "Sure. I got my suspicions."

Anticipation lit in Sarah's veins. "Tell me yours and I'll tell you mine." *Don't let her see the deception.* This kid was good.

Matilda glanced around. "You wouldn't believe me if I told you. No one would."

Just say it, kid! "I'm not like the people here, Matilda," Sarah urged. "You can trust me." She resisted the need to move closer. Stay still. No sudden moves.

The girl's lips tightened. "Rich people can get away with anything." Her gaze bored straight into Sarah's. "Even murder."

Rich people? "Do you mean Pope? Jerald Pope?" He lived near the chapel. He was definitely rich. He had a daughter around the age of the victims. Had Valerie and Alicia stolen her glory at some point?

"Maybe." Matilda ground out the cigarette and kicked the butt aside. "My mom says he's a freak."

"You know those are bad for you." Sarah would have been remiss if she hadn't said as much even as she suppressed the temptation to ask what that last statement meant.

The girl shrugged. "I'm eighteen. It's not illegal in this state."

Not the point, but. "I understand there was a break-in at your house the other day. Is your mom okay?"

Matilda moved her shoulders up and down with that massive dose of indifference only teenagers could dredge up. "We got nothing important for them to take. I've got all the good stuff hidden."

"Good stuff?" Sarah felt for this girl. She had no one looking out for her. Sarah had bought her own big chunk of real estate in that lonely state.

"My grandmother's spell and incantation books." Matilda shrugged. "Stuff."

"Your great-great-grandmother Mattie was Wiccan?"

Those curious gold eyes connected with Sarah's blue ones. "She helped people, just as her daughter did when her time came."

Sarah nodded. "Your grandmother, did she help people, too?"

A shake of the head. "She tried but people didn't believe. She quit, just started pretending it didn't matter."

"Your mother?"

The girl belted out a laugh. "She only helps herself."

"Why does your mother think Pope is a freak?"

Someone shouted to the couple on the dock. Matilda's posture changed, a subtle preparation for an emergency egress. When her attention swung back to Sarah she blinked. "Mom's just crazy, that's all."

Sarah wanted to ask Matilda more personal questions but that would send her running. Her feet were now flat on the ground, her knees slightly bent. She was ready to bolt. "Life can be tough sometimes."

Matilda toyed with the zipper of her jacket. "More for some than others." She focused a look of challenge on Sarah. "You know what I mean."

Not a question. Uncertainty or maybe surprise rippled through Sarah. "I do." The kid had to be guessing. Maybe she'd done some research on Sarah and knew what little public knowledge there was regarding her crappy childhood. "You've read about me, have you?"

Another noncommittal shrug. "I get these feelings about people and . . . things."

Sarah nodded. "Some people have more heightened senses than others. Have a deeper comprehension of the human psyche. You shouldn't be ashamed or afraid of your ability to assess a person or situation."

The girl's gaze held Sarah's. "I'm not afraid of anything. Are you?"

Apprehension tightened in Sarah's gut. How could this kid read her so well?

Before Sarah could question exactly what she meant, Matilda reached into her pocket and pulled out a slender length of leather. She thrust it at Sarah. "You should wear this."

Sarah opened her hand and permitted the item to be

placed in her palm. Attached to the leather strand was a circular metal disc. It burned her skin. Cold, she told herself. Same sensation as being burned. Or maybe it was the healing abrasions from her close encounter with the vines.

"Thank you." She studied the leather necklace that sported a very unique-looking medal symbol. She recognized the design. Pagan.

"It's a protection rune. I want you to wear it all the time. Don't take it off, not even to shower."

Sarah draped the leather around her neck and dropped the medallion beneath her blouse. The metal settled between her breasts. "Thanks."

Matilda looked away, bounced her knees as if antsy. Sarah would be lucky to hang on to her attention another minute, maybe two.

"You think I need protecting."

The girl nodded. Like the other day, she wore the hood of her sweatshirt up, her long dark hair hanging forward on either side of her face. A tattered parka was zipped over that, but no gloves. No makeup; her jeans and shoes had that thrift-store quality that was so fashionable, but, in Matilda's case, was more likely born of necessity. She wasn't exactly too thin, but she had that drawn look Sarah met in the mirror every morning. Not enough sleep and maybe too many dreams.

Maybe too many bad breaks.

"Is he after me?" Sarah prodded. "The devil, I mean." Wouldn't be surprising. Except that she didn't believe in the devil so he was pretty much wasting his time.

"He's real. You must feel him."

Now that was truly eerie. Or not. If Sarah had recorded the conversation and analyzed it, the comment was likely a logical progression of thought. "If you believe he is, then he is."

"Wear the necklace." Matilda pushed away from the rock wall. "You're . . ." She cast around before meeting Sarah's eyes again. "He doesn't like you."

He should get in line. "Thanks for the warning."

"Gotta go."

"Hey," Sarah called after her. The need to talk to this girl a little longer was suddenly a palpable force inside her. "I was about to have breakfast. You want to join me?"

Matilda walked backward enough steps to say, "I don't eat breakfast."

Sarah watched her bound off, hands stuffed in her coat pockets. She touched the necklace through her shirt. This kid knew something. She was clearly confusing what she knew with the stories she'd heard from her mother or even with the rumors about her great-great-grandmother. But, whatever she knew, Sarah had a feeling Matilda was close, very close, to being right.

This killer was a devil . . . and the police weren't going to catch him unless he left a crumb trail.

But Pope? Being rich didn't make him a murderer. What did Matilda know that she wasn't telling? Had her mother serviced him? Worked for him?

Another scenario to investigate.

The bitter cold wind cut through Sarah. She wasn't going to get any warmer standing there.

Fifteen minutes later, she started up the steep drive to the Overlook Inn. At the midway point, a car rounded the up-coming curve. Stepping off the pavement, into the grass and snow, she waited for the black Infiniti to pass.

Instead of passing her by, it stopped. Matilda's warning that the devil didn't like Sarah echoed in her ears. If the devil drove an Infiniti, he was making a better salary than her. Then again, he didn't live in Manhattan.

Tinted glass slid down and the driver's face appeared. Dark sunglasses. Oakleys. Expensive taste.

"Sarah, I left a message for you at the inn's registration desk."

Speak of the devil. Jerald Pope. Sarah gave herself a mental shake. She could safely say that she hadn't expected him to show up. "Sorry I missed you." She gestured to the inn. "I was just on my way back." Duh. He could see that.

The memory of him watching her across the treetops

through his high-powered lens that night suddenly zinged her with a new kind of tension in view of Matilda's comments.

"I wanted to invite you to dinner this evening," he explained. "If you don't already have plans. My family and I would be inordinately pleased if you could come."

Was it possible he hadn't heard the news? She glanced toward town. "Are you sure tonight's a good time?"

"I thought, considering the latest tragedy, you might like to have a night away from . . ." He inclined his head. "Away from the turmoil."

What she really wanted was an opportunity to pick his brain . . . and his daughter's. Maybe even his wife's. And to see just what it was that bothered Matilda about the guy.

"That would be nice. Thank you."

"Seven?"

"Seven."

He smiled. "Excellent."

Sarah watched him drive away. Interesting.

Maybe Mr. Pope was simply doing the socially PC thing. But Sarah wasn't so sure. Everyone was a suspect. Even the rich boat builder and his perfect family.

Rich people can get away with anything. Even murder.

Renewed purpose infused her step. Good thing. The last stretch was straight up; by the time she reached the lobby her legs burned.

There was no one at the registration desk again.

Didn't matter. She already knew about the message Pope had left. If she had any more someone would let her know.

She climbed the stairs a little slower than usual. Jammed the key into the lock and frowned. The door wasn't locked. She twisted the knob and let the door glide open.

The gasp that echoed in the room sounded almost as surprised as Sarah felt. Melody Harvey, hands deep into a drawer, froze like a deer caught in a hunter's crosshairs.

Sarah stepped inside, closed the door, and leaned against it. She'd been looking for this opportunity. Sometimes luck bothered to give her a hand after all.

"I'm sorry." The girl's hazel eyes widened with fear, her

face paled. She gestured to Sarah's bedside table where a note lay. "I came to leave your messages, in case no one was at the desk this evening when you came in."

"That's very efficient of you." It was also a lie.

Melody stepped away from the drawer she'd been rummaging through, humiliation overtaking the shocked terror on her face. "I'm sorry, Ms. Newton. Please don't tell on me."

"Don't worry." Sarah pushed off the door, tugged her hood free of her hair, and tossed her bag on the bed. "I'm not going to tell."

Relief flashed across Melody's face. "Thank you. I am so sorry."

When she would have made a dash for the door, Sarah said, "I wanted the opportunity to talk to you, but I was never able to catch you at the registration desk."

Melody stalled at the foot of the bed, bit her bottom lip. "My parents would totally freak out if they caught me . . . talking to you."

Sarah crossed back to the door and locked it. "I don't think they'll look for you here."

Hands wringing, Melody nodded. "Okay."

"Were you friends with Valerie Gerard?" Though she went straight to the point with her question, Sarah took her time approaching the bed, then taking a seat, so as not to spook the girl. Melody looked ready to bolt, locked door or no.

She nodded. "We graduated high school together."

Melody had the same blond hair and hazel eyes as her younger brother. She was pretty, but not the kind of gorgeous Alicia Appleton had been.

"Do you recall anyone ever being jealous of her? Like maybe when she won academic awards or spelling bees?" Admittedly, it was a stretch to expect anyone to remember that far back, especially when she wouldn't have been more than about nine years old.

Melody shook her head before considering the question. "Valerie was kind of like me. Invisible. Not popular or athletic or anything."

Sarah knew that place very well. "So, to your knowledge, no one had any problems with her, past or present?"

Melody shook her head again but stopped midswing. "When she worked here last summer she had some kind of problem. She wouldn't talk about it, though."

"She worked here?" That was news.

"Only for a few weeks."

Sarah was reasonably sure that if this interview took much longer the kid was going to twist her fingers right off. "If she wouldn't talk about it, how did you know she had a problem? You noticed something different in her behavior?"

More lip-biting. "I . . . sort of walked in on her with my dad once. She was upset. Crying."

Sarah's alert system kicked in full throttle. "Walked in where?"

"The office behind the desk." Melody shrugged. "I asked my dad about it and he said Valerie wouldn't say what was bothering her. He told me not to bother her with it." She stared at the floor. "I don't think he was very happy that I interrupted. He was really worried about Valerie."

Was this why the innkeeper was so rude to Sarah? Had tried to scare her off? He had a secret he didn't want her prying into? Well, well. That certainly shed new light on his behavior.

"Did Valerie have something against your father?" That was about as close as she could get to asking if the two had been involved physically.

Another wag of her blond head. "I don't think so. They usually got along fine. Valerie worked hard. My dad liked her. It was just that one time."

"You're sure there was no one at school who especially didn't like Valerie."

"Positive."

"Not even the people who were up for awards and didn't win because Valerie did."

"Nobody ever said anything."

"What about at church? Did she have any problems at church that you know of?"

Melody glanced anxiously at the door. "I should go before my parents come looking for me."

"Bear with me, Melody," Sarah pressed, knowing she was losing ground. "Anything you can tell me might make a big difference."

Her shoulders lifted as if she intended to shrug but didn't follow through. "She quit going to church, but I don't know why."

Sarah scrutinized her face, her eyes. She was telling the truth. "What about the reverend's niece? Was she friends with Valerie?"

Melody frowned, shook her head. "I don't think so. Tamara doesn't really have any friends. Lately she's been hanging out with Jerri Lynn." She glanced at the door again. "I really gotta go."

Sarah stood and smiled. "Thank you, Melody. If you think of anything else be sure to let me know."

Before Melody made it to the door, Sarah realized there were a couple of other questions she should ask. "What about Alicia? Did anyone have a grudge against her?"

Clearly reluctant, Melody turned back to Sarah. "Not that I can think of." She peered longingly at the door once more. "I'm gonna be in big trouble if I don't get back downstairs."

"One last question." Sarah jerked her head toward the open drawer. "Did you find what you were looking for?"

The heat of embarrassment flooded the girl's face. "I . . ." She moistened her lips. "You're from New York." She shrugged. "I just wanted to see what kind of stuff . . . clothes you had."

Sarah could see a teenage girl doing that, though she wasn't so sure this teenage girl was telling the truth. Particularly since her clothes were in the dresser, not the bedside table. "I hope you weren't too disappointed. I'm not a good example of the latest fashion trends."

"I . . ."—Melody gestured to the door—". . . have to . . . go."

Sarah put her out of her misery. "Thanks for delivering my messages."

A quick nod and the girl was gone.

Sarah closed the door and locked it again.

That was definitely strange. But Sarah wasn't worried about anyone going through her things. She knew better than to leave anything relevant to her conclusions handy.

Two young women were dead. Most of the answers Sarah got when she asked questions were the same. How the hell could two girls with no enemies be murdered in a small town where everyone knew everyone else?

So far the only two leads Sarah had on Valerie Gerard were the falling-out and/or relationship with her minister and some sort of tension with the innkeeper. Alicia Appleton, on the other hand, had only one potential enemy at this point. Jerri Lynn Pope, the would-be competition, if Polly's assessment was correct. If Brady Harvey was to be believed, Polly had been somewhat of a nuisance to Alicia. But Sarah was relatively certain Polly was harmless.

The Pope girl Sarah could check out tonight. The innkeeper, she could talk to most anytime. The minister—considering he'd discovered Alicia's body—wasn't likely taking visitors. That had never stopped Sarah from showing up.

The man would be extremely distraught. Particularly vulnerable to interrogation.

Worked for Sarah.

All she had to do was get past his Nazi wife.

CHAPTER 24

Living Word Church, 9:29 A.M.

Sarah swerved into the church parking area and braked hard.

An SUV, a police cruiser, and a sedan were parked in front of the reverend's home. The sedan was a rental.

Lex August.

Anger, hatred, and a couple other emotions Sarah couldn't readily define erupted inside her.

He was here already. Interviewing the man who'd discovered the body.

Dammit.

She wouldn't be getting anywhere near the house at this point. A deputy was stationed outside. Sarah's name definitely wouldn't be on his access list.

Surveying the street, she didn't see any sign of Conner's Jeep which meant he wasn't here. Had he been ordered off the investigation as well? That would make learning the facts a hell of a lot harder.

"Shit."

Fine. She shut off the engine and got out of the car. Waiting hadn't gone out of style. Neither had badgering. She knew how to do both.

Leaning against her rental, she crossed her arms over her chest and waited. What she would give for a cigarette right now. The nagging need fueled her frustration.

When Lex came out she would demand answers. She

wouldn't get them but maybe a confrontation would cause
him to screw up and let something slip. She could hope.
That strategy had worked for her before.

If it didn't, there was always bribery.

Ten minutes. Twenty, then thirty passed. She didn't care
if it took all day. She wasn't going anywhere.

Snow and ice crunching beneath tires drew her attention
to the lot behind her. Conner's Jeep pulled into a parking
slot. He jumped out and headed her way.

No surprise there. He was back on babysitting detail.
Well, he could forget about it. She wasn't about to be distracted by him a second longer. Heat stirred deep in her
belly as images from last night nudged their way into her
thoughts.

He'd given her a couple of orgasms. So what? He wasn't
the first, probably wouldn't be the last. She owed him nothing. The same as he owed her.

She banished the little voice that balked at her conclusions. This assignment, this man, was no different from any
other. More determination was required to exile the denial
that sprang instantly in reaction to that concept.

Stupid, Sarah. Really stupid.

"Sarah, we need to talk." That dark gaze plowed into
hers. "Now."

"Maybe later, Conner." She turned her attention back to
the Mahaney home. "I'm busy right now."

That didn't put Conner off. "You need to come with me.
The chief is talking about a restraining order and I can—"

The front door of the reverend's home opened and the
chief stepped out.

Sarah straightened. "It'll have to wait." Let the chief take
out a restraining order against her. There were ways around
that scenario, too. *Truth Magazine* had dozens of attorneys.

She stared at the door. Willed Lex to exit before the chief
spotted her.

"Sarah—"

The door opened wide again, cutting off Kale. Her breath
evacuated her lungs.

200200

Special Agent Lex August strolled onto the stoop and down the steps, the black trench coat unwrinkled and gleaming like he'd only just pulled it off the rack at Nordstrom's.

As if he'd sensed her presence, he turned from the chief and settled his gaze on her. Even across the distance of the small yard and broader parking lot, she felt the impact of his stare.

"Hello to you, too," she mumbled. *You bastard.*

"Sarah," Conner said, trying once more but failing to draw her attention. "You should come with me."

"Not a chance." Her gaze didn't waver from the man now striding her way. "Bring it on, hotshot," she added under her breath. She'd waited three years, six months, and eleven days for this moment. Nothing was going to get in her way.

Evidently deciding that he wanted no part in this, the chief opted to wait with his deputy. Just as well. This was between Sarah and Lex.

"Well, well," Lex announced as he overtook her position. "If it isn't the truth seeker." He surveyed her up and down, blatantly displayed his abject disapproval. "How are you these days, Sarah? Still seeing that same shrink?"

"Fuck you, Lex," she snarled. He laughed. *Don't let him bait you.* She reined in her emotions. *Stay in control.*

"I'd hoped you had grown a sense of humor by now. I guess that isn't the case." He adjusted the striped tie that scrupulously matched his crisp navy suit. Not a dark hair out of place. Walking, talking perfection, total attention to every single detail.

Too bad he was all show and no tell.

Sarah made a sound that was nowhere near a laugh. "A sense of humor would be wasted on me," she tossed back, "just like that puny set of balls is on you."

Fury ignited in the jerk's hazel eyes. "What do you want, Sarah? The chief doesn't want you involved in this investigation anymore." He glanced at Conner. "You should go along with your babysitter and play nice." The fury cleared and arrogance took its place. "I'm sure you remember how to do that."

That was when she lost her cool. She got in his face. Let him see the sheer hatred in her eyes. "I remember a lot of things, Lex. Some I'm sure you'd rather I not recall. Shall we play this that way?" She could take him all the way down. Seriously fuck up his glorious reputation.

He chuckled, a dry, thoroughly unamused sound. "You just can't get beyond the past, can you, Sarah? You're scared to death you'll end up just like your mother."

Sarah fisted her fingers. She wanted to slap his smug face more than she'd ever wanted anything in her life. But she wouldn't give him that. That was what he wanted. Something else to release to the paparazzi, to draw attention to her flaws. "I'm here about the case. My mother has nothing to do with this."

"Ah, but she does." Lex stared at her mouth, made her want to puke, before meeting her eyes once more. "Your whole life is about the past. Hasn't your shrink told you that over and over again?"

"What's your problem?" Conner stepped into the mix.

Sarah blinked, glanced at the man who was suddenly at her side looking ready to tear into Lex. Great. She was sick to death of Conner's insatiable need to take care of her. She could damned well take care of herself. She didn't need him or anyone else to do the job.

"Back off, Conner."

"I see you're up to your old tricks," Lex said with a pointed glance at Conner. "There are other ways of gleaning information, Sarah. You don't always have to do it on your back."

Conner had him by the lapels before Sarah could react. "What the fuck does that mean, asshole?"

"I said back off, Conner." This was expressly why she should learn to appreciate vibrators. Men sucked when the testosterone kicked in.

"Kale!" Chief Willard rushed in their direction. "Let go of Agent August, Kale." The out-of-shape chief of police huffed and puffed in an effort to catch his breath. "I don't think the two of you have been introduced."

Conner gave Lex a little push as he released him. "I don't need a formal introduction to know an asshole when I meet one."

Sarah wanted everyone to back the fuck off so she and Lex could finish this. "Chief," she said as calmly as possible, "we're having a private conversation here."

"From where I was standing," Willard shot back, "it didn't exactly sound private."

"Why don't we tell them what the real problem is?" Lex suggested.

"That would be nice," Conner growled, leaning in even closer to the guy.

What the hell? Sarah glowered from one man to the other. This was her battle.

"Sarah, you should explain to these gentlemen the motive behind your obsession with cases like this." The bastard's eyes dared her to ignore his challenge. "Perhaps then they would better understand your tactics."

All attention was on her then.

"My only motive is finding the truth." It infuriated Sarah all the more that a good deal of the ferocity had gone out of her tone. This son of a bitch knew too much about her. He was twisting the situation to suit his needs. His intent was as transparent as glass. He wanted to make her look like a fool. And it would work. She knew all too well.

"Her mother murdered her father," Lex announced, "and seven of his mistresses over a ten-year period. Each time, little Sarah hid in the closet or under the stairs waiting for Mommy to finish up and find her."

Sarah rammed her fist into his gut. Couldn't help herself.

Lex bent forward. Gagged and coughed. The chief stepped between them. Conner manacled her arm, restraining her from doing further physical harm.

When Lex had recaptured his breath, he glared at her with no mercy. The gloves were off now, he was going for the jugular. "All those years," he taunted, "all those lies.

That's what makes the truth so important to you, isn't it, Sarah? You *need* the truth."

His words hit their mark. The rage died a sudden death.

The truth was what it was . . . and she couldn't deny his charge.

The only thing she needed was out of here.

Sarah walked away.

She'd had enough.

Let them believe what they would. Let them depend on that jerk. It was their mistake to make.

"Sarah!"

"Wait, Kale."

When he would have gone after her, the chief grabbed Kale by the arm. "Let her go."

Kale glared at the man, then at Agent Asshole. "What the hell were you doing? She didn't deserve that." Kale's head was still spinning with the reality of what August had said. Sarah's mother had killed her father . . . and seven mistresses? Jesus Christ. There had been nothing about that in the background info the chief and the mayor had given him.

Had Sarah overheard her mother's gruesome activities? Seen things a child shouldn't see? No wonder she didn't believe in people. The ones she'd trusted the most had let her down. From her parents all the way down to this jerk—whom she had obviously trusted with her deepest, darkest secrets.

"She played you, Mr. Conner," August informed him with a fleeting glance at Sarah's car as she spun out of the parking lot. "That's what she does. She digs into an investigation and she uses whoever she has to in order to get what she wants. Information."

Kale was going to beat the hell out of this piece of shit. His chest felt ready to explode. His fingers itched to scrape the parking lot with his self-righteous face. "I don't think you know her quite as well as you think you do."

August smirked. "I know every square inch of her."

Rage detonated in Kale's blood. Had the chief let go of

him already, Kale would have jumped the guy then and there.

"We don't have time to worry about Sarah Newton, Kale," the chief urged. "We have a murderer to find. That's where we need to focus our attention and our energy."

Kale took a breath, grappled for reason. The chief was right. They had to stop this nightmare. If anyone else disappeared . . . he couldn't even go there.

There was no time to worry about Sarah right now. Kale shouldn't even waste a second caring about her feelings. After what she'd said to him last night, he should be finished with her. He'd let her get to him . . . had let her closer than he had anyone in so damned long it wasn't even funny.

And she'd played him off as if he didn't matter.

Yet he couldn't get her out of his head. As hard as he tried, she just kept breaking through every mental barrier he erected.

He could still smell her on his skin. No matter how many showers he took he couldn't wash away the feel of her.

Her world was so different from his . . . he should have known better than to go down that path. He should have recognized that she was only using him.

August's words echoed. . . . *while little Sarah hid in the closet or under the stairs waiting for Mommy to finish up and find her* . . .

Kale could only imagine what Sarah's childhood had been like . . . how difficult growing up with that past must have proven. And then to have it publicly dashed in her face by this asshole.

Kale didn't like this guy. Didn't like his smug face. Didn't like his fancy suit. Kale didn't even like the way he fucking walked or talked.

The truth was, he had no real reason not to like the man. Except for the emotional intensity Kale had just witnessed between him and Sarah.

The two had a history.

August knew all her secrets . . . secrets she hadn't seen fit to disclose in any capacity to Kale despite what they had shared.

Frames of last night's frantic sex in her car flicked one after the other in front of Kale's eyes.

She'd meant it when she'd said it was only sex.

Kale stared in the direction Sarah had disappeared. Would she come back?

Maybe . . . maybe not.

Two young girls were dead. Their killer was running loose.

Finding that monster had to be top priority.

Sarah liked to brag about how she could take care of herself.

He hoped like hell she was right.

CHAPTER 25

Sarah wasn't about to allow Lex August to send her running for cover.

Better men had tried.

Yeah, he'd gotten to her. But when she'd cooled off she had focused her energy on the investigation. The open road had always worked wonders for her attitude and to clear her head. Allowed her to regain perspective and to analyze things more clearly. So she'd taken a road trip. First to Bangor, then to Portland. She'd perused the archives of the newspapers looking for anything on the murders in Youngstown, old and new. She hadn't found anything earth-shattering, but she had discovered one very interesting factoid.

Jerald Pope had graciously covered the funeral expenses for the two young women murdered twenty years ago. Just as he'd helped the Gerard family this time.

Did his generosity make him a suspect or a saint?

There had been only one way to find out.

"Here you are, Sarah."

She accepted the glass of wine. Jerald Pope was a perfect host. Charming. Entertaining. And vastly interesting. As was his wife, Lynda. Dinner had been exquisite.

Beautiful home. Beautiful people.

The empty place setting at the table had been the one glaring imperfection in the evening thus far.

Their daughter hadn't shown.

"I apologize again for Jerri Lynn's absence," Pope said as if he'd read Sarah's mind. "I can't imagine what detained her."

"You know teenagers," Lynda explained, dismissing his concerns. "They can't appreciate grown-up get-togethers."

"I'm sure she found more interesting company." Admittedly, Sarah had been hoping to meet the daughter. According to what she'd learned from Polly, Jerri Lynn Pope was the one who'd had a crush on Brady. Sarah would have liked very much to get a feel for the girl. Was she off celebrating because the competition was dead? Perhaps before this evening was over, Sarah would know what her thoughts were on the latest victim.

Sarah was back on track. And no one, not Lex or Conner, was going to get in her way again.

"I saw you on the news today, Sarah," Pope announced as he set his glass on a table next to the first of two matching sofas. "I could hardly wait until you arrived tonight."

Sarah wondered if he'd seen Blond Barbie's or Blond Ken's stab at interviewing her. "I hope you weren't disappointed."

"Not at all." Pope indicated the elegant sofas stationed across a sleek marble table from each other. "I must admit, I find your background fascinating."

Tension moved through Sarah as she settled on the sofa opposite the lady of the house. Had Pope been digging around in her past? Sarah braced for that possibility as he relaxed next to his glamorous wife. They made a perfect couple. Sophisticated. Handsome. Well educated. And, if Sarah's crappy past intrigued either of them, they were clearly bored with the status quo.

Few people knew about her childhood. The courts and her aunt had seen to that by changing Sarah's last name to Newton, her aunt's surname, after the trial. Sarah hadn't been happy at first. Eventually she'd understood that the move had been a good one.

"Your history is quite fascinating as well." Might as well give him as good as he gave. "Your father was a carpenter. I suppose his love of working with his hands influenced your passion for ship building." Five minutes on Google had given her a detailed history of Jerald Pope.

Pope reached for his wine, savored a swallow. "To be honest, as a young boy I hated woodworking." He chuckled. "But that changed the first time I glided across the water in a sailboat. I was hooked."

Sarah knew that kind of addiction. "Your work has garnered you international acclaim."

"Indeed," he agreed.

"You should come up in the spring," Lynda suggested. "Jerald and I will take you sailing." She swirled the wine in her glass. "There's nothing on the planet like gliding across the water in one of Jerald's vessels."

"I'll do that." Sarah wouldn't but it wasn't polite to say so. Particularly when one wanted to keep the conversation going in the right direction. She sipped her wine sparingly. The road back to the village was dark and twisty.

Despite having lived in New England his entire life, Pope didn't give off the same vibes as the rest of the citizens in Youngstown. There was a worldliness about him that was lacking in others. The same was true of his wife.

"You and Lynda," Sarah broached, "have made quite a name for yourselves with your generous donations."

The two smiled at each other. "It's only fair," the wife offered, "that we help those less fortunate."

"Absolutely," Pope seconded.

Sarah inclined her head and made a show of searching her memory banks. "I think I read somewhere that you"—she looked directly at Pope—"helped the families of the two victims twenty years ago with funeral expenses."

Pope nodded. "I did. The families were devastated. I heard about the troubling financial problems they were having prior to the tragedy. I couldn't take away their pain, but I could lessen the stress in other areas." He shrugged. "It was the right thing to do."

"Unfortunately," Lynda added, "at a time like that, there's

little anyone can do. I'm very proud of my husband for his thoughtfulness."

Another of those shared smiles.

Was it possible for anyone to be this perfect?

"You grew up in Tennessee," Pope said, shifting the conversation back to Sarah, "but you were born in Minneapolis."

Surprise flared before Sarah could restrain the reaction. Only a handful of people knew about that part of her past. Evidently he'd done far more than five minutes on Google looking into her background. "Home was actually a small suburb of Minneapolis."

"You lived above a meat market." Pope inclined his head, studied her a moment. "I find your childhood as ironic as it is fascinating. You were a butcher's daughter."

Inside, where he wouldn't see, Sarah cringed. She hated that term. But her feelings went deeper than that. She hated her father. Hated her past. "I suppose it is a bit ironic." She blocked the idea that Kale Conner now knew all about her past. Along with the chief and the mayor . . . and obviously Pope.

"I'm sure you run into all sorts of strange people in your work," Lynda commented. She pinched her lips together and gave a little shake of her head. "You must feel a very strong conviction to deal with such horrific cases."

What Lynda really wanted to ask was had her mother's decision to murder eight people influenced Sarah's decision to immerse herself in murder and mayhem. Her fingers tightened around her glass. Sarah wasn't going to kid herself here. If Pope had uncovered her humble beginnings, he had the whole story. He was a rich, powerful man. Getting the real story on Sarah had likely been a piece of cake for him.

"I have some stories that would give you nightmares," she admitted. They sure gave them to her. No, that wasn't true. Her nightmares were all related to her own private story. "As far as motive or conviction"—she held the other woman's gaze a moment—"the truth drives me."

"Perhaps you'll write a book one day," Pope offered.

"Perhaps."

"We could write a book, couldn't we, Jerald?" Lynda brushed the back of her hand across her husband's jaw. "Our life has been anything but dull."

Pope nodded in answer to his wife's question. "We've traveled extensively. The deeper and darker the territory, the better."

Lynda laughed. "Africa and Mexico were my favorites."

"The unknown intrigues my wife, Sarah. Whether it's a safari or a venture deep into rugged, uncivilized terrain. She loves a challenge."

"What I love most," Lynda qualified, "is having you at my side wherever I am."

He touched his wife, the slightest caress of her arm. Sarah observed the interaction. Wondered what it was like to have that kind of connection to another human being. Her one stab at a real relationship had ended badly. Today had been further proof of that reality.

After things went south between her and Lex, Sarah had come to terms with the idea that she didn't have the proper foundation for building a relationship. The Popes, the Conners, all had something she didn't: a childhood that included the necessary pattern for developing relationships.

She hadn't gotten that from her parents.

Again, Conner attempted to elbow his way into her thoughts. No way. He was one of them. Sure, the sex had been great but that was where their connection began and ended. Besides, on some level his life was just as screwed up as hers, he just hadn't recognized it yet.

The last thing either of them needed was each other.

"Did you formally study for your chosen profession?"

Sarah blinked. "I'm sorry, what did you say?"

"Of course she studied," Pope said to his wife. "Sarah has spent her life analyzing people. My guess is she has it down to a science. Isn't that right, Sarah?"

"That's right. College and I didn't mix." Probably had something to do with the alcohol and the bad memories of her childhood. She'd leave that part out of the conversation. Not that it mattered. Pope could very well have a copy of her college transcript.

"Are you analyzing us right now?" Lynda searched Sarah's face. The green eyes were stunning with her black hair and porcelain skin.

The question allowed Sarah's tension to recede a fraction. She laughed softly, then allowed her face to show just how dead serious she was. "Of course."

The Popes had a good laugh over that one. But it was the look they shared that gave away the slightest hint of their own tension, at least from the wife.

Sarah made her nervous. Or maybe it was the subject.

Not everyone was immune to the emotional impact of murder discussed so casually.

"Which has been your most difficult case?" Pope asked, keeping the conversation moving.

"Definitely the—"

A door slammed in the foyer. Pope pushed to his feet. "It sounds as if the errant offspring has returned." He glanced at Sarah. "Excuse me."

"It's about time." Lynda watched her husband go, then turned back to Sarah. "You were saying."

Sarah decided to change her answer. "I think the most difficult case has been this one."

Lynda looked surprised. "Really? You've only been here a couple of days. Has this one proven that unsolvable already? The police are equally puzzled, I hear."

"Yes. This one has me and the police bewildered. I can't explain it . . . but . . ." Sarah might as well say it. "Nothing is what it seems. I'm certain we're missing something that's right under our noses."

"My, my," Lynda noted, her tone amused but carefully so, "you've been in Youngstown a mere two days and you've already found us out."

"Don't misunderstand me—"

"No. No." Lynda held up a hand. "You're correct in your conclusion." The polite, collected expression shifted, the change ever so subtle. Her lips tightened. Eyes tapered in unconcealed derision. "Our village is filled with good, decent people but they are very shortsighted and incredibly narrow-minded."

"That's a polite way to size it up." Sarah had found the fire and she wanted to stoke the blaze. She could educate the lady in the ways of small-town America. The smaller the town, the smaller the minds.

"The kids are no different. They run in cliques. You're either in or you're not.", Lynda shook her head in something like disgust, then took a long swallow of her wine. "And if you're not, you're left out."

There it was. The jealousy Sarah had expected. Honest human emotion from someone with the cajones to say it out loud.

"Jerri Lynn has never been accepted here." Lynda stared at the glass in her hand. "I was so disappointed when she didn't elect to go away to college. A change of venue would have done wonders for her."

"Moving on to a new place with new faces can certainly do wonders for self-esteem." Sarah had firsthand experience on the subject.

"That's exactly my point," Lynda agreed adamantly. "That's what I tried to tell her father. She needs real friends. Tagging along after a group that is never going to invite you in or settling for less than what you deserve is self-defeating."

Sounded as if Mommy wasn't happy with her daughter's choices in associates. But then, what mother of a teenager was?

Pope reentered the room, his tardy offspring at his side. "Sarah, this is Jerri Lynn."

Sarah set her glass aside and stood. "It's a pleasure, Jerri Lynn." She offered her hand.

Jerri Lynn shook Sarah's hand and managed a smile but it was less than enthusiastic. Like her mother, she had the infinitely dark hair but the eyes were more blue, like her father's, than green.

"Our MIA daughter got caught up in a grief session at the high school auditorium with her friends."

"It was too sad," Jerri Lynn said, her expression downtrodden. "Alicia's brothers were there." She leaned into her dad. "It was just awful."

"Are you all right?" Lynda asked, the frustration in her expression softening to concern.

"I suppose." Jerri Lynn shrugged. "It was just awful, that's all."

Pope ushered his daughter to the sofa next to her mother. Sarah resumed her seat.

"As difficult as it was, showing your support was the right thing to do," her father assured her.

Jerri Lynn abruptly turned to Sarah. "Is it true they were stabbed through the heart?"

Her parents both jumped to scold her for asking such a thing.

Sarah saw no reason to pretend she didn't know the answer. "I believe that's correct." The news had reported that detail. The kids at school were likely talking about it.

"That would be a gross way to die," the girl said with a shudder.

"I can't imagine any parent recovering from losing a child," Pope offered.

Lynda shivered visibly. "I can't imagine what kind of nightmare this must be for those families."

"Is it true your mother killed your father, Ms. Newton?"

The question caught Sarah so off guard it took her a moment to realize Jerri Lynn had actually posed it aloud.

"Jerri Lynn," Lynda chastised. "Why would you ask something so personal?"

Pope didn't reprimand his daughter this time. Instead he appeared equally interested.

"It's true," Sarah confessed. She couldn't expect people to open up to her if she didn't do the same, but she set the pace and boundaries. It wasn't like Pope didn't have a dossier with all the dirty details. "My mother killed my father as well as seven other people."

"Why?" Jerri Lynn asked in spite of her mother's obvious mortification.

"Because my father was unfaithful. Over and over again. When she'd had enough, she got even."

"Wow." Jerri Lynn scooted to the edge of her seat. "Did you see the bodies?"

"That's quite enough," her father cautioned. "Don't be so forward."

Sarah shook her head. "It's all right. The truth is what it is." She met Jerri Lynn's curious gaze. "Yes. I saw several. I've seen more since. I guess my profession is a little grue-some but it's what I know better than I know anything else."

Maybe that was a little more honest than she'd intended to be.

"Do the police have any clues about the killer?" Jerri Lynn wanted to know. "Everybody says they're totally lost."

"Unfortunately, no clues yet. But they'll figure it out." At least, not unless there was something Sarah didn't know about yet. She'd been shut out of the Appleton briefing.

"I knew that curse stuff was crap." Jerri Lynn scoffed at the idea. "The police are just too stupid to figure it out." A pointed look from her father had her backpedaling. "Sorry. I guess they're doing the best they can."

"Do you think this case will go unsolved like the one from twenty years ago?" Lynda asked, her own curiosity showing.

Sarah weighed the question. "I think this case will go unsolved until they have some evidence or get extremely lucky."

The evening dragged on another hour. Sarah used that time to further analyze the Popes. Jerald was difficult to read. Careful. Polite. The daughter was another story. Out-spoken. Curious. The mother was a little jaded but honest. Sarah appreciated honesty.

When Sarah announced that it was time for her to go, Pope walked her to the door.

"You are a genuinely fascinating woman, Sarah Newton." He helped her into her coat. She'd worn the same black dress from dinner with the Conners. It was the only dress she'd brought on the trip. It was her stock packing item. Wrinkle-free, slinky material. No buttons, no zipper. Just stretchy, clingy material that looked elegant without maintenance.

"Thank you for dinner," Sarah said to her host. "And for a pleasant distraction."

"I would like to ask one last question," Pope said before opening the door for her.

"Ask away." Sarah looped her bag onto her shoulder.

"Do you believe that who we are is entirely genetic?"

That was easy. "Pretty much."

"So you ultimately become some version of who your parents are or were?"

Sarah stiffened. She should have seen that one coming.

"To some degree," she answered carefully, after all, she'd told him to ask, "everyone does." Her pulse reacted to an adrenaline charge. Her heart pounded. Her muscles tensed with the fight-or-flight response.

"If that's true"—he pushed the issue when she was more than ready to let it go—"one with the misfortune of being born to parents who kill, could, in fact, become a killer simply by virtue of DNA."

Sarah couldn't respond for a pulse-pounding moment. She'd asked herself that question a million times. She'd researched the subject. Read every relevant published journal and book.

And the conclusions were always the same.

She could walk out the door and not answer the question. Instinct compelled her to play along . . . see where this went.

"Some say," she ventured, "that we make our own choices regardless of DNA. Their opinion is that those who make the wrong choices use their genetic history as an excuse. Others insist that we do what we're hardwired to do with no

CHAPTER 26

Sarah sat at the intersection of Calderwood Lane and Beau-champ Road.

She stared into the mist swirling around her headlights.

Not once, except for maybe when she and Lex parted ways, had Sarah felt the compulsion to kill anyone.

To actually commit the act.

Okay, so she hadn't really wanted to kill him, but the temptation had crossed her mind. For about two seconds.

But there wasn't a day that passed that she didn't wonder if, forced to defend herself, the act would plunge her into a different reality. One where she couldn't resist the desire to take another life given the proper motivation or not.

Her mother had killed eight people and kept the ongoing activity hidden for a decade.

Sarah's fingers tightened on the steering wheel. Her father had been a cheat who cared about no one but himself. For the duration of his short life, if Sarah had her guess. According to her aunt, he'd always been a no-good two-timer.

Sarah's entire genetic makeup, all that she was . . . was the combination of deceit, uncontrollable urges, and lies.

She understood, even before her shrink had told her as much, that her past was the reason truth was so intensely important to her. She damned sure hadn't needed Lex to tell her so.

And Sarah could live with that.

But, if the trigger for one or more of those bad traits—and

all addicts had triggers for their vices—was ever tripped, would there be any turning back?

The age at which her hair grayed or wrinkles developed or the propensity for illness kicked in—it was all genetic. The color of her eyes . . . her hair . . . her height . . . every damned thing.

Her mother had been thirty when she'd murdered her first victim. Did that make Sarah's upcoming birthday a long-buried trigger? Was she more likely to commit the act at that point, the same as she might expect certain physical changes?

If she knew for certain that would happen . . . was there anything she could or should do about it? Put herself on house arrest? Kill herself before she could kill anyone else?

Did repeat murderers consider killing themselves to stop the compulsion? Or was the power and excitement of the act far too big a rush to miss?

Sarah scrubbed at her eyes. She was definitely losing her perspective, maybe even her mind.

This case hit far too close to home . . . for reasons she couldn't yet discern.

Was staying another day, even another minute, a mistake?

Conner had tried to reach her five or six times.

She wasn't calling him back. He was a distraction she didn't need.

His family, like the Popes, made her too keenly aware of what she'd missed growing up.

And he, Kale Conner, the good-looking fisherman who'd given up his own future to live out his father's dream, was some kind of kryptonite to her.

He made her wonder . . . made her want to be a part of something . . .

Yet, he was ultimately no better than she. He was faking it, too. Pretending that work was all life was about. No wife, no girlfriend. Just his work to keep him company. Oh, and the dog. How was his life so different from hers?

They weren't good for each other. He needed her about as much as she needed him.

Taking her foot off the brake, she headed for the inn. Sleep would do her good.

And maybe for once she'd follow the doctor's orders and take the stupid medicine.

Yeah, right. The ability to function at full capacity was far too important to her.

Chief Willard had shut her out of the investigation. Lex would ensure she didn't get back in. If new evidence had been discovered, the cops might just eventually find the killer with or without her participation.

Maybe Tae was right and she should go back to New York. If she couldn't accomplish anything here, why stay? The only mystery that needed to be solved was identifying the scumbag who liked murdering young women.

No spooks, curses, or boogeymen here.

The fog hovering around the harbor obscured the lights, giving it a definite creep factor and seeming to defy her conclusion.

It was too dark to see much of Bay View Cemetery. Just that foreboding black iron fence.

Were the two crows still waiting on Mattie Calder's headstone?

Sarah shook her head. She'd drifted way off course, intertwining fact with fiction.

Time to set a new one.

The inn stood alone atop that steep hill, the few illuminated windows staring out like pale eyes watching over all of Youngstown.

Tomorrow morning she would need to get a foot in the reverend's door. Or catch him away from the house. Or the niece. The niece might even be better. She appeared anxious to talk. Possibly to get even with her uncle for whatever he had done to her.

Maybe Sarah would catch Barton Harvey in a good mood and go over a few details with him. Like whether or not he wanted to chase her through the woods again.

Yeah, and maybe it would be a pleasant eighty degrees tomorrow.

Not going to happen unless she hopped a plane south.

Her headlights flashed across a silver vehicle.

Jeep Commander.

Conner was waiting for her.

Anticipation shimmered, warming her in ways that should set off any number of alarms. But that didn't happen. Instead, she made excuses for not turning around and driving the other way. Maybe he had news he intended to share on the investigation.

But then he would only give her what the chief had authorized. She could get that on Fox News.

Sarah parked her car and got out. The Jeep was deserted. She glanced at the inn. He would be waiting for her in the lobby.

Or in her room.

Another rush of heat, this one lower, deeper.

The lobby was closed for the night; a small desk light spread its glow across the registration counter, otherwise the room was dark.

Sarah climbed the stairs, listening to the silence. No television noise. No chatter of conversation. Not even the roar of the oil furnace.

But he was here, she didn't have to hear him . . . she felt him.

Sure enough, down the hall, propped in front of her door, was Kale Conner.

His coat lay on the floor at his feet. With his head leaned against the wall and eyes closed, he looked asleep but she knew better.

As she came closer, he lifted his head and turned toward her. She braced for the confrontation.

"You have a message." He unfolded his arms and held a piece of paper in her direction.

She took the paper in one hand and dug for her key with the other. "Thanks." The number on the message was her shrink's. She wadded the note and shoved it into her coat pocket. "You been waiting long?"

He picked up his coat. "Long enough."

She wondered how long they could dance around the real reason he was here. He would want to know if Lex had told the truth . . . how she'd managed to survive . . . et cetera, et cetera.

She didn't want to talk about it.

In her room, she tossed her bag on the floor by the bed and shrugged off the coat. "Have you been authorized to bring me up to speed on the case?"

"No."

Well, that was short and direct.

She looked him square in the eyes. "How much do you plan to tell me off the record?" The man had something on his mind. That was certain.

He dropped his coat onto the chair next to the seriously lacking excuse for a minibar. "Everything."

Surprised, she took a step in his direction. "You're going to break the rules?"

"Yeah."

"Is there some reason you feel compelled to do that?" She took another step; her pulse reacted to his nearness, to merely looking at him. Those broad shoulders . . . lean hips . . . long legs . . . and that face.

His shadowed jaw only made him sexier.

Hadn't she decided that being involved with him like this was a mistake?

"I don't want to talk about it right now." He claimed the final step between them. "I want to talk about you." He hitched his head toward the door. "I've been standing out there all this time thinking about you. And what I wanted to say to you." Sympathy flickered in his eyes. "I'm sorry about . . . today."

Oh, hell no. She didn't want or need his sympathy.

"You're sorry?" Anger scaled her senses. "Why should you be sorry? Lex is an asshole; my past is what it is. None of that has anything to do with you."

"Why didn't you tell me?"

"Tell you what?" She planted her hands on her hips. Her personal life was none of his business. If he wanted to give her information or to fuck, fine. Otherwise, he could go.

He stared at the floor a moment, then met her eyes, his filled with more of that misplaced concern. "About what happened when you were a kid." He exhaled a troubled breath. "Your mom . . . that had to be tough."

"My mother chopped up and buried seven victims. Then she ground my father into sausage. She was nuts. They put her away. End of story." Tension throbbed in Sarah's veins. She never discussed her past with anyone but her shrink. *This* was unnecessary. A waste of time and energy.

"And you were there . . . ?"

If Conner just wouldn't look at her that way . . . maybe she could deal with this. Get past it. But those eyes . . . damn those eyes. "I was there. I heard the screams, the voices. Sometimes I stumbled over body parts. Just another night in the butcher shop."

The memories rammed against her defenses. She closed her eyes, forced them back. Still they came. She'd been terrified of the basement under the butcher shop. Blood-soaked earth. All those bones. All the rotting personal items.

Stop.

She opened her eyes and stared at the man watching her with such overwhelming compassion in those dark eyes. "I got over it."

Silence thickened in the air.

"Did you?"

Her stomach clenched. His voice . . . the way he kept looking at her . . . made her want to let him hold her. To protect her. No one made her feel that way. No one. She had to get this under control. Now. "Enough about the past, Conner." She folded her arms over her chest, banished those weak emotions. "Brief me on the case or fuck me, those are your options."

The heat that flared in his eyes matched the fire that roared inside her. Disrupted her ability to breathe. Even as she ordered herself to pull it together.

"Sarah." He lifted his hand, touched her cheek with such tenderness the urge to cry welled.

She drew away, startled at the unexpected emotion. "Don't even think about it. I don't need your sympathy."

Those eyes . . . those damned dark, dark eyes. Like the night . . . like a place she could fall . . . and just keep falling. "Why won't you trust me?" he urged. "Let me hold you the way I want to. The way I know you need me to."

"I see." Don't give in. Be strong. "You're going to make my ugly past all right, is that it?" No way. As if to defy her, her chest tightened . . . her entire body yearned to lean into him. "I think maybe you'd better pay attention to your own screwed-up existence before you start trying to repair mine."

"Don't try to change the subject. Running away from your problems isn't the answer," he argued quietly. "You can't hide in places like this, on cases like this."

This was priceless. Fury swept away the emotions wearing down her resistance. "Like you don't." She leaned in close, stuck her face in his. "You're so full of shit, Kale Conner. You dropped out of college to take care of the family business. You never went back. You're living your father's life, not yours. How are we different?"

He shrugged those broad shoulders. "I do what I do to take care of my family, not to run away from my past."

"Really?" He was so damned blind. "Then why not go back to school when your brother finishes? Let him take the helm for a while." When he would have argued with her suggestion, she added, "Or are you afraid you can't do it?" She had to laugh. "Why not let Deputy Brighton, or the chief's secretary, make an honest man out of you? Are you afraid of personal commitment, too?" He had no right to throw stones.

"You're right." He held up his hands in surrender. "I put my life on hold to take care of other obligations. Eventually I need to get back to my own goals." He shook his head. "But you, you're the one who's scared. You have no excuse for running away from your life. You have no family obligations. You have choices. Choices I didn't have. And you're pretending they don't exist. It's all about work. It's all about hiding from the emotions that scare the hell out of you."

"Yeah. Yeah. I'm all about work." She glared at him. "And that's the way I like it. Work is my life. That *is* my choice."

He looked away, shook his head. "You don't want to see what you're missing." He stared deep into her eyes then. "Will you feel better about yourself if you solve the mystery every time? Will that make you happy?"

"You want to make me happy, Conner?" She set her hands back on her hips. "Tell me about Alicia Appleton."

He wouldn't look at Sarah now. Good.

"The killer used the same MO as before." Ramming a hand through his hair, he surrendered to her demand. "Cause of death was exactly the same."

Renewed anticipation pushed all the other bullshit aside. "Exactly the same?"

He nodded. "The sick bastard sewed her eyes shut and wrote 'snob' on her torso. She was restrained with glue, just like Valerie."

"Anything else?" Dammit. They had to catch a break here. "Was there something in her throat?"

He continued to look anywhere but at her. He rubbed the back of his neck, the tension obviously getting to him. "Yeah, the missing crown." His eyes met hers then, showed the horror mere words could not convey. "Broken into four pieces. He . . . ah . . . stuffed the pieces into her throat and then taped her mouth shut."

Sarah mentally blocked the images for the moment. It was the only way to maintain her objectivity. "No other evidence, nothing?"

"There was something different this time." He rubbed his eyes with his thumb and forefinger. Like her, he was exhausted. "A drug. They found a beta blocker in the preliminary tox screen. Oh, yeah, and bleach on her skin. It turns out both victims had been washed with a solution containing bleach."

A beta blocker? She frowned. Considered the implications of that strategy. The bleach was a no-brainer. "He was making sure there was no trace evidence left behind." Which meant, he didn't want to get caught any time soon.

Sarah could only imagine what Rachel Appleton was going through right now after hearing the details. Damn this bastard!

"You're sure you're okay?" He searched her eyes, her face. "After what happened?"

They were back to that again. "You mean with Lex?" What did it take to show this guy she didn't need him taking care of her?

Conner nodded.

Sarah grappled for patience. "No, Conner. I'm not okay about it." These people just didn't understand how the game was played. "But I recognize that Lex accomplished his goal and that seriously pisses me off."

Confusion lined his too-handsome face. "I don't understand."

"He ensured that there's no chance in hell the chief is going to allow me even close to the investigation. He's got you second-guessing my stability and feeling all sorry for me. He manipulated all of you and you don't even know it." When Conner still didn't look convinced, she went on, "Trust me, every move Lex August makes, every word that comes out of his mouth, is a tactical maneuver. He eats, sleeps, and breathes this shit."

Fury tightened Conner's jaw. "I should have beaten the hell out of him."

"For what?" She should be flattered that he wanted to protect her honor, but she wasn't. She didn't need anyone taking care of her. "For using me to accomplish his goal?" Conner's gaze collided with hers. "This isn't over. I'll have my move and then he'll be the one pissed off."

A halfhearted shrug lifted one shoulder. Conner suddenly seemed at a loss as to what to say next. "I just needed to be sure you were okay."

How did she get this through his head? "I'll never be okay, Conner, but I can live with it."

"Well." He reached for his coat. "I guess I should go . . . then."

She hated this. She didn't want him sorry or worried. How did she get the old Conner back? The one who respected her ability and wasn't scared to death she'd crack? The one who had sex with her in a car . . . in the cemetery of all places.

"You're leaving?"

He hesitated. "You want me to stay?"

What the hell? Was this guy for real? This was the part that was supposed to be easy. Burn off some of the tension with hot, frantic sex.

She held up her hands. "Fine. Go." This was too complicated.

More of that suffocating silence elapsed between them.

"Well . . . good night."

He really was leaving. Stupidly, her chest tightened . . . ached. What the hell was wrong with her?

Pausing before he reached the door, he turned back to her. "I've never met anyone like you, Sarah." Again he seemed to rummage for the words he wanted to say next. "I . . ." A weary sigh hissed past his lips. "I don't know how to reach you." He searched her eyes, allowed her to see the uncertainty in his. "The crazy thing is, I want to more than I've ever wanted anything in my life."

This was nuts. She walked straight up to him and looked him square in the eyes. "Stop. Just stop. Don't pretend this is something it's not, Conner." That ache deepened, spread through her torso like a raging fever.

"That's the point." He reached out, caressed her cheek. Sarah flinched in spite of the heat his touch generated. "You think you're protecting yourself by keeping your distance but you're wrong. You don't need to be afraid of me." Those warm fingers traced the line of her jaw. "I want to know you. To really know you."

She couldn't move. She could only stare into his eyes, her entire being yearning for more of his touch. For more of those sweet words.

His coat fell to the floor. He cupped her face in both hands. The pad of his thumb slid across her bottom lip.

The air abandoned her lungs. She licked her lips . . . tried to catch her breath. "There's nothing to know."

He leaned down, kissed her cheek so softly, so tenderly she wanted to push him away . . . to stop this rush of intense feelings. She squeezed her eyes shut, told herself to make him go.

"You're so beautiful," he whispered as his lips brushed each closed lid. "I wanted to pound August when he said those things. I wanted to protect you."

Her eyes fluttered open, she searched his. Before she could say anything, he kissed her. Slowly . . . with infinite tenderness. She shivered. Those firm, warm lips left a trail of kisses along her temple, across her forehead.

He pressed his forehead to hers, slid his hand down the column of her throat and toyed with the necklace Matilda had given her. "I don't want to leave you alone tonight."

The ache that had started in her chest and expanded along her torso banded tighter around her heart. She closed her eyes and confessed the truth. "I need you to stay. That's the only way I'll be okay tonight."

If she were lucky he would never know just how honest that final statement was.

He scooped her into his arms and carried her to the bed. Settling there, he held her like a child, rocking her gently. She rested her cheek against his broad shoulder, snuggled against his powerful chest. The sound of his heart beating made her feel . . . safe. Made her want to surrender . . . to trust him.

She lifted her hand to his face, caressed his jaw, trembled at the feel of soft skin and prickly stubble. How long had it been since she'd touched a man this way? Just a touch. She couldn't remember when she'd been held like this . . . as if she really mattered . . . to him.

He kissed the top of her head, then her forehead. She looked up at him and he smiled. "I could hold you like this all night."

Again, she asked herself if this guy was for real.

As if he understood her need for proof, he kissed her again. Even slower, if that was possible. Deeper.

He pulled her back onto the bed with him, rolled to his side and started a fiery path of kisses along the line of her jaw and then down the column of her throat. With more of that painstaking slowness, he undressed her, caressed and kissed every inch of skin he revealed. She let him. All she wanted to do was to feel.

He kissed her hip and she gasped.

"What's this?" He touched the scar on her right side.

The question jarred her from the sweet sensations he'd elicited. She shuddered when the cold, harsh memories invaded the moment.

"Battle scar," she murmured and trembled again. She looked directly into his eyes; saw the same need she felt staring back at her. Need she understood, but there was more in his eyes. And that scared her to death.

"One of your cases?"

She watched his lips as he spoke. Didn't want to talk about *that* but understood he needed to know. "I got too close." Like now, she realized. She looked away from those mesmerizing eyes. "Too personally involved."

What was she doing? Before she could come up with an answer to that question, he started to unbutton his shirt. He took her hand and urged her to assist him. He prompted and teased until she got lost in the task. Together they shoved it off his shoulders and arms. He peeled off the undershirt and her body quivered. He had the most gorgeous body. The boots, the socks, the jeans and boxers, all landed on the floor. The musky smell of hard, masculine muscle triggered another surge of sheer desperation.

He started those slow, sweet kisses again, smoothed his palms over her skin so softly . . . as if she was as fragile as glass and he feared breaking her. More of that confusing tension distracted her. This was . . .

Stop. Sarah closed her eyes. *Just feel.*

He whispered sweet words. Told her over and over how

beautiful she was as he explored every curve and hollow of her body. She followed his example, touching, learning . . . tasting. By the time he settled between her thighs she was already on the verge of coming. He pushed fully into her. She arched her back, pressed her breasts against his muscled chest. Her nails dug into his bare back. For long moments just having him inside her was enough. Her entire being throbbed with pleasure.

Then he started to move. Like his kisses, he kept it unhurried. She felt every inch of him with each slow, attentive thrust and flex. Sweat slickened their skin. Their bodies melded with the building tension until Sarah couldn't resist. She came hard. One last thrust and he came, too.

He collapsed on the bed next to her, pulled her against him, hot, damp flesh to hot, damp flesh, and held her that way. Their frantic breathing calmed . . . their heart rates slowed and the chilly air dried their cooling skin.

Feeling warm, safe, and content, Sarah fell asleep in his arms.

CHAPTER 27

2312 *Beauchamp Road,* 11:09 P.M.

From the mudroom door Jerald watched his daughter preparing a late-night snack in the kitchen. Hadn't she said that she had dinner with her friends after the grief session?

Agony pierced him.

He did not want to believe this was possible. Sarah Newton hadn't become her mother . . . she hadn't killed anyone.

Each time new evidence emerged or new research was released on any type of genetic connection, he rushed to digest it. Each time, his worry deepened.

What had he done?

He rubbed his hand over his mouth. Watched his daughter skillfully peel and slice the apple, the knife far larger than necessary for the task.

Could she have inherited his weaknesses? This nightmare he had lived with for so, so long?

His teeth clenched. Surely fate would not be that cruel.

For years he had been free . . . he had struggled but he'd overcome the urges for the most part.

Every day his daughter had grown into a more intelligent, more beautiful young woman and he had been certain that it wouldn't happen to her.

But now he wasn't so sure.

Lynda insisted she was afraid of her own daughter . . . that something was very, very wrong with her. Jerald had told himself that his wife exaggerated . . . that she was

wrong. That her jealousy of his relationship with their
daughter was the motive for her insinuations.

He closed his eyes a moment. Who was he kidding? He
knew. Damn it. *He knew.*

"Daddy, what's wrong?"

He opened his eyes, met his beautiful daughter's worried
gaze.

"Are you all right?" She placed the knife on the counter.

He nodded, stepped into the kitchen. "Would you like
some of your mother's lobster bisque? It was"—he pressed
his fingertips to his lips and kissed them—"*perfetto.*"

Jerri Lynn giggled. "No, thank you. Just an apple." She
popped a chunk into her mouth.

He needed to confront her with his concerns. His anguish
surged again. He had dreaded this moment from the time
she'd taken her first breath fresh from her mother's womb.

His hands slid into the pockets of his trousers as he
strolled to the kitchen island and propped a hip against it.
"You've been going out at night."

She paused in her chewing, then continued. "It's no big
deal. Just having fun."

"Your philosophy professor left a message for me." Maybe
Lynda had been right. Perhaps they should have sent her away
to school. But he just hadn't been able to let her go.

Her fingers stilled on the next chunk of apple. "Really?"

"Look at me."

She lifted her gaze to his.

"He said you'd missed four classes in the past four weeks.
One more absence and he's going to take disciplinary action."

Whether to avoid a response or simply because she was
hungry, she bit into another piece of apple.

"Who are these friends you've been so preoccupied with?"
All through school she'd had such a difficult time making
friends. She never seemed to fit in. Without effort she had
been an honor student. She hadn't won any awards, those
had always gone to the Gerard girl, but Jerald hadn't cared.
He hadn't needed any plaques or certificates to tell him how

smart his daughter was. Nor had he needed any crowns to show how beautiful she was. She was perfect.

Jerri Lynn shrugged. Sliced off another piece of apple. "The usual crowd."

There was no usual crowd. She was lying to him. That hurt almost as much as the idea that his fears may have materialized. "Who?" he repeated.

She toyed with the piece of apple. "Just Tamara Gilbert." She lifted an uncertain gaze to her father. "Reverend Mahaney's niece. She's cool. She likes me. And I feel sorry for her."

Jerald had to admit that he was glad to hear that she'd made a friend who appeared to want to stick by her, but . . . "Your snow boots are crusted in mud." He wouldn't say the rest. But he knew blood when he saw it. "Have you and Tamara been playing games in the woods?"

Jerri Lynn frowned. "No." She shook her head. "I haven't worn my boots lately."

He motioned for her to follow him.

In the mudroom, tucked behind the woodbox, were her Sorels.

She frowned as she picked up one and checked the boot size. He'd already done that. She and her mother had a matching pair, but Lynda's were a size seven. These—he stared at the damning boots—were an eight. Jerri Lynn's size.

Jerri Lynn peered up at him and shrugged. "Mom must have worn my boots. You know I leave them in here all the time. Maybe Mom didn't want to go upstairs for hers." His daughter made one of those barely tolerant sounds. "Geez, Dad, what's the big deal? It's just mud."

If only that were the case. But it was more than just mud and Lynda hated this time of year. She rarely left the house and certainly didn't traipse around in the woods or muck. Her heart condition prevented her from such risks. Jerri Lynn knew this.

Jerald knew this.

"Come on." She tugged at his arm. "I want to finish my

apple and then we'll have some of that bisque. I guess I'm hungrier than I thought."

"You go ahead." He swallowed at the tightness in his throat. "I'll be along in a moment."

When Jerri Lynn had returned to the kitchen, he lingered in the mudroom.

Was he making too much of this? He really had no valid reason for his concerns. Perhaps Lynda was making him paranoid.

"Ouch."

His daughter's distressed sound caused him to move back to the kitchen. He paused in the doorway in time to see her throw the knife onto the counter. She stared at her left forefinger. Blood oozed and slid downward. She'd cut herself.

When he would have asked if she needed him to fetch a Band-Aid, he hesitated. He couldn't say why he hesitated. Instinct perhaps.

She continued staring, seemingly intrigued, then she licked the drop that slithered into her palm.

His heart began to pound.

She licked again, trailing her tongue all the way up her finger. Then she stuck her finger into her mouth and sucked.

Emotion warred inside him.

As he watched she picked up the knife, studied the crimson smear on the shiny blade. She thrust out her tongue, let it slide carefully over the blade . . .

His breath evacuated his lungs even as he licked his lips.

CHAPTER 28

Monday, March 2, 4:00 A.M.

Hide!

Sarah grabbed her pillow and ran.

Hide. *Mommy will find you.*

Don't listen to the sounds.

Don't let the voices get you.

The blood on the floor stopped her. She couldn't cross the room without stepping in it. It grew and grew, crowding her into a corner until it traced a path around her feet. She screamed!

She had to run.

She slipped, fell into the blood, but quickly scrambled up. Rushing past the kitchen table, she stalled. Her feet seemed to sink into the wooden floor as if it was mud. She blinked. Told herself not to look. But she couldn't close her eyes. Something stared at her from the table . . . something that shouldn't be there.

"Daddy?"

Big fat droplets of blood spilled over the edge of the table. What was wrong with her daddy? Sarah climbed into a chair.

She opened her mouth to scream again but no sound came out. She could only stand there and stare at her daddy's head on the table. Where was the rest of him?

"Sarah!" the voice wailed.

Terror sent goose bumps over her skin. She had to hide.

Hurry! Up the stairs. To her mother's room. She climbed as deep into the closet as she could go, curled into a ball, and hugged her pillow.

Find me, Mommy. Find me!

Sarah!

Sarah bolted upright.

A weight shifted beside her. Suffocating . . . warm.

Someone was next to her!

Sarah scrambled out of bed.

She stumbled.

She gasped for air.

"What happened?"

The voice.

The body moved.

Sarah blinked.

Conner.

She blew out a breath.

Just a dream.

Another nightmare.

"Sarah, you okay?"

"I'm fine." She staggered to the bathroom. Washed her face. Buttressed her trembling body against the sink.

Shit.

She hated those fucking dreams.

She was okay now.

She dried her face. Peed. Then washed her hands.

Pausing at the door, Sarah braced for facing Conner.

Talk about awkward. It was bad enough that he *knew* about her past. The nightmare would only reaffirm his concerns.

Damn.

Deep breath. Just do it.

She sauntered back into the room.

He sat on the side of the bed, the sheet tugged over his lap. "You sure you're okay?"

"Yeah, yeah." She climbed into bed and crawled under the covers. She didn't want to talk about this with him. He'd already succeeded in making her feel completely vulnerable; completely unable to resist him.

"Are we going to talk about this?"

"Nope."

No questions. She did not want any more questions.

He already knew too much.

"I was wrong before." He leaned against the headboard, propped one muscled leg on the bed.

She closed her eyes. Refused to look at him. To be tempted. No matter what he said, the words would only be a lead-in to talking about her past.

"You do what you have to do to survive and I had no right to question your tactics."

Opening her eyes, she admitted defeat. She might as well get this over with. He wasn't going to let it go until he knew the whole story. It would be in her best interests to play off his concerns. "It's not as bad as it sounds." Okay, so that was a stretch. "I never really knew what was going on. I played in the butcher shop during the day. I wouldn't have known the difference between animal blood and human blood." It was all the other stuff . . . the body parts . . . that scared her but she wasn't going into that. "I was usually in bed. When I heard the sounds, I hid. My mother told me to hide when I got scared and she would find me. She always did . . ."

"Always?"

"Except that once." Like in the nightmare she'd just had. "She was filling an order for Jimmy Dean and my dad was the main ingredient."

Suffocating silence.

And finally, "So you got counseling? Like jerkwad said."

Sarah sat up. She stared a moment at his semierect penis and then looked into his eyes. "I did it all. Alcohol, sex, drugs, mostly prescription. *Sex*, cigarettes, more sex, more booze." She puffed out a blast of disgusted air. "And finally I decided that I shouldn't punish myself for my mother's mistakes. And yes." She plopped back onto her pillow. "I've had several shrinks. This one seems to have stuck. Though I don't know why. I never follow her advice. Otherwise I wouldn't be here right now."

He scooted down next to her. "That really sucks."

"No shit." Why didn't he just shut up?

He pulled her into his arms. "You did good, Sarah New-ton." He pulled her closer. "Real good."

She closed her eyes and blocked the echo of his words.

Not real.

She couldn't trust him.

Or his sweet words.

Public Safety Office, 11:05 A.M.

"Don't even try it," Kale said to the man he'd known his whole life, Deputy Rodger Boyd. "We're going in."

"You can go in," Rodger said, stepping into his path. "But not her."

"So shoot me." Kale walked around the determined dep-uty, Sarah right behind him.

No one was stepping on her toes today.

If August got in his way, Conner would beat the hell out of the guy.

The crackle of the deputy's radio warned that he was in-forming the chief.

Kale didn't care what they said. Sarah had as much right to be here as anyone else. She was a part of this investiga-tion. He'd gotten word half an hour ago from Karen Brigh-ton that the next briefing would start at eleven.

Images from a shower with Sarah . . . more sex . . . another shower . . . flashed like a steamy movie trailer. He tucked it away for savoring later.

Maybe she was right and he hadn't been living his own life. But today was as good a day as any to start. Or maybe he'd started last night.

He passed several other deputies en route to his destina-tion, all of whom stopped and stared at him.

Fuck 'em. He'd known these people his whole life. If they didn't trust his actions, then tough shit.

He burst into the conference room where the chief, the

mayor, Kale's fellow councilmen, and the fed were already gathered.

"Sorry we're late," Kale announced. Before anyone could get past the shock of his and Sarah's appearance he dragged out a chair and waited for her to sit. He didn't take his eyes off August. "If we missed anything, we'd like to be brought up to speed."

Kale settled into the chair next to Sarah.

"Kale." The chief was the first to speak. "Don't make me have her hauled out of here by force."

"If she goes," Kale cautioned, "I go. And when I go, I'm going straight out there to those reporters and tell them everything I know." He surveyed the table. "And everything you don't know."

Sarah stared as if she didn't recognize him.

Maybe she didn't. Whatever she thought, he wasn't that go-along guy all the time.

He'd assured her that the people in this village were God-fearing, compassionate folks. By God, he intended for these people to live up to his promise.

Mayor Patterson rose from his chair. "Conner, if you persist in this behavior—"

Special Agent Lex Asshole August held up a hand. "He's right. She should stay."

The chief's jaw dropped.

As did Kale's. What the hell was this guy up to? Sarah had warned him not to trust anything August did or said.

The mayor stood there with his own mouth hanging open for another three or four seconds, before resuming his seat.

No one else said a word.

Chief Willard heaved a sigh. "Well, let's get to it then."

He reviewed the details Kale had already shared with Sarah. She didn't ask any questions. As the chief spoke Kale noticed a timeline had been arranged on the white board usually reserved for community activities requiring law enforcement assistance.

A picture of Valerie, as well as one of Alicia, was accompanied by dates, times, and events. Next to each entry was a list of the persons related in some way to the victim. Beneath all that information were crime-scene photos and the few evidentiary details.

"This morning"—the chief moved on to more recent news—"we swept the scene again." He surveyed those present. "We got lucky."

Kale tensed. They found something? Next to him, Sarah perked up.

Lex August leaned forward. "We found a single boot print in probably the one thawed spot of ground in the whole area."

The chief shook his head. "You'd think the fool stumbled all over the woods looking for that one place to step."

Sarah leaned forward. "Boot? What size?"

August's gaze met hers. "Ladies', size eight. The same as yours."

Tension whipped through Kale. He wanted to rearrange that perfect smile so bad.

"You now believe the unsub is a woman," she said, her gaze never leaving August's.

"That's a possibility." The fed's attention didn't waver. He seemed to be devouring Sarah with his eyes.

It was as if everyone else in the room had vanished. Kale's fury just kept building.

The chief raised his hands. "Before we go getting too excited and making any announcements to the press, there are a few things we need to do."

August turned to the chief. "I'll start the interviews. The list is compiled and prioritized."

"The rest of us," the chief explained, "will divide up into teams and start tracking down leads. One team will run down anyone in the area who is prescribed propranolol, the beta blocker discovered in Alicia's tox screen. That'll take a while since it's a pretty common drug. Another team will get a list of anyone local who competed against Valerie Gerard in that fourth-grade spelling bee, kids and parents, brothers, whatever. And the local competitors in any competitions Alicia Appleton participated in."

"Now that," Deputy Brighton noted, "will take some time."

A rumble of agreement went around the room.

"I want every name," the chief reiterated. "Narrow down those results by anyone who wears a size eight boot." He gestured to the fed. "Agent August has the male equivalent in case we're dealing with a younger male. We'll meet here to compare notes at midnight. No one sleeps until this is done."

The group stood and filed out of the room, a new sense of urgency in their movements.

August rounded the table. "I assume you'll accept my apology for yesterday." This he said directly to Sarah despite Kale standing right next to her.

Sarah didn't know what Lex was up to, but one thing was certain, he never apologized . . . and meant it. "For what? Telling the truth? Not a big deal." She stared straight at him, let him see the delight in her eyes. "Just remember, it works both ways."

Lex adjusted his tie. "I suppose I was feeling a little territorial. You were here first and it has been a while since we've worked together." He glanced briefly at Conner. "How have you been?"

"I've been great." She reached for her coat and pulled it on, then slung her bag on her shoulder.

"Excellent." He smiled that million-dollar smile that had first tugged at her heart strings. "It'll be nice working with you again."

Next to her, Conner shifted. If the glower on his face was any indication, he still wanted to beat the hell out of Lex.

"Lots of things are nice, Lex," she returned. "But working with you in any capacity isn't one of them."

Sarah left him standing there. She didn't look back. Conner was behind her. She could feel him. Her body tingled as she recalled hot, slippery sex in the shower that morning. But the feelings that overwhelmed all else were those confusing ones from the way he'd made love to her last night. So sweetly, so tenderly. No one had ever made her feel that protected, that secure.

She shook off the feelings and memories. She had to focus.

Though she was glad Lex had cleared the way for her to stay, she understood he had a motive. Whatever his agenda, she wasn't going to allow him to manipulate her reactions again.

Outside she and Conner took the usual route to an out-of-the-way parking spot. The press was still camped out front in force.

"Hey."

She hadn't realized she'd been moving so fast until Conner had to hurry to catch up to her.

"Yeah."

"So this thing with you and August," he asked, choosing his words carefully, "what kind of thing was it?"

She rounded the hood without answering, got into the passenger seat of his Jeep. That seemed to be a habit of late. He ended up driving her most everywhere.

Conner slid behind the wheel. "What kind of thing?" he repeated.

"A relationship." She pulled her seat belt into place. "You know, living together."

"Were you . . ." He pulled out onto the street. "Engaged or something?"

"No. Just long-term sex partners."

He braked at a stop sign. "Where are we going?"

The chief certainly hadn't given her any part of the assignments he'd doled out. "West Street."

Conner's brow furrowed in confusion.

"Matilda Calder's house. I have some questions for her."

She wanted to speak to the innkeeper and the reverend. But right now she needed to see Matilda.

Conner drove another few blocks.

"Do you still have feelings for him?"

He didn't have to specify which him. She knew exactly who he meant and the idea was a joke. "Not at all."

"There sure as hell seemed to be some tension between the two of you." He shrugged. "I know you were mad as hell yesterday, but he seemed to be trying to make nice today."

Sarah stared out the window. "What you witnessed yesterday is called hatred, Conner. This morning was tolerance. We both want to work this case, so we tolerate each other. Unless he gives me reason, I won't kill him or anything."

Conner chuckled. "I'm not too sure you would kill anyone. Even if they gave you reason."

He just didn't understand. She turned to face him. Wanted to make sure he really got it. "I'm my mother's daughter, her DNA is fifty percent of my genetic makeup."

He laughed outright then. "You think because she was a killer you'll end up a killer."

"That's scientifically possible."

"Well." He braked for the turn onto West. "That's where we see things differently, Sarah. You believe in science. I believe in people." He looked at her. "I believe in you."

She stared at his profile. Too handsome. Too sweet. Everything about him made her flaws all the more glaring.

"I hope I don't disappoint you."

He pulled to the curb in front of a rundown shack of a house. "I'm not worried." He flashed her a smile then got out.

What the hell was it about this guy that made her not want to fail . . . him?

Forget about it, she ordered.

For now, anyway.

The house should have been condemned ages ago. The entire structure leaned to one side. Three, no four, dead cars had been left unburied in the yard. A dog lay on the porch. Sarah didn't see how he kept from freezing to death.

His tail flopped as they climbed the rickety steps.

"Good fella," Conner said gently before banging on the door.

The house backed up to the woods. Considering the wooded areas between here and the location of the cemetery, it would be easy for Matilda to slip back and forth without being spotted.

"It's quiet in there," Conner said. "Maybe no one's home."

"Knock again."

He banged a little harder this time.

Sarah listened; heard some bumping around. "Someone's up."

Conner beat his fist on the door a third time.

The door flew open. "What the hell is it?"

A woman with stringy black hair and dressed in nothing but a T-shirt glared from Conner to Sarah. But the eyes were the same as Matilda's. This unfortunate being was her mother.

"Is Matilda home?" Sarah summed up the woman in one word. Druggie. Too skinny. Splotchy complexion. Bad teeth. She couldn't have been more than thirty-five. A serious user.

"Who knows?" The woman flung the door open wider. "See for yourself. I'm going back to bed." She eyed Conner once before putting word into action.

Conner entered before Sarah. Another of those protective male gestures.

The living room had few furnishings. A ragged couch and a couple of tables. The mainstay of the decorating was garbage. Empty pizza boxes. Beer cans. Newspapers. Dirty clothes.

"Nice place," Sarah murmured. Poor kid. Living in a dump like this . . . with a mother like that. As crazy as Sarah's mother had been, she'd kept a clean house and she'd taken care of Sarah most of the time.

The kitchen was even worse. Dirty dishes filled the sink, covered the countertops and table. A couple of black flies that miraculously survived the cold crawled around on the window above the sink.

Conner led the way down the hall. As she'd promised, mother was sprawled in bed, most of her ass showing. Some dirtbag lay partially under her. A filthy bathroom was the next door they encountered.

The final door was closed. Sarah knocked but there was no answer. The room beyond the door was quiet. She grasped the knob and turned. The latch released and the door opened.

Unlike the rest of the house, Matilda's room was neat. A white pentagram had been painted with what appeared to be spray paint on the wood floor. Other symbols of her religion hung on the walls. The one bookshelf was mostly empty. Sarah remembered Matilda saying that she'd hidden her stuff.

Her great-great-grandmother's spell books.

The bed was made. The covers old and tattered.

The closet had a couple of T-shirts hanging inside and not much else.

The window that faced the woods was open a crack.

Sarah walked over and peered through the dingy panes. "So this is your way in and out." The girl could avoid running into her mother and her friends and seek the safety of the places she felt safe.

The woods.

And the cemetery.

Sarah turned to face Conner. "Let's go to Bay View Cemetery."

He shook his head. "No kid should have to live like this."

And, the saddest part was that none of the God-fearing, compassionate folks in his village seemed to notice or care.

That was Sarah's cynical side talking. But it was true.

Somehow she would find a way to help Matilda. It was the least Sarah could do for a kindred spirit.

The drive to the cemetery took only three or four minutes.

Sarah opened her door as soon as he'd shut off the engine. She scanned the cemetery. No sign of Matilda.

Sarah had taken only one step from the Jeep when she stopped dead. She stared at Mattie Calder's headstone.

Sitting there watching Sarah . . . or maybe waiting for her to arrive . . . were three black crows.

CHAPTER 29

Noon

In just one hour the the special afternoon prayer service would begin.

Deborah Mahaney stared out the window over her kitchen sink and peered next door at the church's towering stained-glass window. The beautiful rendering of Jesus ascending to heaven gave her comfort even now, in this tragic time.

Today Christopher had a brief, faith-building sermon planned for their grieving congregation.

Evil had struck again and taken another of their sweet children.

Deborah's gnarled hands ached. She rubbed them together.

The memorial service would be tomorrow morning at eleven. Poor Rachel couldn't bear the thought of going through the service days from now. She wanted it behind her.

The ache in Deborah's heart went soul deep. Such tragedy.

As much as she grieved for the Gerards and the Appletons, Deborah had problems of her own, too.

The FBI agent was coming this afternoon. He'd come once already to question Christopher about his discovery of poor Alicia's body. But this time was different. Like that awful Sarah Newton, he wanted to talk to Christopher about Valerie.

Dear God, what am I to do?

Deborah closed her eyes and prayed hard.

How could this be happening? So much time had passed and there had been no trouble. Why now? Poor Valerie was dead. What difference would it make now?

All the difference in the world, Deborah feared.

Her crippling arthritis worsened every year. Poor Tamara was just about to graduate high school. She would be going off to college. That took money. Deborah's medicine and mounting doctor bills took money and insurance.

If Christopher's secret were discovered . . .

God, what would she and Tamara do?

Tamara had suffered far too much already.

Deborah understood that even if the police didn't find that dirty little sin, *she* would. Sarah Newton had a reputation for finding what others missed. She would not stop until she had ruined them.

If Deborah continued to wait . . . it might be too late.

She had watched for a sign, but nothing came.

God often expected his sheep to think for themselves.

Perhaps this was one of those times.

She had to make a plan to save herself and Tamara from Christopher's terrible, terrible sin.

He apparently did not possess the courage to act.

Deborah went to the bathroom and opened the medicine cabinet. She picked up the prescription bottle, turned it in her fingers.

Yes, she had to do something very soon.

CHAPTER 30

Cliffside Care Facility, 2:20 P.M.

Barton clasped the bag in his hand and forced his feet to walk, not run, down the corridor.

Two more doors . . . there.

He walked into the room, closed the door that stayed open when no visitors or facility staff were present.

For a moment he could only lean against the door, his heart pounding harder with each breath.

Was he making a mistake to bring this up?

It wasn't like he would gain anything.

But he had to do it. He could keep this misery to himself no longer.

Barton moved away from the door. The television, he noticed, was muted.

In the long narrow hospital bed, his father lay, the covers tucked neatly around him, his frail eyes staring at the images on the television screen.

Barton moved past the foot of his father's bed. Those faded blue eyes followed him around to the side of the bed. Barton lowered himself into the chair he always selected when he visited. For a long time he simply sat there, unsure how to approach what he needed to say.

Finally, when he could bear the tremendous pressure no longer, he leaned forward and peered into his father's watery eyes.

"Why did you do it?"

Thin lids blinked.

Barton didn't know why he bothered to demand an answer. His father hadn't been able to speak in twelve years.
He'd lain in this very bed since his stroke. Unable to move
even a finger or to utter the slightest sound. Whether or not
he could hear or understand was unclear. He was kept alive
with a feeding tube and intravenous fluids.

Would he never die?

The thought filled Barton's eyes with tears. How could he
be so heartless? He loved his father. Had always loved him.
But after the stroke, this . . . this god-awful thing had become Barton's personal burden.

His father was eighty years old. Living on sheer willpower.

What could they do to him?

Nothing.

He was a mere fragile shell of a human with only a glimmer left of the man who once was trapped inside.

But what would they do to Barton for concealing evidence?

How could he protect his family?

He reached out and clutched his father's cold, feeble
hand. "What am I going to do?"

Closing his eyes, Barton fought the overwhelming emotions.

Today at four the profiler from Quantico wanted to see
him.

What if he had somehow learned the truth?

Barton opened his eyes.

The agent couldn't know the truth. Barton squared his
shoulders, gathered his courage.

There was no way anyone could know.

Not yet.

Barton would be strong for the interview with the federal
agent.

But *she* . . . she was a different story.

She was not bound by the same laws as the agent. She

could dig and sneak around until she discovered Barton's secret.

He clasped the bag closer. It was his curse.

He had to make sure she didn't find out. He had to make her go away.

All of his efforts so far had failed. When she'd gone over that ledge he'd been certain he'd killed her. He shuddered. Had to be losing his mind. He hadn't meant to push her . . . but the impulse had overwhelmed him.

This was what he had been reduced to!

He had to be brave. Perhaps there was a way without going to such an extreme. Whatever it was, he had to find it. He had to find something that scared her enough to send her running.

No one was immune to fear.

All he had to do was find her one true fear and then he could make her afraid.

Then she would leave.

His burden, his secret, would be safe.

CHAPTER 31

Sarah stood, arms crossed, on the periphery of the crowd filing into the Main Street Methodist church for Alicia Appleton's memorial service. Sarah had observed most of the people on her watch-list drift inside.

Clouds threatening snow plotted overhead.

More snow was the last thing they needed.

Trucks, cars, and SUVs lined the parking area, each one dirty from the mixture of snow, ice, sand, and the occasional dash of salt added as necessary, that littered every street and driveway. Welcome to life in Maine.

Sarah had been damned disappointed that Chief Willard hadn't planned a strategy briefing that morning, at least not one she was invited to attend.

If the investigation had discovered additional evidence or learned new particulars on persons of interest since the last briefing no one was talking.

Memorial services were something Sarah didn't typically attend. But she was here for more than paying her respects to the deceased. She was here to analyze the others paying their respects. Not exactly a laudable reason to show, but necessary nonetheless.

She was beginning to think she should have brought two little black dresses. But since she only owned one, it would have to do.

As would the less than sophisticated Converses that were the mainstay of her everyday wardrobe.

Her editor, Tae, had called demanding an update she couldn't really give him.

Primarily because she couldn't explain why she was still here. There was no logical reason. The story she'd come here to follow was basically nonexistent at this point. Sure, there were myths and legends and tales all over this rocky coast. And no doubt many believed those things were as real as any angel or demon or biblical fable. But the truth was out in the open now. Valerie Gerard and Alicia Appleton had been murdered by someone as human as they were. Likely someone they had known, possibly well, or all their lives.

End of story.

Except something wasn't right.

Her instincts were screaming at Sarah to stay. To find the truth. After all, that was the real story.

Maybe it wasn't cloaked in magic or ghosts, but it was thoroughly shrouded in secrets.

Secrets being kept by the most heinous of villains.

Intimates.

People known and maybe loved by the victims.

The mystery here was far more involved than the perp the police were looking for, and certainly more involved than Lex expected. She couldn't label why yet . . . couldn't even put it into words. But she knew it was wrong.

Just wrong. That was all she knew so far.

For the first time in ten years Sarah felt she was a part of something bigger; that her task was more than demystifying bedtime stories.

Conner spotted her across the parking lot and started in her direction. She'd managed to avoid him this morning . . . until now.

After a futile search for Matilda and several attempts to meet with Reverend Mahaney or his niece, and Barton Harvey, she and Conner had parted ways late last evening.

Spending another night with him would have been an

even bigger mistake than she'd already made. She was getting too close . . . allowing him too close.

Sarah'd turned off her cell phone and spent the night reviewing her notes and what few evidentiary details she'd begged, borrowed, and stolen. Then she'd tried to sleep.

Dreams had kept her from achieving that ever-elusive goal.

Only these dreams had been different . . . they had involved *him*.

"I tried to catch you at the inn."

She'd known he would. So she'd left early and driven around. Sarah had found herself at the chapel, or at least as close to it as the police perimeter would allow.

"I had things . . ."

He nodded. "My family's over there." He motioned to his mother's minivan where his father, stationed in his wheelchair, was being hydraulically lowered to the ground. His brother who'd come home from the University of Massachusetts for the memorial service, hovered nearby. "I thought maybe you might like to sit with us. You haven't met my brother Jamison yet."

"Sure." Sarah didn't exactly have an excuse to say no.

Conner looked good in black. Straight-cut suit, crisp white shirt, narrow black tie. Even had the leather wingtips to match. No flannel or boots today. That she noted every little detail was not a good sign.

His gaze traveled the length of her and back.

"It's the only dress I brought," she explained for no good reason. Why should she care if he noticed she'd worn the same thing three times already? Not to mention her coat was not exactly suitable for wearing to church.

"You could wear it every day and the facts wouldn't change."

His hand settled at her lower back as he ushered her toward his family.

Had she just been insulted?

"What facts?"

He smiled. "The facts of how great you look in that dress."

Irrationally annoyed, she pointed out, "That's one fact, Conner."

He leaned closer as they reached the minivan. "The others are private."

"Sarah." Before she could analyze that comment, Polly Conner rushed up and gave her a hug. "You have to sit with me." With a covert glance at her mom, she added in a whisper, "I'll tell you about everybody."

Ellen and Peter Conner greeted her as if they hadn't seen her in ages and were thrilled to have her join them. Conner introduced her to his brother who looked like a younger, carbon copy of him.

It felt . . . awkward . . . too personal.

Conner pushed the wheelchair, his mother walked on one side while his brother tagged along on the other. Polly hung on to Sarah's arm.

The whole situation was somehow uncomfortable.

Sarah was a stranger.

Apparently they hadn't noticed.

"Let's find a seat," Polly urged as the rest of her family headed for the handicapped-accessible entrance.

Having no ready way to disengage herself, Sarah smiled at the girl and went along.

They followed Marta Hanover and her husband up the steps.

Marta glanced at Sarah but quickly looked away.

See? Sarah was not one of them. Why hadn't the Conners noticed?

If that one furtive glance wasn't proof enough, the blatant glares she garnered inside the sanctuary confirmed it.

"Here." Polly tugged her to the wide aisle designed for those physically challenged. She settled on the very end of the pew next to the main aisle and patted the spot beside her.

Conner and his mother entered the row from the other side. When his mother was settled alongside his father, he took the seat next to Sarah.

That his arm went automatically behind her set off another of those gut-level alarms.

Before she could reflect on the maneuver, much less the motive, Polly whispered in her ear. "You see the girl hanging all over Brady?"

Jerald Pope's daughter.

"That's Jerri Lynn. She's been after Brady forever. She and Alicia hated each other. 'Course I can't say much since I had a little crush on Brady, but I got over that and hardly anyone knew."

Jerri Lynn wasn't alone in her efforts to console Brady. Several others, male and female, including Tamara Gilbert, sat around him. But Tamara's presence was merely on the fringes. It was obvious that she was latched onto Jerri Lynn and that alone was her ticket to the party.

"Oh, my God," Polly murmured, still leaning against Sarah's shoulder. "Reverend Mahaney is here without his wife. And he's not sitting with his niece." She bent around to look Sarah in the eyes. "That's weird. They always do everything together." She peeked in the reverend's direction then turned back to Sarah. "His niece is like the biggest nerd in school. Nobody likes her except Jerri Lynn. That's her all over Jerri Lynn," Polly added as an aside, not realizing that Sarah already knew. "Tamara always tells her uncle everything, especially about the youth group members. That's another reason nobody likes her."

Sarah nodded, but her real attention was on Melody Harvey who sat with her parents. Seemed strange that she didn't sit with the other kids her age as her brother did. Maybe she, too, was considered a nerd like Tamara. *Invisible*, that's what Melody had said.

It appeared every police officer on the Youngstown force was in attendance. Except maybe the one guarding the crime scene. The Popes sat together near the back on the other side of the sanctuary.

As if her thought had summoned him, Jerald gave Sarah one of those vague nods of acknowledgment. Sarah returned the gesture. His wife looked regal. She was the only one in the room wearing a hat and dark glasses.

Matilda had been right. Pope was a little freaky. But that

didn't make him a killer any more than his generous donations to the victims' families did. Matilda was just a kid.
Admittedly, one with an uncanny sense of those around her,
but a kid nonetheless. Sarah had to stop allowing her empathy for the kid to filter her assessments.

Sarah shifted her attention from the standing-room-only
crowd to the front where a long table had been arranged in
honor of Alicia. Her senior portrait served as the centerpiece.
More photos, trophies, crowns, and the memorabilia that
represented her too short life spanned the width of the altar.

When the minister stepped up to the podium, the murmur of soft voices and the whisper of fabric in the crowd
settling came to an abrupt stop.

The service began with the minister's thoughts on the
deceased. Close friends and family approached the altar,
one by one, and spoke about the young woman who would
be so sorely missed. Rachel Appleton sat stoically through
every word of every recitation.

Sarah watched her, trying to remember how she'd felt at
her father's memorial service . . . or even at her mother's.
She'd felt numb, uncaring. In a way, relieved.

But not Rachel Appleton. She sat there wearing a brave
face and dying inside.

With the discovery of her daughter's body, Rachel Appleton's life had ended. It didn't matter that she had two sons.
Her daughter had been her life.

Sarah ached for her, sensed with every fiber of her being
that this tragedy could have been prevented . . . somehow.
This woman, a mother who loved so much, gave so much,
had lost a child. Sarah had not known a mother like that . . .
maybe she ached in part for what she'd never had . . . for
what Rachel Appleton would miss.

When the service ended, a few stayed behind to talk, the
rest filtered out. There would be refreshments and grief
counseling available at the high school auditorium.

It wasn't until Sarah stood outside again that she noticed
Lex August. He must have been with the crowd at the back
of the sanctuary.

She could have cared less if she'd ever seen him again in this lifetime, except she wanted an update. She didn't care where it came from as long as it was accurate.

"How did your interviews go?" She walked right into his personal space, toe-to-toe.

There had been a time she would have admired how he looked in a suit, as she had Conner. But not anymore. Because she knew all too well that behind that handsome face and well-maintained physique beat the meager heart of a complete prick.

He adopted that fake smile that seemed to work on everyone else. "Well enough for preliminary groundwork."

Code for: I didn't get shit.

"No new evidence?" She shouldn't get any glee that he'd already been here over twenty-four hours and he hadn't learned anything new—that the killer didn't give him.

But she did.

"Not yet." He adjusted the knot of his tie. "We're still waiting for the final test results and the full-on autopsy report."

"No briefing today?"

He glanced right then leveled his gaze on hers. "Not today."

Lie.

"Really?" She frowned. "At a dead end already?"

Those blue eyes she'd once thought were so gorgeous tapered. "When we have something, you'll get it, Sarah. Don't be a bitch."

Such a turnabout from yesterday. Split personality, maybe? What had she ever seen in him?

She smiled, enjoying every damned minute of this. "Me? A bitch? Never."

Walking away felt good.

Damned good.

Conner glanced up as he closed the side door of the minivan and smiled at her. Perfect white teeth. Truly beautiful eyes . . . and so damned handsome.

"Sarah!"

Her attention turning to the sound of her name, Sarah spotted Polly running toward her and waited.

"Hurry up, Pol," Conner said. "Mom's waiting."

Polly practically bowled Sarah over, cupped her hand over her ear and whispered, "Look over by the picnic tables."

Sarah's gaze went instantly to the row of white picnic tables under the trees beyond the parking lot.

Matilda Calder lingered there.

"She didn't come inside," Polly said secretively. "She thinks nobody likes her." Polly shrugged. "She is kind of weird but I like her. I guess I'm her only friend."

"Thanks, Polly." Sarah patted the hand clamped on her arm. "You'd better go. Your mom's waiting."

"Polly!" her mother called on cue.

Conner's sister rushed to the minivan, and Sarah headed for the picnic tables.

She worried that Matilda would make a run for it but she didn't. She waited, wearing the usual ragged getup, with a cigarette dangling from one hand. Sarah really should buy the girl some clothes. Give her some money for clothes and food, at least. After visiting the house on West Street, Sarah was pretty sure Matilda wasn't getting nearly enough of either. A stop at an ATM would handle that.

"Hey." Sarah's lips stretched wide without prompting.

"You wear it all the time?" Matilda looked at the leather necklace before meeting Sarah's gaze.

Sarah touched the medallion where it rested between her breasts. It fell just beneath the scooped neck of her one black dress. "I do."

"Good." Matilda tossed her cigarette to the ground, uncaring that anyone who saw her would consider the move sacrilegious.

"I went to your house yesterday." Sarah noted again the dark circles under the girl's eyes. Did she have trouble sleeping, too? Judging by the place she lived, probably.

"I know."

"Your mom told you?"

She shook her head, stared past Sarah. "I saw you there."

Sarah glanced back to see what she was looking at. Conner waited near Sarah's car. "Why did you hide from me?"

Matilda cut her eyes toward Conner again. "He was with you."

Sarah folded her arms. "Oh, yeah?"

Matilda nodded.

"You don't like him?"

She shrugged. "His family doesn't like me."

"They don't know you," Sarah argued. "There's a difference."

"I just came to make sure you were wearing the necklace." Matilda took a step back. "I gotta go."

"Matilda, wait. I need to ask you a question." Sarah held very still no matter that she wanted to advance that extra step yawning between them.

"I can't answer it."

Sarah inclined her head. "You don't know the question yet."

"Ask."

"When you say the devil has always been here and the cops can't catch him . . . are you talking about the *devil* or the person who killed Valerie and Alicia?" She purposely didn't mention Pope's name.

Matilda didn't answer, didn't move for a moment, then she said, "They're the same, aren't they."

Sarah's heart thudded hard. "Are they?"

Matilda didn't answer, just stared at Sarah.

"Do you know him?" Sarah's pulse jumped.

"Everyone knows him." Matilda backed up another step. "They just don't realize it yet. Like you."

"Then help me. You said he was rich."

She glanced past Sarah again.

"Just give me a name," Sarah urged. "If you think you know—"

"He's watching me." She suddenly advanced those two steps she'd retreated. She went nose-to-nose with Sarah. "He's watching you, too."

"You're saying it's Pope?"

Matilda shook her head, looked confused. "I don't know. Maybe I'm confusing all the talk and what I feel." She banged her hand against her chest. "But I can feel the evil the same as I can see you." She searched Sarah's eyes. "You feel it, don't you?"

"Yes." Sarah recognized the feeling for what it was. She'd sensed something here . . . *someone* here. "I feel it."

"Then find him. I keep dreaming about the ocean. I think it fuels him . . . makes him feel powerful. That's why he can't leave . . . he needs to be here." She looked past Sarah again, her eyes went wide. "I have to go—"

Sarah looked back at the parking lot's dispersing crowd. "I want to—" She turned back to Matilda.

She was gone.

Sarah's heart hammered. Matilda was scared as hell. She was definitely confused. But her instincts were humming.

Just as Sarah's were.

But she needed more than the ramblings, however heartfelt, of a teenager before casting suspicion on a man like Pope.

"You want to go have coffee?"

At the sound of Conner's voice, Sarah wheeled in that direction.

Irrationally, her frustration heightened. "I'm not in the mood for crowds."

"Who said anything about a crowd?" He searched her eyes, his saying all that needed to be said.

Sarah's attention shifted to the last of the people drifting aimlessly down the church steps.

The Popes climbed into their regal Infiniti. Jerri Lynn hugged Tamara, then dashed over to join her family.

Rachel Appleton, her husband, and two sons drifted into Sarah's line of sight.

Rachel turned and for one fleeting instant she looked directly at Sarah. That ache Sarah couldn't seem to banish swelled. She watched the family walk to the waiting car and settle in. The car drove away.

Sarah blinked, then blinked again, severing the painful

bond. "Yes," she said to Conner. Determination and undeniable desperation bursting inside her. "We'll go to your place. We'll have coffee and then we'll have sex."

When she would have turned to her car, he snagged her elbow, drew her close. "We'll go to my place. Have coffee . . ." He put his face close to hers. "And we'll make love."

She pulled free of his hold and stalked to her car without looking back.

Didn't have to.

He would be right behind her.

He could call it whatever he wanted. Sarah would fortify herself with what Conner had to offer and then, by God, she would find that fucking killer.

For Valerie and Alicia and their families.

For Matilda.

They barely got inside the door of his house before she was tearing his clothes off.

Sarah couldn't explain it. Didn't try.

Thinking was out of the question right now.

She needed to feel.

Between their frantic kisses, he muttered, "Down, Angie."

The dog had reared up to greet her master.

She slinked off to the rug in front of the couch.

"Sorry," he muttered to Sarah.

She didn't care . . . dragged him toward the bedroom.

She hadn't been in there before but she knew the way.

The rest of his clothes hit the floor by the time they reached the bed.

He peeled off her dress, unsnapped her bra, and lifted her onto the bed. She couldn't get enough of his taste . . . of the feel of his skin. Her panties skimmed her legs, caught on her sneakers. She toed them off. Kicked free of the panties.

He burrowed between her legs and thrust into her.

She sighed.

Fear trickled past the other sensations as she realized a cold, hard fact. Here . . . now . . . with him . . . she felt right.

She felt safe.

As if sensing her tension, he kissed her, nuzzled her neck, then he began to move and the fear melted away.

Legs intertwined, bodies joined, she lost herself to the primal heat and motion.

To Conner.

Wednesday, March 4, 2:30 A.M.

The telephone clanged.

Sarah was dreaming . . . sweet, hot dreams.

Her lips parted, lifted.

Skilled hands moved over her skin. Seeking lips tugged at her nipple.

Conner . . .

Another long, loud clang.

The dream faded. The arms holding her released her. The hot, hard body spooning hers rolled away.

"Hello."

Her eyes drifted open at the rough, sexy sound of his voice.

Conner. She was with him . . . in his bed.

Sex. Hot. Frantic. Life-reaffirming.

She was safe. With him. Her stomach knotted with uncertainty. If she got in any deeper—

"What?"

Conner rose up, dropped his feet to the floor. "When?"

Sarah pushed the hair out of her eyes as she sat up. She studied his rigid profile. What the hell had happened now?

"I'll be right there." He placed the handset back into its cradle. Sat stone-still.

"What's wrong?" Adrenaline cleared the last of the sleep from her head.

As if her question had reanimated him, he jumped up, groped for his trousers. "It's Polly. She didn't come home."

"Wait." Sarah scooted off the bed, her pulse scrambling. "Where'd she go?"

"With the other kids to the auditorium."

Sarah pulled the dress over her head, yanked it down her hips. "And?" she demanded as she tugged on her shoes. Please, no . . . not Polly.

He stopped buttoning buttons. Stared at her. Terror in his dark eyes. "No one's seen her since."

CHAPTER 32

Polly was cold.

So cold.

She tried to move. Couldn't. Her hands were stuck between her legs and taped to her feet. She tried to scoot on her butt and fell onto her side. Her head hit a rock. She cried. The tape burned her lips.

God, help me!

Her silent plea shuddered through her. Made her stomach ache. She'd puked before. Almost choked. Had to swallow it or strangle to death. She'd peed her pants.

God, oh God, where was she?

What happened?

She remembered going outside to talk to Matilda. She'd promised to meet Polly there. But she hadn't shown.

Was she here, too?

Polly's heart started that crazy pounding again. Felt like she was going to have a heart attack.

She wiggled, scooted, jerked until she got back up onto her butt. She couldn't see. Something was tied around her eyes.

Listen!

If Matilda was here and taped up like her, then she might make sounds Polly could hear.

The air echoed in Polly's ears. Like she was someplace deep under the ground. She was sitting on rocks. Hard. Bumpy. Not smooth or flat.

It was cold. She shivered. So cold.

She didn't hear anybody else. Just the water. Was she close to the ocean?

She tried to listen harder.

Her body started to shake again. She cried. Didn't mean to. Couldn't help it.

Kale! Please come get me! Mom!

They had to find her. They would be looking. She knew they would.

Her mom and her brothers wouldn't forget her. Her dad wouldn't let them.

Polly's shuddering body suddenly stilled. Her insides got real quiet. Like she couldn't think anymore. Just nothing. No feelings . . . no anything. Then her thoughts came at her all at once.

What had happened to her?

Where was she?

Who had done this?

Memories of going to the memorial service with her family flooded her brain.

Then she knew the answers to all her questions.

The devil had gotten her . . . just like he got Valerie and Alicia.

Matilda had warned her to be careful.

Polly was going to die . . .

She jerked. Tried to get her hands free. Tried to wiggle her feet free.

Help me.

Please, Jesus, help me.

Kale!

Her chest heaved. Mom! Jamison!

Find me. Please, please, *find me*.

CHAPTER 33

As if the dire situation needed any help, the winter storm everyone but Sarah appeared to know about had dropped three inches of snow in the last four hours.

Sarah wished she could give Conner hope.

But in this case there was no precedence for hope.

No evidence that had led to a real suspect.

There was no genuine hope to offer.

Chief Willard called for silence. The assembled mob settled down.

"You have your search areas. Stay with your assigned groups. And for God's sake, be careful out there. We're all worried sick about Polly but we don't need anyone getting hurt and slowing down the search. Now let's get going."

Groups of citizens piled out the exit doors.

More than one bumped into Sarah as they rushed out of the gym. She tiptoed. Looked for Kale. She saw the top of his dark head as he exited with Deputy Brighton and several others whose faces she didn't recognize.

At some point this morning, maybe during that terrifying epiphany, she'd decided to call him Kale.

If she could just find him now . . .

She looked around again. No luck.

"Sarah."

Her attention shifted right. Jerald Pope approached her. She was surprised to see him here. Yeah, he was a lifelong resident but rich guys like him didn't usually get involved on this level. Tossing money around was one thing, but trudging around in the snow and cold was entirely another.

"I didn't see you in the crowd," she said by way of greeting.

He glanced around the gym. "It's a good showing of community support. Many of the people are from surrounding towns."

"Yeah." She glanced at the last of the teams filing out the doors. "I should get out there."

"If you haven't already been assigned to a group, you can go with us." Jerald gestured to where his wife waited with their group. "We'd love to have you join us."

Sarah started to say no . . . but since both his wife and daughter were in his group as well as the Harvey family and another she didn't recognize, she changed her mind.

"Sure."

"You know the Harveys, of course," Jerald said as they walked toward the group.

"Yeah."

"It was important to Jerri Lynn that we be a part of their group."

Sarah just bet it was.

Quick introductions were made and car assignments given. Sarah would be riding with Jerald and Lynda Pope and two of the people she didn't recognize.

She'd hoped to get some time with Barton Harvey since he'd obviously been avoiding her. The swelling in his cheek had diminished but the red had turned a less than attractive shade of blue. Maybe that was why he'd avoided her. He had to know she knew.

As they exited the gym, coat hoods went up and gloves went on. She decided to go for broke. "Mr. Harvey."

He paused. The others kept going. Everyone wanted to get started. Engines roared as vehicle after vehicle rushed from the snowy parking lot.

"I missed you at the inn. I had a question for you."

"We need to catch up with our assigned groups," he groused.

"Valerie Gerard worked for you last summer." Sarah watched his eyes. She had to word her question very carefully or risk giving away her source. "Was she having problems? I understand the two of you had some pretty intense discussions."

His pupils flared. "I've been over this with the chief. Ask him your question."

He turned away. What the hell? "Were the two of you involved?"

Barton Harvey halted. For three beats the snow fell around him and everything else seemed to stop.

Then he walked away, left her standing there without a response.

Whether he knew it or not, he'd just given Sarah his answer. He was definitely hiding something. Something intensely personal . . . to him.

She dashed to the waiting SUV. Mercedes. Black.

Sarah climbed into the back seat with the other two passengers. Loren and Carla somebody.

The ride to Beauchamp Road was silent. The Popes had been given that area since it was their home territory. Judging by the pricey coats the other two were wearing they were from the same exclusive neighborhood.

As they unloaded, Jerald suggested directions for dividing up the area. Loren whatever-his-name-was agreed. He and his wife headed south. In the distance Sarah could see another vehicle doing the same.

"Sarah," Jerald said, "the three of us will take the north end of our sector."

The shore. The water.

The ocean fuels him . . . makes him feel powerful.

"Jerald knows every cave in the area," Lynda explained.

Sarah's gaze settled on Jerald Pope. Rich. Powerful. Lived by the water. Had always lived here. Instinct nudged her. She glanced at his feet, at least a size ten. She had no

plausible reason to consider him more of a suspect than anyone else. Other than the instincts of a kid.

"You're sure you're up to this?" he asked his wife.

She nodded. "I'll be fine." She glanced at Sarah. "I want
to do my part."

Jerald led the way behind his home. The steps carved
from the cliffs would have made going easier had they not
been covered with a fresh blanket of snow.

Lynda's descent was closely monitored by her husband.
Sarah's instincts hummed but she was torn. Part of her
wanted to watch every move Pope made. But the other part
of her, the part that wasn't so certain, kept dragging her attention back to his wife. Lynda looked physically fit. Why
would she not be up to this?

As they reached the shore, Jerald surveyed left then right.
"If we split up, we can work faster. I'll take this side." He
pointed left. "Sarah, why don't you and Lynda take that direction?"

"How far do we go?" Sarah didn't know the area well
enough to comprehend the division of territory. Right now,
focusing on the search was top priority. She could analyze
the Popes an hour from now.

"About two miles." Jerald looked to Lynda. "To the Point.
Sam Drake's team is taking the sector beyond that as well as
the loop that circles the woods."

"We'll meet you back here," Lynda assured him.

Jerald glanced back once as he headed left.

Sarah had to restrain the need to run after him. Was letting him out of her sight a mistake? There was no legitimate
reason to jump to conclusions.

"There are two caves on our side," Lynda explained as
she ushered Sarah to the right. "The Point he mentioned is
the parking area where those who live on the islands"—she
indicated the four small islands that dotted the inlet—"leave
their vehicles to travel by boat out to whichever one they
own."

Sarah nodded, forced herself to focus. She had her flashlight in her bag. She was sure Lynda had one in her bag as well since the chief had gone over the list of items each team needed to ensure they carried.

The walk along the rocky shore was rough going. The snow had melted enough to be treacherous between the rocks since the temperature hovered around thirty-eight degrees. They were very lucky the storm hadn't brought colder air or search efforts would be exceedingly limited.

Sarah kept thinking how devastated Conner's family was. And of Polly's bubbly spirit. If she was out here—Sarah surveyed the foggy shoreline—she would be scared, possibly injured.

Polly would die . . . just like the others . . . if she wasn't found.

Fast.

Sarah didn't want that to happen. An unfamiliar ache rose in her chest. She had to figure this out.

Damned fast.

"The first cave is over here." Lynda pointed to the cliffs. "Access is limited to the first twenty or so feet." She glanced at Sarah. "It's pretty cramped in there."

"Do you want me to go first?"

Lynda shook her head. "I can go first."

As they reached the mouth of the cave, the icy water stood in their path. Only a few inches deep, but without boots that frigid cold was going to suck.

Lynda, realizing the same, glanced at Sarah's Converses. "I think maybe you should stay out here."

"What size do you wear?" Sarah glanced at her waterproof snow boots.

"Seven, but—"

"I wear an eight, but sometimes a seven works." Sarah sat on the closest boulder. "Let me give it a try."

"Eight's Jerri Lynn's size." Lynda tugged off a boot. "Occasionally we can wear the same shoe." She pulled the second one free. "In fact, we both have these boots and sometimes we get them mixed up."

With effort, Sarah pulled the boots on. Snug, but bearable. "This'll work. You stay here and I'll check it out."

"It's been a long time, but I've been in there before," Lynda argued.

"No offense," Sarah insisted, "but your husband seemed worried about you out here. Let me do this. I'm experienced at this sort of thing."

Lynda sighed impatiently but eased down on a big rock of her own. "He worries too much. This isn't the first time my specialist has changed my medication. Jerald frets every time as if it's the end of the world."

Sounded serious to Sarah since she didn't take Jerald Pope as one to worry unnecessarily. Would a man who cared so for his wife and daughter be capable of such heinous murders? Others had. Sarah shook off the thought, turned her full attention on Lynda Pope. "If you don't mind my asking, why do you need medication?"

"It's nothing. Lots of women are affected."

They traded footwear.

"Mitral valve prolapse," Lynda explained. "I was diagnosed a couple of years ago. It's a little more complicated than the usual case. I've been on several different medications over the years, but I'm fine. Really." She tugged on a Converse. "It flares up now and again, particularly if I'm under stress."

Heart condition. Sarah rode out the adrenaline charge, careful not to let the tension show. "What do they give you for that?"

"Last time"—Lynda pulled on the other Converse—"it was propranolol. This time something new." She frowned. "I can't recall the name of it. I just got it two days ago. I haven't even filled the prescription yet." Her gaze collided with Sarah's. "Don't say anything. Jerald would not be pleased if he knew I'd left Bangor without getting it filled."

"Bangor?" Sarah controlled her breathing though her heart rate had sped up.

"That's where I go to see my specialist." Lynda smiled. "Stephen King lives there, you know."

Sarah nodded then stood, couldn't wait to get started. The sooner they covered their sector, the sooner she could find Kale. "You wait here. I'll be back as soon as I've checked things out."

Lynda stood. "No hurry. I'll be waiting."

Sarah resisted the impulse to reach for her cell and call Kale with the news about Lynda Pope's medication. Sarah had to do this right. Polly could be here . . .

As Sarah turned her back, the hair on her neck lifted.

Was she turning her back on a killer?

Or a killer's wife?

CHAPTER 34

Public Safety Office, 9:30 P.M.

Kale was the last to return from the search.

He parked on the street and trudged toward the front entrance.

"Mr. Conner!"

Three reporters, cameramen on their heels, rushed toward him.

He glared at each one. "Don't even think about it."

As he pushed past them, headed for the door, one shouted at his back. "How does it feel to know your sister could be the next victim?"

Kale whipped around, charged up to the guy and decked him.

Shouts accompanied the crowd's withdrawal.

"Come on, Kale."

Two deputies dragged him inside.

"What'd you come that way for?" Charles Collins asked. "You knew they were out there."

Kale glared at the deputy, shook loose of the man's hold. "Leave me alone."

"Sure, man."

Both deputies backed off.

Kale headed for the chief's office. Every damned body in his path stopped and stared.

He didn't want to hear their words of sympathy. He didn't want anything . . . but to find his sister.

In the chief's office, the mayor and the fed were waiting.

The grim expression on the chief's as well as the mayor's face brought him up short.

"What?" He braced. Knew it was bad. Had they found . . .

"Sit down, Kale," the chief suggested.

"Fucking tell me," Kale snapped. It was all he could do not to grab the man and shake the hell out of him.

The fed closed the door.

Kale cut him a lethal look.

"Mr. Conner, you need to sit down." When Kale didn't do as he said, he added, "Now."

Defeat drained the fight out of him. Kale dropped into the nearest chair.

He hadn't had the heart to call his parents before he came here. Because he'd come up empty-handed. They were counting on him to find her.

And he'd failed.

Goddamn it!

"Kale," the mayor began, "Marta Hanover is with your mother and her husband is with your father."

Kale's heart sank into his boots. He blinked to hold back the tears. "What the fuck is it you're telling me?" He looked from the mayor to the chief and back.

Agent August propped himself on the corner of the chief's desk since all the chairs were taken. "At five this evening a dozen roses were delivered to your parents' home, Mr. Conner."

Hours in the cold hadn't numbed him, but that revelation numbed Kale to the marrow of his bones.

"We now believe there is a connection between this delivery and those that came to the . . . others."

The wetness that tracked down Kale's face was the one thing he could feel. Hot, it burned his skin. "Where did they come from?" He didn't ask what the card said because he knew. *Deepest regrets . . .*

"A florist in Bangor. Two days ago, someone left the order in an envelope on the counter, cash enclosed. Unfortunately, the envelope was discarded."

So they couldn't figure out who left it. They couldn't do anything. Kale refused to accept it. "No one saw anyone? No store surveillance? None in the stores nearby maybe caught an entrance or exit?"

"I'm sorry," August said. "There's nothing. Except . . ." The man's gaze bored in Kale's. "Since the order was left to deliver the roses to your parents' home two days ago, we know that your sister was on his list already."

Kale's heart stumbled.

His sister was going to die.

Soon.

Agony twisted his insides as his mind replayed what he'd seen that morning when he and the chief had found Valerie Gerard.

"As if that isn't bad enough," the chief said, his voice lacking any emotion, "Rachel Appleton went and hung herself this morning. She waited until after the boys left for school. Her husband came home for lunch and found her."

Jesus Christ. Kale wanted to scream at God. To demand why he was allowing this to happen.

The door flew open and Sarah burst in.

Deputy Brighton was close behind. "I'm sorry, Chief, I couldn't stop her."

Kale couldn't look at Sarah. He knew what he would see.

Pity. Certainty.

"It's all right, Karen." The chief shook his head. "Just close the door."

Karen did as the chief asked.

Sarah jerked off one of the boots she wore. "Check this against the boot imprint you found at the Appleton murder scene." She yanked off the other one. "They belong to Lynda Pope. She takes propranonol."

"How did you come by these?" August picked up the first boot she'd shed. Studied it, though his face said he'd rather not touch it.

"Doesn't matter," Sarah insisted. "Just do it." She was out of breath as if she'd run a long ways.

For the first time since she'd entered the room she looked at Kale. He couldn't meet her gaze.

While August inspected the boot, the chief said, "Ms. Newton, we have four others here in Youngstown who are currently taking that drug and who knew the . . . girls. We're aware that Ms. Pope is one of them. The others are the Reverend Mahaney and Marta Hanover, Geneva Williams and Loretta Steele. Each of those persons has an airtight alibi for the times the victims went missing. Not to mention one of those five wouldn't be physically capable of carrying out the abduction."

"You've talked to Lynda Pope?" Sarah demanded.

"I talked to her half an hour ago. She'd just arrived home from the search."

Sarah shook her head. "I left her house not more than half an hour ago."

August nodded. "When we arrived she mentioned that her husband was taking you back to the gym." He tapped the boot. "By the way, these aren't a size eight."

"You saw me wearing it, didn't you?" she argued. "You know that sizes can vary."

Kale couldn't take this anymore. He had to do something.

He was on his feet without any idea how he'd gotten there. "I've got to get back out there."

"Now just a minute, son." The chief pushed out of his chair and came around to where Kale stood. "The snow's started falling hard again and the temperature has dropped to well under thirty degrees. You can't go back out there. The best thing you can do is get home and see to your folks."

All the emotions that had drained from Kale suddenly erupted anew. "Are you out of your mind, Chief? I have to find my sister. This bastard is going to . . ." He couldn't say it. Couldn't make his lips form the words.

"Check the boot," Sarah demanded. "I don't give a shit what kind of alibi she has. Check the fucking boot."

Kale couldn't listen to any more of this. He jerked the door open and walked out.

Those same faces, faces he knew, stared at him as he strode to the rear entrance. Voices spoke to him but he didn't listen. He just kept walking.

He had to do something.

He couldn't just go home . . . without his sister.

He pushed out the back door, stormed across the parking lot.

"Kale!"

He didn't slow.

"Kale, goddamn it, stop!"

Sarah grabbed at his left arm, dragged him to a stop.

"Listen to me."

He glared at her. Shook off her touch.

"There's something . . ." She shook her head. "Something about the Popes. I can't explain it. I wasn't even sure what or who it was that kept giving me this feeling until today. Matilda said . . ." Sarah shook her head when he would have butted in, urged him to listen with her eyes. "You have to trust me. I know what I'm talking about. And I'm telling you it's one of them or maybe both."

He almost left her standing there. But the determination on her face . . . in her voice . . . made him hesitate.

The boots . . . his gaze dropped to her feet. She stood there, the snow halfway up to her knees.

Then he remembered she'd pulled the boots off in the chief's office.

She was barefoot except for the socks.

His gaze connected with hers. "You're crazy, Sarah Newton."

"Right now my shrink would probably agree with you."

She was going to get frostbite.

Before his one functioning brain cell kicked in, he acted on instinct.

He scooped her up and headed for his Jeep.

Right now nobody but Sarah seemed to have narrowed down a probable suspect. The others just kept looking for reasons to rule out suspects.

That left Kale with one choice.
Conduct his own interview.
Right after he conducted his own search.
He wasn't a cop.
He didn't need a search warrant.
Or an invitation.

CHAPTER 35

Polly raised her head.

The brush of something soft against the rock whispered in the air. A shoe? Or boot?

Her body froze.

Someone was coming.

Oh, God!

Her mind told her to scream, but her throat wouldn't co-operate.

She was so cold.

Numb.

And alone.

Kale hadn't found her.

The police . . .

She was going to die.

Her head lolled to one side.

Why her?

She wasn't pretty or smart.

She was nobody.

Was it because she talked about the other girls?

A sob choked her.

She whimpered.

The rasp of soles was louder now.

Someone was here.

She lifted her face. Wished she could see.

Maybe she didn't want to see.

Please, please, God, help me. Let someone find me!

The rustle of fabric warned her that whoever was here had crouched next to her.

Fingers twisted in her hair.

She tried to scream. Couldn't.

"The gossip girl."

She shuddered at the cruel voice.

Had to be the devil . . . Matilda had warned her. She'd probably taken off last night to hide like she said she might. That had to be why she hadn't shown up to meet Polly.

A sob tore at her chest. She was going to die.

He put his face close to hers. She tried to draw away. Savage fingers stopped her with a harsh twist.

"You should think before you speak," he whispered close to her ear, the voice barely audible.

The sobs wouldn't stop. She choked and gagged but they just kept coming.

"But," the devil said, "I've decided to give you a second chance."

Quiet! Listen. What was it saying?

"I've decided to trade a gossip for a fraud."

The voice . . . it was . . . male, she was sure of it. A man? No. She trembled. It was the devil.

Oh, God.

"Don't you want that?"

What did he mean? Her body quaked and shuddered. She wanted to run away. To wake up and find out this was just a bad dream.

"You're a very lucky girl, Polly Gossip. A fraud is going to take your place."

He reached between her legs.

She tried to jerk away, tried to scream.

Something ripped.

Her hands were suddenly free from her feet. She tried to work them loose from each other. Couldn't.

"Be a good girl now," he warned.

She stilled. He hauled her to her feet. She stumbled.

Then he was pulling her, one arm wrapped around her

neck. Her feet struggled to keep up but she kept falling against him.

Nausea roiled in her stomach.

Where was he taking her?

What did he mean?

Was he going to kill her now?

She could hear the water.

The waves crashed against the rock.

Air rushed all around her. The gentle spray of something wet hit her face.

She was outside.

Oh, God, she was outside!

Her heart fluttered. She wanted to cry out. She sucked in as much air as she could through her nose. Cold, salty.

Wait.

She inventoried her senses.

Where was he?

The arm was no longer locked around her neck.

She stumbled around, her legs like dead tree trunks.

Her hands shaking, she reached up to her face. Tape across her mouth. Something . . . cloth . . . over her eyes.

She whimpered . . . was afraid any second he would grab her again and tell her that he'd only been joking.

She took hold of the cloth over her eyes with the tips of her fingers and tugged at it. It moved. She pulled it free.

She blinked. Looked around.

The moon peeked from the clouds. The water rushed over the rocks.

Where was he?

She turned all the way around. Didn't see him.

Tears slid down her cheeks. She ripped the tape from her mouth. Cried out at the burn. The sound echoed, reminding her that she was alive.

She stared at her hands. They were taped together with silver tape.

She tried to pull them apart.

The caw of a crow pulled her gaze skyward.

What if he was coming back?

No!

She had to run.

Had to find help.

Her face crumpled with more tears as she stumbled forward.

She had to get home.

Her mom would be worried . . .

She swiped at her eyes and scrambled up the cliffs.

Don't think. Just run.

Run for your life!

CHAPTER 36

Beauchamp Road, midnight

Sarah's cell phone had vibrated at least ten times in the last two hours. She ignored it.

"No one will find the Jeep here."

Kale had taken Sarah to his place where they'd prepared for their own search. Then he'd stopped by his parents' house and gotten a pair of his sister's boots for Sarah to wear. They were a size too large, but they worked.

"You ready?" he asked.

Sarah nodded. "Let's do it."

She and the Popes had searched the shoreline on either side of their house. That left their house, the extensive, rocky shore that separated it from the ocean, and the boathouse.

Getting into the house without getting caught would likely be impossible, but they were prepared for that as well. Sarah would distract the Popes while Kale searched.

Not a perfect plan but not one without some possibility of success.

"Shit." Kale reached into his coat pocket and checked his cell.

Like hers, his had buzzed a number of times. He'd stopped answering the last time the chief called to check on him.

"It's the chief again."

"You know what he wants." He wanted to ensure that Kale wasn't trying anything stupid.

Like this.

Kale stared at the screen of his phone. "He left a voice mail this time."

"Play it." If there was something new they needed to know about, they should be aware before taking this no-turning-back step.

Kale pushed the necessary buttons and set it on speaker.

"Kale, I don't know where you're at—I sent a deputy to your house."

"Great," he muttered.

"You need to come to Bay View Medical Center."

His gaze collided with Sarah's and even in the near darkness she saw the renewed terror.

"Your folks are there with your sister. She's okay, Kale. A little bruised up, but okay."

The words echoed inside the Jeep. Kale didn't move, just stared at her.

"She's okay, Kale," the chief's voice repeated. "He let her go."

Those last four words rang in Sarah's ears.

He let her go.

Public Safety Office, Thursday, March 5, 9:00 A.M.

"Settle down," the chief said. "We've got a lot to cover."

Sarah couldn't sit. She stood by Kale at the door. He, evidently, couldn't sit, either.

Polly was basically unharmed. She had a few scratches and bruises, emotionally she was a mess, but she was alive with no serious physical injuries and that was what mattered. Sarah had spent the last several hours at the hospital with her, Kale, and his family. Sarah had to admit that the community support had been something to see.

The Conner family treated her as if she was one of them. That had felt surreal, still did.

She should be gone by now. But some part of her needed to see how this played out. For Matilda . . . for all involved.

Would anyone in this room pay attention to what Sarah had told them despite the revelations in Polly's statement?

Time to find out.

"As you all know," the chief began, "Polly Conner is, thankfully, safe with her family." A round of applause and cheers broke out across the room. Those closest to Kale gave him a pat on the back or a hug. The chief held up his hands to quiet the ruckus. "We're all happier about that than any words can say."

Sarah was immensely happy, too, but there was a killer still out there. *Get on with it, Chief.*

"Our job now," he finally continued, "is to find this devil before he can grab another of our children."

Devil. The word reverberated through Sarah. Matilda had called the person responsible for the murders the devil. So had Polly, but she'd likely picked that up from Matilda. According to Polly, Matilda was supposed to have met her at the gym last night.

Exactly why they had to get on with this. Another of their children could be missing already. Matilda Calder. Or did no one here consider her one of their own?

"We've learned from Polly that the unknown subject, as Agent August here would call him"—the chief sent a nod of acknowledgment toward the fed—"is definitely male. The unknown subject indicated that he was releasing Polly because he was replacing her with a *fraud*. That means he still has names on his list."

Sarah resisted the impulse to shake her head. The unsub's decision to release Polly wasn't so cut-and-dried. The roses had been delivered. She was supposed to be dead.

Something had changed in the strategy. Did no one see that? Sarah knew killers as well as anyone in this room, better than most. Repeat killers didn't just change their minds and let victims go free. Polly's release was part of the strategy. They just didn't know what part yet.

August stepped forward. Sarah suppressed another urge, this one to roll her eyes. It would be thoroughly uninteresting to hear what he had to say.

"Our unsub is male, as we've confirmed; he's left basically no evidence."

Sarah's mouth gaped. What the hell? What about the boot print or the bleach, not to mention the fucking drugs? She shifted, unable to curb the need.

Kale glanced at her; she kept her attention focused straight ahead. She didn't want to miss a word of what this idiot had to say.

"I believe the minor trace evidence we'd found so far is nothing more than a ruse to keep us guessing."

This was outrageous. She crossed her arms over her chest, hoped like hell August noticed the disbelief written all over her face.

He called off a list of names of those who would begin a second sweep, now that it was daylight, of the area where Polly was found. A villager on his way home from a second-shift job had picked her up on the side of the road. August and the chief were going to reinterview certain persons of interest. Half a dozen other deputies were assigned the task of continuing to screen calls. Hundreds of tips had come in the past couple of days. Devil sightings. Those who'd seen the two dead girls roaming the cliffs. And plenty of others who just wanted to turn in the name of someone they were currently pissed at. The usual. But there was always the chance that something real would come in.

When the chief dismissed the group, Sarah made her way against the tide of those exiting to get to August.

She breached his personal space and demanded, "Are you serious? You're disregarding the evidence and going with this theory?"

He shouldered into his fancy trench coat. "Sarah, the girl said a man abducted her. We don't need to waste time looking for a woman when the evidence to suggest a woman was involved is circumstantial to say the least. And, most likely, is, as I said, a ruse to throw us off his scent."

"Circumstantial?" What the hell? "I gave you the boot. You have the impression of the print found. Are you saying they didn't match? This is no ruse, Lex."

"That imprint was found in a public place. The comparison between the boot you brought in and the imprint taken at the scene is inconclusive. Besides, there's no proof it was made by the unsub. The boots"—he tugged on his gloves—"are a common brand in this area. How many women do you suppose have those boots lying in their mudrooms?"

She wanted to punch the hell out of him. "What about the propranolol?" There were only three women in the immediate area prescribed that drug; one of those just happened to own the boots Sarah had left with August.

"Drugs like that can be ordered on the Internet." August tugged a woolly cap in place. "You know that as well as I do. We're attempting to trace down shipments to this area. Anyone could have ordered it from Mexico or Canada. Again, that may be part of the game. Our unsub may want suspicion cast on someone in particular. Like Lynda Pope. Maybe someone is jealous of her. Have you considered that theory or are you simply going with your gut the way you always do?"

"Damn straight I'm going with my gut." That was the one thing she'd always been able to trust. Sarah understood the number of potential theories here. Absolutely. She also understood perfectly that, just like before, Lex had made his decision and he wasn't changing it.

Unless he was wrong.

Then he'd snag someone else's theory and pretend that was the one he'd really been following all along.

He shook his head but before he could walk away, which was another of his trademark maneuvers, she issued a warning. "Play it your way, Lex. And I'll play it mine."

She didn't give him time to caution her or to threaten to ban her from the investigation. She gave him her back and hit the door.

Sarah had almost made it to the front exit when Kale caught up with her. "What was that about?"

She didn't look at him. "The truth."

With Kale calling her name, she pushed her way out the exit and smack into the middle of the media frenzy outside.

Reporters rushed forward, as far as the barricade the chief had ordered erected would allow.

Several shouted her name.

"What have the police learned from Polly Conner?"

Sarah ignored the guy shouting the question and scanned the group for the lady who'd gotten in her face the other night. Blond Barbie. She pointed to her. "You!" Then she crooked her finger.

Blond Barbie plowed her way through the throng.

Silence blanketed the assembly, microphones extended, cameras rolled.

"Whatever you hear from the others today, mark my word," Sarah said in a loud, clear voice, "the person responsible for these two tragic murders is female. She's out there and she's not finished yet. So keep your daughters at home. Don't let them out of your sight."

She elbowed her way through the reporters, ignoring the other questions shouted at her. She'd made it across the street to her car when a vehicle skidded to a stop not two feet away.

"Get in."

She swung around, glared at Kale. "I'm happy as hell your sister is safe," Sarah said, not about to take any crap from him, either, "but they're wrong. Polly's alive because someone wants us to look in a certain direction. And the hell of it is, it's working." Her revelation to the reporters would let *him* know that it wasn't working, at least as far as Sarah was concerned.

Then Kale Conner did the last thing she would have expected. He climbed out of his car, grabbed her around the waist, and basically tossed her into his Jeep. He thrust his torso through the open door, blocking her escape.

"Scoot over."

Briefly she considered ramming the vehicle into drive and leaving him standing there. But she hated to leave him in the path of all those reporters headed their way.

"Now," he growled.

And he wasn't the enemy. So she climbed over the console, ensuring her butt missed the gearshift.

He slid behind the wheel and barreled away before the crowd of reporters could completely surround his vehicle.

"Are you out of your mind?" he demanded.

"Maybe."

She snapped her seat belt into place and was more than a little thankful that the streets in the area were kept plowed and sanded regularly. With the way he was driving, he would be a danger to anyone in his path otherwise.

"You can't be certain it's a woman."

"They can't be certain it's a man."

"Polly said—"

"Give it a rest, Conner. I know what she said."

"August is right about the boot print, it could have belonged to anyone. The comparison was inconclusive."

Sarah banged her head against the headrest. "Okay, so the boot is circumstantial. Let's throw in the propranolol."

"She has an alibi," Kale countered, "and we can't connect her to the roses. The ones delivered to my parents' home were ordered at a shop in Bangor two days before she went missing."

Bangor? *I just got it two days ago. Jerald would not be pleased if he knew I'd left Bangor without getting it filled.*

"That's where she goes to the doctor."

Kale glanced at Sarah. "What?"

"Lynda Pope. She told me she goes to see a specialist in Bangor. When we were searching for your sister, she mentioned that she'd gotten a new prescription just two days before from her doctor in Bangor."

Kale stared straight ahead. Kept driving.

"Admit it," she demanded. "That's too many coincidences to be circumstantial."

"August has to know that's where her doctor is. They tracked down her prescription."

"Forget it!" It was like talking to a brick wall!

"Is it August?"

She turned to face him. "What?"

He braked for a stop and set those dark eyes on her. "Are you certain there isn't still something between the two of you? Is that why he has to be wrong? You need that conflict to prove something?"

She reached for the door handle. "I don't have to listen to this."

He punched the accelerator, earning a couple of horn blares for the move. "I'm not letting you out of my sight."

Her cell phone vibrated. She started to ignore it but decided that she'd rather ignore him. "Newton."

"So now you've pissed off the FBI."

Her editor. "I don't have time for this, Tae." Had he seen the news clip already?

"Your former favorite fed called me."

Well, that answered that question.

"He threatened to have his director on my back if I didn't get you under control."

"Oh, yeah?" If he was about to insist she come back to New York, he could save his breath.

"Oh, yeah," Tae echoed. "I told him he could forget about it. I don't take orders from him or his director."

Sarah smiled. "I'll try to stay out of his way."

"That would make life simpler."

Yeah, yeah, she knew.

"I'd tell you to keep me updated on the changing situation but I guess I'll have to count on Fox News for that."

She promised to do better and ended the call.

"Is there still something between you and August?"

That Kale had the audacity to repeat the question made her want to slug him.

"The only thing between Lex August and me is animosity."

"What exactly did he do?" Kale shrugged. "Besides being a complete asshole, I mean."

"He screwed up a case. Got an innocent man killed and then used my conclusions on the case as his own to cover his ass."

How could she have ever been that stupid? That fucking blind?

"You're not . . ." Kale began, "still in love with him?"

He didn't just ask that question? "Take me to the inn." She wasn't even responding to that ludicrous question.

"Is that a no?"

Fury blasted her nerve endings. "That's the mother of all nos, Conner."

"Good."

Good? Obviously he was suffering from some sort of post-traumatic stress syndrome over his sister's abduction. He damned sure wasn't making any sense.

"Is it okay if I stop by my office first?" He arrowed her a sidelong glance. "Unless you're pissed at me for asking such personal questions and want me out of your sight like right this minute."

Whatever. "Why not?" What else was she going to do? The cops wouldn't listen to her. Idiots.

She needed to think. To figure out a new strategy. One that would prove her theory. Anticipation filtered past her frustration. She'd made that announcement to the press; that should seriously piss off the killer. All she needed was to watch for the reaction.

Conner and Sons was a block off the harbor, in a back alley. The entrance was tucked between the rear exits of two restaurants. His office was bigger than Sarah had expected.

A young woman, one who looked around the same age as Kale, sat behind the reception desk. "Hey, Kale, I didn't expect to see you today." She smiled a big, shiny-lipped smile. Her eyes went huge with admiration.

He had himself an admirer. Something along the lines of jealousy pricked Sarah. She refused to acknowledge it.

Anyway, the receptionist looked like perfect wife material.

That Sarah's mouth automatically formed a frown at the thought irritated her all the more.

"Christine, this is Sarah Newton."

"Oh, yeah." Christine stuck out her hand. "I saw you on the news a few minutes ago. You look so young on TV."

Sarah gave her hand a quick shake. Opted to take the comment as a compliment. "Thanks."

"I just have to check on a couple of things and I'm off."

Christine gave Kale a big puppy-dog look. "I'm so thankful Polly's okay. I had everyone I know praying so hard."

"Thanks. We appreciate that."

Sarah followed him to his office. "I'm surprised she hasn't hooked and reeled you in already."

He pushed the door shut. "What?"

Sarah jerked her head toward the door. "Christine. She's clearly mad about you."

Kale laughed as he riffled through his messages. "Sure."

Did he not see it? Whatever. Not her business.

As she scanned the numerous photos of him and his father and their crew hanging on the walls, an idea occurred to her. "You could take me for a ride in one of your boats." The inspiration gained momentum even as she spoke.

"If you want. It's pretty damned chilly out there, though."

From the water they should be able to see every cave close to the Pope property, as well as the boathouse and the main house. "I want." She reached for the door. "Hurry up."

"You mean now?"

She nodded. "There's a murderer out there, in case you've forgotten. I want to study the shoreline for any caves we might have missed." She would tell him what she really wanted to do once they were in the water.

He tossed his messages onto his desk. "The chief made me promise I'd keep you out of trouble."

Nothing she hadn't expected. "What's the problem? I just want a tour of the shoreline from the water."

"You will tell me what you're really up to before you actually do it, right?" Those dark eyes nailed hers.

She faked a smile. "You have my word."

After that Sarah wanted to stop by Matilda's house and find out if her mother had seen her. As certain as Sarah was that Matilda was extremely capable of taking care of herself, probably had been doing it her whole life, she still worried about the kid.

Right now Sarah had to see which domino was going to fall.

11:30 A.M.

"So no one comes out here in the winter?"

"Hardly ever. The owner is a summer resident."

They'd decided to stop by Matilda's house first and gotten nothing from her no-good mother. Then Kale had taken Sarah on a tour of the shoreline from one end of the village city limits to the other. He'd pointed out the caves and assured her that each one had been searched. The one where Polly had been held was marked as a crime scene and techs and deputies were still milling about. Sarah had waited patiently through the tour before revealing her true agenda to Kale.

The small island they'd docked at provided the perfect view of the waterfront side of the Pope property.

Sarah reached for her binoculars then dropped her bag onto the porch. She studied the house, zeroing in on each massive window, one at a time.

The family appeared to be home. No company. No evidence that they were packing for a hasty retreat.

Could Lynda Pope carry such a burning hatred that she would kill two innocent young women? Was her husband helping her? Or was he the killer and hoped to point suspicion in her direction? What was the motive? Sure, envy drove people to commit heinous acts at times. But these were people who had it all. Was the thrill gone now? Was this an attempt at infusing excitement into their lives and relationship? Or was getting even for the few things their one beloved offspring hadn't attained in life the goal? Maybe he just wanted rid of his wife.

Matilda had a feeling about him . . . but did that carry any real significance?

Sarah couldn't prove anything. It was just a hunch. A gut instinct that the people inside that house were somehow responsible for the murders.

"You know," Kale said, moving up behind her, "once I knew my sister was safe, I had this overwhelming craving." He fit his body snugly against Sarah's backside.

She lowered the binoculars, her senses instantly going into a whole new zone. His pelvis nestled firmly against her lower back. Even with the fullness of her coat separating them she could feel how hard he was. Her nostrils flared with a sharp intake of breath.

"You're distracting me," she said, her voice, already husky with lust, reflecting just how much.

"Oh, yeah?"

"Yeah."

He leaned down, nipped her earlobe with his teeth.

She shivered. "For chocolate or ice cream or something like that?"

His gloves hit the floor, then his hands slid around to rest on her hips. "No. Not that kind of craving." One of those wicked hands reached up and took her binoculars, set them carefully on the wide railing that encircled the porch.

"I see." She breathed the words.

He pushed up her coat, slipped loose the button of her jeans and slowly lowered the zipper. Another of those delicious shivers rippled through her. He stripped the jeans and panties down her hips, then guided her into a forward lean.

Sarah braced her hands on the railing, closed her eyes as he traced the seam of her ass with deft fingers. A gasp hissed past her lips.

The metal-on-metal scrape of his zipper sent her pulse into an erratic rhythm. The rip of foil assured her he took the necessary precautions.

Then the tip of his penis nudged her. Her body pulsed with anticipation and she pushed away all other thoughts.

He guided himself using those magic fingers, teasing her clit as he worked that hard tip inside her. Her fingers tightened on the railing as he drove fully inside. Her muscles clenched around him. He groaned.

"That's it . . ." He made a pleasurable sound as he slid back and forth, back and forth. "What I was craving."

She spread her feet wider apart, arched her butt to give him deeper access. The friction was driving her crazy . . . that he stretched her so tight never ceased to be a pleasant surprise. He was big . . . big and hard.

With the distance from civilization there was no one to fear seeing or overhearing them. She let herself go.

"Harder," she ordered.

He accommodated her demand.

She cried out . . . felt that building, building sensation, felt her body go taut . . . until the pleasure burst inside her, leaving her panting, hot, wet, and wanting more.

He leaned over her, his throbbing cock still deep inside her, and pressed hard against that spot that made her squirm. "More?" he whispered in her ear.

Was he crazy? "Yes." She moaned. She wanted him over and over until he lost his mind just like she had already.

He straightened, burrowed deeper. She reached up, put her arms around his head and pulled his face to hers. He kissed her, slowly, matching the tiny in and out movements. A little deeper, a little more. She screamed in his mouth. Came hard.

He stopped. Every fucking muscle in her body vibrated with the sensations. Her breasts ached. She moved his hands there so that he could rub them. She pressed his palms with hers, making him caress her more firmly.

He growled with the effort of holding back. She took control, sinking back against him, easing him deeper into her. The rush was amazing, had her gasping for breath . . . and building toward a third orgasm.

He roared with his own plunge toward release. She teased him, grinding, rocking her hips, and he still held back his full, thick length.

She had to have all of him. Pushing away the last of her

reservations, she leaned forward, braced herself, and spread her legs wide apart.

He went in all the way.

They cried out together.

He thrust once, twice more, and then he came hard and fast.

She went on her toes with the impact of her third orgasm.

He held her that way, nestled deep inside her.

Even then, she couldn't resist lifting her gaze to the house across the water.

The truth was there . . . she was certain.

CHAPTER 37

2313 *Beauchamp Road*, 1:00 P.M.

Jerald turned up the volume on the plasma hanging above the fireplace. He instinctively moved toward it as the local news on the hour recapped the latest events. Sarah Newton's image flashed on the screen, a microphone stuck in her face.

"The person responsible for these two tragic murders is female. She's out there and she's not finished yet."

He moved his head side to side. Sarah Newton refused to give up. Part of him couldn't help respecting her doggedness. She would not relinquish until she had the truth.

That admirable trait presented quite the dilemma.

"Daddy."

He turned to find Jerri Lynn standing on the other side of the room watching him, her parka and boots evidence she had only just returned home.

She shook her head, her eyes wide with something akin to shock.

He moved toward her. Wanted to explain that what he'd done was for her benefit.

She backed away. "What have you done?"

Before he could respond, her mother entered the room. "What's going on?" She looked from Jerald to the television screen where more images and comments regarding the ongoing investigation eclipsed the killing storms in the South and the unrelenting floods in the West.

Jerri Lynn ran from the room. Lynda stared after her.

When the clomp of her boots on the stairs had faded, his wife walked quickly to where Jerald stood.

"Jerald, I don't know what she's up to but something very strange is going on around here." She glanced toward the hall to ensure their daughter was still out of hearing range. "We should have sent her away to school. There's . . ." Lynda shook her head, fell silent.

He refused to admit that she was all too correct. That would be pointless now. There were more pressing problems. "What's wrong now, Lynda?"

Her troubled gaze lit with a hint of anger. "You always take her side. She's done nothing but widen the gap between us." Lynda clutched his sweater sleeve. "We need time for us, Jerald. Just the two of us. I can't live like this any longer." Desperation replaced the fury. "I want things to be the way they used to be . . . when we shared everything. Before any of the things . . . that went wrong."

He tensed, reclaimed the calm that he rarely allowed to slip. He knew all too well exactly what she meant. But that was in the past. There was no need to go back there. The pressing matter now was their daughter. "What is it you feel is so strange?"

Again Lynda glanced in the direction of the stairs. "Some of my medication is missing."

His tension escalated. "Your heart medication?" Of course that was what she meant. His wife took no other medication.

She nodded. "And this afternoon I was looking for my other snow boots and I found a knife hidden beneath my Louis Vuitton bag. It was wrapped in one of my scarves." Lynda leaned closer to him and whispered. "Jerald, it was covered in blood. I don't know what's going on . . . but I'm very frightened."

Careful. Don't react. "What did you do with this knife?"

She swallowed hard, the effort visible along the slender column of her throat. "I hid it in the mudroom."

"Show me."

As they moved down the hall toward the kitchen, Lynda paused to ensure Jerri Lynn was nowhere in sight. Music abruptly blared. Her music. She was in her room. Clearly relieved, Lynda took his hand and led the way as if he was unsure of the route. In the mudroom, she lifted the lid to the woodbox and reached inside. She handed him the item wrapped in the silk scarf.

He cautiously unwrapped the knife. Scarlet smeared its shiny blade.

Fear tinged his blood.

There was only one thing he could do now.

He wrapped the scarf around the stained knife once more and tucked it into a canvas bag he used for trips to the market. Setting the bag aside, he reached for his coat. "I'll be back soon."

Lynda's eyes searched his but she did not ask the question he saw burning in hers.

There was nothing to say. He knew what he had to do.

The drive to Bangor took forty-five minutes. Jerald stopped at the gate and entered the necessary code. When the gate slid out of the way, he rolled through the entrance.

River City Storage. The most secure storage facility in all of Bangor. State-of-the-art climate control. Twenty-four-hour monitoring with full-service maintenance.

He parked in his reserved slot and entered the building, which required yet another code. Three layers of security, including biometrics.

Inside, he took the elevator to the sixth floor.

Both sides of the corridor were lined with double entry doors. Each set of doors marked with a number.

Jerald stopped in front of the double doors marked with the number 6.

He entered the code he'd personally selected, 666, then pressed the pad of his thumb to the scanner. The door released, allowing him access to the unit he leased.

Closing the door, he ensured the internal lock was set, then he turned to face his demons.

The clothes he'd worn, from the shoes to the masks, for each encounter were carefully stored in sealed garment bags. The instruments he had used in each of those encounters were packed in their special case, locked and stored on the shelf above the hanging garment bags.

Across the width of the back of the unit was the vault that was absolutely essential to his needs.

Slowly, one determined step at a time, he crossed to that vault. Stored inside were twenty items, each item carefully preserved and labeled.

He had promised himself that when his daughter was born he would stop. No matter how much the weakness haunted him. No matter how intensely he missed the incredible pleasure. He would stop. There was no choice.

Jerald despised those, like Matilda Calder's whore of a mother, who continued to serve their own selfish weaknesses as if they were gods to be worshipped. When the choice was made to bring a child into the world, those weaknesses had to be overcome. No matter the sacrifice.

That child was the only reason he hadn't killed that selfish bitch when she'd tempted him.

His entire life *before,* he had searched for the one thing he had felt missing inside him. *Heart.* When his daughter was born, he'd found that the organ he'd thought nonexistent all those years indeed was present. He'd experienced emotions he'd never known existed prior to that wondrous day.

From that moment forward, his life had been complete.

As challenging as overcoming his own vile weakness had been, he had mastered it. Had never looked back.

Until now.

She had inherited that weakness.

There was no question. No way to deny the reality.

He had no choice.

The only remaining question was the how to save her.

Conviction filled him.

He knew how.

Sarah Newton.

CHAPTER 38

Living Word Church, 4:00 P.M.

Deborah watched her husband kneeling before the crucifix. He prayed so diligently. And yet, no relief had come.

Their worst fears had been realized.

Chief Willard had called. He and that FBI agent would be arriving within the hour to speak to Christopher a third time.

The chief had held a press conference and announced that the Conner girl had identified the suspect as a male.

Now the authorities were going to take a closer look at all male persons of interest.

That was what they considered Christopher.

A person of interest.

Deborah had waited for days now. Prayed and watched unwaveringly for a sign.

Today that sign had appeared.

She had dozed off in her chair and awakened suddenly to find the sun shining through the living room windows. The play of light on the worn wood floors had danced before her eyes. For long minutes she had watched this simple production of nature. A spider had crawled into the open, drawn by the warmth from the sun.

At that same moment Tamara had entered the room. Believing her aunt to be asleep and seeing the spider creeping ever closer, the child rushed across the room, snatched up a magazine from the coffee table and smashed the spider. She had looked up, thinking that the noise had awakened her aunt, smiled and said, "That was a close one."

Deborah had known as she peered into the sweet face of her niece that she could wait no longer.

Despite her gnarled fingers and aching joints, the good Lord had given her a sharp mind.

When danger crept close . . . He expected her to do what needed to be done without delay.

Today.

CHAPTER 39

The Overlook Inn, 5:00 P.M.

A stack of messages in hand, Sarah unlocked the door to her room and let herself in. She shut the door, sagged against it and closed her eyes.

What was she thinking getting involved with him?

This was definitely involved.

Not just sex.

Her body hummed with desire at the mere thought of him.

Not good. Not good at all.

It was a flat-out miracle she'd managed to get away from him long enough to take a shower. He'd insisted that she have dinner with him and his family that night.

If Sarah had half a brain left she would be out of here before then.

Like that was going to happen. She would finish this.

She'd watched the Pope home for hours. The only movement was when Jerri Lynn arrived. And a tow truck. Evidently there had been trouble with the girl's SUV. In case the vehicle was being towed for some purpose that would remove evidence, Sarah had noted the name of the towing company. She'd tried calling the number painted on the vehicle, but she'd gotten an answering machine.

Maybe twenty minutes later she noticed Jerald Pope leaving in his Infiniti. She'd wished like hell she'd been a position to follow him, but she and Kale had been in a boat. By the time they'd gotten back to his Jeep, Pope would have been long gone.

Sarah tossed the messages on her bed, dropped her bag, and headed for the bathroom. Twisting the old knobs, she set the water flow and temperature in the tub. She crossed back to the dresser and scrounged for clothes. She was down to her last clean jeans and panties. The sweatshirt would have to do since everything else was in need of laundering.

Staying this long hadn't been anticipated. But she couldn't leave until it was done. Tonight she would resume her surveillance.

She trudged back to the bathroom and stepped into the shower. The hot water soothed her aching muscles. She was sore in places she'd never been sore before. Her nipples instantly hardened as images and sensations from the trip to the island sifted through her.

Shutting off the water, she climbed out of the tub and grabbed a towel. The fluffy rug tickled her toes. Drying her skin quickly, she reached for the complimentary hair dryer next. When her hair was dry, she swiped on antiperspirant and got dressed.

There was nothing she could do to convince August or Willard of her conclusions on the investigation so that left her with only one choice. Watch her suspects herself.

Lynda and Jerald Pope.

After sliding clean, dry socks onto her feet, Sarah tugged on her Converses. She wondered if Lynda Pope had considered if she would get her boots back when she had Sarah's only shoes delivered to the inn. Sarah had rushed away from the Pope home after the search for Polly before Lynda could ask for her boots or suggest Sarah take her Converses.

If Sarah was right, Lynda wouldn't be needing them anyway.

She stood, grabbed her coat and bag, and headed for the door.

A white envelope lay on the floor next to her door. It definitely hadn't been there when she'd arrived. Sarah bent down and picked it up. Her name was penned across the front in flowing letters.

She dropped her bag and coat to tear the envelope open.

More of those flowing letters streamed across the single, folded page.

> *Hey Sarah,*
> *Sorry I had to go without saying bye, but I couldn't stay. I've always known he was here. I could feel him like a second heartbeat echoing my own. He is marked with 666. Maybe you won't believe me, but please be careful. He's watching you. He uses people sometimes as an angel of light to mislead. Be careful. And wear the necklace. He's very, very close.*

> *Matilda*

Sarah tugged on her coat and shoved the letter into the pocket. The devil, 666. She shook her head. Mixed-up kid.

But damned good at sizing up people. Her instincts were on target even if her beliefs were missing the mark.

A hard-knock life would do that to a person. Make them grow up fast and be wise beyond their years.

That's all it was.

Sarah got in her rental car and headed to the Chapel of the Innocents. In case the area was still considered an official crime scene, she planned to approach from the opposite end of the road. She would stop a good distance away, out of view of anyone who might be monitoring the area, and cut through the woods. Her goal was to reach that ridge overlooking the Pope house.

Since it wasn't quite dark yet, she found the far end of Chapel Trail where it intersected with another narrow road without any difficulty. She grabbed her bag and emerged from the car. Careful to make only minimal sound when she closed the door, she headed into the woods. Snow topped her shoes and, as usual, crowded up her pants legs.

She stayed east, with the sun setting behind her.

By the time she reached her destination it was almost dark. Following her tracks back out wouldn't be a problem. She had her trusty flashlight.

She adjusted her binoculars and scoped out the house. The lights were blazing inside. Perfect.

Her phone vibrated.

Ignoring it crossed her mind, but if another girl had gone missing, she needed to know. She pulled out her phone, checked the screen. *Blocked call.*

Her shrink had never stooped to that level. Neither had her editor.

She flipped it open. "Newton."

A moment of silence elapsed.

"Newton," she repeated, annoyed.

"Sarah Newton," the voice said.

Male, she decided, though it was distorted, almost garbled.

"That's me, asshole. What's up?"

"You're a fraud."

The dead air that followed the statement told her the call had ended even before she checked the screen.

She shoved the phone back into her pocket. She'd been called worse. Just in case, she felt her other pocket to ensure the pepper spray was there.

Focusing back on the house, she spotted Jerri Lynn on the sofa watching television. As Sarah watched, Lynda entered the room and asked her daughter something.

The two argued. Big gestures. Lots of agitation.

"Hmmm."

Obviously neither of them had been her caller. The Infiniti was back in the driveway. So, where was Jerald?

Snow crunched.

She froze.

A split second before she reached for the pepper spray, a hand went over her mouth and nose. An arm banded around her waist. She kicked. Punched. Thrashed. The hand pressed harder against her face . . . there was a cloth in his palm.

Fight!

But her struggles were futile. Her arms grew too heavy to fling. Her legs too leaden to propel.

That was when she noticed the strange smell . . . and how the world suddenly went dark.

CHAPTER 40

9:00 P.M.

Kale said his good-nights to his folks and headed home. Polly was home and a celebratory dinner had been in order.

The only thing that could have possibly made the evening better would have been if Sarah had come.

He'd called her repeatedly and gotten her voice mail. She'd obviously needed some alone time.

As hard as he tried he couldn't keep her off his mind.

His body tightened each time he thought of sex with her.

The kind of connection they shared took a certain level of trust. There was definitely something happening between them.

For a decade he had focused completely on his family's needs, the needs of the business. He had ignored his personal life. Had resented it . . . to some degree. But he'd understood his responsibilities and he had never allowed anyone or anything to get in his way. He'd dated, but never anyone looking for a husband.

He'd watched most of his Youngstown High School graduating class go off to make their marks in the world. And he had stayed behind. Being the good son, the good brother. Not until Sarah Newton arrived had he stopped to think just how much he'd given up.

She'd made him see what he'd denied all those years.

He could never go back. His life needed to be his own once more. His brother had one more year of college and then he would be finished. Jamison could take over the business for a few years. Kale was going to take his turn at life. He hadn't made the announcement to the family yet. But he would.

He owed this new clarity to Sarah.

And he wanted her to be a part of his reclaimed future.

Maybe that was too much to expect . . . but he could dream.

For the first time in ten years, he could dream.

He parked in front of his house and considered that he'd been neglecting Angie. Maybe he'd take her for a run tonight. With all that had happened, food and water and a quick trip to the yard was all the attention she'd gotten lately.

He climbed the steps fumbling for the keys to his door. Leaving the light on would have been a good thing. But that had been the least of his worries recently.

At the door he shoved the key into the lock and would have turned it had he not noticed something out of place a few feet away.

Leaning against the wall was a rectangular white box with a silver ribbon wrapped around it. He picked it up, confusion nagging at his brow. Had to be a mistake.

No card.

He pulled the ribbon loose and opened the box.

A single, long-stemmed red rose lay amid the white tissue paper.

A small white card was tucked next to the rose. He picked it up.

Deepest regrets . . .

He dropped the box. Stared at the card.

The card fluttered from his trembling fingers. He'd just left his parents' house and Polly was fine. He called to check just in case. Then he called Sarah's cell again. No answer. He called the inn. No answer in her room.

Fear knotted deep in his gut.

He ran back to his Jeep and drove as fast as he dared to the inn.

He banged on the door. No answer.

Taking the stairs two at a time, he rushed back to his Jeep. Raced down that winding road. Slammed on the brakes at the stop sign and sat there for a minute.

Where the hell would she go?

The Popes.

He headed for Calderwood Lane.

If something had happened to her . . . it was his fault. He shouldn't have let her out of his sight. He'd known she wouldn't just turn off the need to find the truth until tomorrow.

His heart was in his throat by the time he reached Chapel Trail. A mile past the chapel turnoff he found her car. He climbed out, checked the vehicle. Empty. The hood was cold. It had been parked for some time. It was too dark to figure out which way she had gone from here.

But the Pope home was just on the other side of the woods and his money was on that direction.

This was something he knew better than to try and do alone.

He pulled out his cell and put in a call to the chief.

"Chief, we have a situation."

By the time Kale finished explaining, the chief was already in his truck headed that way.

Kale didn't have to wait long.

The chief stopped his truck on the road in front of Sarah's car and got out. He left the engine running and the lights on. "Still no sign of her?"

Kale shook his head. "I've called her cell phone five or six times. Still no answer. I called the inn again. She's not there. I even called Stanley's gas station to see if she'd called in for assistance. Nothing."

If she'd needed help, she would have called Kale.

Chief Willard stared at her car then turned and gazed toward the chapel. "She could be anywhere."

"I want to talk to the Popes," Kale insisted. "She's convinced Mrs. Pope is involved in all this somehow. If we don't get anywhere with them, we'll have to start a search."

"Guess so."

Kale wanted to shake the man. He seemed distracted. This wasn't the time.

"Come on." The chief started toward his truck. "I'll drive."

Kale worked hard to keep his emotions in check. He just kept seeing those images from the two murder scenes. If something like that happened to her . . .

God, he couldn't even think about it.

"Now listen to me, Kale." The chief put his truck in park in front of the Pope residence and turned off the headlights. "You let me do the talking, you hear?"

"I understand." He'd say anything at this point to get the man in action.

Kale followed the chief to the front door. He pushed the doorbell and they waited.

Another push and movement inside the house told them that someone was coming.

Jerald Pope opened the door, looked from the chief to Kale and back.

"Evening, Jerald," the chief said. "I'm sorry to bother you so late but we're trying to locate Ms. Newton."

Confusion furrowed the other man's brow. "Was she planning to come here?"

The chief shook his head. "We found her car over by the chapel. Looks like she broke down. We thought she might have walked over here for help."

Jerald shook his head. "I'm sorry, gentlemen, but we haven't had any visitors this evening."

"Well, if you hear or see anything," the chief said, "you let us know."

"Certainly."

Before he could close the door, Kale braced his hand against it. "One more thing, Mr. Pope."

Beside him, Kale felt the chief tense.

Pope looked at Kale expectantly.

"Is your wife home?"

Pope nodded. "Did you need to speak with her? Jerri Lynn's here as well."

"Have they been home all evening?"

Pope's confusion shifted to annoyance now. "They have, indeed. Is there more going on here than I know about?"

"No. No," the chief assured. "We're just checking out every possibility. Good night, Jerald."

Jerald Pope bade them a good night and closed his door.

He was lying. Kale was no body language expert, but he knew the man was lying. Sarah's certainty about the Popes was all the certainty Kale needed.

The chief drove Kale to his Jeep. "We'll go back to the office and get a search party started."

He sounded tired. But no matter how tired he was, he couldn't waste time.

"You know Ms. Newton is wrong about the Popes."

"Maybe not, Chief." Kale told him about Lynda Pope's trip to Bangor the same day the flowers delivered to his parents' home had been ordered.

Willard heaved a big breath. "Kale, I'm about to tell you something that only two other people in this whole world know."

Kale wanted to get the search party started, but the chief's tone sounded so ominous he was afraid not to listen.

"Twenty years ago I made a mistake."

Kale silently urged him to hurry.

"I'd been married about fifteen years and things were . . ." He shrugged. "In a rut, so to speak."

Kale had no idea what this had to do with anything. "Chief—"

"Bear with me, son. This has relevance you'll understand in a minute."

Kale summoned a little more patience.

"I had myself an affair."

Had he heard right? The chief had an affair? "Who?" Kale hadn't meant to ask the question, but there it was.

"It doesn't really matter who."

Kale nodded, not daring to ask again.

"The morning I discovered those two bodies," the chief went on, "I didn't get any anonymous call. I came out here to meet my lover."

The chief had lied?

"What happened?" Kale's pulse beat faster.

"She was waiting in her car down by the road. We rushed up to the chapel for privacy. We liked going there. Early in the morning like that we didn't have to worry about being bothered."

"And you found the bodies."

The chief nodded, his face grim. "For a few minutes we were both in shock. Two poor girls lying there with blood everywhere . . . gaping holes in their chests. We were just sick. Stumbling around. She was crying. Hell, she was hysterical. I was torn all to pieces. But I was a cop. I had a job to do."

"What did you do?"

"I sent her home and I covered our tracks. But first, I called your father and asked him to say he'd had coffee with me that morning. I needed an alibi . . . just in case. Peter questioned me." The chief shook his head. "I couldn't tell him the truth and involve him, too. I finally confessed I'd been seeing someone and . . ." He sighed. "Peter hasn't spoken to me since."

At least now Kale knew the answer to that ancient question. But that didn't matter now. What mattered was finding Sarah. "Chief—"

"I couldn't let anyone find out," the chief said, cutting him off. "I still loved my wife. I had two kids. I couldn't risk my job." He blew out another of those burdened breaths. "So I tampered with evidence. There were footprints. But in order to conceal her presence—we'd made one hell of a mess stumbling around—I had to make a mess of the snow around the bodies and the tracks leading up to the chapel."

Damn. "You made a mistake."

"I did. But there's one thing that was certain, Kale." He looked Kale straight in the eyes. "They were men's footprints. At least a size ten and a half or eleven. The person who'd been there before us was no woman. It was definitely a man."

Kale didn't know what to say to that. Polly had said the voice was male. The chief insisted the murderer twenty years ago was a male. "But you said there was no connection between what happened twenty years ago and now."

The chief heaved another of those labored breaths. "Do you really believe what we saw that morning was the work of a woman?"

Kale just didn't know. All he knew was that they had to find Sarah.

Before it was too late.

CHAPTER 41

Find me!

Sarah's eyes tried to open.

Something got in the way.

She reached up to wipe her eyes . . . something slick covered them.

Adrenaline rushed through her.

The arm holding her, the hand over her mouth and nose . . . the strange smell.

She tried to sit up . . . couldn't do it.

Her heart thumped hard.

Fraud.

She ordered her mind to be quiet!

I've decided to trade a gossip for a fraud.

Polly Conner had sobbed through the statement. Someone else was going to take her place.

A fraud.

Sarah Newton . . . you're a fraud.

The fight-or-flight instinct detonated inside her.

Be still, she ordered.

Assess the situation.

Pictures of mutilated bodies filed one after the other through her head like an out-of-control slide projector.

Her hands and feet were bound . . . separately. There was . . . tape over her mouth and eyes.

She felt groggy . . . there had been a cloth or pad in his hand. It must have been loaded with some sort of inhalant.

How long had she been unconscious?

Focus. Get up. Get loose. Get the hell out of here.

She braced her right elbow on the hard ground. Pushed with all her might.

Her sluggish body eased upward.

She maneuvered into a sitting position. Pulled her knees up to brace herself.

Her fingers touched the tape on her eyes. She found the edge and pulled.

A scream blasted into her mouth with the sting to her eyelids.

She blinked. Dark.

The tape on her mouth was next. She peeled it off. Grimaced.

Looking around again, she still couldn't see. She drew in a deep breath but her olfactory senses weren't in proper working order yet.

Wherever she was, she was cold as hell. Her body shivered.

She twisted her hands. Tape around her wrists.

What about her ankles?

Okay, think!

Listen carefully for sound while working on the tape around your ankles.

Her fingers went to work on the tape around her ankles.

It took forever . . .

Finally her feet were free.

She scrambled up to a standing position. Tried to run. Fell flat on her face.

The coppery taste of blood filled her mouth.

Shit.

Busted lip.

She scooted up onto her knees, took it slow standing up. Waited a minute to find her equilibrium.

One step at a time she felt her way around her prison.

Rock walls. Rock floor. Cold. Damp. She inhaled deeply. Musty or . . . water. It smelled like stagnant water.

Cave.

She was in a cave.

Her brain urged her feet to run, but she resisted.

She had to run the right way or risk getting completely lost.

She stumbled.

Hit the ground, knees first.

Her knees throbbed.

Calming herself, she felt around to see what she'd fallen over. Soft. Lumpy.

A bag.

She fumbled for an opening.

Her hands dove inside.

The familiar contents sent another adrenaline surge rushing through her veins.

Her bag.

She felt for the flashlight . . . found her cell phone.

Her pulse reacted, catapulted with hope.

Okay, okay, you need the light to get the fuck out of here.

She found the light, clasped it as well as the phone in her hands. She pushed to her feet. Using her thumb, she turned on the flashlight.

Her eyes squinted against the light.

When her vision had adjusted, she looked around.

Something shiny on the ground.

She walked closer.

Her breath stalled in her lungs.

Knife. Bloody.

An alarm roared in her head.

Don't panic. Don't touch the knife. Evidence.

But what if . . .

Fuck it.

Run.

Using the flashlight she stumbled around until she could hear the surf. She followed the sound, it got louder and louder.

Suddenly she was outside . . . on the rocky shore. Water pooled around her ankles.

The moon peeked from behind the clouds.

She didn't recognize the area . . . didn't see any of the islands.

Don't stand here like an idiot!

She started running. Didn't matter which way.

Up the cliffs . . . there were trees up there . . . probably a road somewhere.

She climbed, letting the moonlight guide her . . . fell repeatedly. Didn't stop until she reached the tree line.

Use the phone.

Her cell phone and flashlight were still clutched in her bound hands. She dropped the light, worked the phone into position where she could flip it open. The screen didn't light up . . .

"Son of a bitch!"

The battery was dead.

She dropped it, picked up her flashlight, and headed into the woods.

There had to be a road or a house . . . or something.

She would find help.

On cue her body shuddered.

If she didn't freeze to death first.

CHAPTER 42

Public Safety Office, Friday, March 6, 5:50 A.M.

It was almost daybreak.

Kale paced the lobby. They'd called off the search two hours ago to wait for daylight.

He'd raised hell when the chief first mentioned taking a break to wait for the sun to come up. But, like him, the deputies participating in the search were half frozen.

It was the right thing to do . . . but he couldn't bear the thought of Sarah being out there in the cold . . . or worse . . .

Being tortured.

The chief was already reorganizing the groups, laying out the new search grid.

Kale needed him to work faster. He needed the sun to fucking come up.

Agent August strolled past him, hands shoved deep into his trouser pockets. He glanced at Kale. "She's a survivor, you know."

Kale gritted his teeth. He didn't want to hear anything this prick had to say.

"Two years ago she had a little meltdown." August studied Kale's face as he spoke, analyzing, concluding. "A total mental break, they say. She spent seven days in a padded room. But she came back. She'll come back from this."

Kale hadn't intended to, but he blinked. The burn of emotion wouldn't be assuaged any other way. He didn't know if anything this asshole said was true . . . but he knew that Sarah had to be the strongest woman he'd ever met. Who wouldn't have a meltdown considering the kind of work she did and how invested she got? Or if you considered her childhood.

August smirked and shook his head. "You shouldn't get so hung up on her. She'll go when the investigation is wrapped up and you'll be left here wondering what the hell happened."

Kale took a swing at him. The bastard dodged in the nick of time.

"Conner!"

Hands held him back.

August just laughed.

Kale wanted to kill him.

The front entrance doors burst open. "I need some help over here!"

All eyes swung to the door.

Jimmy Tate, Sarah leaning against him, stumbled into the lobby.

Kale's heart swelled. He rushed to her.

"Sarah! Are you all right?"

She blinked. Stared at him, her pupils wide.

Shit! He lifted her into his arms.

She was freezing.

Where the hell was her coat?

"We need to warm her up!" Kale shouted to anyone listening.

People started clambering around him.

"Let me go." Sarah struggled against his hold.

"We need to get her to a hospital," Kale said to the chief.

"No." She struggled some more. "I'm all right. Put me down."

He had no choice but to do as she said or risk dropping her. She staggered. He steadied her.

She searched the faces until she found the chief's. "I can take you to where I was held."

Kale shook his head. "First, we go to the hospital."

"Listen to her," August urged. "If she needed immediate medical attention, she would tell you."

Sarah pushed away from Kale. Glowered at August. "Chief,"—she looked directly at him—"take me now before my memory is muddled with other influences."

"Where'd you find her?" the chief asked Tate.

"I was on my way to work," Jimmy told him. "Found her way down on 52. She was trying to climb outta the ditch. It's a miracle I saw her. She'd about frozen to death. I wanted to take her to the ER but she made me bring her here."

"Why the hell didn't you call?" Kale demanded.

"I don't have no cell phone," Jimmy growled. "She wouldn't let me stop nowhere. She wanted to come straight here."

"We're wasting time," Sarah argued, her voice quivery and weak.

Kale jerked off his coat and wrapped it around her. She shuddered. Damn it! She needed medical attention. He didn't care what she or anyone else said.

"Get the lady some coffee," the chief shouted. "And let's take her where she wants to go."

After a few wrong turns in the woods, they found the location where Sarah had dropped her cell phone.

Sarah pointed to the shore. "Down there."

Kale didn't want her to go back down there but there was no stopping her. Now that she had some caffeine in her veins she was taking no orders from him. Or anyone else.

At the mouth of the cave, the chief halted the progress. "Agent August, you, Kale, and Ms. Newton come with me." He surveyed the rest of the group as they ambled closer. "Karen, you call the State Police and tell them to get their lab techs down here. And call Billy Jackson and let him know we're out here."

This cave wasn't technically in Youngstown town limits, so the local police needed to be contacted.

The chief glanced at Kale. "Let's see what we've got here."

Sarah led the way.

The powerful flashlight beams bounced around the dark interior. Kale spotted the bag she carried everywhere. He started to reach for it.

"Don't touch nothing," the chief reminded.

"Over here, Chief," August shouted.

Kale stayed close to Sarah. The agent's flashlight was focused on an object on the ground.

Silver glinted . . . big-ass knife . . . bloody.

The chief studied it a moment, then surveyed the area around it.

A piece of white cloth lay on the ground nearby. Small, empty tubes that had once held glue. A partial roll of duct tape. Empty food containers. A woman's shoe. And eyeglasses.

All kinds of evidence.

Anticipation burned inside Kale.

'Bout fucking time.

They were going to get this bastard.

CHAPTER 43

2312 *Beauchamp Road,* 11:00 A.M.

Jerald watched the security monitor in his study as the police cruisers braked to sudden stops in front of his home. Five, no seven deputies spilled out of the vehicles and formed a perimeter around his home. Chief Willard and Special Agent Lex August approached his front door.

He'd expected them hours ago.

Some things took time, he supposed.

When he'd gotten his passport years ago he'd had to provide his thumbprint. It should have been an easy process with the federal agent's assistance to match the prints on the evidence to him.

Apparently they had taken the route of caution, not wanting to jump the gun and risk double-jeopardy complications.

Understandable.

The doorbell sang its greeting, echoing through the house. He had ensured his wife and daughter were away this morning.

That made things simpler.

Less traumatic for all involved.

His primary goal was to ensure they were both protected.

No matter the cost.

Enjoying a final look at the home he had so lovingly designed himself, he took his time arriving at the front door.

At least now he had no reason to worry about the carpal tunnel surgery. His hands would no longer be of any use to him.

When he opened the door, Chief Willard stepped forward. Jerald was surprised his service revolver remained holstered.

"Good morning, Chief." He glanced at the agent. "Agent August. How can I help you this morning?"

"Jerald, I have a warrant here to search your property." Willard held the official document in his hand. "We'll need your full cooperation."

Jerald stepped back, opened the door wide. "Be my guest."

He got a glimpse of Sarah Newton waiting near one of the police cruisers. He smiled, gave her a nod.

Perhaps she didn't know it yet, but this was a game she could not win.

CHAPTER 44

Deborah watched, transfixed, as Jerald Pope was escorted, hands cuffed behind his back, into the Youngstown Public Safety Office.

She blinked, returned her attention to the reporter touting the breaking news.

"More to come in this gruesome story. For now, according to Chief Willard of the Youngstown police, after discovering overwhelming evidence early this morning, master boat builder Jerald Pope has been arrested for the murders of Valerie Gerard and Alicia Appleton. Back to you, Scott."

The reporter's image was replaced on the screen by her colleague's back at the station. He wore a grim face for the camera. "Thank you, Marcia. That news comes from Youngstown, where it appears a frantic investigation into the disappearance and murder of two young women is finally coming to an end."

Deborah turned from the television, shock settling over her. She walked numbly to the kitchen and picked up the prescription bottle. She stared at the few remaining tablets inside.

What had she done?

Fear slithered around her throat and tightened like a noose.

She rushed to the window and gazed out at the church

where Christopher was working on the upcoming Sunday's sermon. Soon he would grow sleepy and eventually lose consciousness.

Think rationally, she told herself.

There were two options.

She could call 911 and stop this now before it was too late. But then she would likely go to prison for the rest of her life. Christopher would understand and forgive her as she had forgiven him, but the rest of the world would not be so forgiving.

The other option, if chosen, would play out as set in motion, leaving her and Tamara well provided for, financially. Their futures would be assured. The chances of the police discovering the truth were minimal. The insurance was more than adequate for their current and future needs.

But Deborah knew her Father in heaven would know.

And He would not forgive her.

As much as she had no desire to spend the rest of her life in prison, she had a greater desire not to spend eternity in Hell.

Deborah reached for the phone.

The Overlook Inn, 12:15 P.M.

Barton stared at the television set.

Was it possible?

Was the nightmare finally over?

If an arrest had been made, the investigation would end.

He looked heavenward and repeated a mantra of thanks.

Sweet Jesus, was it really over?

But Jerald Pope? Incredible.

Barton hurried into his private office and unlocked his desk. He grabbed the plastic bag in the bottom drawer and removed the bane of his existence from it. Now that the danger had passed, he had to decide what to do with it.

Destroy it once and for all.

He'd kept it all these years . . . just in case he needed to prove that he'd found the journal and learned of the secret inside. But now, that was no longer necessary.

Perhaps he would burn it . . . or bury it with his father when he eventually passed.

No waiting. He would act today.

Since he'd only just cleaned out the fireplace, his wife would be suspicious if he started a fire before evening. No, that wouldn't work.

Bury it. Yes. He would bury it. Time and the elements would destroy the filthy pages. They would decompose and return to the earth where they belonged.

He had a minor yard task or two. Some of the landscape lighting needed repairs. His wife would think nothing of him doing those chores. But just to be safe, he would wait until she was away from the inn. She had errands. Perhaps he would insist she do them this afternoon.

A relieved sigh whispered past his lips.

He didn't have to worry about the police anymore. Or that annoying Sarah Newton. Lucky for her. He'd racked his brain coming up with a plan to scare her away. That business was no longer necessary.

Finally, he could rest easy again.

CHAPTER 45

Until he could be transported to the county jail, Jerald Pope was being held in the conference room. Two deputies were stationed in the room with him, another two outside the office.

Every single piece of evidence they had found was lined up in a neat little row.

The shoe had belonged to Alicia, the glasses to Valerie. The knife and the other items had been covered in Pope's fingerprints and both victims' blood.

Too neat.

Sarah stood outside the rear entrance, wishing again she had a cigarette.

Her instincts still leaned toward a female perpetrator. But, of course, no one wanted to hear that. They had their murderer. Sarah, herself, had been forced to admit that it was a man who called her cell phone and then snatched her.

Of course it was a man. He was covering for someone. His wife or his daughter? Sarah's every instinct insisted that was the case.

Didn't anyone consider it a little strange that the first two victims were murdered and the last two escaped unharmed?

This was utter and complete bullshit.

She jerked the door open and went back inside.

"Hey, I was looking for you."

She met Kale's worried gaze. "Are you sure you're okay?"

If he asked her that one more time . . .

"I'm fine. Just . . ." Why bother even saying anything to him? He was like the others. He wanted this case over.

"Come in here." He pulled her into the closest office and closed the door. "Talk to me."

What was the point?

"Come on, Sarah, say what's on your mind."

"Don't you find this all too easy?" She turned her hands up. "The neatly placed evidence. The fact that Polly and I escaped when the other two didn't. Think about that."

"Sarah." Kale leveled a weary gaze on hers. "You can't seriously think he's innocent after what they found in that storage unit in Bangor."

Yeah, yeah. She knew. Twenty perfectly preserved human hearts. "Yes," she agreed, "he's a sick monster who obviously killed a whole hell of a lot of people, including the two young women from twenty years ago. I just don't think he killed Valerie and Alicia."

The federal authorities were assuming jurisdiction over that aspect of the Pope case. Which was no surprise. August was probably in the men's room whacking off right now in celebration of the huge case he'd cracked.

"Sarah," Kale said patiently, "why would he accept responsibility for these two murders? Why would he let himself be caught? No one was ever going to catch him. Don't you see that what you're proposing is a little crazy?"

Crazy. Possibly.

"Why would he do that?" Kale asked.

"To cover for someone else. Think about that. That's not crazy. That's anything but crazy." She paced the small room. "The murders were motivated by envy. That's a very female motivation. The boot print, the propranolol, the roses. None of it is even remotely consistent with his previous MO."

"August asked him about that," Kale argued. "He said he'd quit killing a long time ago, but the temptation overwhelmed him and he had to kill again. He changed his MO to try and make it look as if someone else committed the murders. He didn't say a woman, but that could have been his ultimate intent."

Sarah wasn't buying it.

"What blows me away," Kale went on, "is that he had all that stuff, the tools he used to kill those people, the clothes he wore—all of it—right there in the storage unit. That's sick."

666.

The code for his storage unit.

He's the devil.

. . . he uses people sometimes as an angel of light to mislead . . .

The unexplained pieces fell into place and suddenly it all made sense to Sarah. Jesus . . . Matilda was right.

"I have to talk to him."

"Whoa." Kale took her by the shoulders and made her look at him. "You know they're not going to let you do that."

Sarah knew what she had to do. "Yes they will."

She waited for Kale to step out of the way; the instant he did she was out the door. She hunted down August.

"I need to speak with you." He looked at her, as did Chief Willard. "Privately."

When he didn't readily agree, she gave him a look that warned of severe consequences.

"Give us a moment," August said to Willard.

Kale stood in the corridor watching as Willard exited his office. Sarah didn't have time to placate him. She closed the door and turned on August. "I want to talk to Pope."

August smirked. "No way. You know how this works, Sarah. We're not going to do anything that might weaken or somehow damage our case. He's off limits."

"You either let me talk to him or I'll go outside right now and tell all those reporters how bad you fucked up three and a half years ago." There wasn't a day went by that she didn't remember.

"What would that accomplish?" He tried to pretend she was suggesting an impotent reprisal.

"You made a mistake. You leaked the information about that suspect *after* I warned you that he was innocent. You ignored me and the facts I presented and, because you did, he was murdered."

August's expression hardened. "But we got the bad guy in the end."

"Yeah," she confirmed, her jaw tightening, "the bad guy I urged you to consider before anyone innocent was murdered." She laughed. "Then you took credit for my conclusions."

He scrubbed a hand over his jaw. "All right. All right. I'll give you a minute or two with him." He shook his finger in her face. "But don't fuck this up just to get back at me."

She made a sound of disbelief. "Are you kidding? That's your MO not mine."

His glare intensified. "This thing between us is done now. You talk to Pope and then we're even."

She nodded. "Absolutely."

August jerked the door open and cut a path through the people crowding the corridor.

"What was that about?" Kale asked.

Sarah paused, looked into his eyes. "Just trust me." Then she followed the route August had taken.

When she reached the conference room door, he was ready to let her in. "Remember what I said."

"Yeah, yeah."

He opened the door and she went inside. "Step outside, gentlemen," August said to the deputies.

They looked at each other then at Sarah, but they didn't argue.

Before the door closed Sarah heard Kale demand, "What the hell are you doing?"

August would handle him . . . for now.

"Sarah." Pope smiled. "I would stand but—" He pulled at his wrists which were handcuffed to the chair arms.

She dismissed his apology with a wave of her hand, then settled into the chair directly across from him. "I have a few questions for you. Just to satisfy my own curiosity."

He inclined his head, analyzed her. Looking for the lie, as she so often did. "How can I know that you're not recording this conversation?"

She stood, peeled off her sweatshirt, and turned all the way around. "No wires." When she'd faced him once more, she pulled the sweatshirt back on. "Do I need to take off my pants, too?"

A grin lifted one corner of his mouth. "Not necessary. Oddly, I trust you."

"I'll bet you do." She eased back down in the chair.

For a moment they stared at each other, both analyzing.

"How did you manage to kill so many without ever getting caught?" That was a hell of a record. Seemed like a good way to get him talking while at the same time lowering his guard.

"I traveled a lot then. All over the country." His expression grew distant as he contemplated his past. "I always chose my victim while I was away. Never anyone close to home. And I planned extensively to lessen the likelihood of making a mistake."

Anyone in the business of murder had to admire a man so precise. "Your victims were random?" With that many murders involving the same MO, one would think the feds would have noticed a connection. Typically when a pattern emerged, comparisons were done among the various jurisdictions.

"Oh, no, you know better than that. A serial killer is never truly random. There is always a distinctly similar motive driven by his compulsion."

She had known he would understand what he was. "So, how did you choose them?"

"I needed to satisfy the urge, but I didn't want to eliminate anyone who contributed to society. You never know when someone might turn out to be the one who invents the cure for cancer or who turns around global warming."

She got it now. "So you selected those who were a burden to society rather than vice versa. Prostitutes, thugs, et cetera."

He nodded. "Very good, Sarah. You understand me quite well."

"When did you know you were a serial killer?"

"Aha. The million-dollar question." He drew in a deep breath. "When I was perhaps seventeen, I began to feel the compulsion to cause pain. It was controllable then. By the time I was nineteen, it kept me from sleeping, haunted my nights ruthlessly."

"Is that when you started to kill?"

He shook his head. "No, I conquered the demon by spending endless hours planning. I didn't start killing until a full year later. I decided that if I was going to kill, I would plan the perfect murder." His lips widened into that charming smile again. "And I did, repeatedly, for the next eighteen years."

"I'll bet you had a schedule, too."

"Absolutely. I was allowed one kill per year." He paused. "I'm sure you've already calculated and understand that eighteen years of killing is not twenty."

"I wondered if perhaps the two extra murders were the two young women found at the chapel twenty years ago."

"Those two were a rather unfortunate necessity."

Sarah didn't know whether to be surprised or not that he'd just openly admitted to having killed those two women. "I thought you never killed close to home."

"Never. But I didn't choose them. They were an unforeseen complication."

"How's that?"

"To that point, I had been somewhat careless in storing my memorabilia. I had designed a special storeroom beneath the water at my boathouse. Those two drunken revelers had gotten lost that night. They'd docked at my boathouse and taken refuge inside. When I discovered them early the next morning, they had passed out but it was obvious they had found the entrance to the storeroom. One had even attempted to pick the lock. I couldn't take the risk that one or both would speak of the strange hidden door they had found."

"So you killed them, using no particular MO, and left their bodies to be discovered in a public place."

"Precisely. Such careless mutilation was not my style. But I couldn't resist taking their hearts."

"That's why you moved everything to the storage unit," she suggested. "I suppose even a serial killer has to do housekeeping from time to time."

He smiled. "Yes. There were things I needed to get in order. It was unfortunate that two lives had to be sacrificed as a result."

Unfortunate, yes. Sarah wondered if this man, this being, even had a heart. "Is the number 666 indicative of how you feel about yourself?" That was certainly no coincidence.

He laughed softly. "Don't doubt my understanding of who and what I am, Sarah. Though I have tried to be a good father and husband, deep down I have always fully comprehended what I am. I chose that code as a sort of irony. So many worry about the devil taking their souls and holding them prisoner in hell. Isn't that what I've done?"

She could see the irony, yes.

"After twenty years," she redirected, "what awakened the demon?" Two decades of meticulous control and then the man who planned every detail so carefully suddenly gets sloppy? No way.

"The first temptation came in the form of that whore on West Street."

"Matilda's mother?" Sarah tensed. Was this what Matilda had been talking about?

"A few years ago she attempted to seduce me in a public place and then blackmail me." He made a disparaging sound. "It didn't work, of course." His gaze locked with Sarah's. "She has no idea how close she came to being a victim of someone besides herself."

"But you resisted," Sarah suggested.

"For the child's sake." Jerald shook his head. "In hindsight, perhaps the child would have been better off if I had acted on the impulse."

Sarah studied him a long moment. "If that was a few years ago, why kill again now? Who pissed you off this time?"

"I believe we've reached the end of constructive conversation, Sarah."

His expression closed as surely as if he'd pulled the blinds or locked a door.

"You're afraid to talk about it," she challenged. "Afraid I'll figure out the truth."

He leaned forward as far as his constraints would allow. "I know what you're afraid of, Sarah Newton."

Tension stiffened her. "How would you know anything about me?"

"I know everything about you. From your humble, gruesome childhood to your boring college days and everything in between and after. Most information about one's life, every little secret, is easily attained with the proper incentive."

Fury roared through her. "You're right," she agreed. "I do believe we've reached the end of constructive conversation."

She pushed up from her chair and started for the door.

"Don't worry, Sarah."

She paused, looked back at him. "What would I be worried about?"

"You're not a killer."

"That's right," she tossed back. "I'm not. But you are."

"Exactly my point. There's one thing a natural-born killer knows and that's another killer."

"I appreciate your vote of confidence." She reached for the door.

"You think about it often."

Enough. But some tiny little seed of doubt wouldn't let her walk away without hearing him out.

No . . . wait.

. . . one with the misfortune of being born to parents who kill, could, in fact, become a killer simply by virtue of DNA.

He'd said those words to her. Sarah recalled distinctly

that tense conversation. And now she knew exactly what he'd been saying. "You're worried about your daughter."

The flare of surprise in his eyes told her she'd nailed his deepest, darkest fear.

"Why would I worry about Jerri Lynn?" He schooled his expression. "She's the perfect daughter. An honor student. She's never been in trouble in her life."

A triumphant smile slid across Sarah's face. Now she understood. "You're afraid she's like you."

Something dark and sinister lit his eyes then. "Perhaps you're mistaking your own fears with mine. Whether or not you will inherit your mother's penchant for killing is something *you* think about often."

He struck that nerve, unerringly. "Perhaps," she confessed. "As any offspring of a killer would."

"There are conflicting theories regarding the DNA issue, as you well know," he rebutted, unwilling for her to have the last word. "But there is one sure way to be certain of yourself."

Don't let him see you sweat. Don't even ask what he means.

She should let it go . . . move on. But there was more here.

The truth.

"I know you want to ask how."

She could say no, but he would recognize the lie. "Say what you have to say, Pope. I have things to do."

He smiled, believing he'd won. "Yes, of course. As I was saying, the test is simple. The next time you're in a tight spot, see where instinct guides you. If the first instinct is to kill, then you may have a problem on your hands."

"Is that why you're here," she challenged. "Because your daughter failed the test?"

Pope's jaw tightened. "I would do anything to protect my daughter, that's true."

As any parent would. That was his point. "What about your wife?" Might as well cover both possibilities.

Just when Sarah was certain she couldn't be surprised

any further by the man, he did just that. Sadness settled over his face.

How could a killer feel such a broad range of genuine emotions?

"We're finished here." Pope looked away from her.

Sarah had gotten all she was going to from him.

She exited the room.

Besides, her creep meter had topped out.

"Satisfied?" August wanted to know.

"Yeah. He's all yours." Even if you don't have the right killer.

She was out of here.

If these people were too stupid to see the facts, then tough shit.

She found her coat and bag near the dispatcher's desk and headed for the rear exit.

Kale waited for her outside. Or maybe he'd been out there for his own purposes. Whatever. He was currently in her path.

"What was that all about?"

She took a breath. "That was about confirming my conclusions. Jerald Pope did not kill Valerie or Alicia."

"Did he say that?"

"No. But it's the truth. When someone else goes missing, you and your friends will figure it out. I'm out of here."

She walked past him.

"Just like that."

She hesitated. Shook her head. This was why she never got tangled up in relationships. Not since that one stupid mistake.

"I guess this thing between you and August is still there."

And there was the jealousy card. Perfect. He was a guy, what did she expect? He would rather assume she was still hung up on another guy than to believe for a second that she could simply live without him.

Sarah turned around. "You see, Conner, this is why I don't do relationships. They're messy and one person always wants it more than the other."

Those dark, dark eyes reached deep into hers, maybe deeper than anyone had gone before. "You don't want to know where this"—he gestured to her then to himself—"can go?"

She thought of how it felt to be with him, so damned intense. And of his family who had that whole Disney Channel thing going on, something she'd never had. So tempting . . . but what if it wasn't real?

She wasn't setting herself up for that kind of letdown.

"Good-bye, Conner. It's been . . . real." For the first time she meant that in the truest sense of the word. Real. But too big a gamble to dare to depend on.

He didn't try to stop her.

She was glad.

The emotions that choked off her ability to breathe would pass.

By the time she reached the inn she'd just about given up on avoiding the tears.

Damn it.

She would have gone inside but something in the backyard lured her attention there. Barton, the innkeeper, was digging . . . or burying something near a cluster of bushes. He patted the dirt with his shovel, chunked a little snow on top of it, and then strode off to the barn.

Strange man.

She went inside and packed her stuff. Dropped her key at the unmanned registration desk and headed for her car. She had no idea where everyone was. More importantly, she no longer cared. She was out of here.

Outside she groaned. Nightfall had awakened the fog. It had risen in full force. Great.

That wasn't stopping her.

Her suitcase was in the trunk before she remembered she had to get a receipt. Tae would raise hell if she came back, again, without a receipt.

But if there was no one in there, she couldn't get a receipt. Maybe the innkeeper was back at his post by now.

She'd almost made it to the door. Through the window she could see Barton Harvey behind the desk.

It was dark. Not to mention it was foggy as hell.

She should leave.

There was a flight at nine. She could make it.

But then she'd never know what the innkeeper had been up to. She'd recognized that he had something to hide since she'd gotten here. It was more than his dislike of her. It was probably that strange incident between him and Valerie Gerard. And definitely his weird behavior. Not to mention his wife's overprotectiveness.

What would it hurt to check it out? If the family's goldfish had croaked, she'd soon know. But if he was burying something else out there . . . she'd know that, too.

She would check to see what the digging was about and then she'd get her receipt and go. No big deal.

Maybe he'd found a dead rat or something and had decided to dispose of it. Or maybe he'd planted seeds. But that didn't explain him dumping snow on the spot.

Her curiosity wouldn't be put off. She made sure he was still behind his desk and she hurried around the corner of the inn. Once she stepped about ten feet from the building, the landscaping lights no longer illuminated the darkness. Even if he looked out now, he wouldn't see her. It was completely dark over in those bushes. The moon was hiding behind the clouds. She was wearing black.

Go for it.

It was probably nothing. Maybe she just wanted to get back at old Barton for being such a dick the whole time she was here. Served him right. Maybe he'd buried his stash of *Hustler* magazines.

She knelt against the rocks bordering the cluster of bushes and dug out her flashlight. She wasn't about to reach in there without looking first. After confirming the location of the recently disturbed earth and snow, she tucked her flashlight between her knees. She glanced back at the inn, noted that Harvey was still behind his desk, his back turned to the window.

Do it. She turned on the flashlight and aimed its beam on the spot; hopefully, her body would block most of the light.

Her fingers dug into the cold soil. She had to be out of her mind to do this.

Maybe she was crazy. Most people wherever she went ended up thinking so.

It really didn't matter what kind of secrets the innkeeper had. Hell, it could be that dead rat she'd already considered. But that old familiar story instinct just wouldn't let it go. Maybe she would—

Her fingers encountered a texture different from that of the dirt. Hard. She adjusted the beam of light.

A book?

A journal.

She opened it. Shook off the page. Boldly scrawled handwriting filled page after page.

A date at the top of one page caught her eye. February tenth, twenty years ago. A diary?

That packing sound that loose snow made when compressed by a footfall whispered against her eardrums.

She froze.

Sarah heard the thwack before she felt the pain.

The blast erupted in the back of her head.

Lights burst in her retinas.

Then nothing.

CHAPTER 46

7:00 P.M.

Kale wasn't letting her leave like this.

He wasn't giving up that easily.

He parked next to her car. She was still here. Anticipation wired him.

He still had a chance.

As he jogged across the parking lot another vehicle arrived. He recognized it. Mrs. Harvey. She and her kids climbed out, grocery sacks in hand.

Inside, he glanced at the reservation desk. Deserted. He bounded up the stairs. Her door was closed. He banged on it. No answer.

"Sarah!"

Still no answer. He tried the knob. Locked.

He started to bang again and a scream stopped him.

He bolted for the stairs. Took them two at a time.

The lobby was still empty.

"Dad!"

Brady's voice. Kale followed the sound through the kitchen and to the mudroom.

Barton Harvey lay on the floor, blood pooled around his head. Bags of groceries had spilled around his motionless body. Brady was on his knees next to his father. Mrs. Harvey and her daughter were holding each other, sobbing.

"What happened?" Kale dropped to the floor next to

Brady and checked Mr. Harvey's carotid pulse. Faint, but there.

"I don't know." Brady shook his father. "We just found him this way."

"Call nine-one-one," Kale instructed. He started to lean down to inspect the man's wound when something registered in the corner of his eye.

Black. Bag.

Sarah's bag lay on the floor near the door to the garage.

Terror ignited in his chest. Even as Brady spoke to the operator, Kale hit the speed-dial number on his cell for the chief.

Kale swallowed back the panic. He had to reach the chief. He had to let him know this wasn't over.

CHAPTER 47

Sarah's eyes opened and her head exploded with pain.

She groaned. Shut her eyes tight.

What the hell?

She tried to move. Her arms and legs wouldn't cooperate.

Cold. Whatever she was lying on was cold as hell.

Another cave?

Shit.

She tried to think how she'd gotten here.

A shuffling sound echoed around her.

Sarah tensed.

Someone was coming.

She ordered her body to move.

Didn't happen. She wasn't restrained. But her body felt so heavy.

Whoever was coming was close.

She squeezed her eyes shut and held her breath.

Don't move. Don't breathe.

Hands landed on her shoulder. She tried not to tense. Play dead.

"Ms. Newton?"

Recognition flared. She opened her eyes, tried to see in the dark.

A click followed by a blinding light hit her face.

"Thank God."

Sarah blinked. "Chief Willard?"

"Come on. Let me get you out of here."

Disbelief or maybe just plain old relief kept her gaze glued to him.

"Take it easy," he said as he helped her to her feet.

"How . . . how did you find me?" Her body shuddered and shook from the cold. The world spun with each move she made.

"Let's not worry about that right now," the chief urged. "Let's just get you out of here. This has to stop now."

A piercing wail rent the air.

The chief froze.

Sarah sagged against him.

The flashlight's beam moved about before hitting legs running toward them.

What the hell?

The impact caused the chief to grunt and stagger back. The flashlight clattered onto the rocks.

Without his support Sarah crumpled to the ground. Her head spun wildly.

"I told you not to interfere," the voice scolded as the chief collapsed into a heap.

The glow from the flashlight's beam highlighted the knife protruding from his chest.

Sarah blinked. The chief was . . . stabbed. Shit. She needed to get out of here.

Couldn't manage the strength. Her arms shook when she tried to push up to a sitting position.

A blow to her abdomen made her gag.

"Get up!"

She tried to identify the voice but her brain wasn't working right somehow. Definitely female.

"I said get up!"

Another slam into her gut.

Sarah gagged, coughed. Then pushed herself into a sitting position. She looked around, the world tilted. The pain in her skull screamed.

"You almost ruined everything," the cruel voice taunted. "You and that fool." She moved to lean over the chief.

Grunted with the effort of tugging the knife from his chest. "He should have listened to me and let me finish this. All he had to do was cover any mistakes I made. Fool."

Sarah couldn't see her face . . . but she now recognized the voice.

She moved from the chief's motionless body to where Sarah lay. She stared down in disgust. "Bitch," she snarled.

Sarah stared up at Lynda Pope who clutched that big knife in her hands.

"Why'd you kill the chief?" Sarah swallowed back the taste of bile. "He was on your side . . ." Something Sarah had missed. She'd just thought the chief was too stubborn to listen to her.

"Don't worry about him," she snapped. "You have bigger problems." She waved the knife in Sarah's face.

Oh, well, Sarah mused. The story of her life.

Despite the pain, Sarah did what she always did, she questioned. "You should've been thankful your husband took the fall for you. You could have gotten off scot-free. No one suspected he wasn't the killer except me, and I was leaving."

"You are so stupid."

Her foot connected with Sarah's rib cage. This time she puked.

Great.

Sarah raised a shaky hand to wipe her mouth. Her equilibrium wouldn't find its footing. Her stomach roiled. She knew the symptoms. Concussion.

Fucking great.

"That was the plan," Lynda scoffed. "Those self-serving little bitches would die, all the evidence would point to Jerri Lynn." She laughed, an evil, grating sound. "I knew Jerald would try to save her. All I had to do was strike once more after that and ensure Jerri Lynn looked guilty. With her father in custody, there would be no escape. You were actually a great help to me. If only that idiot hadn't jumped the gun." Lynda kicked the chief's motionless body. "Now things are . . . complicated."

Since he didn't even grunt, Sarah assumed he was dead.
Or well on his way. Damn.

"How're you going to explain this?" she prompted. Keep
her talking. Form a plan.

"I have a new plan," Lynda explained in that condescend-
ing tone she had mastered. "Poor Jerri Lynn was so distraught over her father's arrest. I tried to reason with her but
she wouldn't listen. She blamed the entire situation on you.
She ran from the house ranting madly. Of course, I called
Ben and told him. He rushed to save you and, well, you both
lost in the end. And Jerri Lynn just couldn't live without her
father so she came home and took a whole bottle of my
medication. When I discovered her and tried to wake her,
she, of course, was dead, too."

"There's this thing," Sarah decided to mention, "called
divorce. You couldn't take that route?"

"I loved him." She sighed. "I waited so long for him to
choose me over her, but he never did. I gave him opportunity
after opportunity. Until I'd had enough." Lynda laughed.
"Then all I wanted was for him to suffer. He forced me to
bring that selfish brat into the world and I wanted him to
know the pain of losing her. With them both out of the way,
everything is mine."

Damn, what kind of mother hated her child that much?

"How did he force you to have a child?" Sarah had to
get this spinning-room problem under control so she could
make a run for it . . . or defend herself somehow. The longer she could keep Lynda distracted, the more time she
had to pull herself together.

Lynda sighed again. "He was gone all the time. I never
saw him. So I found myself a distraction." She gestured to
the chief. "He wore a uniform, carried a gun, it was fun . . .
for a while. It didn't mean anything. But Jerald got suspicious and started pressing the issue of a child. For a while I
put him off, but then, when those two girls were murdered
and left at our regular meeting place, Ben and I decided we
were better off as friends. I knew Jerald had figured it out. I
knew it was a warning."

"Took you long enough to figure out a plan," Sarah muttered. "What were you afraid of?" Had Lynda known Jerald was a killer? If so, that made her one sick bitch.

Lynda reached down, grabbed a handful of Sarah's hair and gave her head a shake. "You know who my husband is! I had to wait for the perfect time. When she was old enough . . . when all the circumstances were perfect. Otherwise I'd be dead!"

Sarah gave her head a moment to stop exploding in agony. "Good point," she agreed, biting back the groan of pain. So she was a sick bitch.

Lynda crouched down to Sarah's eye level. "After the Enfinger development came to town, people started talking about the curse. I knew the time had come. I began my role. I made Jerald think I was afraid of our daughter. That she was somehow trying to hurt me or to frame me. It worked like a charm. He was so convinced he took her SUV away the other day. She came home to find a tow truck waiting to haul it to storage. Imagine the poor child's surprise. How could daddy be so cruel?" She said the last in a high-pitched whine.

Sarah thought about that a moment. "Your husband is a very smart man. I can't believe he would be fooled so easily."

"No more talking." Lynda shoved a small plastic container at Sarah. "Take these."

Sarah reached out, took the container. Prescription bottle. She couldn't read the label without more light. "What is this?"

"Don't you know?"

Propranolol. Panic flared in Sarah's stomach.

"Now, take them," Lynda ordered. "All of them."

Sarah's mind frantically searched for a way to keep her talking or to somehow get out of this . . . but she couldn't think.

"Do it!" Lynda positioned the tip of the knife against the side of Sarah's neck.

It would take time for the pills to enter her bloodstream.

Maybe if she went along the bitch would get overconfident and . . .

Sarah was fucked.

"I still don't understand how you got the chief to help you." She was grasping at straws, but she was damned desperate.

Lynda made a derisive sound. "All I had to do was threaten to tell his wife and my husband and he did whatever I asked. After all, he wasn't killing anyone, I was. He whined and cried about it, but he did what he had to. I think he was more afraid of Jerald finding out than his wife."

Sarah tried to summon another question, couldn't get her brain to work.

"Take the pills!" Lynda jabbed her with the tip of the knife.

Sarah opened the bottle and looked at the dozen or so pills left inside. More irony. She'd considered doing this very thing, only with sleeping pills, several times as a teenager. But she'd backed out each time. Maybe this was the Big Guy's way of letting her know He really did exist and she should have started respecting Him long ago.

"Pour all of them into your mouth." The knife tip pierced Sarah's skin.

She tipped her head back and let the pills fall into her mouth.

"Now drink."

Sarah reached for the bottle of water Lynda offered, the nasty taste already leaching into her mouth. She untwisted the top and took a sip, trying her best to keep the dissolving pills from going down her throat.

"Swallow!" Another gouge with the knife.

Fuck it. Sarah downed a gulp of the water, let the lethal dose slide down her throat. She tossed the bottle aside. "Happy now?" The panic welled and welled.

Lynda smiled. "Yes."

She pushed to her feet, turned toward the chief and shook her head. "He should've listened."

Sarah bolted into action.

The world tilted again as she rushed to her feet. She flung herself at Lynda.

The two tumbled to the rocks. The knife clanged and scooted across the rocks.

Lynda grabbed Sarah's hair. Pain erupted and Sarah screamed. They rolled. Sarah punched and kicked. Lynda pulled her hair harder, banged her head against the rocks.

Sarah's hold on the bitch loosened as blackness threatened. The pain was overwhelming.

She was going to die.

"That's right," Lynda taunted as she settled astride Sarah's stomach. "Die!"

No fucking way.

Sarah bucked. Lynda wasn't expecting the move. She reeled sideways. Sarah bucked harder. Flung her body weight against her enemy, then rolled. Sarah was suddenly on top. Lynda reached frantically for the knife. One hand on the bitch's throat, Sarah reached out with the other and snagged the knife. She settled her weight fully on the woman's chest, using her thighs to trap the bitch's arms against her sides.

She smiled at the panic in Lynda's eyes. "Now who's going to die?"

Rage rushed through Sarah's limbs, making her stronger. Making her want to kill this bitch more than she'd ever wanted anything in her life.

If your first instinct is to kill . . .

Pope's words echoed in Sarah's head.

She hesitated. Stared into the face of the bitch who had killed three people, two of whom had been innocent victims . . . she had terrorized an entire village. She had been prepared to kill Sarah . . .

She tossed the knife aside.

Lynda grinned with triumph. "I knew you couldn't do it."

"Shut the fuck up." Sarah grabbed two handfuls of the bitch's hair and banged her head against the rocks a couple of times. When her eyes rolled back in their sockets, Sarah figured that was enough.

But she wasn't taking any chances. Keeping one hand on

the bitch's neck, she reached for the duct tape lying on the ground. She grabbed the end between her teeth and pulled a good length free, then tore it off. She scooted backward, manacled her prisoner's hands together. As she tore off another length of tape, Lynda came to enough to try and fight. Sarah banged her head against the rock twice more and Lynda went lax.

"Bitch," Sarah muttered.

She wound the tape around Lynda's wrists several times before doing the same to her ankles. She didn't bother taping her mouth shut. If she woke up, let her scream.

Sarah moved over to the chief, checked for a pulse. Nothing. She put her cheek to his face, felt for breathing. Nothing. Her head still spinning, Sarah attempted CPR until she became too groggy. Still no pulse.

Shit.

The pills. She had to find help. Sarah tried to stand. Didn't make it.

Wait. The chief would have a radio or cell phone. Sarah dug around in his pockets. No radio . . . her fingers wrapped around what felt like a phone and relief rushed through her. She could call for help once she got outside.

She managed to stand and then stagger toward what she hoped was the mouth of the cave.

The ground tilted under her feet. The rock walls moved and shook.

By the time she was outside it was almost impossible to keep her eyes open.

She fumbled with the chief's phone. Kept dropping it. What the hell?

The pills. Shit. All the adrenaline was amplifying the affect.

Sarah dropped the phone and did the only thing she could. She shoved her fingers down her throat. She gagged. Repeated the process. Then she puked.

One more time. Gag. Puke.

Hopefully she'd gotten rid of some of those fucking pills.

Groggy as hell, she reached for the phone again. Couldn't make it work. Shit! The keypad was locked. Her heart thumped. She didn't know the right password or code.

Dammit!

Get up. Walk. Find help!

Sarah struggled to her feet. After three attempts she managed to stand.

One foot in front of the other.

Again.

Keep going.

Her mouth felt dry. The ground kept moving. Her vision was narrowing.

"Damn."

She fell forward in the snow. Told herself to turn her head to the side so she could breathe.

Maybe she did . . . maybe she didn't . . . she couldn't say for sure.

She thought about Kale Conner and his family . . . about how it felt to be with him . . . she should have been nicer to him . . .

She must have turned her head because she could see the moon reflected in the water. She could hear her heart beating. Slower and slower.

She was dying.

Tae would be pissed.

Her shrink would nod and say she suspected it would happen.

Kale would be sad.

Something hot rolled over her nose and onto her cold, cold cheek where it rested against the snow.

A tear.

Shit.

Then Sarah did something she hadn't done since she was nine years old . . . she prayed.

Please, God . . . let him find me.

"Sarah."

Her lids fluttered helplessly. Had someone said her name?

"Sarah, wake up."

Sarah struggled to force her lids open. Finally she managed a narrow crack. She smiled. "Matilda." Sarah licked her lips. Her mouth was so dry. "I thought you were gone."

"You needed me."

Sarah tried to laugh but the sound was more a grunt. "No shit. I think I might be dead already." As if on cue, her lids grew too heavy to keep open.

"Stay awake, Sarah!"

Sarah jerked at the loud command. Her lids fluttered open again.

"You have to stay awake," Matilda told her. "If you go to sleep you won't wake up. Ever."

"Sorry . . ." Sarah needed a drink of water. "I can't . . ."

"Stay awake, Sarah. I'll send help."

Silence echoed around Sarah. She focused on opening her eyes once more. She blinked. Where was Matilda? Had she imagined her?

Sarah tried to stay awake like Matilda said . . . but she just couldn't . . .

Funny . . . she was pretty sure she was dead since she couldn't feel her heart beating anymore.

She couldn't feel . . . anything . . .

CHAPTER 48

A steady beep, beep, beep filtered through the haze.

Was she in the fog?

Sarah told her eyes to open so she could see.

Didn't happen.

Her head felt like it weighed a ton.

She tried to lift her arm, her right, then her left.

That didn't happen, either.

Go for something little.

She wiggled her toes, or tried to.

She wasn't sure if it worked or not.

Okay, focus.

Open your eyes!

Bright light.

Her lids clamped shut.

Shit. She was dead.

Wait. There had been something in the light.

Working up her courage, she forced her eyes open one more time.

Damn, that light was bright.

She blinked a couple of times.

Something blocked the light.

A face.

"There's my girl."

Tae?

Okay, she wasn't dead. Tae was too mean to die.

"We thought we'd lost you."

Was that emotion she heard in his voice?

She licked her lips . . . tried to swallow. Her throat was seriously dry.

"Where am . . . I?"

"Well, it ain't the Waldorf-Astoria, sweetheart."

Now that sounded more like Tae.

"What happened?"

"I'll let your friend give you the official details. Right now all that matters is that you're back." Tae squeezed her hand. "My time's up. But I'll be back soon."

He was gone before she could say anything. What did he mean his time was up?

She didn't know how long he'd been gone when warm fingers closed around hers. Her gaze moved upward and dark, dark eyes held hers.

Kale.

"You scared the hell out of me."

Her heart did something weird. Not quite a flutter. "Sorry."

Flashes of memory from those minutes in the cave bounced around in her head. None of it fit together.

"Lynda Pope is in custody. Your buddy August got the whole story out of her. The chief, unfortunately, didn't make it."

Panic started to well in Sarah's chest. She was alive. Okay. Calm down.

"Barton Harvey is a couple floors down from you," Kale told her. "He's been charged with assault and battery."

Sarah tried to frown but it hurt. There was something she should remember about the innkeeper. "Why's he here?"

Kale lifted an eyebrow. "You don't remember?"

She started to shake her head but a burst of pain warned her not to. "No." Damn.

"You found where he'd buried his father's diary and he popped you on the back of the head with a shovel."

Damn, and she didn't even remember. Asshole.

"He claims he realized he'd overreacted and dragged you into his mudroom to call for help, but then someone bonked him on the head. Of course we know now that was Lynda.

"Looks like you were right," Kale concluded. "It was a woman."

Yeah, yeah. "I'm always right."

Kale chuckled, the sound rusty and weary. "That's a fact, lady."

Sarah felt her lips smile. She loved his voice. Even when he sounded so tired. Her smile drooped. "Wait. What's the deal with the diary?" She vaguely remembered finding a journal or something in the dirt.

"Oh, sorry." Kale cradled her hand in both his. "Deputy Brighton cleared that up. Barton found the journal a few years ago. He read the journal notes about those two murders twenty years ago and thought the entries meant that his father had committed the murders. He couldn't ask his father because he'd had a stroke and can't speak or respond in any way."

"Why was his father keeping a journal?" She needed Kale to get to the point. Her head was killing her and she was so damned tired. The only thing keeping her focused right now were those dark, dark eyes of his. She loved looking at his eyes.

"Barton's father and the former chief of police were planning to write a book about Youngstown's first murders. Mr. Harvey kept the notes in that journal. Then when Chief Boggus passed away, Mr. Harvey decided not to move forward with the project. All this time Barton thought his father was a killer and he was trying to protect him."

There was still a part missing. "But why did he make Valerie Gerard cry?" Melody had told her about that. Funny Sarah could remember that but she couldn't remember the innkeeper hitting her in the head with a shovel.

"Apparently, he found Valerie at his desk and he yelled at her. It was nothing. But even his daughter was worried that you suspected her father and she broke into your room to check up on your activities." Kale shook his head. "She fell apart when August questioned her and said it was her fault because she told you what happened with Valerie. The whole family's been walking an emotional tightrope since you got here."

The really dumb part was that it was their reactions to Sarah that made her suspicious in the first place. "So it wasn't Harvey who was involved with Valerie?"

Kale moved his head side to side. "It was the Reverend Mahaney."

So that was the reason Valerie stopped going to his church. Wait, Tamara had told her something about that. "Did his niece turn him in?"

Kale frowned. "His niece? No. His wife had gotten worried that his secret would be discovered so she decided to take care of the situation. She gave him an overdose of his heart medication."

That was seriously screwed up. "Is he dead?"

"No, Deborah saw where Pope was arrested and she called nine-one-one. Just in time."

Sarah was sure she would absorb and assimilate all this later. Right now it was just too overwhelming.

The memory of Lynda forcing her to take those pills bobbed to the murky surface of Sarah's mind. "Lynda gave me an overdose of the propranolol." As if she'd only just remembered and the symptoms had been delayed by her lost memory, she suddenly couldn't breathe.

"We know." Kale squeezed her hand. "You don't know how close we came to losing you. We were almost too late."

Sarah blinked, didn't understand.

"I went to the inn looking for you and found Mr. Harvey. We started searching for you then. I knew you'd been right all along. I couldn't find the chief and I had a hell of a time convincing August, but he finally came around."

Sarah searched her memory banks. "I beat the crap out of Lynda. Then I tried to help the chief."

Kale nodded, his eyes suspiciously bright. "I know. We found you facedown in the snow . . . I . . ." He cleared his throat, looked away. "You were barely alive. It took a hell of a lot of prayer and some skilled work here at the ER to reverse the effects of the propranolol. The doc said if you hadn't thrown up . . . you might not have made it."

"I'm lucky you found me in time." She didn't want to

think about the fact that she'd prayed for the first time in about twenty years.

She'd keep that part to herself. For now.

"Luck had nothing to do with it."

Wait. That was right. Matilda had found her. "Did Matilda tell you where I was?"

Kale frowned. "Matilda? No." He hitched a thumb toward the other side of the room. "She's here. She wants to see you."

Sarah didn't understand. "But she was there. She must have told you where I was. She told me to stay awake . . . but I couldn't."

The confusion in Kale's eyes told her he had no idea what she was talking about. "I talked to Pope." He fell silent a moment; judging by the quiver of his lips, he was conquering his emotions.

"You talked to Pope?"

He nodded. "I told him what you suspected and that if he didn't help me, you would become one more victim of the women in his life. I wasn't sure which one it was."

"And?" Damn, this man had to learn how to get to the point.

"He told us where you'd likely be. Said he felt compelled to do the right thing."

So, she owed her life to God and to Jerald Pope.

This was all too strange.

"I guess the investigation is closed then?"

Kale nodded. "August left as soon as he knew you were out of the woods."

It was nice to know he'd cared enough to hang around and see whether or not she died.

"Have they said when they're letting me out of here?" She felt like hell, felt weak as a kitten actually, but she despised hospitals.

"A few more days. Until you're strong enough and the effect of the drug is gone completely."

"I guess I can deal with that."

"There are others waiting to see you." Kale looked at her

hand, where he held it in his own, before meeting her gaze again. "I guess I should give someone else a turn."

That's when she noticed all the flowers. Twenty, no, at least thirty, arrangements. Including red roses.

"Wait." *Deepest regrets.* "Who sent the roses?"

"You want me to check the card?"

"No. I mean to the parents of the victims?"

"Oh, yeah. It was Lynda. She does it every time someone passes away. The whole covert order in Bangor was about making it look as if Jerri Lynn was setting her up. Apparently, Jerri Lynn had gone with her that day."

"I can't believe so many people sent flowers," Sarah muttered.

"And you thought nobody liked you."

Duh.

Instinct nudged Sarah. "Why don't you look at the card with the roses?" She needed to know.

"Sure." Kale crossed the room and pulled the card from the greenery. *"Deepest regrets."*

Sarah's pulse stumbled.

"Jerri Lynn Pope."

Sarah cleared her throat. "That's weird."

Kale shrugged. "You have to remember, both her parents are accused of murder. She's pretty much alone now."

"Yeah." Sarah knew how it felt to be suddenly alone. She also knew that Jerri Lynn was one weird girl . . . from one bizarre family. Although Sarah felt bad for Jerri Lynn on one level, there was still something she didn't trust about the girl.

"I've been holding on to something for you." Kale reached into his pocket and pulled out the necklace Matilda had given Sarah. "It seemed important to you and I didn't want it to get lost. They took it off you in the ER." He placed it in her hand.

"Thanks." The rune felt cool against her palm. "Matilda gave it to me."

"Matilda and about a dozen other people are in the corridor waiting to see you," Kale told her, "but I thought I should fill you in first."

Sarah blinked, overwhelmed with all the information and emotions. "I appreciate that."

"By the way," he added, "my parents have offered to take Matilda in, if she'll agree. Polly loves her like a sister and has convinced them to help."

Now there was some good news. Something to celebrate. Sarah's heart felt glad.

Kale stared at their joined hands a long moment. Then he lifted his gaze to hers. "I was coming after you, you know. I didn't want you to go." He looked down again. "I won't beg you to stay, because that wouldn't be right. But . . ." That dark, dark gaze met hers once more. "Fuck it. I'll beg. I really want you to stay. Think about it, Sarah, okay? Seriously think about it."

That was something she could definitely promise him. "Deal."

This was going to be a new beginning for her. She was never going to worry about DNA or genetics again. She was who she was. No matter who or what her mother and father were.

Sarah considered that Jerri Lynn faced the same dilemma. So far she hadn't killed anyone. Even though Sarah had considered the girl a prime suspect . . . but now she knew the truth.

Instinct nudged her.

Or did she? Something still didn't feel right. Maybe it was the drugs.

Kale kissed her forehead, dragging her back to happier thoughts. "I'm glad to hear that."

Sarah smiled. Maybe it was the knock on the head or the medicine or a combination of both, but she suddenly wondered where this guy had been all her life.

The door opened. "Kale, let somebody else in!" Polly flashed a grin at her. "Hey, Sarah!" Then the door closed as if someone had pulled the girl back.

Kale managed to smile. "You heard that. I've got to let the others have a turn."

Damn, Sarah was finally Ms. Popular.

Sarah held on to his hand. "I don't want you to go." But she needed to see Matilda and Polly and whoever else was out there. "Can you send Matilda in next?"

"I can try."

He let go of her hand long enough to cross to the door. He stuck his head out and murmured to those waiting outside. When he drew back into the room, he pulled Matilda in with him. She wore her usual goth getup. Sarah was seriously glad to see her. A smile dragged at her chapped lips.

"You made it," the kid said quietly as she moved up to Sarah's bedside. "I knew you would."

Sarah searched her face, wondered if she should even ask. "How did you find me?"

Matilda's gaze locked with hers, a frown lined her brow. "I don't know what you mean."

Okay, so she'd imagined the whole thing. "I dreamed you were there with me. You kept telling me to stay awake."

Matilda searched her eyes. "I was really worried about you." She placed her hand atop Sarah's. "I could feel how bad it was for you. I . . . I was afraid for you." She squeezed Sarah's hand. "So I closed my eyes and thought of you. I saw myself protecting you and bringing you back safely." A faint smile tilted the girl's lips. "I guess it worked. Kind of like prayer."

"You were right about Pope," Sarah told her. "He's pretty much the devil. He and your mother had a run-in. I guess that's why you got those bad vibes about him."

Matilda shrugged. "I get feelings about people all the time. No big deal. It's just the way it is. My instincts about him were just stronger than most."

Yeah, Sarah mused, no big deal. Though she still didn't believe in all that ESP junk or woo-woo stuff, she knew Matilda was a very special young lady.

"I should go back out there." Matilda glanced at the man waiting a few feet away. "Polly and a bunch of other people want to see you, too."

Sarah tried to smile but her lips quivered. "I'll see you later."

Matilda leaned down, kissed her on the forehead, then whispered in her ear, "The police couldn't get him, but you did. You're special, Sarah Newton."

Before Sarah could speak, Matilda had hurried from the room.

Warm, salty tears slid from Sarah's eyes. She wasn't special. Matilda was the one who was special.

Kale hovered over Sarah once more. He took her hand. "You okay?" He swiped the dampness from her cheeks with warm fingers.

"Yeah. I'm good." She searched his eyes, wanted him to see the truth in her words. "I'm better than I've ever been."

He kissed her nose. "Good." He glanced at the door. "Look, there's going to be a riot out there if I don't let Polly in here."

"On one condition," Sarah told him.

"What's that?"

"Kiss me." What was he waiting for? "I almost died. I deserve a real kiss, at least."

He kissed her.

He'd found her.

Or maybe she'd found him.

Either way, she was never looking back. She had a new philosophy. The truth is always going to be what it is, but she now knew it could be altered by many things, life, hope . . . and even prayer.

And by certain . . . special people.

The truth is what it is, but sometimes it was not what it seemed.

The truth was, it was time to get over the past and make herself a future.

Sarah had come to find a killer, and she had. But the *truth* was, she'd found far more.

She'd found Kale.

She'd found herself.

CHAPTER 49

Strange.

Jerri Lynn Pope walked along the massive entry hall.

There was no one left of her family but her.

She was like an orphan.

She drifted into the kitchen and rummaged in the fridge. She should eat. It was well past lunch. There was a lot of change going on in her life. She needed her strength.

There was no one to take care of her now. She had to learn to take care of all her needs.

Cheese, fruit . . . nothing appealed to her.

When she noticed the thick slab of filet mignon her father had intended to grill today, she smiled. That would work.

Jerri Lynn grabbed the dish, set it on the counter and went in search of a knife.

She selected a butcher knife and studied the glint of light from the windows on the blade. She loved those mesmerizing glints. Loved the way they flashed so brightly.

On second thought she grabbed the bowl of salad and her favorite dressing from the fridge.

Perfect. Steak and salad.

She sliced into the thick meat; red ran from its tender flesh. She shivered. She lifted a small piece, considered its color and texture, then popped it into her mouth.

She chewed. Closed her eyes and moaned.

There was nothing quite as good as raw meat.

She thought of how her own blood tasted whenever she cut herself. Would human flesh taste as good as the steak?

Jerri Lynn's pulse reacted to the concept. She studied the red trickling down the knife blade.

One day soon . . . very soon . . . perhaps she would know for sure.

"I found the pajamas."

Jerri Lynn looked up as Tamara padded into the kitchen. Tamara struck a pose to show off her new loungewear.

Jerri Lynn smiled. Her one true friend. "You look delicious."

Tamara grinned. "Thank you."

Perhaps one day soon Jerri Lynn would know many new things.

EVERYWHERE SHE TURNS

CHAPTER 1

Huntsville, Alabama
Saturday, July 31, 6:30 A.M.

Women.

Bitches. Every fucking one of them.

The world was about to be rid of one more stupid bitch.

All he had to do was catch her.

Laughter burst from his chest as she darted from the alley, plunging into the dark cover of the woods in a last-ditch effort to save herself.

Did she really think she could escape him that easily?

Stupid, stupid bitch.

Not in this life.

In this life, he was the killer. And she . . . well, she was the victim.

The only decision that remained was the manner of death.

Slice open her silky white throat?

No. Too cliché.

The memorable mark of a truly magnificent killer was at its core quite simple . . . *originality.*

He allowed her a few precious seconds. Just enough to provide a fleeting glimmer of hope. Then he charged into the damp, dense woods, using the trampled underbrush she'd left in her wake as his path.

She should just face the one undeniable fact close enough to feel its hot brush on the nape of her fragile neck.

She was dead.

Within the hour her heart would slow to a complete stop . . . heat would begin to seep from her flesh and the final image captured on her retinas would fade to black.

His face would be that last image.

At that trauma-filled moment, when her brain released the massive dump of endorphins that gifted the dying with an eerie calm as their entire pathetic lives flashed like a bad movie trailer through their impotent minds, she would recognize her one fatal mistake.

She shouldn't have gotten in the way.

Bravado . . . curiosity . . . whatever it was that made her dare to step out of her place, it was just another bad choice in a long line of bad choices littering an insignificant existence mere minutes from being over.

Even now as he grew nearer and nearer, so shockingly near he could hear the humid air raging in and out of her desperate lungs . . . could feel the sheer terror throttling through her veins . . . she still couldn't help herself.

She had to glance back. To see the truth that had been right in front of her for the duration of her short life.

He smiled.

This was going to be fun.

CHAPTER 2

Johns Hopkins Hospital
Baltimore, Maryland
10:30 P.M.

Dr. CJ Patterson fished in her purse for her keys as she neared her ancient Civic. In twenty-three minutes she would be home, five minutes after that she would be out of these scrubs and soaking in a tub full of hot, steamy water with an open bottle of chilled Sorraco uncorked and parked within reach.

Forty-two patients in fourteen hours.

A twelve-car pile-up on Interstate 695 had kept the ER buzzing for the final three hours of her too-long shift. Half a dozen cops were still attempting to interview the victims capable of answering questions.

"Just another Saturday night in Charm City." She reached for the door, but something in the corner of her eye snagged her attention. "Oh, damn."

Flat tire.

The second one this week. CJ heaved a disgusted breath. She had to get new tires.

Another reality hit on the heels of that one. She slapped her forehead with the heel of her hand. "Double damn."

Who had time to get the other flat tire repaired? Certainly not a third-year resident who worked ten or more hours most days and who spent the rest of her time studying for boards.

Damn. Damn. Damn. Plowing her fingers through her hair, she pulled her ponytail free, glanced around the gloomy parking garage and considered her options. Getting someone here to repair one or both tires would take hours on a Saturday night.

"Forget it." She did an about-face and headed for the nearest exit. There was always a cab or two waiting within hailing distance of the ER entrance on East Monument Street. She'd get a ride home and deal with this in the morning when she'd had some sleep. Tomorrow was her first day off in two weeks. Too bad it was Sunday because she had a million things to take care of and the business world of nine-to-fivers had no appreciation for her frenzied schedule.

She pushed through the north exit of the staff parking garage into the muggy night air. Someday, when she had money, she might actually have a decent ride. One with good tires. And reliable air-conditioning.

Such was the life of a medical resident—every aspect of one's personal life was about the future.

Sweat had dampened her skin by the time she reached East Monument. At the ER's street entrance she stopped, stepped back from the curb before an arriving ambulance mowed her down. Lights and sirens, not good. Hard as she tried not to linger . . . to look, her efforts were futile. Two of her colleagues rushed out to connect with the emerging paramedics and the patient strapped to the gurney.

CJ forced her attention back to the taxi a block or so beyond the ER's drop-off point. The arriving patient was in good hands. CJ's shift was over.

She had to learn that even the most committed physician needed boundaries. She couldn't save the world alone. Especially without sleep.

At the passenger side of the taxi, CJ opened the rear door and gave her home address to the driver. She collapsed into the seat, tossed her purse aside, and snapped her safety belt into place. Blessed relief hissed past her lips.

Finally.

"Tough night?" The driver lowered the volume of the jazz radiating from the taxi's speakers as he rolled out onto the deserted street.

"Long, long night," CJ explained. But that was the reality of choosing a career in emergency medicine. The ER was not the place for those who preferred banking hours and neatly scheduled appointments. Strange. Maybe the reason she loved the adrenaline-charged life of an ER physician was related to her drama-filled childhood. Wasn't all that one did connected to the environment of the formative years?

Obviously she'd been lunching with the psych residents way too much.

The driver had his own theories about tonight's frenzy. He offered a lengthy discourse on how the full moon always made the crazies come out. CJ didn't bother telling him just how right he was.

The full moon—

Tires squealed. Metal crashed. CJ's head jerked left, then right, banging the window as the taxi absorbed the momentum of an oncoming car crossing the intersection against the light.

For an endless, paralyzing moment there was no movement, no sound, other than the murmur of the jazz still whispering from the speakers.

"Son of a bitch!" The driver whacked his fist against the dash.

CJ shook off the shock, released the safety belt and rubbed at the dull ache in her right temple. The other car had broadsided the taxi. Both vehicles now sat in the middle of the intersection, steam rising from the hood of the offending vehicle.

Swearing profusely, the driver scrambled across the seat and out the passenger side door.

CJ shoved that hot bath out of her mind for the moment and flung her door open. She caught up with the furious taxi driver as he confronted the driver of the other car.

"You didn't see the light? What are you? Blind?"

CJ looked from the dazed driver climbing out from behind the steering wheel to the passenger emerging from the backseat. "You two okay?" Both occupants were male. Caucasian. Young, twenty, twenty-one.

"We gotta get to the hospital," the passenger shouted at no one in particular. He turned all the way around, staggering drunkenly, as if he needed to get his bearings.

An instant mental inventory of causes for his imbalance, from illegal substances to head injuries, quickened CJ's pulse. "Call 9-1-1," she instructed the taxi driver, who was still cursing and stomping his feet.

"Are either of you having difficulty breathing? In pain? Lightheaded? Nauseous?" Moving toward the passenger, CJ visually assessed the car's driver. Looked a little dazed and confused as if he wasn't sure this was real or just a bad dream. No apparent injuries.

The passenger wore a black Bob Marley T-shirt. Now that she was closer CJ could see that the T-shirt and his hands were as bloody as hell. Her pulse quickened. His inability to regain his equilibrium persisted.

"Is he calling the cops?"

CJ ignored the driver's question. "Where'd the blood come from?" she asked the Bob Marley fan, who appeared focused on her blue scrubs. No visible signs of injury. Eyes were glassy. His long dark hair was stringy, but not wet or sticky. Where the hell had the blood come from?

"My brother." He grabbed her arm, tugged her around the open passenger door. "He needs help."

There was another passenger?

CJ pushed the guy aside and maneuvered her way into the backseat.

Damn.

Blood. Lots of blood.

Third passenger was a kid, not more than nine or ten. His Hannah Montana pajama top was saturated in crimson. She tugged the top up and out of the way to get a look at his torso. He didn't flinch. Didn't moan.

Deep penetrating chest wound.

Shit.

She needed more light. Bracing her hand on the seat, she leaned closer. Something wet oozed up between her fingers. Blood. *Shit. Shit. Shit.* The seat . . . she checked the knees of her scrubs . . . the damned floorboard . . . blood was everywhere.

Instinct kicked in and training overrode emotion.

Patient had no other visible injuries.

Not breathing.

Oh, hell.

No pulse.

Adrenaline detonated in CJ's veins, sharpening her senses.

"Help me get him out of here!"

The older brother stuck his upper body into the car. "What?"

"You and your friend," CJ commanded, "help me get him out of the car and on the ground. Hurry!"

The two men scrambled into unsteady action. CJ cradled the boy's head and neck as the brother and his friend lifted him out of the backseat.

"Put him down over there." She jerked her head toward the front of the taxi. The headlights would help her see what she was doing. Streetlights weren't enough.

"You! Taxi guy!" CJ shouted at the man still on his cell phone. He stopped explaining their circumstances and stared at her in question. "Tell them I need an ALS unit. We have full trauma arrest." She turned back to the boy. The battle was very nearly over. "Tell them to hurry!"

"You can help him, right?" The older brother dropped to his knees on the pavement next to her.

"We have to control the bleeding." CJ needed this guy focused on his little brother, not distracting her.

"You know what this means?" his friend yelled as he paced back and forth in the middle of the street. "The cops are coming. We gotta get outta here."

"Shut up!" the brother screamed.

"Give me your hand." CJ reached out to him. His eyes were wild with fear and whatever had him buzzed. His hand shook as she gripped his wrist and covered the wound with his palm. "Keep pressure there. It slows the bleeding."

Not that this kid had much left to leak.

CJ started chest compressions.

"They'll take us to fucking jail," the friend railed. "I ain't going to jail. This is your fault, not mine!"

"I said," the brother warned, "shut the fuck up."

CJ tuned out the heated exchange. Focused on keeping the boy's heart pumping. She had no idea how long he'd been in full arrest, but he didn't have a chance in hell of surviving if—

Blood seeped from beneath the kid's left shoulder, spreading ominously over the pavement.

Shit.

She stopped the compressions.

"What're you doing?" the brother demanded. "Keep . . ." he motioned with his free hand ". . . doing . . . whatever. That's what you're supposed to do, right?"

CJ didn't answer. She carefully rolled her patient onto his right side. Her breath fisted in her throat, refused to fill her lungs.

Exit wound: left scapula. Major blood vessels . . . the heart . . . all lay smack in the middle of the path the bullet had taken. The puddle of blood on the pavement indicated that every chest compression she'd executed had sent more of what little blood remained in his slim body out that exit wound.

"Do something!" the brother wailed.

Where the hell was that ambulance? "Did you tell them to hurry?" CJ shouted to the taxi driver.

He nodded frantically. "They're coming! They're coming!"

"Help him, goddammit!" the brother shouted in her face.

CJ flinched but kept her focus on the kid. She lowered him onto his back. "We need pressure on that wound!"

The brother obeyed the order and she resumed chest

compressions. The kid would likely die anyway, but he would damned sure die if she didn't try.

Just . . . hang in there, kid.

"Don't you get it?" the brother's paranoid friend yelled. "The kid's dead. Nobody loses that much blood and lives. She's only doing that"—he waved wildly at CJ with both hands—"to keep you from freaking out. The kid's fucking dead, man."

Big brother shot to his feet. "If you don't shut—"

"Gun!" the taxi driver screamed. "He's got a gun!"

Don't listen. Don't look. Focus.

The distant shrill of sirens accompanied the screaming between the three men.

"Tell him," the friend shrieked at CJ, "that you can't save the kid!"

"Is that true?"

She ignored the brother's demand. Mentally marked the necessary rhythm.

He stuck his face close to hers. "IS THAT TRUE?" he screamed in her ear.

"I'm doing all I can," CJ admitted without looking up. She braced for his reaction, but didn't stop the only option she had available to help the patient.

"If he dies," the brother warned, "you die." He jammed the gun in her face.

Fear bumped against her sternum.

Ignore the fucking gun! Lift. Compress. Repeat.

The sirens grew louder and louder. Nearly here. *Thank God.*

The friend started backing away. "I'm out of here. I'm not going to jail."

A police cruiser skidded to a stop on the other side of the taxi and the lowlife driver took off.

"He's running!" the taxi guy bellowed to anyone listening. "The driver is running. Stop him!"

Compress. Lift. Repeat.

"Drop your weapon!" *Cop.*

The unloading paramedics were shouting questions at

CJ. "Full arrest," she called back. "Deep penetrating entrance wound mid-torso. Exit wound left scapula. Massive blood loss." *Get that Advanced Life Support unit over here!*

"Drop your weapon!" the cop repeated.

"He's . . . only nine years old," the brother pleaded, his words directed at CJ and barely audible amidst all the shouting. "You can't let him die."

CJ couldn't help herself. She lifted her gaze to his. No matter that the gun was still pointed at her, there was nothing reassuring she could say. The resignation that claimed the brother's posture, his eyes warned his intent a split second before he acted.

There was no time to react.

The explosion from the gun shattered the night.